FALLEN ANGELS

www.rbooks.co.uk

FALLEN ANGELS

Valerie Wood

BANTAM PRESS

LONDON · TORONTO · SYDNEY · AUCKLAND · JOHANNESBURG

TRANSWORLD PUBLISHERS
61–63 Uxbridge Road, London W5 5SA
A Random House Group Company
www.rbooks.co.uk

First published in Great Britain
in 2007 by Bantam Press
an imprint of Transworld Publishers

A CIP catalogue record for this book
is available from the British Library.

ISBN 9780593059999

Addresses for Random House Group Ltd companies outside the UK
can be found at: www.randomhouse.co.uk
The Random House Group Ltd Reg. No. 954009

The Random House Group Limited supports The Forest Stewardship
Council (FSC), the leading international forest certification organisation.
All our titles that are printed on Greenpeace approved FSC certified
paper carry the FSC logo. Our paper procurement policy can be found at
www.rbooks.co.uk/environment

Typeset in 12/14pt New Baskerville by
Kestrel Data, Exeter, Devon.
Printed in the UK by
CPI Mackays, Chatham, ME5 8TD.

2 4 6 8 10 9 7 5 3 1

For Peter, Ruth, Catherine and Alex.

CHAPTER ONE

'Get your hands off me, Billy Fowler! In God's name, what 'you doing? Tek it off me!'

Lily struggled and swore as her husband pulled the noose tighter round her waist. He had asked Daisy to pass him the rope from the back of the cart and when she did so he had swiftly made a loop and flung it over Lily's head.

She had known he was up to something from the minute he had ordered her and Daisy out of the cart in which they had been travelling since before daybreak. It was now mid-day and both she and her daughter were exhausted and hungry. Lily could barely stand, her legs were so cramped and her body ached so much.

'Are you listening to me?' she demanded. 'Tek it off, damn you! Why are we here? Why've you brought us to this place?'

'Shut your face!' Billy Fowler was shorter than Lily, with a pot belly and a temper which outdid hers. He fastened the end of the rope to the shaft and securely knotted it. 'You'll stop here till I come back. I need a drink.'

He'd driven into the inn yard and enquired of a stable lad how much it would cost to leave the horse and cart for the afternoon. Money had changed hands as Lily watched suspiciously. Billy had woken her early that morning, and ordered her and Daisy to hurry and get ready; woozy with sleep they had left home even before light had broken as a faint glimmer on the horizon beyond the sea which was almost on their doorstep.

'What game're you playing, Billy?' she said now. 'What 'you up to?'

'No game,' he said with a grim laugh, 'and you'll find out soon enough.'

'Fetch us some water,' she called after him as he headed towards the inn door.

He grunted and walked on. Lily looked down at her daughter. 'We'll be all right, Daisy. Just try and get this rope undone, will you?'

Daisy nodded. She was fair and thin, nothing like her dark-haired mother. 'What's he doing, Ma?' Her voice was croaky with tiredness and she plucked ineffectively at the rope which held her mother fast. 'Why are we here? Where are we?'

It was a question they had asked Billy constantly on the journey but one that he had refused to answer. Lily pressed her lips together. She didn't trust him one jot, but their days were dull and monotonous, which was why she had compliantly climbed into the cart that morning, hoping for an outing.

'We're in Hull, I think,' she answered. 'Onny I don't know why. We'll find out when he's ready to tell us. If I could onny get this damn rope off. It's nipping me no end.'

Her son Ted had stayed behind. Billy had given him orders to feed the hens and goats and dig over the vegetable plot, telling him brusquely to make sure he did it properly or there would be trouble when Billy got home that night. The boy, at thirteen sullen and silent, watched from the doorway of the cottage as his mother and sister climbed into the cart.

Billy had bought the flat, two-wheeled open vehicle at a knock-down price. It had slatted sides and was without any shelter from the elements, and he had fashioned the driver's seat from a wooden box. A coil of rope and several empty sacks were in the back and Lily had spread the latter out for her and Daisy to sit on, grumbling at Billy as she did so and saying she hoped they were not going far as the weather didn't seem promising. It was cold and damp, but as dawn broke and the sky lightened, she and Daisy twitched their nostrils as the smells of spring cheered them.

They had driven into the coastal village of Withernsea and then along the road towards the thriving market town of Patrington. Lily had perked up, thinking this was their destination: she would enjoy that. But Billy had driven straight through without stopping, ignoring her questioning, and taken the road to Hedon, another market town where he had stopped at a hostelry to buy a jug of ale. He'd drunk thirstily from it and then handed it to Lily; she'd taken several deep gulps and given it to Daisy to finish off.

They'd continued along a turnpike road where Billy had to pay for their passage; Lily saw the tops of ships' masts and tall cranes beyond the marshy land and guessed they were travelling alongside the Humber estuary to the large town of Hull, a place she had never been.

Lily winced as a pain shot through her belly. Hope that's not a sign of summat, she thought, biting her lips together. Babby's not due for ages. She tried to put her fingers between the rope and her belly to ease the tightness. Mebbe the rocking of the cart has disturbed it. Why's he tied me up? Does he think I'll run away? God knows I would if I had somewhere to run to. She began to worry about the long journey back. Would Billy pay for a night's lodgings? Somehow she doubted it. And what was his business here anyway that he needed her and Daisy to be involved in it?

Billy came back bearing a jug of water and a hunk of bread. 'Here,' he said, thrusting them towards her. 'Get that down you.'

Mother and daughter drank thirstily and shared the bread. 'You going to tell me what this is about, then? My patience is stretched to its limits. What 'you up to, Billy Fowler?'

They had had a ferocious argument just a few days

before, one of many, but this time it had centred on Daisy and the child that Lily was expecting. He'd told Lily that the girl would have to find work, as a kitchen or laundry maid in one of the farmhouses. He'd suggested too that Lily should try to get rid of the baby. 'I can't afford to keep all these bairns,' he'd bellowed at her.

She'd shouted back. 'You should've thought of that afore asking me to come here. You knew I'd got two childre' and besides, Ted earns his keep. You mek him work all 'hours God sends.'

He'd said nothing more but she knew he was stewing with resentment, and wished with all her heart that she had never married him but had stayed as she was, a young widow living in her home village of Hollym, able to work and given parish assistance for the two children.

Her husband, Johnny Leigh-Maddeson, whom she had known since childhood, had been passionate about joining the army. 'It's my ambition, Lily,' he'd pleaded when she'd wept over his plans. 'I'll get leave, and I'll save my pay to bring home.' And because she loved him she knew she couldn't hold him back. After they were married and when she was expecting Ted, she lived with her widowed mother in the cottage where she had been born. Johnny was sent to Ireland and returned when Ted was six months old and she immediately conceived with Daisy. He came back again in time for his daughter's birth and thought she was as bonny a bairn as the flower she was named for and a month later was once more recalled to his unit.

'Sorry, lass,' he'd said, hugging Lily close. 'But that's 'way it is when you're married to a sodger. But I'll be back,' he promised. 'Never fear.'

She saw him just once more when Ted was three and Daisy already walking and talking, and then never again. Though Johnny hadn't been a good hand at writing, she had previously had grubby notes from time to time which said he was missing her and longing to see her and the children, but then there was only silence.

10

Nearly three years passed before Lily wrote to his commanding officer who replied briefly that Johnny had been posted to Afghanistan where there was conflict but that he couldn't give any further information. Two more years went by and she was giving up hope that she would ever see him again, but asked the parson if he would write to the regiment for her, thinking that a letter from him would carry more weight than hers; the reply he received gave the grave news that Johnny's regiment had suffered heavy losses in Afghanistan and had been posted to India. They had no record of John Leigh-Maddeson and must presume that he was missing, possibly having died in action. She was devastated by the news and felt that all hope had gone.

She met Billy Fowler at the Plough Inn in Hollym where she worked in the evening to supplement her parish relief and the money she earned as a washerwoman in the big houses of the village. She was poor and she was lonely after her mother's death, and she worried about the children's not having a father. Billy became a regular at the inn; he seemed to be a quiet man and often asked her to go out walking, which she refused to do. Eventually he tried to persuade her that she should come and live with him in his cottage just a few miles up the road at Seathorne. 'I've got a bit o' land,' he'd said. 'Enough to live on.'

'You'd have to marry me,' she told him. 'I'd want that security. And I'd have to bring my bairns.'

She had seen doubt in his eyes, and he'd asked how long it would be before her son could work. Ted was eleven by then and she told Billy that he was already doing jobs in farms after school and at harvest time.

'So what happened to your husband?' he'd asked.

'Dead,' she'd said regretfully, knowing that no one could ever take Johnny's place. 'He was a sodger. I've not seen him in years. My bairns don't even remember him. He was posted to Afghanistan so I reckon them foreigners killed him and nobody found his body.'

The parson had seen no reason why they shouldn't be

married if there was no objection after the reading of the banns, which there wasn't. Billy didn't buy her a wedding ring, 'because,' he said, 'you've got one already,' which should have warned her of the type of man he really was: mean, miserly and with no warmth or laughter in him whatsoever. She rued the day she had met him as soon as she set eyes on the dismal hovel he called a smallholding which teetered on the edge of the eroding cliff.

She was used to the sound of the sea having lived only a mile from it all of her life, but never had she lain awake trembling in her bed, hearing the crash and thunder of the waves battering the cliff beneath them and waiting for what seemed to be the inevitable fall on to the sands below.

'Come on, then,' she said now as she stood defiantly in front of him in the inn yard. 'Spit it out! What can you buy here in Hull that you can't buy nearer home? And why've you tied me up?'

He gave a thin lopsided grin. 'Not buy,' he answered, jiggling the rope which held her. 'Sell!'

'What?' Lily struggled to free herself but he pulled the rope tighter. 'Damn you, Billy Fowler. Tek it off!'

He sneered. 'I'm sick o' you and your bairns. I told you I haven't come to buy. I'm here to sell. I'm selling you for 'best price I can get and I'm throwing in that bairn for free, cos I don't want her either.'

Daisy began to cry but Lily was speechless. He'd gone off his head. He must have done. 'You can't do that,' she yelled when she got her wits back. 'You can't sell people like you sell cows or pigs!'

Billy gave a harsh laugh. 'I've heard as you can. Some years back a fellow from Patrington sold his wife at Hull market. Got a good price for her from all accounts.' He jiggled the rope again and freed it from the shaft. 'So come on, my beauty. Let's be off. Let's see how much we can get for you.'

CHAPTER TWO

'You're mad,' Lily protested, struggling to get free. 'Law will say that you are.'

'I don't think so.' Billy grinned, a tic flickering on his top lip. 'There's no law says a man can't sell his own wife and besides, I just told you, it's been done afore so there's a press— press something or other, which means you can do it again.' He tugged on the rope, forcing her to move on or be cut in two.

'I'm expecting a babby!' she shouted at him. 'Your babby.'

'Should get more for you then, shouldn't I? Like selling a horse in foal or a goat in kid. A real bargain!'

Lily stumbled after him out of the inn yard and into the Market Place. Canvas stalls crowded round a magnificent church. The vendors were shouting their wares, holding up squawking hens in one hand and dead rabbits in the other. Stallholders were selling hot pies and baked potatoes and from them came a delicious smell, reminding Lily that she was hungry. They had had little breakfast and since then only the hunk of bread.

Daisy was weeping and catching hold of her. 'Ma, he can't do this to you! It's not right. Shall I run and fetch a constable?'

Billy grabbed her wrist. 'I heard you, you little varmint. You'll stop here wi' me or I'll sell you to somebody else and you'll not go wi' your ma.'

13

He trudged on past the church, looking for the best place to stand and make his pronouncement. There were hundreds of people milling about, buying, selling, and all of them bargaining. Some were carrying sacks of potatoes; others had fur or fowl in wicker baskets. There were poor people dressed in rags, others who were clean but shabby, and yet others who were well dressed and just looking at what was going on around them. A group of gypsies ran by leading several horses and putting them through their paces, showing them to advantage.

'That's what I oughter do wi' you,' he muttered. 'Onny I don't suppose you can run being as how you are.'

'I'll kill you, Billy Fowler,' Lily yelled at him, tugging on the rope. 'As soon as I get this off me, you'll wish you'd never been born!'

He ignored what she was saying and plodded on, pulling her behind him, until he came to a more open place at the west end of the church, where several people, men and women, were standing on boxes and airing their views on the state of the country or the plight of the poor, or inviting those who would listen to come and be saved by the Lord.

Billy eyed them, assessing the situation. One man had come to the end of his address and was looking about him. He had been preaching of hell and damnation but no one was listening. Whatever he had had to say wasn't of sufficient interest for anyone to stop. He stepped down from his box and Billy hurried towards him.

'I'll give you threepence for 'loan of your box for an hour,' he said.

The man sniffed and wiped his nose on his sleeve. He was thin-faced and didn't look as if he'd had a good meal in a long time. 'Threepence'll buy me nowt. Sixpence,' he said. 'For half an hour.'

Billy turned away. 'An hour, then,' the man called.

'Done,' Billy said, reaching into his pocket.

'Are you selling or preaching?' the man asked, taking

14

the money from him and clutching it tightly in his hand. 'They're an ungodly rabble.'

'Selling,' Billy said briefly. 'But nowt that you'd want.'

'No,' the preacher muttered as he walked away. 'All I want is a square meal and a place in heaven.'

Lily shouted after him. 'This fellow won't help you with either; he's destined for hell fire.'

'Shut your face,' Billy growled, and pushed her up on to the box. 'If you don't be quiet I'll tek your lass and drop her in 'Humber.' He lifted a warning finger. 'I mean it, don't think I don't. And I'll leave you to fend for yoursen.'

She was silenced and pulled her shawl round her. It had belonged to her mother and was worn in places but voluminous and warm. She was beginning to feel ill. Her back ached and her body felt heavy. She licked her dry lips. I hope to God I'm not starting in labour. 'Daisy,' she said in a low voice. 'Try and get me a sup o' water. There'll be a pump somewhere about. Ask somebody to lend you a cup or a jug.'

Daisy dashed away to one of the stalls before Billy could stop her and Lily saw her talking to the vendor. He looked across towards Lily and, handing Daisy a cup, pointed down the street.

'What's she up to?' Billy muttered. 'If she brings 'law here . . .'

'She's fetching me water,' she barked at him. 'For God's sake, Billy. Unfasten this rope. It's cutting me in half.'

'Not likely,' he said. 'I know you. You'd run off, scream-ing and shouting for 'constable.'

'You've said that 'law won't do anything, so why would I send for 'constable? Anyway,' she added bitterly, 'they're all men so they'd do nowt.'

'That's right.' Billy stuffed his hands in his pockets and waited for Daisy to come back, which she did a few minutes later, bringing a brimming cup of water.

Lily drank it in one quaff and, breathing heavily, said, 'I'm starting in labour.'

'Don't give me that,' he snapped. 'It's just an excuse. You're not due.' He wrapped the rope round his wrist and, lifting both hands to cup his mouth, began to shout.

'*Wife for sale! Wife for sale!* Fine specimen of womanhood. Sound in wind and limb. Good teeth; a bit proud but a strong master can soon knock that out of her. Wife for sale! Wife for sale!'

Lily screamed at him and yanked on the rope, nearly pulling him off balance. 'Hellhound. Viper. Scum!' She launched herself at him, and, being above him on the box, knocked him to the ground, falling on top of him and flailing him savagely with her fists.

A crowd gathered, all talking excitedly and urging others to come and watch the scene. 'How much d'you want for her, mister?' somebody called out. 'Or will you pay 'em to tek her away?'

Billy struggled to stand up and dragged Lily to her feet. 'I'll tek five guineas,' he said, shrugging into his coat. 'She's a good worker when she's a mind, and childbearer,' he added. 'She's got a girl here,' he pointed to Daisy, 'nearly ready for work. She's included in 'price.'

Some of the men muttered together, pursing their lips and discussing whether she was a bargain.

'It's against 'law,' a woman's voice called out. 'And you should be ashamed o' yoursen.'

There was loud guffawing amongst the men. 'Wonder how much I'd get for mine,' a man laughed. 'I'd be prepared to give her away, 'cept she warms my bed.'

There was much ribald comment mingled with the voices of women berating them, and then the crowd parted as a uniformed constable appeared on the scene.

'What's going on here?' He wore a blue tailcoat fastened with metal buttons, matching blue trousers and a top hat. He nonchalantly swung a wooden baton in one hand. 'I'd call it an affray.'

'No, it's not, constable.' Billy spoke up. 'I'm within my rights. There's nowt to say that I can't sell my wife if I want

16

to. She's part of my goods and chattels.' He ducked as Lily took a swipe at him. 'There was a case some years back where a man sold his wife at Hull market.'

The constable took a notepad and a stub of pencil from his pocket. 'Name?'

'Lily Fowler,' Billy said. 'Formerly Leigh-Maddeson.'

'Why'd she change her name?' the constable asked.

Billy gazed blankly at him. 'Cos she got married. That's what women do. They change their names.'

'But why did she change her name from Lee to Lily?' the constable persisted.

'I didn't,' Lily said in exasperation. 'Leigh was a middle name! Now, get on with it and arrest this man who, in a moment of madness, I agreed to marry and who is now off his head and should to be taken to 'asylum!'

'He seems perfectly sane to me.' The officer put away his writing materials. 'And as far as I know, perfectly within his rights to sell you if he should so wish.'

The crowd nodded, murmuring in agreement. 'Quite right.' 'Took her on as lawful wedded wife.' 'Can sell her just 'same as an old chair.' 'Or a horse or a cow, it's all 'same.'

'What am I bid?' Billy climbed up on the wooden box, holding Lily tight by the rope.

Daisy clung on to her mother's skirt. 'Are you all right, Ma?' she whispered. 'What are we to do?'

Lily didn't answer. The fall from the box had left her breathless and once more the pain in her back struck deep.

'Come on!' Billy urged. 'She's a fine specimen of woman-hood. Who'll give me five guineas?'

'Sixpence,' a man called out amid general laughter. 'Though I don't know what my missus'd say if I took her home.'

'Is she good in bed?' a young voice shouted and Billy turned towards the sound.

'Now, young fellow, wherever you are. Things like that

are not discussed in public,' he said disapprovingly. But then he winked, shaped a woman's curves with his free hand and made a suggestive movement with his hips.

'What's this? What's happening?' Another voice rose above the laughter. 'Who's the woman?'

Some of the crowd drew back to let a slim, pale-faced man through. 'Why's she tied up?' he asked. 'Has she stolen summat?'

'No, sir,' Billy answered. 'Never in her life. She's honest through and through. Got a temper on her, though, which needs to be curbed, and I've not mastered that, which is why I'm selling her. She needs a younger man than me to subdue her. I want a quiet life.' He dropped his voice to a wheedling tone. 'She's too strong-willed for me. But look at her.' He turned to Lily. 'Ain't she a beauty?'

Lily lifted her chin and stared straight back at the man who was looking at her. Though he was quite handsome, he had an angular arrogant face and she thought that if he paid out money for her, she'd be off as soon as the rope was loosened. She and Daisy. But she was feeling very queasy and wondered if she could outrun anybody. Dammit, she thought uneasily. I'm starting in labour and it's far too early. I'll lose 'bairn for sure, but mebbe that won't be a bad thing under 'circumstances.

'Give you five shillings for her,' the man called out.

'Come now, sir. That's an insult if ever I heard one.' Billy scowled. 'Good-looking woman like this! No, two guineas then. Young lass is included.'

'Don't want the girl, she's too young.' The man turned away.

'Now, sir,' Billy said hastily, thinking that this was the only offer he'd had. 'Think of what a bargain. Young lass is nearly ready for work. Is ready in fact,' he assured the crowd in general. 'It's just that her ma wanted her to stay by her, but she's old enough at twelve.'

Daisy shook her head in dismay. She wasn't yet twelve.

And she didn't want to leave her ma. What would become of her?

'Ten shillings then,' the man called out. 'But without 'girl. I don't tek bairns.' He turned and glared at the crowd who were muttering against him. 'I don't deal wi' childre'.'

'She comes wi' me!' Lily called out. She wanted this over and done with so that she could go and lie down somewhere. 'We'll both come for ten shillings and work for our keep.'

Billy looked baffled. What was happening? Somehow Lily was taking charge. 'A guinea then,' he shouted. 'And all right, I'll keep 'girl and tek her back wi' me.'

'No!' Daisy shrieked. 'I won't go. I'm stopping wi' my ma!'

'Twenty shillings, sir,' Billy said desperately. 'There you are, a bargain.' If he didn't sell her, what would he do with her? She'd be a hellcat for sure. 'Fifteen, then.'

The stranger came towards them, jingling money in his pocket. 'Ten bob. Tek it or leave it.'

'Tek it!' someone in the crowd shouted. 'You'll not do better'n that. Folks in Hull don't part easy wi' their money.'

Billy hesitated. He didn't want to take Lily home; she'd make his life a misery and he'd be the laughing stock of Holderness.

'Right! Done,' he said, holding out his hand. 'You strike a hard bargain, mister.'

'And you're a blackguard,' the man said, handing over ten shillings, and adding in a whisper, 'It takes one to know another. Now get out of town, back to whichever sewer you came from.'

Billy pocketed the money and, with a furtive glance at Lily, stepped off the box, threw the end of the rope to the buyer and scurried away.

Lily made to go after him, but the man held her back. 'Swine!' she screeched at Billy's back. 'Cockroach! Get back to your dunghill! I hope you fall into 'sea.' She stopped

19

short in her shouts of abuse as another pain racked her and she doubled over. 'Don't know who you are, mister, but I need some help.'

'Jamie's the name,' he said, frowning. 'What's up wi' you? Are you sick?'

'I'm sick all right,' she gasped. 'Sick to death o' men and Billy Fowler in particular.' She adjusted her shawl and took a deep breath. 'What you lookin' at?'

Jamie lifted her shawl. 'You're pregnant,' he said accusingly. 'He didn't say you were pregnant. You're no good to me!'

She lifted her hand and struck him across his face. 'I didn't ask to come here. You got what you deserved for your ten bob. You're no better than Billy Fowler! Go after him and ask for your money back and I hope you kill each other ower it.'

He stroked his reddened cheek. 'There's no wonder he wanted shut o' you!' He looked her up and down. 'Come and find me when you're rid of 'bairn. I might have a job for you.'

'Don't, missis.' A woman's voice came from the middle of the dwindling crowd. 'You'll be worse off than you were afore.' The speaker disappeared in a flurry of skirts and shawls. Jamie shrugged.

'Suit yourself.' He glanced down at Daisy. 'Better take care o' your ma. There's a chemist across 'street. He might be able to help.' He turned abruptly and left, pushing his way through the crowd.

Lily sank to the ground. 'Daisy,' she groaned, 'get me somebody, quick. I'm losing 'babby.'

CHAPTER THREE

Oliver Walker peered between the coloured glass jars and bottles that were sitting on shelves in his father's shop window. Something was going on across King Street. A crowd had gathered and he stood on tiptoe, craning his neck, but could only see the top of a woman's head: her shawl, in fact, for he couldn't see her face.

'Something's happening out there,' he told his father. 'There are a lot of people milling about. And not just the market people.'

'A trader?' His father carefully poured a dark liquid from a large bottle into a small one, and then put a cork in the top. 'Or a preacher telling them to save their souls?'

'Save whose souls?' Oliver's mother, Martha, came into the shop from an inner door with a shopping basket over her arm, wearing an outdoor coat. 'There's nobody out there worth saving!'

'Oh, come now, my dear,' her husband gently chided. 'That's a little harsh.'

'Riff-raff!' She grimaced. 'From 'bottom of 'heap, most of them. I'm going shopping,' she declared. 'I'll be back in an hour.'

Oliver raised his eyebrows at his father as she went out of the door, but his father didn't respond. Charles Walker was used to his wife's opinions and although he didn't approve of most of them he had learned over the years to

21

mainly disregard them. It made for a quieter life, he had discovered.

'There's a man there now,' Oliver commented, still looking out. 'He must be standing on a box. I could see a woman before.'

His father came and stood beside him. 'Preacher,' he said. 'There was someone there earlier. But that poor fellow didn't get a crowd. He just stood there talking to himself.'

'That's why I don't think it's a preacher,' Oliver said. 'They never get such a crowd. This fellow must be selling something special to attract so many people.'

'Go and see then, if you want to,' his father smiled, indulging his sixteen-year-old son. 'But we must get these mixtures made up. Customers will be coming in for them.'

'All right.' Oliver took off his white coat and rolled down his sleeves. 'I'll just take a look. Shan't be a minute!'

He dashed out of the shop, setting the bell jingling. A few minutes later he was back. 'You'll never guess, Pa! It's a man selling his wife! Isn't that appalling? He's got a rope round her waist, like you would with an animal, but the worst thing is I saw her shawl swing open, and . . . and I think she's expecting a child.'

His father put down the spoon with which he had been about to measure a quantity of white powder into a paper cone. 'You're not serious!' he exclaimed. 'Should we send for a constable?'

Oliver shook his head. 'There's one there already, but I don't think he's doing anything about it.'

'It's surely not possible! It must be against the law.' His father rubbed his chin. 'Though something tells me I've heard of it happening before. Yes,' he exclaimed. 'I have. My father told me about it. A countryman came into Hull and sold his wife; but that must have been – oh, twenty years ago; surely people have more respect these days?'

The door crashed open and his wife looked in. 'What did I tell you? Riff-raff. There's a man out there selling his wife! Country folk by 'look of 'em. He's asking five guineas

22

for her! Disgusting!' She flew out again, leaving the door open.

Oliver carefully closed it behind her. 'Is there anything we can do?'

His father looked at him from over the top of his spectacles. 'No,' he said. 'If the constable is there and it's not against the law – though that would surprise me – then it's nothing to do with us. Perhaps the wife is willing.'

'She didn't seem willing.' Oliver gave a wry smile. 'She was calling her husband some very choice names.' Then his smile faded. 'There was a little girl with them. She looked very frightened.'

'How old? Now that would worry me.' Charles looked grave. 'It surely wouldn't be permitted to sell a child. That would be abhorrent.'

'I don't know.' Oliver shrugged. 'Ten – eleven. She was just a scrap, really. Not much on her.'

'Mmm. Perhaps they're desperate. A great many people are. If they're country folk they've perhaps come to town looking for work and found none.' Charles sighed. 'Little we can do, I'm afraid.'

They both continued with the job of getting medication ready for their customers, and after a while Oliver glanced out of the window again. 'They've gone,' he said. 'At least the crowd has. I wonder what happened.'

'Ma!' Daisy bent over her mother. 'Who can I ask? I can't leave you here. What shall we do?'

'Give us a hand up, Daisy,' Lily said. 'Pain's easing a bit.'

Daisy put her hand under her mother's elbow to help her and Lily leaned against the railings.

'You all right, missis?' A woman hailed them and came over. 'I saw what happened back there. Monsters, both of 'em. I'd hang 'em up by their shirt tails if I had my way.'

Lily gave a contemptuous grimace. 'I could think of worse things to do to 'em; especially that scabby, sneaking scoundrel of a rogue who's my husband. If I ever get my

hands on him he'll be sorry.' She gave the woman a searching glance. 'I've started in labour. Do you know where I
could go for help? I've no money. Not a penny.'

'Where do you live?' the woman asked. 'Are you from
round here?'

Lily shook her head. 'First time I've been. We're from a
place called Seathorne. Near Withernsea,' she added, seeing
the blank expression on the woman's face. 'On 'coast,' she
elaborated, when the woman frowned and shrugged.

'Never heard of it,' the woman said. 'What 'you doing
here?'

'I wish I knew,' Lily groaned. 'It wasn't my idea.'

'Well, I think 'best thing you can do is go to 'workhouse
infirmary. They might tek you in till you've had 'babby;
but I doubt they'd let you stop, not if you're not from these
parts. I'll show you where it is if you like. It's not far from
here.'

'Workhouse!' Lily let out a gasp of anger and frustration.
How had she come to this? 'I can't do that! I've never sunk
so low!'

'I don't know where else to suggest. Not if you've no
money.' She looked about her meaningfully and then back
at Lily. 'What do you want to do? I can't hang about. If you
don't want to go, then I'll have to be off.'

'No. Wait! I'm sorry,' Lily said and grimaced as a pain
shot through her.

'You'll not want to give birth out here!' The woman
seemed anxious. 'I think you'll have to be quick.'

'Yes.' Daisy took her mother's arm. 'We'll go there. It
don't matter, Ma. Nobody will know us. There's no shame.
It's not your fault.'

Lily made a huge effort, leaning on Daisy as they followed
the stranger across the square and down a street to another,
wider street full of shops and banks and imposing offices,
until they stopped at a pair of wooden gates outside a
dilapidated building. 'This is never it?' she said, dismayed
at its condition.

'Aye, it is,' the woman said. 'They've been on for years about moving it somewhere else, but nowt ever happens. I don't know what it's like inside,' she added. 'Thank God I've managed to avoid it. All 'best, anyway,' she said. 'I'll have to be off. I hope they can help you.'

'So do I,' Lily said on a shallow breath, 'because I don't think I've got long.'

The woman scurried off and by her nervous manner Daisy felt that she wanted to get away from them; that she was frightened of her mother's giving birth whilst she was there. I'm frightened too, she thought. What if Ma dies? What'll I do without her? She turned wide eyes to her mother. 'Shall I knock, Ma, or shall we just go in?'

The gates were half open and people were going in and out. Poor, ragged people, Daisy saw. They looked as if all hope had been knocked out of them.

'We'll go in,' her mother said. 'See if there's anybody in authority. Please God, they'll tek me.'

As they went through the gate into a large yard somebody called to them. Down some wooden steps which led from a hay loft, a young lame boy was being hauled by his scruff by a thin-faced shabby-looking man. The man dropped the boy, who scurried off, and shouted at them. 'Who are you? You're not resident here.'

'I'm Lily Fowler and this is my daughter.' Lily looked at him and any hope of sympathy she might have cherished died immediately. 'I'm – I'm pregnant and I've started in labour. I need a bed or a midwife.'

'You'll be lucky!' He came towards her. 'Where you from?'

'Near Withernsea,' she began, but he interrupted.

'Withernsea! That's not in this district! You can't stop here. You'll have to go back where you came from.'

'But I can't! We've been abandoned. I've no means of getting home.'

The fellow took her by the arm and roughly turned her

towards the gate. 'Out!' he said. 'We can't tek you. We're full up as it is.'

'But where can I go?' Lily cried. 'I can't give birth out in 'street!'

'Go to 'vagrant office,' he said, pushing her out. 'They might give you summat.'

'I'm not a vagrant,' she pleaded. 'And I'm not asking for a handout. I need a woman to help me, or a doctor.'

He guffawed. 'A doctor! Who do you think you are? You shouldn't have got yourself in this fix in 'first place.'

Lily clutched imploringly at his coat, but he was already closing the gate. 'Now, gerroff,' he said. 'Afore I send for 'constable.'

She bent low, screwing up her face and biting on her lip. 'What am I going to do,' she muttered. 'Billy Fowler, may you rot in hell.'

'Can somebody help?' Daisy begged people passing by. 'Is there anybody who can help my ma?'

Most people hurried past, but one woman slowed down. 'Won't they admit her at 'workhouse?'

Daisy shook her head and began to cry. 'He said we had to go back where we came from and we can't do that.'

The woman lifted her umbrella and banged on the work-house gate, which had been locked behind them. Another man opened it. He appeared to be someone in authority for he wore a grey wool coat and a black, though rather stained, top hat. 'Yes, madam?' he said politely, for the woman was neatly dressed. 'What can I do for you?'

'This poor woman needs help immediately,' she said. 'And she's been turned away.'

He opened the gates again to admit them, and giving the woman a fawning smile said, 'I'll attend to the matter.'

She gave a little sigh of satisfaction and turned to Lily. 'I'm sure you'll be all right now, my dear,' she said, and hurried away up the street.

'Now then,' the man said sharply. 'Are you a Hull resident?'

'No,' Lily gasped. 'But I just need to lie down some-where. I don't want to stop here and I'll leave just as soon as my labour's over.'

The man frowned. 'You're not a Hull resident? Well then, I can't help you. This establishment is for 'paupers of Hull; 'Board of Governors wouldn't thank me for tekking folks in from far and wide. Heaven knows we've little enough room as it is.'

He put his hand on the gate and opened it wide, and, with a sweep of his hand, made to usher her out.

'I hope you can sleep at night,' Lily hissed as she passed out of the gate. 'Are there no decent folk anywhere in this town?'

He shrugged and closed the gate behind her. Then he opened it a crack. 'There's a sick dispensary in John Street,' he muttered. 'You could ask there.' The gate slammed shut.

'We don't know where that is,' Daisy cried. 'We'll have to ask somebody.'

'It might be on 'road where we came in,' Lily muttered. 'That was 'main thoroughfare.' She put her hand to her mouth. 'Help me, Daisy. I feel sick. Let's try to get back to that church. Mebbe there'll be somebody there, 'parson or 'churchwarden or somebody.'

Daisy put her arm round her mother's waist and they staggered back towards the square. 'I'm bleeding,' her mother groaned. 'If I don't survive this, Daisy, you must try to get back to Ted. Tell him what's happened. Tell him about that wicked reprobate who did this to me and tell him to report him to 'authorities.' She took a shivering breath. 'And if I do survive, I'll have my revenge. Just see if I don't.'

Somehow they reached the church gates and Lily took hold of the railings. 'Go inside and ask for help,' she gasped. 'I can't go any further.'

Daisy ran down the path towards the heavy doors and Lily bent low. She groaned as another pain struck her.

'You all right, love?' a woman's voice asked and Lily shook her head. Then another voice asked, 'What's up? Is she drunk?'

'No,' the first voice said. 'I think she's – are you in labour, missis?'

Lily nodded. 'Yes.' Her voice grated. 'My daughter's run into 'church to fetch help.'

But Daisy was running back. 'Door's locked, Ma,' she said breathlessly. 'I've hammered 'n' hammered, but nobody's answering.'

'Side door,' someone said. 'That'll be open.'

Lily raised her head. A small crowd had gathered round her and even some of the market traders were looking over to see what was going on.

'She can't stop here, poor lass,' a young woman said. 'It's not decent. I'll run to one of 'shops. Surely somebody will tek her in.'

There was a murmur of approval and the woman sped off. A trader turned up with a cup of water which Lily gratefully sipped. Then the crowd parted to make way for a middle-aged man in a white coat.

'Can I help you?' he asked her. 'I'm not a doctor, but I am an apothecary and I have a small room in my shop where you might like to rest.' He took her arm as she nodded. 'My name is Charles Walker. Come, it isn't far. We'll take care of you.'

CHAPTER FOUR

Billy Fowler scurried back to the inn where he had left the horse and cart. 'Ten bob,' he muttered. 'Should've got more'n that for her! Won't buy much won't ten bob.'

Nevertheless, it bought him a meat pie, followed by a roly-poly pudding and several tankards of ale. Then, because he had a long journey home, he bought a bottle of rum and downed a large glass of it before going to collect the horse and cart. He gave a penny to the stable lad, who looked at it askance, muttering something derogatory about country peasants, before putting it in his pocket.

He drove out of the town over a rickety old bridge and then pulled over. 'I'd mebbe be better going back 'other way,' he muttered. 'Pike keeper on yon road might remember me coming in wi' 'wife and 'young lass.' He decided therefore to travel on the older turnpike which was several miles longer but preferable, he thought, to enquiries from the toll keeper regarding the whereabouts of his wife and daughter.

He took a swig from the rum bottle and set off. It was a bright afternoon with no sign of rain, though the sun was low in the sky, and he reckoned that he would be home by nine o'clock. 'I could even,' he muttered, as he trundled along the Holderness road, 'go across country, over Humbleton Moor to Roos, and save paying an extra toll at Hedon.' I'll see how 'time is going when I reach Wyton Bar,

29

he meditated. Though there's no hurry. I've had my dinner and there's nobody at home to nag at me for being late.

It was then that he remembered Ted, Lily's son, who would be waiting for him. Now then, he mused. What tale am I going to spin about his ma? Do I say she's run off? That she and his sister decided to stay in Hull? The problem occupied him for the next few miles as they rattled along, going at a fairly brisk pace despite the narrowness of the road compared with the one they had travelled on coming into Hull, for it was raised above the common land and as there had been no rain for the last few weeks the ground was dry.

He paid at the first tollgate and took another swig from the bottle before he moved off again. 'Aye, I think that's what I'll do. I'll go across country; I think I know 'way. It might tek a bit longer but it don't matter, I'm in no hurry.' And so he continued, muttering and talking to himself and taking glugs from the rum bottle. He stopped once at a roadside trough so that the horse could take a drink while he relieved himself, and almost fell over as he drunkenly climbed back into the cart.

The journey took longer than he had anticipated and the sky was darkening as he reached the village of Bilton, and the air felt heavy with the threat of rain. Soon it would be time to make a decision. Should he continue on along the turnpike towards the village of Preston and the town of Hedon, or should he turn off on a side road which, although free, would be much harder going. 'I'll have to pay at Wyton Bar,' he grumbled to himself, 'and then again at Hedon if I go on 'new road to Patrington.' He jingled the money in his pocket. 'I'll have nowt left at this rate.'

'Going far?' the toll keeper at Wyton Bar asked him. 'We're in for a drop o' rain if I'm not mistaken.'

'Not far,' he slurred, feeling tired and dizzy.

'Haven't seen you about afore,' the keeper said. 'Not from round here, are you?'

'No,' Billy muttered. 'Just visiting some folks.'

'Oh, aye? Who's that then? Somebody at Humbleton?'

Billy glanced at the signpost. 'No, some folks at Sproatley.'

'Sproatley? I used to live there afore I got this job. I worked for 'Constables.'

Billy nodded. He had heard of the landowners of Holderness who lived in a great house on the edge of the village of Sproatley. 'Have to be going,' he said. 'Afore 'rain starts.' He shook the reins and the horse reluctantly moved off.

'Watch out if you've any money,' the keeper called after him. 'There's some rogues about.'

Billy glanced over his shoulder. 'Don't have any,' he shouted back. 'I'm onny a labouring man.' But after turning a bend, he took his money from his coat and pushed it down into his breeches pocket. Then, a little further on, he stopped and extracted the florins, hiding them under the sacks in the corner of the cart.

It started to rain as he arrived in Sproatley and by the time he reached the road leading to Humbleton it was lashing down. He put his coat collar up but within minutes he was soaked.

'Blast it,' he shivered. 'Nivver expected this.' He pulled up and reached over to get a sack to cover him; as he caught it up he heard the rattle of coins as the florins rolled on the floor of the cart.

'Damn and blast,' he cursed, climbing down. 'I'll have to find 'em.' He searched in the gloom, his hands sweeping the boards of the cart. He found one and put it in his pocket, but couldn't find any others. 'Have to look in 'morning when it's light,' he muttered. 'Can't lose it. No point in going all that way if I'm gonna lose it.'

His thoughts jumped back to Ted. He'd got rid of Lily and Daisy, but what was he to do about her lad? 'I should nivver have married her,' he surmised. 'I was talked into it, I reckon. She was that persuasive.' But he remembered how attracted he had been to Lily when he first met her. 'It was her eyes,' he muttered. 'Finest eyes I've ever seen on a woman, and them hips! But I'm best on me own without having a woman telling me what to do; telling me to get washed when I'm not mucky; allus mekking 'house tidy. There's no need for it. No need at all.

'I'll send 'lad off to look for 'em. Reckon on that I waited and they didn't turn up. He can walk into Hull, young lad like him. It'll onny tek him just over half a day; or get 'carrier from Patrington if he's any money. I'll not pay for it. I'm done wi' that, financing them as doesn't belong to me, and wi' a bit o' luck he won't come back either.'

He was beginning to shiver as the cold and the wet penetrated his clothing. He took another drink and peered ahead of him. It was as black as pitch and there were no landmarks to guide him. 'I can't even see 'road,' he muttered. 'There's not a house or a barn showing a light. I could be in 'middle of 'field for all I know! Whoa up, Dobbin!' he shouted as the cart hit something solid and ground to a halt.

He climbed out and groped about in the darkness. 'Daft beggar!' he complained. 'He's run into a wall or a bridge or summat.' He felt along the side of the cart and down to the wheel. It had become jammed fast on a brick wall which, when he felt along the top of it, he realized was the top of a small bridge, probably over a dyke or a ditch. He pulled and pushed but couldn't budge the wheel. Cursing, he groped towards the horse and began to unfasten the leather traces to release the animal from the shafts.

'Can't see a damned thing,' he muttered, his fingers cold and clumsy. 'I should've brought a lantern.' The horse snickered, shaking its head and curling its lip. 'Don't you take a nip out o' me, you owd devil, or I'll tek me belt to you,' Billy snapped, pulling roughly at the straps.

He grabbed at the animal's collar as he released it and felt it making a bid for freedom. 'No, you don't,' he warned. 'Don't think you're leaving me out here on me own cos you're not.'

He awkwardly held the straps with one hand and led the horse to the rear of the cart, where he felt about at the side of the road for a tree or a bush where he could tie it up. He found a spindly bush and hooked the straps over it, then turned his attention to freeing the wheel. The rain ran down his neck as he tugged and heaved and shook it, and then he went to the front of the cart to push. There was a creaking and grinding as at last it came free and he felt a brief moment of triumph. He rolled it off the bridge, put the horse back into the shafts, climbed aboard and shook the reins. The cart jerked and tilted as the horse moved on and Billy only just saved himself from being tipped out.

Wearily he climbed down again and searched with his hands around the wheel. A spoke was cracked; but that won't matter, he thought, and felt below the vehicle along the axle. 'Damned linchpin's gone! Must have fallen out when 'cart hit 'bridge.' He realized that within another few yards, the wheel could have come off altogether.

He put his hands to his head. 'Now what am I going to do?' He heaved a great sigh. 'By heck! I'm stumped and no mistake. I'll have to leave 'cart here and ride 'hoss home. But suppose somebody comes along and pinches 'cart? It's a good 'un; worth a bit.'

He stood there in the wet and the darkness, rueing the wrong decision that had made him come across country, but never thinking that it was his own streak of meanness that had decided him to cut across the hummocky plain of Holderness on unfamiliar roads and narrow tracks; to cross dykes and ditches with wide open fields and meadows on either side with barely a tree or a hedge for shelter. Muttering and mumbling, he unhitched the horse again and pushed the cart under what felt like scrubby undergrowth. He fished about in the back to find the coins, but felt nothing but the soaking wet sacks, which he wrung out and draped round his shoulders.

He hadn't ridden since he was a youth and he scrabbled

about trying to jump or climb on to Dobbin's wet back. But the horse was having none of it and he shied and skittered until he broke free from Billy's restraining grasp and cantered off, the sound of his hooves thudding in the darkness until it gradually faded away.

Billy stamped, cursed and kicked at the cart, but missed his footing and fell full length. 'I'm at 'end of my tether,' he muttered, slithering about on the muddy road, almost weeping with anger and frustration. 'I'll have to find some shelter and then in 'morning I'll try to get a lift. But where in God's name am I?' He started to shout. 'Is there nobody living in this godforsaken place? Help. Help!'

Ted stretched and yawned, rolled off his mattress and looked out of the window. It was a grey and dreary morning, with no breaks in the low cloud at all. The sea was the same colour and the sluggish white-tipped waves rolled monotonously towards the cliffs, thudding softly against them.

'So where is everybody?' he murmured. 'Two days they've been gone and Fowler said they'd be back 'same night.'

Ted never addressed Billy Fowler by name and only ever thought of him as Fowler. He disliked him intensely and knew that the feeling was mutual. He frowned. Where had they gone that would take so long? His mother hadn't been expecting to stay away. She would have said if she had and left him something to eat. He had seen the puzzlement on her face and heard her asking Fowler where they were going, but he hadn't answered.

He riddled the fire and put on more wood, swung the kettle over the flame, and then slid back into his bed on the floor. No sense in going out just yet, he thought. Nowt much to do and anyway I'll hear them come back and can nip out sharpish.

He didn't sleep but only ruminated on his future. I'll leave, I think. There's no point in stopping here. I'm old enough to work. When they'd lived in Hollym he had started occasional work on the farms, but about the same time that his mother had married Fowler work had fallen off and he had been unable to find other employment. Though he had disliked Fowler on sight, he had thought that he could help out on his smallholding, until such time as something else came his way.

To his horror, and he felt to his mother's too, the 'smallholding' had turned out to be nothing more than a hovel standing on the edge of the cliff and in imminent danger of falling into the sea. There was a small scrappy plot of land behind the cottage where Fowler had made a half-hearted attempt at growing vegetables. Two goats were tethered in a small grassy area which also supported a dozen or so hens and ducks. Fowler had told them that he had once had land at the front of the house, but that it had crumbled away into the sea.

'I can't stand goat's milk,' Ted's mother had told Fowler when they first arrived. 'Can't we have a cow?'

'Aye, if you pay for it,' had been his reply, and because Lily had managed to save a little money for emergencies it was used to buy a milch cow.

'This is yours and Daisy's,' his mother had whispered to Ted, 'so you've got to look after her. Mek sure she gets 'best grass. See if you can find somebody who'll let her feed in their meadow. If there's plenty of milk I'll mek some cheese. It might be 'best nourishment we'll get.' She had added in another whisper, 'I think I might have made 'wrong decision here, Ted lad. But we're stuck wi' it.'

That had been eighteen months ago and had it not been for his reluctance to leave his mother and sister in the clutches of Fowler, Ted would have left to look for work elsewhere. But he had dug over the vegetable plot, dragged seaweed up the cliff and added it to the heap of cow pats, goat droppings, fowl dung and night soil to rot down. With this he had mixed ash and soot until he had a rich compost and by the following summer he had harvested a good crop of potatoes, cabbages and leeks, and in a bucket of sand

and compost had grown the biggest carrots he had ever seen.

The kettle started to steam; he rolled out of bed and made a pot of tea, then cut two thick slices of bread and spread them with blackberry and crab apple jelly which his mother had made last autumn. It was tart to the tongue as she had had little sugar to sweeten it and make it set, but she had added honey from a jar which one of their former neighbours had given her when they moved to Seathorne.

He stood munching on the bread and drinking his tea, gazing out of the window at the dreary sky. 'Wonder where they've got to? Shouldn't mind if *he* didn't come back. Ma and Daisy and me could get along fine wi'out him; till 'house falls over anyway. Don't know how we'd manage then.' He chewed over the possibilities of getting a job with one of the local landholders and being given a tied cottage, but he knew very well that hopes of that were negligible. 'Perhaps we could go back to Hollym, mebbe get our owd cottage back if nobody else is living in it. We're in Withernsea township just 'same as afore.'

He drained the pot of tea, had another slice of bread, and then dressed, putting on his coat and boots. As he laced up his boots he heard a sound outside. 'That's 'hoss,' he muttered. 'They're back.'

He unbolted the door and opened it, letting in an icy blast of wind. He looked out but could see no one. Then he heard the whinnying of the horse from round the back of the cottage where there was a lean-to wooden structure which passed as a stable. He closed the door behind him and went out, wishing that he'd got up earlier to let out the fowl as Fowler would be sure to grumble that he'd done nothing but lie abed.

But there was no one there. The cart wasn't there either, but only old Dobbin, who had settled himself behind the wooden wall. 'What's up, owd lad?' Ted stroked the horse's neck and unfastened the trailing reins. 'What's happened? You've been tekken out of 'shafts, so what's going on? Have you run off? But why would you do that? You're a docile old fellow usually. Nowt much bothers you as a rule.'

He rubbed the animal down with a sack as he was talking to him; his coat was very wet. He fetched an old horse blanket to put over him. He fed him and went to open up the ducks and hens and feed the goats. Then he walked across to their neighbour's meadow with a pail in his hand to milk the cow. 'Don't understand it,' he mumbled. 'Hope that owd bugger hasn't been up to summat; or mebbe he's tipped 'cart over and they're all lying in a ditch somewhere. But then Dobbin would still be fastened up in 'shafts.' He went back again to look at the straps after he'd seen to the cow, and saw that they had been unfastened and not torn away.

By midday he was becoming very anxious; he climbed on the horse's back and rode a short way down the road to look for any sign of them. Wherever they've been they'll have to walk back, he thought, so I hope they've not gone further than Patrington. And Ma in her state won't be able to walk fast. That's it, he decided. Summat's happened to 'cart, mebbe a wheel's dropped off, and they're having to walk and it's tekking a time cos of Ma. He frowned and bit his lip. But then, why's 'hoss come back on his own?

He turned about and rode back. Most of Seathorne village had succumbed to the sea some years before and the remaining few straggling buildings appeared to be deserted, or he might have enquired of somebody if they'd seen his family.

As he rode towards the cottage the roar of the sea was like thunder. The horse skittered about, afraid of the wildness of the wind that had risen and the crashing of the waves against the cliffs. Ted slid down from his back and led him towards his shelter. 'Don't be afeared, owd lad. Sea'll not get you here. It'll get me first if I stay much longer in yon hovel.'

He walked to the edge of the land and peered over. 'Spring surge,' he muttered as he watched the swirling, sand-lashed foam batter the cliffs. A chunk of boulder clay slithered down from the top, gathering up an avalanche of loosened debris, rocks, pebbles, shingle and clumps of grass, and depositing them into the buffeting waves.

Ted glanced back to the cottage. 'Will it last 'night? Dare I stop another night or will I finish up in 'sea?'

The horse whinnied and Ted looked towards the muddy track. Somebody was walking unsteadily along it. A bedraggled and weary figure who staggered from side to side.

'Fowler!' Ted shouted. 'Is that you?' Without waiting for an answer he shouted again. 'Where's my ma? Where's our Daisy? What's happened?'

CHAPTER FIVE

'Where's my ma?' Ted went towards Fowler. 'Where've you been?'

'Mind your own ruddy business,' Fowler grunted. 'Get out o' my way, you recklin'. I need my bed. I'm just about all in.'

Ted put his fist towards Fowler. 'It is my business. Tell me where she is. Have you left her somewhere? Is she sick?'

Fowler sneered. 'She's sick all right, and so will you be if you don't shift out o' my road.'

'I'm not moving till you've told me where they are.' Ted drew himself up. He was the same height as Fowler, prepared to fight him if necessary. 'Where've you been? Patrington?'

Fowler's lip curled. 'Further than that, and they're not anywhere that you'll find 'em.' Maliciously he stared at the boy. 'And you can pack your things and clear off. You needn't think you're stopping here wi' me cos you're not.'

Ted felt sick and angry. What had Fowler done? His mother wouldn't have just gone off without telling him. He grabbed hold of Fowler's coat and felt the wetness of it. 'You'll tell me where she is first or I'll drop you ower 'side of 'cliff.'

'You and who else?' Fowler jeered, pushing him away. 'You've nowt on you, you little ratbag.'

Ted tightened his grip, almost lifting Fowler off his feet.

39

Though he was thin, he was stronger than Fowler, and had large hands and feet. Fowler was flabby and indolent and only ever moved slowly. 'We'll see,' he said, pulling him towards him. 'Tide's in – you'd get a soaking.'

Fowler wrenched himself away. 'They've stopped in Hull if you must know. Your ma said she wasn't coming back. Fed up wi' 'country, she said, and wanted to stop in town.'

'I don't believe you. Ma's a countrywoman! Never been in town in her life. You've left her there, haven't you?' Ted shouted. 'Left 'em both on their own! How will they get back? Where's 'cart? Hoss came back on his own. Summat's gone on that you're not telling me.'

'Axle broke.' Fowler shrugged. 'I had to push 'cart under a hedge. Damned hoss cantered off. I've walked from God knows where. Miles I've walked; now get out o' my way!'

'And that's where you left Ma and Daisy? In 'middle o' nowhere?'

Fowler grinned. 'I just told you. She's stopped in Hull. Last time I saw her was in 'Market Place.'

'But – but she's—' Ted didn't like to mention his mother's condition. He knew, of course; but it wasn't something to be talked about, and certainly not to Fowler. The very idea of his mother and him together made him want to vomit.

'In 'pudding club! Aye, I know that, don't I? And that's why I wanted rid of her; aye, and that sister o' yourn as well. Now I'm shut o' them both.'

Ted threw himself at Fowler, knocking him to the ground. 'You've killed 'em,' he yelled. 'You're a murderer!'

Fowler levered himself up, thrusting Ted away. 'Daft young beggar! Course I haven't killed 'em! I've sold her. Told 'chap what bought her he could have your lass as well for 'same price.'

Ted rocked back on to his heels. 'You never! I don't believe you. You wouldn't do owt like that.'

'Why wouldn't I?' Fowler got to his hands and knees. 'It's not against 'law; anybody'll tell you that, and I'm sick to death of having somebody telling me what to do in me own house. I like being on me own.' He looked up at Ted. 'So like I just said, you can clear off; pack your things, such as you've got, and go. Go on! Beat it!'

Ted saw red. His mother sold! That couldn't be right. It had to be against the law. She wouldn't have gone willingly, that was for certain, and she wouldn't have left him. He grabbed Fowler by his jacket, pulling at him and shaking him violently. 'I'll kill you,' he shouted.

Fowler tussled with him as he rose, throwing wild punches to Ted's face and swearing. 'You haven't got 'strength,' he rasped, kicking out with his boot, catching Ted on his shin and making him wince. 'Mammy's little milksop. Think you can fight, do you?' He lashed out, a glancing blow which struck the side of Ted's cheek. 'I'll show you how to fight.'

Furious, Ted threw himself at Fowler, catching him off balance. They both fell heavily, and Ted, on top of the older man, rained blows on his head until Fowler called out, 'All right! All right!'

They drew apart and Ted, breathing heavily, stared at his opponent. In those few seconds he was unprepared for Fowler's fist as it landed under his chin. He drew in a sharp breath as he reeled and Fowler, with an unexpected spurt of energy, sprang to his feet and launched a boot at his ribs. 'That'll larn you to mess wi' me, tha young varmint.' He stood over Ted as he lay curled up, winded. 'Now clear off and don't come back.'

Ted started to rise, saw Fowler's boot poised to kick again and caught it, bringing the older man crashing down. They rolled over and over on the muddy ground, slithering and sliding, punching and kicking, but Fowler was tiring and Ted felt that the blows aimed at him were lessening. He pulled back his fist to aim another blow, but Fowler saw it coming and rolled over, trying to get to his feet. 'Young whelp,' he snarled. 'Get off into Hull and find your ma and tell her how you tried to fight, but hadn't got 'marra.'

Ted jumped to his feet and grabbed Fowler. 'Haven't got

'marra? Haven't got 'marra? I'll show you what I've got, you clodhopping lumpkin.' He shook Fowler and they shouted abuse at each other, pushing, shoving, aiming blows, and skidding on the wet and muddy cliff top.

Ted's cold hands grasped Fowler's jacket; it was soaked with rain and mud and he could barely keep a grip. He had pulled back a fist to aim another blow when his feet skidded from beneath him. Fowler started to laugh derisively but his laugh turned to a startled shout as Ted's feet became entangled with his and he too began to fall. They had rolled about on the quaggy ground oblivious of how close they were to the cliff edge. Fowler's arms began to flail as he fought to get a grip with his feet.

It was almost like slow motion, Ted thought, as, flat on his stomach, he gazed over the brink. One minute Fowler was there and the next he was falling backwards, first his head, shoulders and body and then his legs and feet disappearing over the edge.

'He's done for,' Ted muttered. 'It's not my fault. I couldn't have hauled him back.' He thought guiltily that even if he had been able to, he didn't know if he would have stretched out a hand to Fowler. 'I can't see him. He's gone straight into 'sea.'

The sea below him roared and lashed, foamy crests of wild water crashing against the cliff. He felt the sting of sharp sand as the spume spattered against his face. I hope nobody thinks I knocked him over. I know I said I'd kill him and throw him over, but I didn't really mean it, and anyway, it might have been me gone down instead of him. He wouldn't have helped me back either. Pushed me, more like. He glanced round nervously. Still, it's a good job there's nobody about to see us fighting or they might think I'd done it on purpose.

The waves were battering all along the cliffs as far as he could see. There was no shore at all; the sand was completely covered by deep water. 'What'll I do?' he muttered. 'If I go into 'village for help, by 'time I get back wi' somebody it'll be too late. And what if they start questioning me; what if they ask me what he was doing standing right on 'edge? What'd I tell 'em then?'

He got to his feet and the enormity of the situation made him shake. He put his hand to his mouth. Is it my fault? No, it's his. He shouldn't have said he'd sold my ma. No decent man would have done that. I didn't want to kill him, not really. If he'd just tummelled over accidental like, I wouldn't have been that bothered. I didn't like him. Hated him even. But still!

He stood dithering with uncertainty. I wish Ma was here. I don't know what to do. He looked again over the edge but could see nothing but battering waves; the sky was darkening and a huge rain cloud was hanging threateningly overhead.

'Nobody'll ever find him now anyway.' He bit into his lip. 'Even if they put a boat out. He'll be washed up further down 'coast. Mebbe at Kilnsea or Spurn and nobody'll know him down there.'

He made a sudden decision and with one last look over his shoulder he ran towards the cottage. He took a blanket from the bed and wrapped a clean flannel shirt, his other pair of trousers and a pair of socks into it and rolled them up into a knotted bundle, and he went outside to the wood pile and found a stout stick and threaded it through the knot. He stopped and considered. What to do about the hens and goats, and the cow which was over in John Ward's meadow? Nowt's ever straightforward, he pondered. I can't just leave them.

He nibbled on his fingers as he cogitated. But I can't take them with me either. I'll take 'hoss and ride him into Hull. He sighed and put down the bundle and went into his precious vegetable plot. He'd only just started planting seeds and beans so he reckoned that not much would be wasted. He scurried across to the henhouse and began to unravel the chicken wire which surrounded it. The hens rushed squawking on to the fresh piece of earth and began scratching about. He went inside the henhouse and came out with two eggs; one he cracked and swallowed raw and the other he put into his coat pocket. He unfastened the goats from their tether and let them free. That just left the cow, and he was sorry to leave her; they hadn't had her long, having swapped her for the old one, a clutch of eggs and a basket of vegetables. He knew that she would let John Ward know that she needed milking the next morning. He had often found her standing near the fence next to Ward's yard and he was certain that the farmer would milk her when no one else came to do it.

Back inside the house he beat up the other egg into a cup of milk and drank that, then picked up his bundle of clothes. 'Nowt else to take,' he murmured. 'And I'd best be off now rather than wait till morning. Nobody'll see me now that it's nearly dark.'

His eye caught Fowler's rubber coat hanging behind the door. Fowler hadn't thought fit to take it when he set off on the journey to Hull, and Ted recalled how wet his jacket was. I'll take that. It's no good to him where he is, he told himself, and he gave a shudder at the thought of his stepfather's body being washed down the coast. He put on the coat and was glad of it when he stepped outside, for the cloud had opened up and heavy rain was pelting down.

He closed the door behind him and went to the shelter, fetching out the agitated, nervous horse, tacking him up with an old and worn saddle, and placing the blanket across his neck. He put his foot in the stirrup and jumped on his back, setting his bundle in front of him. 'Cheerio, Seathorne,' he muttered as he wheeled round towards the track. 'Shan't be seeing you again. Not if I can help it, anyway.'

As he rode off he heard a crashing, reverberating thud and lifted his head thinking it was thunder; then it came again, a slithering, rumbling sound, like muffled drums. He glanced over his shoulder and his mouth dropped open. The cottage door, which he had closed, was swinging wide, banging against the frame. The ground in front of the cottage where a moment ago he had been standing had fallen away, leaving nothing beneath it but broken cliffs .and foaming turbulent water.

CHAPTER SIX

Lily leaned heavily on Charles Walker's arm. Hope to God it isn't far, she worried, or I'll give birth out here in 'street. Daisy scurried at her side, patting her arm and whispering that she'd be all right now.

'Here we are,' the chemist said. The door to his premises was already held open to admit them by a young man who ushered them through to a small room behind the counter: a room with a wall full of shelves containing bottles in blue, green, black and clear glass. It smelled very clean, like soap, just as her old kitchen at Hollym used to do on washdays. There was a narrow bed along a wall with a white sheet and a blanket folded neatly upon it and on the other wall was a sink with a tap.

'I can't pay you,' she gasped. 'My husband's abandoned me. Sold me, he did.' In spite of her anger and pain, or perhaps because of it, she began to weep. 'I'm destitute, yet 'workhouse turned us away.'

'A terrible place. You wouldn't want to be in there. But don't worry about that now,' he said gently. 'First we must make sure that you are delivered safely of your child.'

'I won't be. It's too early, and besides I took a battering coming in 'cart. We've come from 'coast, near Withernsea.'

He led her towards the bed. 'I'm not a doctor,' he told her again. 'I'm a chemist, an apothecary. But I'll send my son for a midwife; I know of one who lives nearby. Your daughter can stay with you until someone comes.'

'Thank you, sir,' she breathed, and thinking again of the expense added, 'but I don't want to be a bother. Do you have a wife who could help me instead?'

Charles Walker cleared his throat. 'She's out at present.' He thanked his luck that she was, for she would have had something to say if she had been here.

Lily suddenly bent double with pain. 'I think it's too late anyway.' She retched and he hurriedly fetched a small bowl and a towel. 'Oh!' she gasped again. 'Leave me, sir. And you, Daisy, go away. This is not for you to see. I'll manage on me own.'

The chemist ushered Daisy out of the room and into his shop. 'Is the pain very bad?' he asked on his return a few minutes later. 'I can give you something to ease it.'

She gave a groaning laugh. 'I don't think you can. There's nowt to ease 'pain o' childbirth.'

He gave a small smile. 'Indeed there is. The use of chloroform is very effective.'

She gazed at him from watery eyes. 'Aye, I heard summat about it. But that's not for 'likes o' me. I couldn't afford owt like that. Can you spread an old sheet or newspaper on 'floor? I don't want to mek a mess on your nice clean floor.'

'It will wash,' he said. 'It's washed every day with carbolic acid to kill any germs.'

She swallowed and squeezed her eyes tight as another pain creased her. 'This is bad,' she muttered. 'Mebbe I'll have that midwife after all.'

He nodded. 'My son has gone to fetch her. He'll be back in just a moment. She lives only across King Street.'

'I don't know where that is.' She breathed heavily. 'This is my first visit to this town.'

He raised his eyebrows, and then turned his head towards the door at the sound of a jangling bell. 'That'll be Oliver back again. Just a minute.' He hurried out and returned immediately with a woman, older than Lily, perhaps in her late thirties, who bustled in, took off her shawl and rolled up her sleeves, then washed her hands in the sink as the chemist went out of the door and closed it quietly behind him.

'Now then, dearie.' She turned to Lily. 'Let's have a look at you.'

Daisy had stood on guard behind the counter. Mr Walker's son had asked her to mind the shop whilst he slipped out to fetch the midwife. 'Shan't be a minute.' He grinned. 'Two shakes of a lamb's tail, that's all.'

She wondered how he knew that old saying. He surely wouldn't have seen any lambs here in Hull, except those brought to market. He wouldn't have seen them frisking in the meadows as she had, jumping with all four feet in the air when they were only a few weeks old.

She gazed about her. Such myriad bottles, boxes and containers, and narrow chests with small wooden drawers, each with a brass plate engraved with a name on it. Names she couldn't even pronounce, let alone understand. Many of them began with ph and she blew through her lips as she tried to say them. A pair of brass scales, some tweezers and several spoons of different sizes stood on the counter. Muslin, adhesive plasters, bandages and scissors were in a box on a shelf underneath.

He'd returned within a few minutes, closely followed by a woman, who looked at her and commented, 'You've got an assistant, Oliver!' So then Daisy knew his name.

'Will my ma be all right?' she asked him shyly when the woman followed Mr Walker into the other room.

'I don't know.' He came round the back of the counter to stand next to her. 'I don't know about this sort of thing. But I expect so, now that Mrs Moody is here. She's well respected. That's why my father asked her. It was lucky she was in.'

'Is this your shop?' she asked. 'Your father's, I mean.'

'Yes.' He smiled. 'I help him. I'm his unpaid assistant. Until I pass my exams and then I'll be his junior partner.'

She sighed. 'That's nice,' she said softly. 'I don't know where my father is. Ma says he's dead.'

Oliver frowned. 'But I thought – I thought . . .' He pointed vaguely across the square towards the church. 'Wasn't that your father who – who sold your mother?'

'No!' she said vehemently. 'He's not! That's Billy Fowler. Ma married him when my da didn't come back. He was a sodger,' she explained. 'Ma says he was killed in Afghanistan – or somewhere foreign, anyway.'

'I see,' Oliver said solemnly. 'I'm sorry. And don't you like your stepfather?'

'No, I don't! And Ted doesn't like him either.'

'Who's Ted?'

'My brother.' Her mouth trembled. 'His name is Edward really, but we allus call him Ted. He'll wonder what's happened to us when we don't go back.' She turned anxious blue eyes up to him. 'What do you think Billy Fowler will do to him when he gets home? He won't want him there. He didn't want either of us; he didn't want this bairn that my ma is having either.'

Oliver took a breath and wondered if this act of kindness on their part might have brought them more difficulties than they had anticipated. 'What's your name?' he asked.

'Daisy,' she said. 'Daisy Leigh-Maddeson.'

'I'm Oliver Walker, Daisy,' he said. 'And I think that your brother will be able to look after himself perfectly well, and that he'll probably come to look for you and your mother.'

She smiled at him. 'Do you think so? Ma says that he doesn't have 'brains he was born with. But he's all right really.'

Oliver laughed. 'All mothers say that. My mother used to say it to me – Ah!' he exclaimed as the door jangled open. 'Here she is!'

As Mrs Walker came through the shop door, so too did Mr Walker emerge from the inner room. She looked suspiciously about the shop. It was as if she could smell trouble. Then she spotted Daisy behind the counter and stared at her.

'Who's this?' she demanded. 'We don't allow people behind 'counter!'

Mr Walker and Oliver spoke at the same time.

'This is Daisy.'

'Her mother is in labour.' Mr Walker indicated the door behind him. 'Mrs Moody is with her.'

'In our dispensary!' Mrs Walker looked horrified at the idea. 'Molly scrubbed it out only this morning!'

'Yes.' Charles Walker gave an apprehensive smile. 'Wasn't that a good thing? That's why I like it cleaned every day. We just never know when we might need it for emergencies.'

His wife glared at him. 'We don't have the facilities for women in – in those circumstances. Why isn't she at home?'

'She's from out of town, Mother,' Oliver cut in. 'She was taken ill and brought here.' He avoided saying that his father had been sent for and had brought her here himself.

'Well she can't stay,' she stated. 'Not once she's been delivered. She'll have to go home.'

'We can't go home,' Daisy said in a small voice. 'It's too far, and anyway . . .' Her words trailed off as she saw Oliver give a warning shake of his head.

'We'll talk about that later,' Mr Walker said briskly. 'She's in no fit state to go anywhere right now.' He smiled down at Daisy. 'In the meantime would you like to help us?' When she nodded he said, 'Go through into the kitchen and wash your hands and face. Molly will give you some hot water and maybe even a cup of chocolate if you ask her nicely. Mmm,' he pondered. 'Perhaps she'd better make a large jug. I'm sure your mother and Mrs Moody would like some too; and then when you've had that you can go with Oliver on a few errands and deliver some prescriptions.'

He looked at his wife, whose face had set as if in stone. 'It's the least we can do,' he said quietly. 'She's only a child, and she's had a difficult, worrying morning.'

She didn't answer, but swung round, with her basket still on her arm, and barged through another door into what Daisy assumed was their private rooms.

'Come on,' Oliver said to Daisy. 'I'll come with you and introduce you to Molly. You'll like her, she doesn't bite.'

Ten minutes later the midwife put her head round the door. 'Mr Walker. Can you come?'

He stopped counting out some tablets into a box, and went towards her.

'She's having a bad time,' she said softly. 'I can't save 'child, but if you could give her a drop o' laudanum or mebbe a whiff o' chloroform to help her over 'pain, I can deliver her of it.'

He nodded. Going first to lock the shop door, he went back into the dispensary and washed his hands at the sink. Then he took a pair of steps and climbed up, reached to the top shelf and handed down a bottle to Mrs Moody. On the ground again, he poured a few drops of the liquid contents on to a pad of folded muslin and approached Lily, who was lying on her side on the bed with the sheet over her.

'I don't know your name,' he said.

'Lily,' she breathed. 'Lily Fowler it is now, though I'll not be known by that any more.' She took a deep breath and gave a silent cry, her face creased with pain. 'I'll – go back to my other name when this is over.'

'Well, Lily,' he said, 'would you like me to give you something to ease your suffering? Chloroform is perfectly safe.'

'Aye, why not?' she whispered hoarsely. 'It can't hurt 'babby, cos she's just told me it won't live. I knew that anyway. Yes,' she said. 'I'd be glad to have summat. This is worse than giving birth to a living child. It can't help itself out like a full term one.'

51

'I know,' he said softly, and leaning over her, he said, 'Take a nice deep breath, Lily, don't fight it, and you'll just have a little sleep.' He put the pad over her nose and mouth. 'Breathe in, and when you wake up it will all be over and you can begin your life again.'

CHAPTER SEVEN

When Lily's eyes fluttered open she was on a narrow bed with a pillow beneath her head and a warm wool blanket over her. She gazed through half-open eyes round the darkened room which was lit by a low oil lamp, wondered vaguely where she was and then drifted off to sleep again. When she woke again it was morning, the lamp had either burned out or been turned out, and she could hear voices calling, the clatter of hooves and rattle of wheels, and all the bustle of life going on outside in Hull's Market Place.

I must have been here all night, she thought. But where's Daisy, and what about 'babby? Somebody must have— Her thoughts were interrupted when the door opened and Daisy came in.

'I've brought you a cup o' tea, Ma.' She smiled. 'Molly's just made it. It's that hot it's steaming, look!'

Lily sat up. She felt refreshed after her sleep, though her body was aching. 'I don't know who Molly is,' she said, 'but she's an angel. That's just what I need.'

'She works here,' Daisy said. 'She told me she's general dogsbody to Mrs Walker; but she likes Mr Walker. She says he's a proper gentleman.'

Lily blew on the tea. 'So he is,' she murmured. 'I reckon I'd have died without him.'

Daisy observed her solemnly. 'Babby died, Ma. Mr Walker said we'd to think of it as nature's way.'

'Aye, poor bairn,' Lily sighed. 'I reckoned that it would; it wasn't ready for this world. But mebbe just as well for I don't know what I'd have done wi' another bairn to feed. As it is, Daisy, I still don't know what we'll do. We're in a fix and no mistake.'

Daisy said nothing, not telling her mother that she had heard raised voices last night after Mr Walker had closed the shop, and he and Oliver had gone through to their parlour for supper. She had stayed in the kitchen with Molly and the cook, who had eyed each other but made no comment, at least not in her hearing. It was Mrs Walker who was doing most of the talking; her voice was shrill whereas Mr Walker's was low and subdued, and although she could only catch occasional words she guessed that the subject under discussion was how soon she and her mother would be leaving.

'We might have to leave today, Ma,' she said. 'I don't think we'll be allowed to stay any longer.'

Lily shook her head; her dark hair tumbled about her shoulders and Daisy thought she looked beautiful. 'Course we can't,' she said. 'Why should these folks keep us here? Mr Walker's been very good to tek us in. He'll need this room for his work.' She swung her legs off the bed, clutching the teacup in her hand. 'I feel a bit dizzy,' she murmured. 'I'm not sure if I can stand up.'

There was a knock on the door, and Molly entered carrying a tray. 'I've brought you a bit o' breakfast, missis,' she said. 'Sorry, but I don't know your name.' She nodded at Daisy. 'I know this is Daisy.'

'Lily.' Lily gazed at the tray. It had a teapot, a sugar basin and a milk jug on it, and a plate of eggs and bacon. 'Lily Leigh-Maddeson. I'm going back to my first husband's name. I don't want to hear my second's ever again.'

Molly drew near. 'I heard,' she whispered, her eyes wide. 'Is it true? That he tried to sell you?'

'Tried!' Lily exclaimed. 'Well, money changed hands. But whether it's legal I can't say. He said it was, but I'd

54

never heard of it afore.' She took the tray which Molly held and drew her legs back on to the bed. 'This is good of you.' Her voice dropped low. 'Does Mr Walker know I'm eating his vittles?'

'Oh, aye. He said as I'd to bring you a good breakfast as you mebbe wouldn't know when your next meal would be.'

'I don't.' Lily was hungry, not having eaten since she and Daisy had shared the bread the previous day, and set to to demolish the breakfast, mopping up the egg yolks with a slice of bread. 'If I'm stopping in Hull I'll have to look for work, but if I'm going back to where I belong then it's a long walk.'

'I heard Mr Walker tell his wife that you weren't fit to be moved yet.' Molly nodded her head knowingly. 'He said you'd had a difficult time.'

'So I did, and I was glad of whatever it was he gave me, but that doesn't mean that I should stay on here.' She wiped the corner of her mouth with her finger. 'I'd like to pay him back somehow if I can. Will he let me do summat? I could wash 'floor in here.'

'There's no need,' Molly said. 'I have my instructions on how it's to be done. He's very particular, is Mr Walker. He'll come in to see you, I expect, when he's finished his breakfast and you can ask him if you like.' She went towards the door. 'If you bring 'tray back when your ma's finished, Daisy, you can fetch her some hot water for washing. You'll want to freshen up, I expect?'

Lily thanked her and said that she would. She finished eating, after asking Daisy if she'd like some of the bacon.

'I've had mine,' the girl answered. 'Just 'same as yours. Eggs weren't as fresh as ours, Ma,' she whispered. 'And 'bacon was salty.'

Lily agreed, but added, 'I've never had my breakfast in bed afore, Daisy; that was a real treat. Now that we're fed we're ready for whatever 'day throws at us.' She handed her the tray. 'Fetch me that hot water, there's a good lass, and I'll have a wash. Then I'll thank Mr Walker and we'll be off.'

'What do you think you and your daughter will do?' Charles Walker asked. 'When you're ready to leave, I mean. I could go with you to the workhouse and plead your case if you'd like me to.' He gazed anxiously at her and she wondered why he would feel at all responsible for someone he didn't know. He had a pleasant face, she mused, though worried-looking, and she wondered if that was on her account or if he always had a troubled countenance. His eyes were deep brown and his forehead was wide where his hair was receding.

'The only difficulty with applying at the workhouse,' he continued, 'is – well, there are two really: one, you are not from the area, and two, the building is very overcrowded. There's to be a new workhouse built on Anlaby Road which will accommodate more residents.'

Lily felt tears spring to her eyes. What a dilemma. She didn't want them to have to go to the workhouse, where they'd certainly be separated; Daisy would be sent out to work in one of the mills as a pauper worker, whilst she would probably have to pick oakum, unless she could get a job outside.

'If I could find work I could perhaps afford a room,' she began. 'I'm a good housekeeper, or I could work in an inn, I've done that afore. I don't suppose . . .' She hesitated. Dare she ask this question when he had been so good to them already? 'I couldn't ask if you'd let Daisy stop wi' you for a bit? Just until I found work? I don't mean for nothing. She'd work for her keep. She could scrub floors or run errands. She's a good girl.' She gazed at him imploringly. 'She wouldn't be any bother.'

He had opened his mouth to speak when the shop door bell jangled and they heard voices. 'One moment,' he said quietly. 'I'll just see who this is.'

He went out of the room and as the door swung open she

56

heard a woman's voice. Daisy slipped in. 'It's Mrs Walker,' she whispered. 'She's in 'shop wi' two men. She looks a bit fierce.'

'Does she?' her mother whispered back. 'Is it summat to do wi' us, do you think?'

Daisy nodded. 'She wants us to leave. I heard her telling Mr Walker. They were arguing about it this morning; he says you should stay a bit longer.'

The door opened again and Martha Walker entered. She was thin-faced and bony and dressed in outdoor clothes: a long black coat with a grey shawl over it and a dark grey bonnet which covered most of her light brown hair.

'I'm Mrs Walker,' she announced. 'I've made arrangements for you. There's transport waiting to take you elsewhere. You'll be looked after until such time as you've recovered from your ordeal.'

Lily rose from the bed where she had been sitting. 'That's very—' she began. Kind, she had been going to say, but there was something in the woman's demeanour which suggested that kindness was probably not one of her traits. 'Thoughtful,' she said. 'Most thoughtful, Mrs Walker,' she added. 'I'm very grateful to you and Mr Walker.'

Mrs Walker sniffed as if to say *And so you should be*, but she pursed her lips and then said, 'It'll be most appropriate, I'm sure you'll agree, and the only option open to you under 'circumstances. I understand you were turned away from 'workhouse yesterday?'

Lily nodded and swallowed. 'Yes.' What has she in mind? she thought. Where is she sending us? Mr Walker can't know about it or he wouldn't have asked me what we were going to do.

'Well, this place won't turn you away. I've been personally to ascertain that there's a place for you, and there is,' she said with a hint of triumph in her voice. 'So I've booked it.'

'And Daisy?' Lily asked quietly. 'Will they take Daisy?'

Mrs Walker turned to look at Daisy. 'Oh, no! They'll only

take women who are . . . well, who are – like you. Anyway, if you're ready, 'men are waiting outside to take you.'

'I can't go without Daisy,' Lily said in alarm. 'Wherever this place is, surely she'll be able to come? It'll not be for long, onny a day or two. I'll get work as soon as I'm able.'

Mr Walker had come into the room and overheard their conversation. 'Daisy can stay here,' he said firmly, not looking at his wife. 'She can help Cook and Molly; they'll find something for her to do.'

Mrs Walker drew in a sharp breath. 'Well!' she huffed. 'I don't see why—'

'It's only for a short time, my dear,' he said placatingly. 'And as Mrs Fowler says she hopes to find work and a room, it's the least we can do to help someone in such a dreadful situation.'

Lily could have wept with gratitude. What a generous kind man he is. However did he come to be married to such a hard woman as this? But still, she thought apologetically, at least she's taken the trouble to find someone else to take me in and give me shelter for a few days. She didn't have to do that; she could have just turned us out into the street.

'She's very lucky there's a place for her,' Mrs Walker said sourly. 'Very fortunate.'

'Begging your pardon, ma'am,' Lily said, 'but what is this place?' Suspicion was lurking. Mrs Walker wanted rid of her, that much was obvious and she didn't blame her for that, but where was she sending her?

'It's a temporary place,' Mrs Walker hedged. 'A charitable institution.'

Lily glanced at Mr Walker, who had a resigned expression on his face and gave a little shake of his head. 'I'm sorry that there seems to be nowhere else,' he murmured. 'It is the times in which we live. There is no provision for people who fall into a desperate trap through no fault of their own.'

Lily wrapped her shawl round her. 'I'd better be off then,'

she said quietly. 'I don't want to detain you any longer. I'm more grateful than I can say, Mr Walker. I hope one day I can return your kindness.' She kissed a tearful Daisy and told her to be a good girl. 'I'll leave her in your safe hands,' she said, looking at the apothecary. 'Until I come back for her, which I hope won't be long.'

She felt dizzy again and swayed on her feet. I must have lost a lot of blood, she thought. I feel weak. 'I'm ready. Thank you.'

Mr Walker led the way out of the room and into the shop where Oliver was standing behind the counter. Out in the street was a small waggon with two men waiting by it. They turned as the door opened and Lily felt their eyes appraise her.

'You must drive carefully,' Charles Walker told them. 'This young woman is not yet recovered from childbed.'

Young woman, Lily pondered as she was helped into the waggon. I'm barely thirty and feel ancient. Married at sixteen with Ted on the way. What does life hold for me now? But I'll think on it whilst I'm at this place and then come back for Daisy.

'Where are we going?' she called to the men driving the waggon. 'Where 'you tekking me?'

The driver laughed and the other man turned to her and grinned. 'Don't 'you know, darling? Didn't them good folk tell you?'

'No, they didn't,' she retorted. 'I wouldn't be asking, would I, if they'd told me?'

He gave her a wink. 'Nice place,' he said. 'They'll larn you to be a good girl in there. That's what they think, anyway.' He chortled.

She leaned towards him. 'What do you mean? I 'don't know what you're talking about.'

'Come off it,' he said cynically. 'You'll rest up for a bit, then you'll be back on 'streets again. We've seen it all afore, haven't we, Jack?' He turned to his companion, who nodded and muttered something incomprehensible.

'Back on 'streets? But,' she licked her dry lips, 'I'm a married woman.'

He shrugged and appraised her again. 'I'm not blaming you, missis. Everybody's got to scratch a living one way or another.'

'For God's sake,' she screeched. 'Where are you tekking me? I'm not a street woman! My husband's abandoned me. I've no means of getting home.'

He turned and looked fully at her. 'Then I don't know why you're going to this place. We were just sent out to pick up a woman. We thought you were like 'others. It's a home for fallen women,' he added. 'Hope House. A refuge. They're shown 'error of their ways and when they're cured they're sent back to their friends or family. If they have any,' he sniffed. 'And if they'll have 'em.'

She was aghast. I'm a respectable married woman. At least I was until that toad Billy Fowler brought me to this. What am I to do?

They had left the busy town and were now travelling through the outskirts. Lily sat pondering. Do I ask them to take me back? But then what should I do? Throw myself on the mercy of the Walkers? She won't want me, that's for certain, and why should she? I need a day to recover before I can try for work. Perhaps this place won't be so bad. Mebbe they'll give me a bed for tonight and I'll leave tomorrow. But will they take me in if I tell them that I'm not a street woman but just fallen on hard times? Fallen! Aye, I've fallen right enough. That's what I am after all. A fallen woman.

CHAPTER EIGHT

The waggon drew up outside the front door of an ordinary three-storey house with clean lace curtains at the sash windows. There was no garden or paved area and the door opened out on to the street. As Lily was helped down a woman in a plain grey gown and bonnet stood waiting to greet her.

'Come along,' the woman said. 'Don't be afraid. There's no one here to bully or intimidate you.'

Lily gazed at her. As if anybody could, she was tempted to say, but held her tongue. She would find out what went on here before she asserted herself; and she needed to rest. She badly wanted to lie down. She was led into a small hall and then into a room which held two hardback chairs, a desk and another chair behind it. The woman sat in the desk chair and asked Lily to sit down in one of the others.

'My name is Mrs Grant,' she said. 'I understand you've recently had a miscarriage.' She looked down at a sheet of paper on the desk. 'I take it that it was an untimely deliverance and therefore not registered?'

Lily nodded, suddenly beset by emotion. Poor little bairn, she thought. Poor little bairn! Was it a girl or a lad? Nobody said and I didn't ask, but maybe it was too soon to say. She thought of Ted. What would become of him? Would Billy Fowler send him away? He had no affection for him, none at all, and neither did Ted like his stepfather. She no

61

longer thought of her husband as Billy, but in rancour gave him his full name. She wiped away a tear with her shawl. 'It didn't go full term,' she muttered.

'Had it lived, would you have cared for 'child in spite of any difficulties?' Mrs Grant raised her bushy eyebrows and Lily wondered if it was a gesture of surprise or just an involuntary action.

'It wouldn't have been 'bairn's fault – 'circumstances, I mean,' she answered. 'Childre' don't ask to come into this world.'

'Do you think that it's God's will?' Mrs Grant's eyebrows shot up again. 'Don't you consider that men have much to answer for in their pursuit of pleasure, and women too for allowing them that indulgence?'

'Aren't you a married woman, Mrs Grant? Don't you understand about a husband's rights?'

Mrs Grant drew herself upright. 'I'm not married,' she said primly. 'I'm the housekeeper here, and called Mrs as a courtesy.'

'Well, Mrs Grant, if you were a married woman, you'd realize that there's no shame in coupling; it's part of married life. Difficulty arises when a child's born and there's little money to raise it,' she said wearily. 'Or if 'husband refuses to accept it.'

Which is what happened with us, she acknowledged. Billy Fowler didn't want this child. All he wanted was for me to housekeep and cook for him, and share his bed. He didn't want the responsibility of another human being.

'I don't understand you!' Mrs Grant said. 'You speak as if you were a married woman. Do you have a husband?'

'I did,' Lily admitted. 'Until yesterday morning. He brought me into Hull from where we lived and sold me in Hull Market Place.'

The woman clasped her hands in front of her face and gasped. 'Sold you! But – how could that be? Surely it isn't lawful?'

62

'Whether it is or not, that's what he did. He said that somebody else had done it some years back so that made it legal and it was what he was going to do.'

'So who bought you?' Mrs Grant's eyes were wide, her eyebrows working furiously. Lily watched them in fascination, then shook her head.

'Some young fellow. I can't remember his name, but when he saw I was pregnant he said I was no good to him.'

'Well, you can't stay here; there's been some kind of mistake. This place is not for you. This is a house for fallen women – unfortunate women who have succumbed to a life of degradation. We aim to show them 'error of their ways and send them home to their families.'

'And what if their families don't want them?' Lily's spirits plummeted. 'Then what? Back on 'streets?'

Mrs Grant set her mouth in a thin line. 'We try to find them work. Work where they can gain respect and rebuild their lives.'

'That's what I want,' Lily exclaimed. 'Please! Let me stay just for today, till I've recovered from my confinement. Then I'll find work and repay you. I've a young daughter waiting for me,' she pleaded. 'What'll happen to her if you turn me away?'

She saw the woman hesitate and added, 'You say you onny tek fallen women. Well, I've fallen as low as I can get. There's nowhere lower than 'gutter and that's where I'll be if you show me 'door. I'd walk back to Seathorne, but I know he wouldn't tek me in, and neither would I want him to.'

As she spoke, she again felt dizzy and bent low; her ears began to ring and sparkling stars filled her head and seconds later she blacked out, crashing on to the floor.

She heard Mrs Grant calling for assistance and tried to lift her head, but the room was spinning and with a low groan she lay back on the floor. She felt arms lift her and carry her out of the room and was conscious of white walls and brown doors, stairs and another room, and then being put into a bed where she sank back with a sigh. 'I'm bleeding,' she whispered.

Another woman dressed in black stood over her. 'When did you miscarry?' she asked.

'Yesterday, I think,' Lily murmured. 'I'm not sure.'

The woman put a cool hand on her forehead. 'She's very hot.' Her voice sounded very faint and far away to Lily. 'She might have childbed fever. Bring her some cool water to drink and wash her down. And bring some more sheets.'

Lily succumbed to the pleasure of being given sips of water, then being washed and covered over with a soft blanket. 'I'm sorry,' she muttered. 'I'm being a trouble.'

'We'll do what we can for you,' the woman in black said. 'But we're not nurses. Rest now and I'll look in again later.'

'Thank you,' Lily breathed. 'I'm very grateful.'

She spent the rest of that day and all of the next feverish and restless, drifting in and out of sleep, yet conscious of the fact that if she made an attempt to wake up, she might be considered better and asked to leave. Each time she heard the rattle of the door knob, she closed her eyes and didn't respond when spoken to. Nevertheless, she did feel weak, as if the terminated pregnancy had depleted her energy, whereas after the births of Ted and Daisy she had felt rejuvenated.

I had something to look forward to then, she brooded in her waking moments; a new young life and a hope of my husband coming home. Now I have nothing. I don't know if I'll ever see Ted again, or whether Daisy and I will survive.

On the third morning a young fair-haired woman brought her a tray neatly arranged with a bowl of gruel, a thick slice of bread on a plate, a spoon and a knife. She sat up in bed and knew she was back to normal. Her fever had gone and her body felt rested. 'Thank you,' she said.

'You're a fine one, ain't yer?' The girl opened the curtains, letting in a stream of light. 'When I was brought here they didn't put me to bed!'

'I'd childbed fever,' Lily told her. 'Why were you brought here?'

She shrugged. 'Usual thing! I was "rescued" off 'streets.'

'Didn't you want to be?' Lily tucked into the soothing gruel.

'Not bothered really. I was persuaded to come. But I was doing all right. I don't know owt else. How am I supposed to live otherwise? There's no work. I'll not go into 'work-house and pick oakum and I've nowhere else to go.'

She was a pretty girl, Lily thought, bright and chirpy. She was dressed plainly in a grey dress with a white apron over it, which Lily guessed might be the standard wear for the residents here. 'Don't you have any family?' she asked. 'No ma or da?'

'Yeh.' The girl nodded. 'But I had a bairn and his father wouldn't marry me, so my da turned me out. Ma would've let us stay even though we already had my sister's bairn at home. But Da said enough was enough and we had to go.'

'So what happened to your babby?'

The girl's face clouded. 'I fostered him out. But he died.' Tears glistened in her eyes and she dashed them away. 'Anyway,' she shrugged again, 'that's that. They brought me here to learn me for other work.' She sat on the edge of Lily's bed and gazed into space. 'Don't know what else they think I can do.'

'What's your name?' Lily asked. She felt sorry for her. The girl's position was worse than her own. My two children are fit and healthy – at least they are at the moment.

'Betty,' the girl answered. 'What's yours? You're not from round here, are you?'

'Lily. I come from a place on 'coast; and I'm not here for

'same reason as you. I'm an abandoned wife and I had a miscarriage. I was rescued too,' she said. 'Somebody took me in and then they sent me here. I'll be leaving today though,' she added. 'I'll have to find work of some kind. I've a daughter to care for.'

'There's no work in Hull,' Betty said gloomily. 'Mebbe scrubbing floors 'n' that, but I don't want to do that. I'm a bit particular.'

Lily finished off the bread. Not so particular if she earned her living as a street woman. 'I'd rather scrub floors than sell myself,' she said.

Betty got up and took the tray from her. 'You might find that's all there is,' she said cynically. 'Women don't have much choice.'

She's right, Lily thought as she swung her legs out of the bed and gingerly stood up. They get into trouble and there's nobody to help them. At least Johnny married me when we found out I was expecting Ted, but then we were going to be married anyway. I never wanted anybody else but him, and he felt the same, I know he did. She sighed. She still loved and missed her soldier husband; she always had, even though she'd married Billy Fowler.

'Are you well enough to leave?' the woman in black asked when Lily presented herself downstairs. 'We're not so unkind that we'd turn you out before you're ready.'

'You've been very kind,' Lily told her. 'And I'd like to repay you. What can I do? Wash 'sheets mebbe; clean 'room that I slept in?'

The woman, Mrs Thompson, hesitated. 'Well, you could spend the morning helping the staff. Some light housework perhaps?'

'Yes, I can do that,' Lily said. 'I've never stayed abed afore when I had a child. There was never anybody to wait on me.'

How hard it was, she remembered, especially after Ma died; her mother had always helped her with looking after

66

the children until her final illness, and then Lily had had to cope on her own. The parish helped her when she reached rock bottom, but she took work wherever she could, always taking the children with her, since she was never able to afford to pay a childminder.

She brushed the stair carpet and swept the hall, washed the paintwork on the front door, then scrubbed the doorstep until it was almost white.

'That will do, thank you.' Mrs Thompson came out to her. 'You've more than repaid us. The driver is going into the Market Place after dinner to pick someone up, if you'd like a lift back.'

Lily washed her hands, tidied her hair and collected her shawl. The dinner smelt good. She sniffed; beef. Will they offer me a bit of dinner before I go, I wonder?

A place had been set for her at the large wooden kitchen table. She sat next to Betty, who had set the table for eight: herself, Lily, Mrs Grant, Mrs Thompson, Cook, the maid of all work and two young women, who from their appearance Lily guessed had also been 'rescued'.

The two young women made swift inroads into the beef and dumplings as if they hadn't eaten in a long time, and then looked up eagerly as they were offered treacle pudding.

One of them was very young, Lily surmised, barely sixteen, and the other not more than eighteen. Though their hands and faces were clean, they were dressed in what could only be described as rags: thin skirts with torn hems and unkempt frilled bodices that had seen better days. The younger girl shivered constantly and bit on her fingernails.

'After we've eaten,' Mrs Grant said to them, 'we'll find you some more clothes to wear. Yours are onny fit for 'rag bag.'

Both girls glanced at Betty, who surreptitiously pointed a finger at her own neat gown as if she was showing them what to expect.

'I like what I'm wearing,' the older girl stated flatly. 'It came from Rena's. It was a supper gown once.'

'Never! Not in a million years!' Cook pronounced. 'Even I can tell that and I know nowt about fashion.'

The girl scowled at her. 'No, I can see that! Rena told me this skirt was made for a nopera singer.'

'Well if you're so fond of it, Lizzie, you can keep it once it's been washed,' Mrs Thompson said mildly. 'But whilst you're here you must wear something more suitable, especially if we're to find some other employment for you.'

Lizzie glared at her too, but said nothing, only glowering at them all in turn through narrowed eyelids. Lily hazarded a guess that Lizzie wouldn't be staying long in this establishment. She'll be off as soon as she's satisfied the pangs of hunger and forgotten the pain of her bruises. The girl's thin arms were black and blue and she had a fading yellow bruise and cut beneath one puffy eye.

The younger girl, Cherie, scrunched her arms about her waist and said she would like something warm to wear. 'It's that cold at night out on 'streets,' she said huskily. 'I thought I was going to freeze to death.'

'And how much worse it would be in winter,' Mrs Thompson murmured. 'But we're hoping that you won't go back to that life, Cherie. We'll find you something else to do.'

'Huh!' Lizzie groused scornfully, and pushed her empty plate away. 'Like what? There's nowt else for such as us wi' no money or place to live. We know we can earn summat out on 'streets. Enough to buy us a meat pie or a glass o' gin, anyway.'

'So don't you want to stay?' Mrs Thompson asked in the same mild manner as before. 'You don't have to. Nobody is forcing you.'

Lizzie pouted and tossed her head. 'I onny said I'd come cos of Cherie. I knew she'd get ill if she didn't get warm and have a bit of a rest and a proper bed to lie on; and she wouldn't come wi'out me.'

They're living on the streets, Lily thought in horror. They've no place to stay. She took a deep breath of trepidation. Is that my fate? Is that what will happen to me?

CHAPTER NINE

'Drop me off in 'Market Place, will you?' Lily asked the waggon driver, thinking that she might as well go back to where she had started in this town, for she knew nowhere else.

'You didn't stop long,' he said. 'Are you a hard case?'

'A hard case? What do you mean?'

'Well, some of 'women who go there just have a bit of a rest and a hot dinner, and then they're back on 'streets again. It's called 'temporary home for fallen women so they can't stop 'em leaving. It's not like at 'female penitentiary where they've to stop for two years; they've to do washin' and ironin' and such like in there to earn their keep.'

'I see,' Lily said thoughtfully. 'And in 'temporary home, do some of them go back to their families?'

'Oh, aye,' he said chattily. 'Sometimes they do, or else they're found other jobs. Committee's going to try and buy 'house next door cos they're running out of space wi' just the one. They'll have room for fifty women then.'

Fifty! So many unfortunate women – or girls, she thought. That's all Cherie and Lizzie are. Poor girls who have to earn a living out on the streets.

'What 'you going to do, then?' he asked as he drew to a halt in the Market Place close by a golden statue of a man on a horse. 'Going home?'

Lily shook her head. 'I've got no home. I'll have to look

70

for work and then a room. Where should I try, do you think?'

'Don't know, missis.' He pursed his mouth. 'Try one of 'inns or mills. You might be lucky, you know, if somebody hasn't turned up for work.'

I've lost track of 'days, she thought. We came in on Friday, and the market was busy, as it was on Saturday when they took me to Hope House. Today it was quieter with fewer people and traffic about, just a few carts and waggons, a brougham parked outside a hostelry, a man with a donkey, and only one or two stalls in the long street.

'Good luck then,' the driver said, moving off. 'Hope you find summat.'

She vaguely lifted a hand as he drove away and walked down the side of the church towards King Street. Then she looked across to the parade of shops where the apothecary had his premises. Dare I go in? she wondered. And if I do will they expect me to take Daisy away with me?

As she watched, the shop door opened and Mrs Walker came out; she brandished an umbrella and scurried away from the square, towards the street which held the workhouse. Should I go in and ask if they'll keep Daisy for a bit longer? Mr Walker won't know I've been ill and not able to look for work. She sat on a side wall and peered through the iron railings, out of sight of anyone watching from the shop window, and pondered on what to do. Then the door opened again and Oliver Walker came out. He had a box tucked under his arm and another in his hand, and he turned to the door as if waiting. Daisy emerged; she was smiling, and she too held a box in her arms. Lily saw them both laugh about something and then go off in the same direction as Mrs Walker. She's not unhappy, Lily thought. She seemed very merry. I've not seen her smile like that in a long time. Not since I married that blackguard Billy Fowler.

She moved off her perch on the wall and went back the way she had come. She had noticed an old inn across from

71

the golden statue and thought she would ask there if they had any work.

Outside the inn there were now several hansom cabs being loaded with luggage. A delivery van pulled through the archway towards the back of the building. A well-built woman with a clean white apron over her black skirt was giving orders to a man in a leather apron and at the same time shouting instructions to a young girl. She politely dipped her knee to several people leaving the hostelry, who departed with her good wishes for a safe journey.

'Now young woman, what can I do for you?' she asked briskly when Lily approached.

'Beg pardon, ma'am, but do you have any work for me? I'm stranded in Hull and I've a young daughter to—'

'Sorry, I've just took somebody on for cleaning. Come back at 'end of 'week and if she hasn't shaped up I'll talk to you.' The landlady broke off to tell a young lad to get upstairs and bring some luggage down. 'And look sharp about it,' she harangued him. 'Folks have a train to catch and 'cabby's waiting.

'Sorry, m'dear,' she said to Lily. 'But you see how it is?'

Lily thanked her and backed away. This obviously wasn't a good time, but when was? She walked along the street and saw another hostelry and enquired there, but the answer was the same. Nothing available; come back next week. How do I live in the meantime? No job means no food or money to pay for a room. She called in at a few shops, greengrocers and butchers, to ask if they required a cleaning woman but she didn't have any luck there either.

She avoided the smarter shops, milliners and drapers, as she had caught sight of her reflection in a shop window. I look like a country bumpkin in this old skirt and shawl. She drew herself up; she was a tall woman and striking-looking, she knew, but her old clothes dragged her down and made her look frumpish. There had been no new clothes when she had married Fowler, nor money forthcoming to make any. The clothes she was wearing were the ones she had had when she was married to Johnny.

It was now well into the afternoon and some of the shops were closing, so she wandered further down the thoroughfare, past another church, and cut down a narrow side alley into the cobbled High Street, which was closely built with imposing houses, warehouses and inns. Running between some of the buildings were narrow lanes which on investigation she found led down to a river.

'This must be 'River Hull,' she murmured, and glancing south along it saw that it led into the Humber estuary. The river was full of coal barges, small ships and keels loaded with timber and other commodities. She turned away. 'Nowt here for me,' she muttered. 'If I was a man I could try for work on a ship.' She gave a wry smile. But I'm not a man and I've a daughter to consider. Dear God, she thought. What am I going to do?

She called at other inns but was turned away and in near despair stopped outside two more. Both were ancient timber-framed hostelries. Signs above the entrances pronounced one to be the Yarmouth Arms, the other the George Inn. A narrow alley ran between the two buildings and she cut down it into a large yard, determining this time to be assertive. Stabling with haylofts or accommodation above ran around the yard, and she scrutinized it carefully. The light was fading and she would soon need somewhere to sleep.

'Got any jobs for a hard-working woman?' she said breezily to the man who opened the rear door of the George. 'I can draw ale, measure gin, scrub floors . . . !'

'Possibly,' he said, and she held her breath in anticipation. 'But my wife takes on 'staff and she's away till tomorrow. Come back tomorrow night about seven and you can talk to her.'

'I couldn't help you out tonight, could I?' She gazed at him pleadingly. 'I'm desperate for work and somewhere to stay.'

He shook his head. 'Staff don't sleep in; you'd have to find your own room if she teks you on.' He started to close the door. 'Come back tomorrow. I'll tell her to expect you.'

Lily wanted to weep but she gritted her teeth and walked away. I'm that tired; I'll have to find somewhere to sit down.

The alley came out at the other end of the Market Place, where the name on the wall had changed to Lowgate. Between the two main streets lay myriad narrow lanes and courts, all crammed with poor housing. Lily shuddered; she had always considered Billy Fowler's cottage to be a hovel, but at least we had fresh air, she thought. Not like the poor souls who have to live down here. They probably never see daylight.

She sat down on the steps of a bank to rest her feet and watched as workers tramped their way home. Many of them were poorly clad and there were barefoot children with tearful weary faces shuffling alongside the adults.

Is this what is in front of Daisy? Working in a mill or a factory? How am I going to feed and clothe her? I can't expect Mr Walker to keep her. Tomorrow I'll go and ask him what he thinks we should do. I'm willing to work. I'll do anything. *Anything*.

A fair-haired man came up the steps, glanced at her and then sat down on the step above. What's he up to? she thought. Waiting for somebody? He doesn't look like a down and out. She turned towards him. 'Are there any soup kitchens in this town?' she asked.

He stared at her. 'Onny in winter. Not this time o' year. Why – ain't you had no dinner?'

'Yes. I ate at dinner time,' she said. 'Midday.'

'Think yourself lucky then,' he said brusquely. 'There's folk in this town that don't eat from one day to 'next.'

He looks as if he's fed well enough, she thought, although he wasn't fat, but rather quite lean. But he didn't have a hungry look; on the contrary, he seemed satisfied, and his manner was complacent.

He came and sat next to her. 'I've seen you afore,' he said, contemplating her. 'Where've I seen you?'

'Nowhere,' she answered, but knew that he had, for she had just recognized him. She began to rise from the step, but he put out his hand to hold her back.

'Hang on,' he said. 'Don't rush off. I do know you! Your husband sold you to me last week!'

'Scabby scurvy dogs!' she said vehemently. 'Both of you! Blackguard,' she spat out. 'You should be ashamed of yourself.'

'Hey, hey!' he protested. 'What if I hadn't bought you? You'd still have been with him. I did you a favour.' He looked her up and down. 'I thought you were expecting? Have you lost it?' He clutched at her skirt, forcing her to sit again.

Lily put her head in her hands and thought quickly. Maybe he could give her a bed for the night. But I shan't share it with him, oh dear no. She lifted her head. 'Yes,' she told him. 'I miscarried. I'm not well. I need somewhere to stay.'

'What happened to your lass? The one that was with you.'

'Somebody's tekken her in. But they couldn't tek me as well.'

'So where've you been since then?' he asked.

She heaved a great sigh. 'Home for fallen women. Hope House. Somebody sent me.'

He started to laugh. 'Oh, yeh! I know it. Some friends o' mine often stay there. Listen,' he said, 'I told you to ask for me when you'd got rid of – you know. So why didn't you? You belong to me. I bought you fair and square. Ten bob I gave for you.'

Lily got to her feet. 'Go jump in 'river!' she said, any hope of a bed for the night fading rapidly. 'Whelp! What are you? A procurer of women!'

'I've been called all sorts o' names.' He looked up at her. 'Most of 'em true. But I meant it when I told you to get in touch. You look 'sort of woman who'd not stand any non-sense.'

'Huh!' she said. 'What? When I allowed myself to be sold!'

'Ah, yes. But you didn't have a choice, did you? Not when you were expecting a babby and you had your daughter wi' you. I reckon you'd have given that husband a whack or a lash of your tongue if you'd been able to.'

'I'd have roasted him alive,' she spat. 'And he knew it. That's why he tied me up wi' 'rope.'

'Sit down,' he said. 'I want to talk to you. I've got a proposition. What's your name?'

She sank wearily back on the step. 'Lily,' she said.

He nodded his head as if in thought, pursing his lips. 'Lily. It's got a nice ring to it. *Miss Lily*. Mmm.'

Lily gazed at him suspiciously. 'What 'you on about? It's Mrs, not Miss. I'm a – was a – married woman. Been married twice.'

'Have you?' he said vaguely. 'Well, I'm not bothered about that. Listen,' he said again, 'I've got a house – well, I don't live there, but you can stay tonight if you like – no funny business, honest,' he added as he saw her suspicious glare. 'I've got my own place. I've onny just tekken this other house on. Fellow that had it had to move away in a bit of a hurry, and he owed me, so he let me have it. It belongs to Broadley,' he said, but the name meant nothing to her.

'It's a house,' he urged. 'A sort of rooming house, but I need somebody to keep an eye on it. You know, run it for me.'

'Oh!' It sounded promising but she was still wary of him. 'A kind of housekeeper, you mean?'

He hesitated. 'Yeh, summat like that. What do you think? Do you want to come and see it? It's onny round 'corner from here.'

'I've no money,' she said. 'You'd have to pay me if I work for you. Can I bring Daisy – my daughter?'

'Erm, not tonight you can't. But we'll talk about it later.'

He'd risen to his feet and as he did so a man passing by wearing a business suit and top hat greeted him. 'Anything doing, Jamie?'

'Not tonight, sir,' he answered. 'Mebbe tomorrow.' He put up his thumb. 'About 'same time?'

The man nodded and walked on. Lily stood up; she was taller than Jamie. 'All right,' she said. 'I'll come with you. But I'm warning you, if you try owt—'

'I won't. You have my word, and if you don't like what's on offer, then you can just leave.'

'Why me?' she asked as they walked along the street. 'You don't know me or owt about me.'

'I said, didn't I? You look 'sort who wouldn't stand any nonsense.'

She gave a sceptical smile. 'Or mebbe it's because everybody else knows you and nobody trusts you. That's it, isn't it? You're too well known.'

He made no answer, only sighed, and they continued walking until they came to a square of houses, mainly run down, but some with lace curtains at the windows. 'It's just down here, that one on 'corner.' He took a key from his pocket. 'It needs money spending on it,' he said. 'Landlord won't spend owt so I'll do it up as soon as I have some.'

He ran up the steps to the front door and inserted the key in the lock. 'Come on in.'

Lily cautiously followed him inside. The hall was dark, for the rooms off it all had their doors closed. He knocked on one and called, 'It's Jamie!'

'Come in, Jamie!' a girl's voice replied. 'I'm on my own.'

They entered the room. It was furnished with a bed and a chair, a desk and a chest of drawers. At the windows hung red velvet curtains and swaths of lace. There was a strong smell of perfume. A young woman was curled up on the bed; she wore a shabby dressing robe beneath which Lily glimpsed bare white legs.

On seeing Lily behind Jamie, she drew her wrap round her. 'Ooh!' she squealed. 'You didn't say you'd brought visitors.'

'You—' Words almost failed Lily as she took in the scene. 'You *pander*. Whoremonger! This is a bawdy house!'

CHAPTER TEN

Ted didn't know the way to Hull. He'd never been, though he had a rough idea of where it was. If I go towards Hollym and then to Patrington I'm bound to pick up a sign for Hull. But I'll have to go on 'old roads cos I've no money for 'turnpike if I have to pay. He hadn't a single penny in his possession. He'd never had any money. Fowler had always said that he had to work for his keep, and Ted would rather that than feel beholden to him.

He rode through his former home village but didn't see anyone. The sky had darkened with low black clouds and the rain had kept everyone indoors. A dog barked as he passed one of the cottages but no one came out. I'll ride on to Patrington, he thought, and then look for shelter. He was cold and shivery but at least Fowler's rubber coat kept out the rain.

'Come on, owd lad,' he said to the horse. 'Can't you go a bit faster?' He urged him on, digging his heels into his thin ribs, but Dobbin skittered and skidded on the muddy uneven road and Ted had to be content with a slower pace, keeping his head down and his collar turned up to stop the rain running down his neck.

Just before he reached Patrington he noticed a brick barn with a damaged roof standing off the road, and decided to seek shelter. The rain was still lashing down and he could barely see the road in front of him. A gate hanging off its hinges opened on to a yard; he dismounted and led the horse towards it. 'Come on,' he said. 'Let's go and get dry. We'll go off again in 'morning afore anybody finds us.'

He pulled open the large barn door and sniffed at the scent of threshed grain. The threshing floor was of beaten earth and covered with a fine yellow dust, and dry except in one corner where the roof had caved in and the rain was coming through. 'This'll do us,' he said to his equine companion and the nag snuffled against his shoulder.

There were some empty sacks in one of the two bays and he gathered them up along with a bundle of threshed straw and made himself a bed. He took off his wet coat and hung it up, then took the saddle and blanket off Dobbin's back, shook the blanket and put it loosely over him again. Steam rose as the horse shuffled off, nosing about on the floor, and Ted lay down on the sacks. 'I'm jiggered,' he muttered. 'What a night. What am I going to do? Where will I finish up? Will I find Ma and Daisy, and what will Ma say when I tell her that Fowler's dead?'

He rolled over from side to side, unable to settle as he thought of the consequences of his fight with his stepfather. Will I be blamed? But nobody knows I was there. He sat up and stared across the blackness of the barn. 'If anybody says it's my fault, then I'll be branded a murderer! Will I be hanged?' He put his hand to his thin neck, gingerly stroking it. 'It'd mebbe be best not telling Ma what's happened,' he muttered. 'But on 'other hand, perhaps she'd like to know. She'd be right glad to be shut of him, I'm sure of that.'

He lay down again as exhaustion overtook him. I'll think about it tomorrow, he mused, as sleep finally claimed him.

Daylight creeping through the broken tiles and the ventilation holes in the walls woke him the next morning. Dobbin nudged him. He opened the door and let the horse out to graze on the grassy verge of the yard. I wish I could eat grass, he thought, I'm that hungry. His stomach rumbled but he knew there would be nothing to eat; he'd just have to drink water as soon as he came to a stream and fill up his empty belly in that way.

He arrived in Patrington as workers, mainly women and children, were streaming towards Enholmes cotton mill to work. No one took any notice of him and he continued on towards the next village of Ottringham, where he saw a road sign showing him the way to Hedon and Hull.

The road was narrow in places with deep ditches on either side, whilst the waterlogged land towards the Humber was dotted with pools of glistening water where seabirds had settled and grey herons stood motionless. As he approached Hedon the road became wider and better and he saw a toll house ahead, but when he spoke to the toll keeper he discovered to his relief that he could lead Dobbin through without charge.

He stopped to rest the horse outside the town and to stretch his own legs. His hunger had become a dull ache in his belly and he took a long drink from a stream. There had been a good deal of traffic on the turnpike road: ponderous broad-wheeled waggons pulled by teams of heavy horses, single-horse carriers' carts, a mail coach, and a pony and trap driven by a young woman who had lifted her whip in greeting to him.

In the town he asked someone the way to Hull and was given two alternatives. 'I want 'quickest,' he said.

'Then tek 'new road,' the stranger said. 'You'll not have to pay if you walk through 'toll bar.'

'I need food,' Ted told him. 'I've not eaten since yester-day.'

The man shook his head. 'You get nowt for nowt,' he said sagely, but took his rucksack off his back and unfastened it. He brought out a loaf wrapped in a brown paper bag and tore off a hunk. 'Here, lad. Have this and welcome. Where're you going?' he asked curiously.

'I'm going to look for my ma and sister. They went to Hull and didn't come home.'

'Big place is Hull,' the man replied. 'But mebbe they

didn't want to go home. Mebbe they like it there. Plenty o' work for women, that's what I heard anyway.' He winked. 'If you're not too particular.'

Ted nodded and thanked him for the bread which he bit into ravenously, but it wasn't enough and only reminded him of how hungry he was.

It was after midday when he reached the town; he passed a military garrison, then crossed the bridge over the River Hull and saw how it opened up into the wide brown Humber estuary. The country boy saw too, for the first time in his life, tall factory chimneys belching out sooty black smoke, windmills, church towers, massive warehouses, impressive brick buildings, and shops of all kinds; and he smelt the overpowering stench of fish and seed oil, glue, blubber and slaughter yards.

He put his hand over his nose and mouth. Ma would never want to stay here, not if she was given the choice. He felt nauseous from the smells and with hunger and he looked round wondering where to go and what to do next.

Carriages rattled by, as did delivery waggons and donkey carts, and as he trotted on towards the town he came to an area packed with market stalls selling all manner of goods – livestock, vegetables, flowers, meat and fish – and some of the stalls had braziers where sausages were cooking on the hot coals.

He swallowed and licked his dry lips as the smell reached him. Standing with his mouth open, he watched people queue up to buy. He dismounted and led Dobbin nearer, but someone told him to move the horse and make room and he backed away.

I've no money. How can I buy food? He thrust his free hand into the pocket of the coat and felt about. Nothing. Only a piece of rag. He felt in the other. What's this? His heart raced as he felt something metal caught in the seam. A penny. A penny! His spirits lifted as the prospect of food rose in front of him.

The stallholder cooking the sausages was placing two of them on a slice of thick bread to hand to a waiting customer. 'How much?' Ted called out. 'How much for 'bread and sausage?'

'Threepence,' the vendor called back. 'Best sausages in 'town.'

'How much for sausage on its own?'

Desperation must have shown in his voice for the trader looked up. 'Tuppence,' he said.

'I've onny got a penny,' Ted's voice cracked. 'What can I have for a penny, mister?'

'One sausage, no bread,' he answered, flipping over the sausages. 'I'm here to mek a living, mate.'

'I'll have a sausage then.' Ted's mouth was starting to drool.

'You'll have to get to back of 'queue. There's other folks here before you.'

'Oh, sorry!' Awkwardly, holding the horse's reins by one hand, Ted joined the queue of people waiting to be served, some of whom looked at him in annoyance as Dobbin stood against them.

'Why don't you tie him up somewhere,' a woman shouted at him, ''stead of fetching 'hoss shopping wi' you!'

He gazed at her. 'I don't want anybody pinching him,' he explained. 'He's worth a lot o' money.'

A man guffawed. 'Aye, to 'glue factory,' he spluttered. 'They'd give you a bob for him. Then you could afford a pound o' sausages!'

Ted stared in dismay and felt tears gather in his eyes. He bit on his lip. 'He's all I've got,' he mumbled. 'I can't sell him.'

Another woman looked at him. 'Are you from 'country?'

He nodded, unable to speak but wondering how she could tell.

'Watch out for yoursen, then,' she said. 'There's some villains about who'll pinch your hoss and leave you holding 'reins in your hand wi'out you even knowing he's gone!

What 'you doing in Hull?' she asked. Her accent was flat, not dissimilar to that of Holderness, but not the same either.

'I've come to look for my ma and sister,' he said. 'They came in last week and nivver came home.' Some warning flashed into his mind that he shouldn't give away the fact that he had seen Fowler since then. 'My stepda said he was going to sell my ma. I thought he was joking but they nivver came back.'

'Hey, I remember that,' another woman said as the queue shuffled up. 'There was a woman. Her husband tied her up wi' a rope. She was pregnant 'n' all.'

'She was!' Ted agreed, relief spreading over him that they had come here after all. 'Do you know where she went? Did somebody buy her?'

The woman shook her head. 'They were over in King Street.' She pointed past a church towering above them. 'I went to see what was going on when I heard all 'commotion. Didn't stop, though. I've plenty o' troubles of my own wi'out watching ower other folk's predicaments.'

It was Ted's turn at the head of the queue and he waited for the sausage to finish cooking. The trader forked it and put it on a slice of bread. 'Go on,' he said, taking the penny. 'And don't forget to pay me back when your ship comes in.'

Ted thanked him gratefully and sank his teeth into the succulent, thick, fatty sausage. The bread was hard and crusty but he didn't mind that as long as his hunger was satisfied. He moved away from the stalls and sat down with his back against a wall near a row of shops and put Dobbin's reins over his foot. He heaved a sigh as he finished eating, and licked his greasy fingers. He could think now of what to do next, whereas previously all he could think of was food, and how to get some.

He looked about him. At one end of the long street via which he had come into the town, a statue on a plinth was glinting in the sunshine. Opposite him was the large church

– a cathedral, he thought – and when he looked the other way the street narrowed past fine shops – umbrella sellers, spectacle makers, gunsmiths and fishmongers – and other premises such as banks and offices towards another church which jutted out into the road.

He heard the sound of drums and saw a platoon of soldiers marching down the street, and guessed they were on their way to the garrison. He saw the flash of steel, and a handful of scruffy small boys marching alongside the platoon swinging their arms in ragged unison.

I could be a soldier, he mused. Like my da. Like the father he couldn't remember.

Then he saw a group of dark-skinned, foreign-looking men wandering about the market stalls, and surmised they were off one of the ships which he had seen moored in the river. Or I could go to sea. But not fishing, he thought. I wouldn't want to be a fisherman, but I wouldn't mind sailing on a big ship to foreign parts. The men crossed over the street towards where he was sitting and he got to his feet. They said something to him that he couldn't understand and he shook his head. They laughed and patted the horse's neck and moved on.

He watched their progression down the street. Yes, he thought. If I can't find Ma or our Daisy, I'll try for a ship and sail away.

Daisy skipped across King Street intent on carrying out her errand in the shortest time possible, just to show that she could. She was delivering medication to one of the doctors who had his surgery in Lowgate, near St Mary's church.

Mr Walker had asked her if she could do the delivery for him as it was very urgent, Oliver was out on another errand and Mr Walker himself was busy. She felt proud that he had asked her to do it on her own and because she liked him, and he was so very kind to her, she wanted to please him.

I wish that I could work for him, she thought as she hurried along. I'll soon be old enough, but Ma might want to go back home to Holderness when she comes back. I don't, though. I like it here in Hull – there's so much to see and do.

She had accompanied Oliver on various errands around the town on Saturday and again this morning. On Sunday he had taken her for a walk to the pier and shown her where the theatres and music halls were, although he had told her that he wasn't allowed to go as his mother thought they were sinful. There were shop windows to look in, too, but she didn't do that now as she wanted to get back as quickly as possible to please Mr Walker.

Daisy had also helped Oliver, under careful scrutiny, to dispense medication; counting out tablets and putting them into small bottles, weighing out powders and pouring them through cones into paper bags.

Mrs Walker didn't help in the shop and although she didn't speak to Daisy very much she didn't seem to mind her presence; but perhaps that's because she thinks I won't be staying much longer, she mused. Ma will surely be back soon. Mr Walker had told her that she would come back when she was recovered. She had asked him what would they do then but he had shaken his head, looking very solemn, and told her that he didn't know.

I could go to work in a shop, she thought, glancing in at a draper's, or in a flower shop. I know about flowers. But then she realized that she didn't know the names of the exotic flowers which were in the next window. She had never seen anything like them before. They were not country flowers, anyway, she decided. They were too large and colourful.

She delivered her parcel and turned round to go back, then stopped for a minute to watch some soldiers marching past. She waved to them but they didn't wave back. Perhaps they're not allowed to, she thought. She walked along a little way, keeping in step with them, and when they had passed on she looked both ways in order to cross the street.

There was a grey horse standing by the side of the road with a boy waving beside it and she gave a little smile, thinking how like Ted he was. Then she stared and stared. It was Ted, and he was waving at her.

CHAPTER ELEVEN

'What 'you doing here? Have you come on Dobbin? Why didn't you bring 'cart? Does Billy Fowler know you're here?' Daisy was amazed to see Ted and also very pleased; she wanted to hug him but didn't as she knew how embarrassed he would be.

Ted shook his head. He was immensely relieved to see her. 'I don't know where Fowler is.' He felt a slow flush rise up from his neck to his face as he lied. 'Dobbin came back on his own. Where's Ma?'

'I don't know,' she confessed. 'Somebody came and took her away to some place. But she's coming back,' she assured him. 'She said that she would.'

'So where are you stopping?' Ted stared at his sister. She was too young to be on her own.

'Oh!' Daisy put her hand to her mouth as she remembered Mr Walker. 'Wait here for me, Ted,' she said urgently. 'I've just got to dash back and tell Mr Walker I've done his errand. No, I know. Come wi' me.' She beckoned eagerly. 'You can wait outside 'shop.'

'Have you got a job o' work?'

'No. I'll tell you in a minute. Come on, I've got to be quick.'

She led the way down by the side of the church to where a square opened up. 'Wait here,' she said. 'You can sit on 'church wall till I come back. You will, won't you?'

she said anxiously. 'You won't go away?'

'No, I won't. Is there any chance o' summat to eat, Daisy? I'm starving hungry. I've had nowt but a bit o' sausage since yesterday.'

'I'll ask Molly,' she said before dashing away, leaving him wondering who Molly was, and how it was that his young sister knew these people and could find her way round the town after such a short time.

He had to wait ten minutes to find out. He watched the shop door where she had run in and presently it opened, a man looked out and across at him, and then Daisy came out holding a plate and a cup.

The cup held milk which he drank straight down, wiping his mouth with the back of his hand when he had finished. The plate held a slice of meat pie, still warm and running with gravy.

'It's what we had for our dinner,' Daisy told him as he took a bite. 'They eat ever so well at 'Walkers' house. We had a treacle pudding but there's none left. Oliver ate 'last bit.'

'Who's Oliver?' Ted spoke with his mouth full.

'Their son. He's sixteen and going to be a chemist like his da.' She sat next to Ted on the wall and clutched her chin in her hands. 'I hope I can stay here,' she said. 'When Ma comes back, I mean. She lost her babby,' she told him.

'Lost it?' he said. 'How come?'

'I mean it wasn't born alive,' she explained patiently. 'It was too little. I didn't see it cos 'midwife took it away. But Molly said that it was too young to be born.'

'Oh!' Ted said. 'Do you mean like that ewe of John Ward's that aborted a lamb, or when that kitten was born dead?'

'I think it was aborted,' she said seriously, nodding her head. 'That's what Molly told Cook when she thought I wasn't listening. She said there was no wonder when Ma had been tied up. She said if she'd had a husband like that she'd have swung for him.'

Ted swallowed hard, and felt the pie lodge like a stone in his chest. 'Tied up? What happened?' he asked. 'What did Fowler do to her?'

Daisy told him in great detail and with some embellishments what had happened after their arrival in Hull. 'And then this man came along and said he would buy her and then when he saw she was expecting he changed his mind, onny it was too late cos he'd already given Billy Fowler the money and he'd scarpered.' She took a deep breath and continued, 'I expect Billy was scared of what Ma might do to him if she caught him, but by then she was feeling right bad and we were trying to find somebody to help us.'

She told him what had happened at the Walkers', and then started to cry. 'I was that frightened, cos I thought that Ma might die and what would I have done then, cos I couldn't have found my way back to Seathorne. Not that I would have wanted to go back to *him* anyway!'

Ted put his arm round her in an unexpected show of affection. 'It's a rum do, Daisy, and no mistake, but you'll be all right once Ma gets back from where Mrs Walker sent her. I suppose she did it for 'best,' he said, for Daisy had confided that she thought Mrs Walker didn't want her mother in their house any longer than necessary. 'And she didn't know our ma, after all. It's a bit tricky tekking in a stranger; especially if you've got some money 'n' that and you don't know if they'll pinch it.'

'I know.' Daisy wiped away a tear. 'And Mr Walker and Oliver have been really nice to me and let me help them in 'shop; I suppose that was so I didn't get in Mrs Walker's way, though I've done a bit o' dusting as well.'

'You've earned your keep then,' Ted said. 'You've not been a burden to 'em. Listen, Daisy. I'm going to tell you summat. I wasn't going to but I think I'd better; onny you've to promise not to tell anybody but our ma when she comes back, otherwise it's 'end of me.'

He scratched his chin, which was beginning to grow

dark and slightly bristly, though as yet he had never had to shave. 'I told you that I hadn't seen Fowler, didn't I? Well, to begin with, 'hoss came back on its own, but later on . . . later on, Fowler did come back. He was fair staggering. I thought he was drunk onny he wasn't; he said that he'd had to leave 'cart somewhere cos it had got stuck and Dobbin had bolted and he'd had to walk back. It took him a long time, I think, cos he's not very fit. And then . . .' He hesitated, unsure of whether he should tell the truth. 'Then he told me that he'd sold Ma in Hull Market Place, and I was that mad I hit him.'

'Did you, Ted?' Daisy's eyes shone with excitement. 'Did you really?'

'Aye.' He nodded, pressing his lips together. 'I did. And then we had a fight. And then . . . well, neither of us noticed where we were going and it was that wet and clarty on 'cliff top we were slithering about all over 'place.' He turned to look at her. 'And then he went ower. Fell ower 'cliff and into 'sea. I didn't mean it to happen,' he said earnestly. 'And if there hadn't been a high tide he'd have been all right and just landed on 'sands. But there was, and – and he must have been swept away cos I couldn't see him.'

Daisy stared open-mouthed at her brother. 'So,' she breathed, 'is he – is he dead?'

Ted hunched his shoulders up to his ears. 'Dunno. I suppose so. Drowned. He must be. Tide was running high. A spring surge, I think. Anyway, that's not all. I decided that I'd leave in case anybody found his body and thought I'd done him in, when really it was an accident; and I was just riding away on 'owd hoss when I heard this crash, and when I looked back I saw that 'cliff in front of 'cottage had slithered ower and 'front door was swinging ower 'edge.' He paused for breath. 'So I reckon it'll all have gone ower by now and folks'll think that's how Fowler died – if they ever find him.'

Daisy said nothing for a moment but sat pondering. Then she said in a small voice, 'I'm not sorry. I didn't like him.' She turned to look at Ted. 'But do you think you'd be blamed for it? Cos I'd swear that you wouldn't ever do owt like that!'

'But you weren't there, Daisy,' he said miserably. 'So you wouldn't know.' He handed her the empty plate which he had been clutching. 'So I'll have to leave. Run away to sea where nobody'll know me.'

'But what about Dobbin?' she asked, stroking the horse's neck. 'What'll you do about him?'

'I don't know,' he said irritably. 'I've got more to think about than 'blooming owd hoss!'

They both sat in silence for a few minutes, then Daisy said, 'You could sell him to 'gypsies. I saw them in 'market when we first came.'

'What?' Ted raised his head to look at her. 'Are you still on about 'damned hoss?' Apologetically he patted Dobbin's neck.

'It's just that you'll need some money,' she said, 'and you can't tek him with you if you're going to sea, and me and Ma won't want him cos we'll have to find work.'

He saw the sense in what she was saying although he wouldn't have admitted it. 'I can't wait till next market day,' he groused. 'I'll have to be off today.'

'There's Oliver,' she said suddenly. 'Let's ask him.' Before he could stop her she was running across the square to catch Oliver before he went inside the shop.

'This is my brother,' she told him, bringing him across, and Ted stood up from the wall and nodded to him. 'He's going to sea and needs to sell our old horse. Where do you think he should go?'

Oliver looked doubtfully at Dobbin. 'I don't think you'll get much for him,' he said. 'Does he pull a rully or—'

'Aye, he's a good strong hoss,' Ted was quick to point out. 'He's a bit thin, I know, but he's got stamina. He's good for a few years yet.'

Oliver scratched his dark head. 'There's a horse dealer in Dagger Lane, or there's the gypsies . . .'

'See, I told you,' Daisy said to Ted. 'But he can't wait until market day,' she explained to Oliver.

'He doesn't need to. They camp on Dock Green. I'll take you if you like,' he told Ted. 'It's not far.'

Ted agreed, and whilst Oliver slipped back to tell his father where he was going he mused that he would rather sell Dobbin to the gypsies, because the horse dealer might ask questions about where the horse had come from. And, he thought, with a tension tightening inside him, the horse wasn't really his to sell as it had belonged to Billy Fowler.

Daisy came too, walking between the two boys and glancing up from time to time at each of them. Ted walked with his head down, looking at his boots and leading Dobbin by the reins, but Oliver walked tall and told them about Dock Green. 'It's used for all kinds of events,' he said as they went along the Market Place and towards Castle Street. 'People like to walk there on a Sunday to hear the speakers giving out their opinions, and then in October the Hull Fair comes and pitches there. You'd like that, Daisy.' He looked down at her, smiling. 'It's great fun. The gypsies camp on the edge of Dock Green and most of them leave after the fair is over, but some stay and they buy and sell horses.'

The grassy area was mostly empty with just a few school-boys kicking a ball about, but pitched right on the edge were a few tents, or benders as Oliver called them. Several horses and ponies were tied up to stakes in the ground, and there were small cooking fires burning.

'We have a horse to sell,' Oliver said to a man who came out of one of the benders. 'Are you interested?'

The gypsy shook his head and Oliver turned away, but the gypsy called him back. 'How much d'you want for him? He's no flesh on him.'

'He's wiry and strong,' Ted told him. 'He's a good worker.'

The man came and ran his hands over Dobbin's flanks

and then opened his mouth to look inside. 'Give you five shillings,' he said.

Ted and Oliver both gave a dry laugh, whilst Daisy gave a gasp. 'He's worth more'n that,' she said.

'No thanks,' Ted said testily. 'I'm not giving him away!'

'Don't be in a hurry,' Oliver muttered to him. 'They like to bargain. How much are you willing to take?'

'Dunno,' Ted grunted. 'But more'n five bob.'

'A guinea?' Oliver murmured, and when Ted nodded he told the gypsy, 'We want twenty-one shillings for him. We'll ask one of the others.' He'd noticed two other men watching, one of them smoking a pipe and listening and the other, a younger man, eyeing up the horse.

'Seven and sixpence then,' the first gypsy said, and when Oliver shook his head offered another shilling. Oliver refused again, and the younger of the other gypsies came over.

'I'll give you ten bob for him,' he said. 'He looks sound.'

Daisy gave a sigh. That's what the man had paid for her mother. Surely she was worth more than an old horse.

The first man started to object. 'This is my deal,' he said, shaking his fist.

'Twelve and six then,' Oliver told him, 'otherwise we sell to your friend here.'

'Twelve shillings. My last offer,' the gypsy said.

Oliver glanced at the second gypsy, who shrugged and turned away. He looked at Ted, who nodded. 'Aye, all right,' he said reluctantly. 'I'd mebbe not get more from 'horse dealer.'

The gypsy counted out the money from his pocket. 'The saddle and blanket?' he said. 'They come with the hoss?'

'You can have 'saddle,' Ted agreed, 'but not 'blanket. I might need that.'

'You'll look after him, won't you?' Daisy asked the gypsy, stroking Dobbin for the last time. The man smiled, his teeth white against his dark skin. He patted her fair head. 'Don't you worry, little *chavi*. He'll have a nice time with the Romanies. We know how to look after our hosses.'

Oliver turned round to look at the gypsies as they walked away. 'They're in cahoots,' he told Ted. 'There's money changing hands. They've got a bargain between them.'

'Aye.' Ted shrugged. 'I guessed he was worth more, but I can't afford to wait.'

'Why the hurry?' Oliver asked curiously.

'I've nowhere to live, and no money,' Ted answered. 'That's why I'm going to try for a ship.'

'But you've no experience? Did – erm, did your step-father want rid of you too?'

'Yeh,' Ted answered vaguely. 'At least, he allus did; but he didn't come back and now 'cottage has fallen into 'sea.'

'Fallen into the sea!' Oliver looked amazed. 'Why? How?'

'It's been standing on 'edge of 'cliff ever since we went to live there,' Daisy interjected. 'Ma was allus afraid of it going over with us in it. It's 'erosion,' she explained. 'Most of 'village has gone over, even 'vicarage. But they're building some new houses further back for when 'railway line comes to Withernsea,' she finished, pleased to be able to impart some knowledge.

Ted grunted. 'If it comes,' he said. 'Why would folk want to come to that miserable place?'

'Cos of fresh air,' she said indignantly. 'And for town bairns to play on 'sands.'

Oliver laughed. 'And to see the sea! I've never seen it. If the railway goes to Withernsea I'll definitely go, Daisy, and perhaps you'd come with me to show me the sights?'

She gazed adoringly at him. The railway line wouldn't be coming for ages. It was only being talked about. But if Oliver meant what he said, then it implied that they would still be friends. She nodded. 'Yes,' she said huskily. 'Course I will.'

'Well I'll not be here,' Ted said, lifting his chin in a deter-mined manner. 'I'll be sailing on 'sea by then, and not just 'German Ocean either. I'll be on other seas as well; sailing round 'world.'

CHAPTER TWELVE

'It's not a brothel!' Jamie objected. 'It's a house of pleasure.'

'Pleasure!' Lily gasped. 'Who for? Not for 'poor lasses who work here it isn't!'

'They don't have to come,' he barked back. 'They can stop out on 'streets if they want to, but they'd rather be here where it's warm than out there in 'rain and cold. Ask her.' He pointed to the girl on the bed. 'Ask her where she'd rather be!'

The girl pulled herself up, her head against a greasy-looking pillow. 'I'd rather be inside than out there.' She waved a thumb towards the window. 'But what I'd really like is my own little house and a husband to look after me.'

'Huh!' Lily said contemptuously. 'Cry for the moon, you might as well. Surely there's a better way to make a living?'

'Show me it then,' the girl pouted. 'Cos I don't know of one.'

Lily was silenced. She didn't know of one either, not yet at any rate. But I don't know the town; I don't know what there is here. I'm a stranger, a countrywoman.

'Do you want to stop tonight or not?' Jamie asked her. 'There's plenty of room. We'll talk tomorrow.' He gave a shrug. 'Then if you want to leave, you can.' He gazed at her from sly blue eyes. 'But don't forget you owe me ten bob before you go.'

She took in a breath. 'Where would I get that sort of money?'

'I don't know.' His mouth lifted but he wasn't smiling. 'I paid out in good faith. Rescued you from that fellow you called a husband, so you owe me.'

He turned to go and this time he did smile as he reached the door. 'Onny kidding, Lily.' He gave her a wink. 'But you and me, we could work well together. Think about it.' He opened the door, nodded to the girl on the bed and left.

'Scum!' Lily muttered.

'He is,' the girl said. 'And if you owe him he'll want it back, never mind him saying he's onny kidding. But on 'other hand, he's not as bad as some. He's never violent towards his girls – at least . . .' She hesitated. 'There were some rumours a while back, but I don't know if they were true.'

She swung her legs off the bed. 'His ma was on 'streets. Jamie used to find her customers—'

'What?' Lily said in disgust. 'His own mother?'

The girl nodded. 'He had grand plans for starting up a place like this and putting her in charge.' She laughed. 'But then his ma married one of her customers and went all respectable. A grocer's wife she is now and Jamie's banned from seeing her.' She sighed. 'I wish one of my customers would marry me.'

'What's your name?' Lily asked.

'Alice,' she said. 'I used to work here when 'other fellow and his madam had it!' She screwed up her lips. 'Now they *were* scum!'

'His madam?' Lily said. 'What do you mean?'

Alice glanced at her and smiled; she was pretty, Lily thought, but very pale, with shadows beneath her blue eyes. 'My, you are an innocent, aren't you? Miss Emerald we had to call her, though it wasn't her real name, o' course. My, you should've seen her.' She grinned. 'Thick red hair, fancy clothes, and she allus wore an emerald round her neck. Don't know if it was real. She ran 'place, kept 'customers sweet and looked after 'money. But he got into some kind of trouble and they had to leave town. I heard that Jamie offered to pay 'rent that was owed if he could take it over.'

'And, erm, has Jamie got many girls living here?' Lily asked.

'Just me at 'minute.' Alice stretched her arms above her head. 'A couple of others have gone away, shall we say. But they'll be back. They'll be back when they need to eat or are cold working out on 'streets.'

'I met some girls,' Lily said slowly. 'When I was at 'home for fallen women. It was a mistake,' she added hastily when she saw Alice's eyes widen. 'I shouldn't have been tekken there. I'd had a miscarriage, but it was my husband's child. He abandoned me and my daughter. But these girls,' she went on. 'They were street girls. Cherie, one of them was called, and she was onny young—'

'I know her,' Alice said, 'and her friend Lizzie. They'll not stop there; them good folk think they'll go home or get other jobs, but they won't. Mark my words,' she said seriously, 'they'll be back on 'streets afore you can say Jack Robinson. Anyway, I've got to get ready for work. But I'll show you round first if you like. You can have 'pick of 'rooms if you're stopping.' She looked directly at Lily. 'You don't seem 'type, somehow. How is it that Jamie found you? Were you living rough?'

Lily heaved a breath. 'Not exactly. My husband put me up for sale in 'Market Place. It was Jamie who bought me.'

Alice stared. 'Was that 'ten bob Jamie was talking about? God! Is that all he thought you were worth? Your husband, I mean?'

'It's all he was offered. It seems wives are worthless.'

'Women, you mean!' Alice said sourly. 'My da said I was worthless when he threw me out. Mind you, I was glad to go. I didn't want to end up like my ma. Just a drudge, she was.'

Lily's mind was ticking. 'Do you reckon that Hope House has 'right idea? They mean well, those women who run it, I'm sure; but 'girls who go there seem to be just gathering their health and strength before they go back on 'streets again.'

'Yeh. It's not as if it's their own place,' Alice said. 'They're not comfortable there. They can't call it home, can they? They're under an obligation to keep on 'straight and narrow. I know there's some as will welcome 'chance, but most will leave, like you say, and go back to work on 'streets again.'

'But if they were somewhere where they were with folks they could trust and be comfortable with,' Lily said slowly as an idea formed, 'and if 'men they met were vetted first so that they were not afraid of being hurt—'

'Look, I'll have to go,' Alice interrupted, pulling on a grubby skirt. 'All 'best spots will have gone. I'll show you where everything is. There's a privy out at 'back. We share it with 'houses on either side. On 'top floor there's an attic with a tin bath if you want to haul water up there, and, as I said, tek your pick of 'rooms. They're all a bit scruffy, not been cleaned in years, and there's bedding in a cupboard.'

She seemed to be in a hurry so Lily told her that she would find her own way round the house. It was taken for granted that she would stay the night. Where else would I go? she thought. At least I'll have a bed to sleep in. And then I'll think of what to do tomorrow.

To her eyes the house was enormous. There were three rooms downstairs which had been turned into bedrooms, a fourth which held a large wooden table and cupboards, and then a very dirty kitchen with a stone sink and an ancient cooking range. All the rooms had oil lamps in them and the kitchen had candlesticks and holders on every surface – all of which were also covered in thick candle wax.

Upstairs on the first floor were a further three bedrooms,

with washstands and free-standing cupboards, which when Lily opened them were found to contain grubby finery, gowns and shawls, and off-white petticoats. All the rooms smelt strongly of stale perfume.

On the attic floor were two more rooms. One had been used as a store room and was piled with broken chairs, old cushions and pillows with the feathers spilling out of the ticking; the other had a tin bath half full of scummy water standing in the middle of the floor, with a heap of grey sheets or towels beside it.

Lily shook her head. 'This could be a palace,' she murmured. 'It must have been somebody's home at one time, and now it's come to this.' She went across to a window which faced on to the square and looked down. There were a lot of people loitering about, both men and women. Some of the women were sitting on the steps of the houses and many of them were barefoot and bare-legged and sitting in what Lily thought a provocative manner with their skirts pulled up to their knees.

As she watched, she saw men approach them and some of them were invited into the houses. Others linked arms with the women and walked away, laughing and shouting to their companions. Some of the men looked like seamen, dressed in wide trousers and short reefer jackets, and many of them had a dark foreign look about them.

'It's a brothel quarter,' Lily muttered. 'However did I get to be here? First thing in 'morning I'm leaving!'

She chose what she thought was the cleanest room on the first floor and looked in a cupboard on the landing to see if she could find clean bedding. She was a fastidious woman even though she had always been poor, and didn't at all relish the idea of sleeping in someone else's sheets. 'Especially when I know what they've been up to,' she muttered darkly. She fished about in the cupboard and brought out several blankets which appeared to be clean though they smelt and felt damp.

'Well, beggars can't be choosers,' she told herself,

spreading the blankets across the bed. 'And I'll be glad to put my head down and my feet up.'

She fell almost immediately into an exhausted sleep, which was punctuated by dreams of chasing Billy Fowler with a rope. Once she called out Daisy's name and sat up, unable to recall where she had left her, and then as she remembered that she was with Mr Walker she lay down and fell asleep again.

In the middle of the night she heard shouts and screams and loud laughter and turned over, putting her head beneath the blanket. 'Damned whores,' she murmured. 'How am I supposed to sleep with that racket going on?'

She was drifting off again when she heard a loud thudding; she groaned and slid further under the bedclothes. 'No place for a respectable body,' she groaned, hunching her shoulders up to her ears as the banging continued. Then she sat up in bed, exasperated. 'For God's sake,' she shouted. 'It's 'middle of 'night!'

'Lily!' She could hear her name being called. 'Lily!'

Am I hearing things? Who knows my name? I'm dreaming. I must be. But no, there it was again, and again came the banging.

'It's somebody at 'door! Who is it? Nobody knows I'm here.'

She slipped out of bed and into her shoes, dragging a blanket round her shoulders and carefully easing her way downstairs. It was pitch dark and she kept hold of the stair rail until she reached the hallway. The banging had dropped to a steady dull thump on the door.

'Who is it?' she called. 'Who's there?'

'It's me.' The voice was no more than a croak. 'Alice. Let me in, for God's sake!'

'Where's 'key?' Lily called back. The door was locked but there was no key in the lock. 'Where's it kept?'

'Hanging on 'wall to 'left of 'door. About halfway up. Be quick, Lily, please.'

Lily slid her hands up and down the wall and then felt

the nail and a key hanging on it. 'Just a minute. It's so damned dark I can't see a thing.' She fumbled about trying to fit the key into the hole, then in it went and she turned it. The mechanism needed oiling, but as it creaked she pushed against it until she heard the satisfying click.

She cautiously opened the door. 'Don't you have your own key?' she began, but stopped when she saw Alice slumped on the step. 'What's happened,' she said, bending down to her. 'Have you fallen?'

'Help me in, will you?' Alice looked up at her. One eye was closed, the other bruised and bloody; her lips were swollen and there was a cut across her face.

'Whatever's happened?' Lily helped her up and brought her inside. 'Who did this to you?'

Alice gave a soft groan. 'It's one of 'hazards of this game,' she muttered through her distended lips. 'But I never thought it'd happen to me. What am I to do?' She started to cry. 'I daren't go out there again. I'm scared that I'll die.'

CHAPTER THIRTEEN

There was no hot water, for the cooking range was stone cold and hadn't been lit in a long while, but there was a water pump over the sink and Lily strenuously pumped the creaking handle until she was rewarded with a thin stream of brackish water, which after some perseverance ran fairly clean into a tin bowl she had located in one of the kitchen cupboards.

She found a sheet in the landing cupboard and tore a piece off it, and went through to Alice who was lying, weeping, on the bed.

'This'll hurt a bit,' Lily told her, 'but I'll try and get 'blood off and clean you up a bit.' She gently dabbed away at the cuts with the wet cloth, and carefully trickled cold water over Alice's swollen eyes. 'You'll have a couple o' shiners tomorrow,' she said. 'You could do with some red meat to put on them. If you've any money I'll go and find a butcher in 'morning and get you some beef steak.'

Alice gave a muffled groan. 'He didn't pay me, did he? Took what he wanted and then beat me up. I don't know how I got back.'

'Why didn't you bring him here? I thought that was 'whole idea of having a house.'

'He wouldn't come,' Alice said. 'I met him by 'New Dock and invited him back. He looked as if he might have had some money. He was just off a ship anyway. But he said

103

no; he was scared of being trapped, I think, or of 'house being raided by 'police.' Her swollen mouth quivered. 'He was horrible to me, Lily. I thought I was going to die.' She broke into a spasm of weeping. 'A few weeks back a young lass was fished out of 'Humber,' she gasped. 'I knew her by sight. She'd been beaten up and then pushed into 'river.'

'Hush, hush.' Lily stroked her head. 'Don't think about it. You're safe now.'

She felt desperately sorry for her. Alice was only young, eighteen at the most. Lily looked back at her own life when she was that age. Her husband was away it was true, but she had his return to look forward to. She had a child and a one-roomed cottage which she could almost call her own. And in a village, she thought, everybody knows what their neighbours are doing; they know if they are sick or in trouble with 'law. There are few secrets. But in a large town it's different. What if I hadn't been here? Where would Alice have gone for help?

'Will you stay with me, Lily?' Alice begged. 'I don't want to be on my own. Please!'

Lily agreed and climbed back upstairs to fetch her blanket. 'I'd give owt for a cuppa tea,' she murmured. 'If I can find some wood I'll see if I can get that range going in 'morning. It'd warm 'place up as well.' The house felt cold and damp and had a musty smell.

What am I thinking of she thought as she lay huddled next to Alice, whose sobs were lessening. I'm leaving. I'm not stopping here. But where shall I go? What shall I do? And what shall I do about Daisy? And Ted? Is he still at Seathorne with that blackguard, or has he left? Thrown out, more likely. Then she too began to weep as the events of the last few days overwhelmed her.

She fell into a troubled sleep and was awakened once more by someone hammering on the front door. 'I'm coming, I'm coming,' she shouted. 'Just a minute.'

She wrapped the blanket round her, blinking at the brightness of the morning as it streamed through the window. She went barefoot to the front door, unlocked it and opened it to find Cherie and Lizzie standing at the top of the steps.

'What 'you doing here?' Lizzie said in amazement, her mouth dropping open.

'I might ask you 'same thing.' Lily opened the door wider to let them in. 'Had enough hot dinners to satisfy you?'

'I would have stopped at that place,' Cherie said wistfully, 'but Lizzie wanted to leave and I wasn't going to stop on me own. So we decided to come away as soon as we'd had our breakfast.'

'Just as well you didn't leave before breakfast,' Lily said laconically, 'cos there's nowt to eat here.'

'So why are you here?' Lizzie asked again. 'I didn't know you were on 'game.'

'I'm not!' Lily said sharply. 'So don't be thinking it. I've just had a bed for 'night. Alice is here,' she told them. 'You know her, don't you?' When they both nodded, she said, 'Come and take a look at her and see what can happen when you're in this line o' work.'

She led them into the room where Alice was trying to sit up. Her eyes were swollen slits and she peered towards the two girls. 'I'm so stiff,' she mumbled. 'I ache all over.'

'Best stay in bed, then,' Lily told her. 'Unless you've owt special to get up for?'

'Jamie will be coming for some money.' Tears trickled from between Alice's eyelids. 'And I haven't any to give him. He'll turn me out for sure.'

'What happened?' Lizzie asked, as Cherie's face turned even paler than it was already. 'A customer, was it?'

Alice nodded, hardly able to speak. 'I shan't be able to work for a week!' she whispered.

'I'm scared,' Cherie said in a small voice. 'What'll we do?'

'I'll talk to Jamie when he comes.' Lily was tight-lipped. She was angry. Angry with Jamie, with the man who had done this to Alice, with Billy Fowler who had put her in this predicament. Surely somebody can do something! 'It isn't fair!' she said bitterly. 'It just isn't fair.' Three pairs of eyes turned in her direction.

Lizzie shrugged. 'Who ever said it was? Nobody's ever done owt decent for me and I'll not do owt for anybody else. Except for Cherie,' she added. 'Onny for her. I'll look out for her.'

'Why?' Lily asked. 'Why for Cherie and nobody else?'

Lizzie eyed her bleakly. 'Cos she can't look out for herself. She needs somebody to watch out for her.'

Lily nodded. Lizzie seemed so hard and indifferent, yet she had a weak spot which the vulnerable Cherie had penetrated. She turned to Alice, who was resting her chin in her hands. 'Who watches out for you, Alice?' she asked.

Alice shook her head. 'Nobody,' she said. 'I've allus looked after myself. Never had anybody.'

They all jumped as the front door crashed open and a voice called out, 'Morning, ladies!'

'Jamie,' Alice muttered and slid down under the blanket. 'Tell him I'm ill.'

'You are ill,' Lily said firmly. 'Don't worry about Jamie. I'll deal with him.'

Jamie came jauntily into the room. His fair hair was tousled by the wind, but he was well dressed in a grey tailcoat and dark trousers, rather fancy for a working day, thought Lily, who knew nothing about fashion. He raised an eyebrow when he saw Lizzie and Cherie.

'You're back then.' He grinned. 'Didn't think you'd last long being pious.'

Lizzie opened her mouth to retort, but Lily forestalled her, asking sharply, 'Do you always come into a woman's room without knocking?'

He glared at her. 'It's my house,' he snapped. 'Why shouldn't I?'

'Manners maketh man,' she retaliated. 'Have you never heard o' that? No, course you haven't. Now tek a look at

Alice seeing as you're here and then come wi' me. I want to talk to you.'

Jamie looked down at Alice huddled under the blanket. She didn't attempt to open her eyes, which would have been difficult anyway, because she didn't intend to look at Jamie in case he asked if she'd been paid.

'You're in a mess,' he said. 'Was it anybody we know?'

She shook her head. 'A seaman,' she whispered hoarsely. 'Never seen him before.'

'A foreigner? Or local?'

'He had a funny accent,' she answered wearily. 'But I don't know where he was from.'

He began to ask her more questions but Lily interrupted him. 'Leave her be,' she said. 'I'll tell you what you need to know. Come out here wi' me.'

She went out of the room and he followed her into the kitchen. She faced him. 'She could've been killed,' she said. 'But it wasn't here in 'house. They were out on 'streets somewhere. Near to 'dock, I gather.'

He made a disgruntled tutting sound. 'Why didn't she bring him back here? What's 'point o' me paying rent on this place if they're going to stop outside?'

'He wouldn't come,' she explained. 'Alice thought he was afraid of being caught by 'police.'

'Mmm.' He screwed up his mouth. 'Well, sometimes places are raided, but onny if there's been trouble; if men have been robbed or owt, then 'constables keep watch.' He glanced slyly at her. 'Have you decided to stay, then? Going to watch over 'em like a mother hen?'

'I might,' she said calmly. 'It depends. I'd have to mek a few rules first.'

He snorted. 'You're forgetting. You owe me. I'm 'one who meks rules.'

'And it's you who stand to mek a profit.' She glared back at him. 'And you won't do that if these girls go out on 'streets looking for customers and get a beating. Much as I hate 'thought of it, they're safer if 'customers come here.'

107

He rubbed his nose. 'Well, that's what used to happen when 'other couple ran it, but 'police were allus sniffing round. They're up and down 'square all 'time.'

'Aye,' she said derisively. 'I gathered it's hardly a street of respectability. Women parading about and men on 'lookout. It's disgusting!'

'So it might be,' he sneered. 'But it's life. It's what happens. And you're a part of it now unless you can pay me back what you owe.'

'Nowt to stop me just disappearing out of Hull and going back to 'country,' she said.

'Oh aye? And what about your daughter?' he asked. 'How're you going to feed and clothe her?'

'Don't think I haven't thought about her,' she said softly. 'And that's why I've decided to stop here.' Her eyes had a luminous look; he saw a flash of green and then gold. 'But there are conditions, and if you agree, I'll make this into 'most respectable bawdy house in town.'

'Bordello,' he said. 'It sounds better.'

Lily shrugged. 'Means 'same thing. Do you want to know or not?'

Jamie nodded. 'Go on then. Tell me your grand plan, though what it is I can't imagine. You're just a country peasant. How do you know what folk in town want?'

'First of all I'll tell you what I want,' she answered. 'And for a start this place needs cleaning up. You can't expect anybody who's anybody to come to a slum like this. Whole place needs scrubbing out; 'curtains need washing, 'bedding needs washing. It stinks like what it is,' she said, wrinkling her nose. 'But it needn't cost you,' she added, for she saw alarm on his face. 'I'll do it, and those girls in there will help me.' She pointed towards the hall and Alice's room. 'That's if they want to stop. You'll bring soap and carbolic and you'll bring coal and wood to light 'range so we can have hot water, and light fires in 'other rooms as well, and when we've finished we'll want clean clothes.'

'Don't expect much, do you,' he snapped. 'How am I expected to pay for all of that?'

'Oh, I expect you'll find a way,' she said sweetly. 'You don't seem 'type who'll stick fast at owt so simple as finding money. Anyway, you'll get it back as soon as 'customers start coming in.'

'And what do you want out of it?' Jamie gave a crooked grin. 'Will you go on 'game as well? Make a bob or two on 'side?'

Lily eyed him narrowly. 'If anybody had suggested that to me a week ago I'd have given him a worse black eye than Alice has, but I'm in an odd position and I have to mek a living and if 'onny way is working in a house of ill repute, then I'll do it. But the answer to your question is no, I won't be giving myself to any man, for money or not, and I'm mekking that clear right from 'start. My job will be to look after those girls, manage this house, keep it in order and try to keep 'police sweet. I'll look after your money and mek sure you get paid. But them girls will need to be paid as well and so will I.' She gazed squarely at him. 'So do we have an agreement or not?'

He raised his head and surveyed her. He scratched his neck and then his chin and she noticed that he'd cut himself shaving as there were spots of blood on his neckerchief.

'Right,' he agreed. 'We do.'

CHAPTER FOURTEEN

They agreed on the basics, with Jamie's priority to bring in wood and coal so that Lily could light the range. She'd also told him that he should fetch bread and meat so that they could eat. 'We can't work on empty stomachs,' she said. 'And if we're to clean this hovel out we'll need sustenance.' He'd complained, but she ignored his mutterings and added that he should also bring some red meat for Alice's eyes.

After he'd gone she went back into Alice's room where she found Lizzie and Cherie sitting on the end of her bed, both looking very miserable.

'Cherie says she wants to go back to Hope House,' Lizzie said plaintively. 'She's scared of being beaten up like Alice.'

'Then you should go,' Lily said firmly.

'But I can't go without Lizzie.' Cherie's lips trembled. 'I'm scared of being on my own.'

'How come you're working on 'streets?' Lily asked. 'You're onny a bairn.'

Cherie bit on her lips. 'Da died some time ago, and then my ma died, so landlord turned me out of 'house cos I couldn't pay 'rent. I couldn't get a job o' work and then I met Lizzie.'

'When was this?'

'Onny a couple o' weeks back.' Lizzie answered for

Cherie. 'She was wandering about near 'pier. I thought she was going to chuck herself over.'

'I might have done,' Cherie whispered. 'But then Lizzie gave me some of her supper.'

Lizzie nodded. 'I'd made a bit o' money that night and I'd bought a meat pie.' She shrugged nonchalantly. 'So I shared it.'

Lily gazed at Cherie. She had an air of innocence about her. Like Daisy, she thought. 'So then you went to work on 'streets together?'

Cherie glanced at Lizzie. 'No,' she admitted. 'I haven't. Not yet. Lizzie did it for me. I daren't, you see.' Tears glistened in her eyes. 'So Lizzie has been keeping us both on what she's earned.'

'That's why we went to Hope House,' Lizzie told her. 'I thought they'd get Cherie some other kind o' work, but they wanted me to stop as well and I didn't want to.' She shrugged again. 'I was going to slip out when nobody was looking, onny Cherie caught me leaving and said she wouldn't stop on her own.'

'And have you been working for Jamie as well?'

'On and off,' Lizzie said. 'When it suited me; I came back here cos I thought Cherie would be safer than out on 'streets.'

Lily nodded thoughtfully. So Cherie is still innocent and Lizzie has been protecting her. How easy it is to jump to wrong conclusions about people.

'Well, young ladies,' she said softly, 'I have a plan. If you're willing we can work together, stand together and mek a better life for each and every one of us.' She told them briefly of her discussion with Jamie. 'I already know what Alice wants; she wants her own little house and a husband to look after her.'

Lizzie snorted derisively. 'Fat chance o' that.'

'So what do you want, Lizzie?' Lily asked.

'Well, not a man for a start!' Lizzie laughed shortly. 'I've had enough o' them to last me a lifetime. They think they're using me, but they're not: I'm using them. They want summat I've got so they've got to pay for it. But what I'd really like,' her mouth pouted and she gazed dreamily about her, 'is a shop that sells nice clothes: gowns 'n' cloaks 'n' that. Not a second-hand tat shop like Rena's I don't mean, but one that sells new clothes for folks wi' money. I'd be 'best-dressed woman in town then, cos I know about fashion,' she said defiantly, 'even if I don't have 'money for it.'

She would be too, Lily considered, for there was a certain air about the way she wore her worn shawl and swished her torn skirt. She was still wearing her own clothes, whereas Cherie wore the grey dress given to her in the charity house.

'And what about you, Cherie?' Lily asked. 'What'd please you?'

Cherie looked down at her hands and twisted them to-gether. 'I don't know,' she whispered. 'I felt safe when I was at home with my ma and da, even though we had nowt much. When they died I thought my brother would ask me to live with them, but his wife said she'd enough mouths to feed as it was and that I had to fend for myself or go to 'workhouse.'

Lily shuddered. Having seen the place she could under-stand Cherie's preferring a life out on the streets.

'So what I'd really like,' Cherie continued, 'is a place where I'd feel safe again. It's not that I don't want to work,' she added hastily. 'I worked in 'flour mills and cotton mills until I was dismissed and then I couldn't find another job o' work. But I'd want a place to come back to.'

'Why were you dismissed?'

'Cos I'd got to fifteen and they tek on younger bairns for less money.' She hesitated. 'But I was allus falling asleep,' she said. 'I was that tired all 'time and they said I was a danger to myself. I might have fallen into 'machinery, you see.' She yawned. 'I'm tired now,' she confessed. 'I could just crawl into that bed wi' Alice.'

Alice shifted up in the bed. 'Come on then. I've slept wi' more than two in a bed afore now.'

In a minute, Cherie had slipped off her boots and slid in beside Alice. Lily looked at Lizzie. 'Well,' she said. 'It looks as if it's just you and me to set about this place. What do you think? Are you going to stop here or tek a chance out on 'streets?'

Lizzie grinned. 'I'm going to stop.' She took off her shawl and rolled up her sleeves. 'Let's get started. We'll chuck out all 'rubbish, and then when Jamie comes back wi' fuel we'll get 'fire going and then them two,' she nodded towards the bed, 'can get themselves up to help us scrub out.' She looked at Lily. 'We've told you what we want, Lily. But you haven't said what you want.'

Lily heaved a sigh. It seemed as if all she cared for had gone for ever. Her beloved Johnny was the only man she had ever wanted. Billy Fowler had been meant to fill that gap in her life, but marrying him had been a terrible mistake. Ted and Daisy were the ones she had to think about now. Daisy was safe for the moment, but could Lily bring her here, to a house of ill repute? And as for Ted, will he ever find me? For surely he'll come looking when he discovers that Billy sold me.

'I have a son and a daughter,' she replied. 'They're the ones that I care about. I must work to give them a home.'

Lizzie looked aghast. 'You can't bring them here! It wouldn't be right!'

Lily laughed. 'Got some morals, have you, Lizzie?'

'Aye,' Lizzie said, looking offended. 'I have!'

Whilst Lily raked out the old ash from the kitchen range and then scrubbed it clean of ancient cooking grease, Lizzie found a sweeping brush and a pair of steps and swept the ceiling and walls free of cobwebs. 'Phew,' she exclaimed, wiping her face with a dirty hand. 'We'll need a bath when we've finished in here.'

'And we shall have one,' Lily said. Her face and hands were covered in soot and coal dust. 'As soon as this fire is

113

going we'll set 'pan on top and fill that tin bath upstairs wi' hot water.'

Lizzie leaned on the brush and contemplated. 'I've really enjoyed myself,' she said. 'I never thought that having a clean sweep would make me feel so satisfied.'

'Aye.' Lily dusted herself down. 'It does. When I had my own little cottage – it was onny one room, mind – I kept it clean as a new pin. I felt right proud of it, and when 'agent came to collect 'rent he allus used to say it was a pleasure to come into it.'

'How did you manage to pay 'rent?' Lizzie asked. 'If your husband was away?'

'Parish helped me, and I worked. Did washing in farmhouses, and I worked in 'local hostelry. I nivver stuck fast because after my ma died I used to worry about leaving 'bairns on their own. I'd put Daisy to bed, but Ted was a young varmint; he'd pretend to be asleep but I allus knew that as soon as I was out of 'door he'd be out of bed and off outside to play.' She shrugged. 'But what could I do? I had to work. Anyway, my neighbour had a garden where he grew vegetables and I persuaded him to let Ted have a small patch of earth to grow things.' She smiled as she reminisced. 'So that's what he did, and often when I came home later Ted would be flat out on 'rug in front of 'fire, still with his muddy boots on and his face and hands dirty, just worn out with 'exertion of working outside.'

'So where is he now?' Lizzie asked.

Lily put her hand to her face and squeezed her eyes tight. 'I don't know,' she said. 'I don't know.'

Jamie came back a little later with a sack of coal, kindling and a barrowload of wood. 'I've asked 'coalman to call regular,' he said. 'But go sparingly with 'coal – it's costing me a fortune.'

Lily looked at him. 'We've got to do this properly,' she told him. 'Otherwise you'll have a bawdy house just like 'rest of 'em down 'street. If you want gents to come here they won't want to be sitting in shabby surroundings.'

He bit on a piece of loose skin on his finger and said nothing for a second. Then he nodded. 'All right. You get it looking tidy. Then tell me what you have in mind.'

'It needs a lick of paint,' she said. 'Then I want things changing round. I'll have that room that Alice is in, then I'm handy for 'front door and seeing who's coming in and going out. That middle room can be a sort of parlour where folks – men,' she said reluctantly, 'can sit and have a drink or even a bite of supper.'

'Supper!' he exploded. 'You want to give 'em supper! I'll tell you they'll want to be off home as soon as they can afore their wives miss 'em.'

'Not all of them,' she said patiently. 'And I thought we could give them a drink or supper before they . . .' She pointed upstairs. 'Before they . . .'

'Tek girls upstairs,' Lizzie said pointedly. 'It's no use beating about 'bush, Lily. That's what they'll be coming for, supper or not!'

'Yes, I know,' Lily admitted. 'But I thought mebbe we could make it more sort of high class.'

Jamie stared at her. Then he blinked. 'There are places like that,' he said. 'But I hadn't thought – but then . . .' He pondered. 'Why not? I'd need to spend more money, though. To mek it suitable.'

'And you'll need more girls,' Lizzie said practically. 'It can't be done with just me and Alice.'

'And Cherie,' Jamie said.

'Not Cherie,' Lizzie and Lily said together.

'She's not experienced,' Lizzie said.

'I've got other plans for her,' Lily added.

Somebody hammered on the front door. Jamie looked alarmed. 'Sounds like 'constable,' he whispered. 'Go and placate him, Lily. Tell him it's a rooming house.'

She raised her eyebrows at him and went down the hall to the door, opening it with a half-smile on her face, prepared to be amiable. But it wasn't the constable but a young fair-haired woman in a grey dress.

'Hello,' she said. 'What 'you doing here?'

'Everybody asks me that,' Lily sighed. 'It's Betty, isn't it? You'd better come in.'

Lizzie and Betty eyed each other. 'Didn't think you'd stick it out,' Lizzie mocked.

'Lasted longer than you, anyway,' Betty retaliated.

'I didn't intend stopping,' Lizzie snapped. 'I onny went cos of Cherie.'

'What's going on, then?' Betty asked. 'Why are you here, Lily? I thought you said you weren't in this line of work.'

'I wasn't,' Lily said. 'I'm not. There's been a change o' plan. Perhaps you'd like to hear about it?'

'Mebbe,' Betty said in a non-committal way, and Lily thought that her tone of voice wasn't as harsh as Lizzie's. It was as if she had conquered her lowly accent and tried to improve herself.

Lily outlined the plans for the house and the customers they wanted to attract. 'Businessmen,' she said. 'Tradesmen too, but not any riff-raff who might use violence.' She told her about Alice being beaten and Betty shuddered.

'It's what I'm scared of more than owt – anything,' she said. 'Even more than catching disease.' She looked at Jamie. 'We've had our arguments, I know,' she said, 'and you've taken advantage of us, but I'd like to stop and give it a try.'

'You can,' Jamie said. 'But that's on condition that you and Lizzie don't fight.'

'I'll not fight,' Betty countered. 'It's degrading!'

'Ha, listen to milady,' Lizzie said. 'Who do you think you are?'

'That's enough!' Lily spoke as if they were children. 'I'll not have any bickering. We've got to work together. If either of you've got a complaint you come to me and I'll try to sort it out.'

Jamie grinned. 'Good! I'll leave you to it, Lily. Last thing I want is two she-cats scrapping.'

'And that's enough of that sort of talk,' Lily said sharply. 'We'll have some respect, Jamie, if you please.'

He pulled a face. 'Sorry,' he said, giving a mock bow. 'I'll try to remember.'

'Before you go,' Lily said, 'I'll give you a list of what we need. Cushions and antimacassars and suchlike to cover up 'shabby furniture. Then when we're ready you can tek Lizzie with you and you can get us all some new clothes.'

'New clothes!' he gasped. 'I'm not made o' brass.'

'Not *new*,' she explained. 'Second-hand! Lizzie will know what to get, won't you, Lizzie?'

The girl's face brightened. 'Yes,' she said. 'Course I will.'

'As for you, Betty,' Lily said, 'I've got something else in mind for you.'

CHAPTER FIFTEEN

The following day, Lily put down her sweeping brush and duster, washed her hands and face in warm water, brushed her hair with a hairbrush she had found in a cupboard and announced she was going out.

'Where're you going?' Lizzie paused in the act of draping a shawl over a chair in the room now known as the parlour. Jamie had brought a bagful of shawls and curtains and various pieces of material which they had soon found a use for, and already the room had taken on a different appearance.

'I'm going to see Daisy,' Lily said. 'Poor bairn will think I've abandoned her.' And I don't know what Mr Walker will think if I tell him where I'm working, she thought. I'll feel so ashamed.

She borrowed a shawl to put round her shoulders, marched down the steps of the house, and, keeping her gaze straight in front to avoid any eye contact with young women loitering around the other houses, walked briskly down the street. Halfway down she noticed an old woman sitting on a doorstep; she held her chin in her hands, her bony elbows propped on her knees, and she turned tired eyes towards Lily as she passed.

On the corner of the street two constables stood swinging their batons as they conversed; they looked towards Lily as she approached them. She nodded her head regally and gave a slight smile. 'Good morning,' she said and was gratified to see them touch their helmets with their fore-fingers, though they had rather confused expressions on their faces.

Just as well to have the law on our side, she thought, though I don't doubt they'll be knocking on the door before long. Great heavens, whatever am I doing in a situation like this? I'm an honest, law-abiding, good-living woman. Or at least I was. And once again she cursed under her breath the name of Billy Fowler who had brought her so low.

She lifted her chin and straightened her shoulders as she opened the door of the apothecary's shop. Oliver was behind the counter with his back to her, tidying up the shelves. He turned round and smiled as he recognized her.

'Mrs Maddeson! How nice to see you. Are you feeling better?'

'Thank you, I am,' she replied, thinking how polite he was for such a young man. How tongue-tied my Ted would be, greeting a woman. 'Is your father in?'

'Regrettably not,' he said. 'He's gone to see a patient. Dr Brown sent for him.'

'Oh!' She'd worked herself up to this visit and now she'd have to come again. 'Could I see Daisy then? Please,' she added.

'Of course.' He came round to her side of the counter. 'You're not going to take her away from us, are you?'

She looked at him in surprise. 'Well, I asked your father if she could stop until I found work. I didn't want to impose—'

'We've enjoyed having her here,' he said. 'And I met your son,' he added. 'He's not at all like Daisy, is he?'

'You met Ted? When?' she asked breathlessly. 'Is he here? In Hull, I mean?'

'Erm, I'm not sure where he is now.' Oliver fidgeted. 'Daisy will tell you about him. I think she's with my mother

119

at the moment. Would you like to come through to the house?' He opened a door and invited her into a dark hall-way. 'I can't leave the shop but I'll just let my mother know you are here.'

Oh, no, she breathed. Not Mrs Walker.

Oliver called out, 'Mother! Can you come a minute?' There was no reply so he called, 'Molly! Are you there?'

The maid came scurrying through another door from the back of the building. 'Molly, will you take Mrs Maddeson through to my mother, please? She's come to see Daisy.'

'Are you tekking her home?' Molly asked the same question as Oliver had. 'She's settling in nicely.'

'Is she?' Lily said. She had thought that Daisy might be fretting for her, but it seemed that she wasn't.

Molly tapped on another door and waited a second before opening it. 'Mrs Walker,' she said, putting her head round the edge. 'Mrs Maddeson is here to see Daisy.'

Mrs Walker must have said something to her, for Molly then ushered Lily into the room. She blinked in astonishment, for there was Mrs Walker in a chair with her feet on a footstool and Daisy standing behind her brushing her long straight hair.

'Forgive me if I don't get up, Mrs Maddeson,' Mrs Walker said. 'I have a bad headache and Daisy offered to brush my hair to try to relieve it.'

Lily smiled. Little minx, she thought. She loved to brush my hair and pin it up for me and then she would chat and I'd find out that she wanted something from me. I wonder what it is she wants from Mrs Walker.

Lily dipped her knee to Mrs Walker, who she thought seemed less brusque and more amiable with her hair undone and hanging down her back.

'I trust that Daisy has been useful to you, Mrs Walker? It was most kind of you and Mr Walker to tek care of her while I was unwell.'

Mrs Walker gave a slight nod. 'I hope that you've recovered from your ordeal and are returned to health?'

120

'Yes, ma'am. I'm as fit as I ever was.' Lily glanced at Daisy, who smiled demurely and kept on brushing Mrs Walker's hair. What's she up to? And how come she's offered to do Mrs Walker's hair? I didn't think Mrs Walker would have even spoken to her.

Mrs Walker half turned towards Lily. 'And have you found yourself a position? A job of work?'

Lily hesitated. 'I have,' she said quietly. 'It will do me for 'time being anyway, though it's not anything I'd have thought of doing.'

'What kind of work? And somewhere to live? Somewhere you can take your daughter?'

'That's why I wanted to talk to Mr – well, you and Mr Walker, ma'am.' Lily stumbled over what to say. She could hardly tell this woman she was going to be ruling over a brothel, or a *bordello* as Jamie would have it. 'It's housekeeping work, Mrs Walker, and I'll have to live in.'

Mrs Walker pushed Daisy's hand away and turned round to face Lily. 'So what you're saying is that Daisy can't go with you. Have you tried for other work?'

'Yes,' Lily said. 'In 'hostelries and 'inns; but there was nothing that would tide me over so that I could pay for a room for Daisy and me.' She bit on her lip. Perhaps I didn't try hard enough, but what more could I do? 'I thought if I took this job I'd be able to save up enough to pay rent on a room and then look for other work.'

'A housekeeping position isn't to be sneezed at,' Mrs Walker said sharply. 'There's many a woman would be glad of a job like that.'

'Yes, but Daisy—' Lily began.

'Where is this position? Would it be with anybody I know?'

Lily swallowed. She was convinced that it was a street of brothels, but would Mrs Walker be aware of it? 'It's a house in Leadenhall Square,' she said. 'At 'end of 'main street. Lowgate, I think it's called.'

Mrs Walker's face paled and a look of disbelief came into

her eyes. 'Leadenhall Square!' she croaked, glancing from Lily to Daisy. 'Fasten my hair back, Daisy,' she commanded, 'and then go and ask Molly to bring in some coffee.'

Daisy quickly knotted Mrs Walker's hair behind her neck and with a smile at her mother she dipped her knee to Mrs Walker and went out of the room.

'Do you know what kind of street that is?' Mrs Walker hissed when they were alone. 'It's a street of whores!' She stared at Lily, who was shocked at her frankness. 'I suppose you wouldn't know, as you're a newcomer to 'district, but I'm telling you that it's 'worst street in Hull and no decent woman would work there!'

'I didn't know.' Lily's voice quavered. 'Somebody took me. Offered me a bed for 'night, and a job running 'house. I thought it was a lodging house until I got there.' She closed her eyes and pressed her hand to her mouth. 'It was 'same young fellow who paid my husband. He said I had to pay him back if I didn't stay. I don't know what else to do,' she said, swallowing a sob. 'I seem to be digging a deeper and deeper hole to fall into, and I've got Daisy to consider.'

'Daisy can stay here.' Mrs Walker spoke in a no-nonsense tone of voice. 'She's proved very useful and I'd be willing to employ her. She's young but I can train her in 'way I want.'

Lily was astonished at the suggestion, but before she could comment Mrs Walker continued, 'My husband was angry when I sent you to 'home for fallen women. He said you were a good-living woman who had come to grief through adversity and no fault of your own.'

'He was right,' Lily whispered. 'These last few days have been a nightmare. I keep thinking that I'll wake up and be back in my own village again.'

'Well, you won't.' Mrs Walker's face was set. 'Not unless you can find somebody to take you and if they did what would you do then? Go back to your husband?'

Lily shook her head. 'No.' She took a deep breath.

122

'When I was in Hope House, Mrs Walker, I met some young women who worked on 'streets. They've turned up at this house in Leadenhall Square. One of 'young women already living there had been beaten up by a customer and they were all frightened.'

How much should I tell her? she wondered. How would she understand, a woman like her with a house and a husband and money to spend? She had noticed as she came into the room that although it wasn't lavish, the furniture was good and solid; there was a patterned carpet on the floor and velvet curtains at the window.

'I had an idea,' she continued, 'that if I turned 'house into a nice place, then 'girls could stay there and . . . and gentlemen could visit them, and they'd have no need to go out on to 'streets.'

'It'd still be a brothel.' Mrs Walker sniffed, but then swiftly put her finger to her lips as Molly brought in a tray with a coffee pot and two cups and saucers.

Lily hadn't been asked to sit down and had remained standing, but now Mrs Walker said, in Molly's hearing, 'Please sit down, Mrs Maddeson. I'd like to discuss Daisy.'

'Y-yes,' Lily began. 'But about Daisy working for you, Mrs Walker. She's onny been with you a few days; and you know she's not yet twelve.'

Mrs Walker nodded. 'Leave 'coffee pot, Molly,' she said. 'I'll pour. I'm aware of that,' she answered Lily when Molly had left the room. 'But she's got nice manners; she's a credit to you, I'll say that. She was sent in with 'tea one day and poured without spilling, and she's helped Mr Walker in 'shop; and it came to me that perhaps we could do with a girl who was adaptable. And,' she added, 'better that she's young and not one experienced in 'ways of womanhood who might think of tekking a fancy to my son. I know these young girls,' she said sagely. 'That's why Molly is older. We don't want temptation putting his way.'

Lily hid a smile. 'It'll come his way sooner or later, Mrs Walker. It's human nature, after all.'

'But not until after he's served his time with Mr Walker and become an apothecary.' She drew her lips into a thin line as she poured the coffee and said firmly, 'I want 'best for him and for him to marry well so that he can carry on in Mr Walker's footsteps.'

'He's your only child, is he, Mrs Walker?'

'He is.' Mrs Walker's eyes clouded. 'I had a daughter but she died. There's been no more.'

'I'm sorry,' Lily said. 'It's hard to lose a child.'

It was as if a shutter had come down on Mrs Walker's expression, for Lily could read nothing in it. I don't understand her, she thought. Why has she invited me to have coffee with her? She could have taken me down to the kitchen to discuss Daisy.

'I'll keep Daisy here.' Mrs Walker sipped her coffee. 'She'd be starting work at twelve anyway. Earlier than that if she was working in a mill or a factory. I'll supply her with her work clothes, caps, aprons and suchlike and take payment for them out of her wages.' She looked across at Lily. 'If you're going to take that work you won't want her with you.'

'Why, no,' Lily began, 'but I shan't—'

'If you decide to take it, I must ask you not to tell Mr Walker.' Mrs Walker pursed her mouth. 'My husband wouldn't approve at all.' She took a breath and gave a little shake of her head. 'I'm more understanding in these matters. That's why I arranged for you to go to Hope House when I thought that you were – when I mistakenly thought you were—'

'Yes. Yes, I do understand.' Lily helped her out of her confusion. 'When you thought I was a woman of ill repute.'

But there's something more, she pondered. Why hasn't she shown me the door? Why hasn't she changed her mind about Daisy when she's just learned that I'm to be running a disorderly house?

'Who will you be working for, Mrs Maddeson? Not that I'm likely to know them,' Mrs Walker added swiftly. 'But just so that I can be aware and steer away any difficulties should they arise. Mr Walker occasionally has to give medication to women like that.'

'There won't be any difficulties, ma'am,' Lily said. 'I'll be discreet. I wouldn't want my daughter to know 'nature of 'business. But I onny know the man as Jamie. First time I met him in 'Market Place he said everybody would know him.'

Mrs Walker gave a nervous swallow in her thin throat and she wet her lips with the tip of her tongue. 'I've never heard of him,' she said. 'But then I never expected to.'

Lily finished her coffee and stood up. 'You've been very understanding, Mrs Walker,' she said. 'And I appreciate that and your kindness to Daisy.'

'Oh, I've not been kind,' Mrs Walker asserted. 'I just saw her potential. I'll expect her to work for her keep and her salary. I'll try her out for three months and mebbe by then you'll know if you're staying in that place or if you have a change of fortune and go on somewhere else. Now, I expect you'll want to speak to your daughter. I'll give her half an hour off and you can tell her that I'll employ her from today.'

Lily waited in the shop for Daisy to come from the kitchen. When she did, Lily noticed that she had tidied her hair neatly under a bonnet which wasn't her own, though she still wore the shabby skirt and shawl she had been wearing when they left home.

They walked out into King Street and Daisy tucked her arm into her mother's. 'Are you better now, Ma?' She looked up at her. 'You look better.'

'Aye, I'm well rested now. The people in that place that Mrs Walker sent me to looked after me right grand. They put me to bed, and fed me when I'd recovered. Now then, Daisy,' she said. 'Mrs Walker wants to employ you.'

'I know.' Daisy gave a cheeky grin. 'I tried to be helpful to her and Mr Walker and I told her that I'd allus wanted to be a maid to a grand lady.'

'You never! You've never mentioned that to me!'

Daisy's eyes sparkled. 'That's cos I'd not thought of it afore. But Molly sent me in to tidy Mrs Walker's room and mek 'bed, and while I was in there I thought that would be a nice sort of job to have. And while I was there I sorted out her jewel boxes which were lying on a dressing table—'

Dressing table! Lily thought. We've never had such a thing, let alone jewel boxes.

'And then she came in. She was angry at first to see me there – mebbe she thought I was pinching summat – but when I showed her what I'd done – I'd put her brooches together, and her necklaces – she said that Molly wasn't very good at that sort of thing, and told me to tidy her cupboards and drawers. And do you know, Ma?' Her voice became animated. 'She's got some lovely things.' She put her hand to her mouth and leaned towards her mother. 'You'd never guess to look at her, would you, but she's got lots of lovely lacy petticoats and *under-drawers*,' she added in a whisper.

'Daisy!' Lily admonished her. 'If you want to work there you must learn to keep quiet about such things. Now,' she said firmly. 'Tell me about Ted. You've seen him?'

Daisy nodded solemnly. 'I'm not sure if he meant me to tell you, Ma. He might be in trouble. Billy Fowler is dead. Ted's run away to sea cos he thinks he killed him!'

CHAPTER SIXTEEN

The sea had encroached on the land along the eastern coast of Yorkshire for centuries and many villages in the Bay of Holderness had been consumed. Where the waters licked or battered the base of soft boulder clay, the weakened low cliffs slid down on to the sands leaving a jagged edge on the grassy top and making narrow bays and small coves below. Mostly the sands were covered when the tide rushed in, but here and there, where the boulders and clay had been heaped in the fall, there were small inlets where it was possible to stand and claw a way up the cliff out of the reach of the approaching waves.

It was into one of these inlets that Billy Fowler had been carried and he grabbed with all his strength and vigour at a heap of boulder clay, holding on tightly as the sea washed over him, making him retch, cough and splutter. 'By, I thought my end had come,' he gasped. 'Thought I'd had it.' He took several deep breaths, for he had been dragged under water several times as the sea carried him away from where he had fallen.

He looked up at the slippery mud-red cliff above him; he could see no handholds, just here and there tufts of grass which might, if he grasped them, pull out by their roots and deposit him back in the water again. 'I'll have to wait till tide turns,' he muttered. 'If I tummel down cliff I might not be so fortunate as to survive next time. I'll not chance it.'

But he was cold and shivery and although the heavy rain which was lashing down couldn't make him any wetter than he was already, it added to his discomfort. He was up to his waist in water and his hands were blue with cold as he clung on.

'It's that young peazan that's brought me to this,' he groused. 'He'll be up there in my house, thinking I'm a goner. By, I can't wait to see his face when I turn up.'

His legs were so cold he could barely feel them, and each time a wave rushed in it swept over his head. He struggled to get up higher on the tumbled boulder clay and managed to straddle it. Then he heard a rumble and looked up. Another chunk of cliff was falling, slithering down the rock face towards him. He put his head down between his arms to protect himself and felt the battering of stones, sand and clay as with a splash, slosh and splodge they hit the water.

Another wave of frothy spume thundered over him and as he lifted his head to take a breath he gave an exclamation of elation. The fallen clay and boulders had filled in the gap between himself and the cliffs, making it possible to scramble towards the place where a steep but navigable path had been formed.

He clawed his way over the heap, and then attempted to climb, sometimes slithering down again on the slippery treacherous surface. He paused halfway up to gain his breath. 'At least I'm out of 'water,' he gasped. 'And if it teks all night, I'll get there.' The sky was dark and ominous with the rain and he had lost track of the time and how long he had been in the water.

At last he reached the top of the cliff and lay panting on the grass. He lifted his head and looked about him. There was no sign of his house; the sea must have carried him a considerable distance. He shuffled away from the edge. The cliff top was so cracked and fissured that it wouldn't be long before that too would crumble and fall.

He lay on the wet grass and surveyed his surroundings, trying to get his bearings. The area was flat with no positive landmarks, but as he narrowed his eyes he could see across the land to the post-mill at Hollym and the disused church of St Nicholas. His eyes followed the horizon, coming to rest to his right and seeing his neighbour John Ward's farmhouse and meadow in the near distance.

'So where's my house?' he muttered, sweeping his gaze towards the sea. 'What's that?' A stable or loose box leaned precariously near to the cliff edge. 'That's my hoss shelter!' He rose clumsily to his feet. 'So where's my house?' He started to run, stumbling in his haste. 'It's nivver gone ower!'

He reached the derelict shelter and looked about him. Straw and hay were blowing about and where his house should have been were but a few spars and boulders, bricks and pantiles, for over the years he had patched up the old cottage with whatever had been to hand. He peered over the edge. It was now almost too dark to distinguish details, but what he did identify halfway down the cliff was a chair and a bed, a chimney pot and some smashed white crockery which gleamed in the gloom.

'Them was hers,' he muttered. 'Brought 'em wi' her. Rest was mine and now it's gone. It's all gone and I've nowt left.' He turned in bewilderment to look about him. 'Nowt at all. Where shall I go? Where shall I sleep? In stable wi' 'hoss. But where is he? Where's 'hoss?'

He stumbled back to the shelter. 'He were here before I had 'fight wi' yon lad.' His eyes flickered about him, noting that the saddle had gone. 'Where is he? He's gone off wi' hoss, that's what! Wi' my hoss!'

He shivered uncontrollably, his teeth chattering. 'I've got to get warm. Get these wet clouts off. I'll go to John Ward. See if he'll help.'

Billy Fowler had had an acrimonious relationship with his neighbour for many years, but the animosity had lessened once he had brought Lily to live with him. She had made friends with the old man and his wife, baking them a pie with the apples they had given her, and they

129

had allowed her to keep her cow in one of their meadows with their stock.

He trudged towards their farmhouse. They're going to ask me where she is, and her bairns. What story can I tell them? I have to get dry. I'll reckon that I'm concussed at first and get my memory back when I'm warm.

He reached their door and thumped on it. 'Help,' he called in a weak voice. 'Help!'

'Who is it?' Mrs Ward called and he thumped again.

'Billy Fowler! Help me.'

'Just a minute.'

He heard her calling to her husband and he banged again. 'Help me!'

The bolt was drawn and the key turned, and Mr Ward looked cautiously out. 'What is it? What do you want?'

'Cottage's gone ower. I've been in 'sea. Got washed ower 'side.' He was beginning to feel ill as he stood outside their door. 'For God's sake let me in.' His legs buckled and he fell to his knees, grabbing Mr Ward to save himself, almost dragging him down. 'I've lost everything,' he wailed. 'Me bed, me chair. Everything belonging to me has gone ower 'edge.'

They managed to drag him inside and towards the fire. Mrs Ward clasped her hands together. 'But dear God! What about your wife and her bairns? Don't tell me they're drowned!'

Billy's whole body shook and Mr Ward helped him off with his sodden coat. 'Fetch a blanket,' he told Mrs Ward. 'He's going to get pneumonia if he doesn't get these wet clouts off.'

Mrs Ward brought a blanket which he wrapped around himself, stripping off to his skin beneath it whilst she heated a pan of water on the fire. 'Brandy and hot water, that's what he needs,' she told her husband. 'You've got a drop left in 'cupboard.' He looked askance at her, but he went to fetch it.

Then he sat opposite Billy by the fire and threw questions

130

at him. 'So where were you when 'house went ower? Were you in it or outside?'

'And where was Mrs Fowler and her childre'?' Mrs Ward wrung her hands in dismay. 'Don't say they were in it when it went ower! They'll be dead for sure.' Her voice broke. 'That poor lass and her bairns.'

'Not 'young lad,' Mr Ward broke in. 'I saw him wi' 'goats late afternoon and then a bit later saw him riding off on 'owd hoss.' His eyes narrowed as he gazed at Billy. 'Haven't seen his ma or 'little lass about for a day or two, though.'

'She's not been well,' Billy muttered. 'She stayed inside and 'lass looked after her.'

'So 'lad's safe at any rate,' John Ward said slowly. 'Where was he going? Will he be back? We'll have to send out a search party for Mrs Fowler and her daughter.' He nodded his head as he contemplated. 'I'll tek 'trap ower to Withernsea and find somebody to tek a boat out.'

'It'll be useless tonight,' Billy mumbled. 'I was washed down 'coast. I was stuck at 'bottom of 'cliffs for hours,' he exaggerated. 'If it hadn't been for another fall which cleared a path, I'd still have been there.' He gave a deep sigh. 'Doubt if I'd have survived 'night.'

'But we'll have to look for 'em,' Mrs Ward insisted. 'They might be stuck on 'cliffs, same as you were.'

John Ward gazed suspiciously at his neighbour. 'Hours, you say? Well, 'house was still there when I went to lock up 'hens. I was earlier than usual, cos of 'weather. I'd have noticed if it had gone ower. That's when I saw Ted riding off, just afore I came inside.'

Billy put his hand to his head. 'It seems like hours,' he said in a faint voice. 'Mebbe it wasn't. I onny know that I was half drowned and got washed up on to some boulders. I had to cling on for dear life,' he said plaintively.

'That's as mebbe.' Mr Ward got to his feet and went towards the door where his outdoor coat was hanging, with his boots standing neatly by the side of it. 'But if you survived, happen your wife and 'little lass are doing 'same.'

'Can I stop 'night?' Billy whined. 'Then in 'morning when my clouts are dry I'll go to 'parish and ask 'em to house me.'

'You'll not go to 'land agent, then?' Mr Ward paused with his hand on the latch. 'He'll need to be notified to tell 'maister.'

'He can go hang,' Billy muttered. 'All 'time I've been living on 'edge I've had to pay full rent, nowt knocked off for 'land I've lost!'

'Not 'maister's fault,' Mrs Ward butted in. 'He's losing land as well. And he'll have lost your rent now 'cottage has gone ower.'

'Well, he can seek me out,' Billy grumbled. 'I'll not go lookin' fer him. He'll not house me anyway. He's got nowt that I want. Not out here anyway. No, I'll ask parish to find me summat. I heard tell they're going to build new houses in Withernsea. I'll ask 'em for summat temp'ry till they're ready.'

'And how will you live and pay 'rent?' Mrs Ward was astonished.

'I'll work as a labourer,' he said. 'Do odd jobs. I'll manage,' he muttered, forgetting for a moment that he was in company. 'Now I'm on me own wi' onny meself to cater for, no other mouths to feed.'

He looked up to find both Mr and Mrs Ward staring at him. 'So.' Mr Ward's jaw was slack. 'You reckon they're dead then? Mrs Fowler and young Daisy?'

Billy shook his head sorrowfully. He sighed a deep sigh. 'I reckon they are.'

CHAPTER SEVENTEEN

'Poor bairn!' Lily wept when Daisy told her that Ted had gone to look for a ship in case he was blamed for Fowler's death. 'He wouldn't have done it deliberate. I know he wouldn't, even though he couldn't abide Billy Fowler. And was he sure that he drowned? I wouldn't put it past him to pretend that he was dead just to put 'fear o' God into Ted.'

'Ted said he leaned right over 'edge and all he could see was 'foam. All of 'sands was covered over, he said.'

Lily wiped her eyes on her shawl. 'Well, I can't pretend my heart is broken and now I can't speak ill of 'dead, even though I'd like to. He was a dowly ill-mannered man wi' no kindness in him.'

'Why did you marry him, Ma?' Daisy asked. 'If you thought that?'

'Because when he used to come into 'hostelry of a night, he seemed amiable enough, and I thought he was lonely like me.' She turned to Daisy. 'Women do get lonely.' She gave a soft smile. 'Even if they've got bairns to comfort 'em. And I missed your da,' she added in a low voice. 'Even though we didn't see much of him I allus thought of 'time when he'd come breezing in through 'door and all'd be right with 'world. But as 'years went on I had to admit that he probably wouldn't be coming back and that I'd have to find a father for my bairns.'

133

'We hadn't known him, Ma.' Daisy put her hand into her mother's. 'So we didn't miss him, though sometimes I thought it would be good to have a da, like some of 'bairns I knew. And Ted felt 'same; but not Billy Fowler. We'd rather have done without than have him.'

'Well he's gone now and I'm a widow again.' Lily felt fresh tears sting her eyes, but they weren't tears for Billy Fowler. It was a sorrow come back, even though it had never really gone away, for her dearest Johnny.

'I can't do anything about Ted,' she said, swallowing hard. 'He'll probably be away on a ship by now, but,' she wagged a finger, 'if you should see or hear a whisper that he's back in Hull, you must tell me.'

Daisy nodded. 'Will we stay here in Hull now, Ma? I want to. I like working for Mr and Mrs Walker.'

'No point in going back,' Lily said. 'What or who would we go back for? If Ted had been there, then I might've done. We could mebbe have managed between us, though not at 'Seathorne cottage. I reckon it'll go over afore long if it hasn't already. No, I'd have gone home, back to Hollym, and tekken a chance there.' She sighed. 'But it's not to be. And you've 'prospect of a better life here, Daisy.' She squeezed her daughter's small hand. 'You be a good girl and work hard for Mr and Mrs Walker and you'll do all right.'

Lily made her way back from King Street towards Leadenhall Square. The town was busy with hustling people, noisy with the clip-clop of horses' hooves and rattle of wheels on the cobbles. She heard a shout of 'Stop thief' and saw a small ragged boy running along the road with a rabbit hanging from his pocket being chased by a shopkeeper in a bloodstained apron. She watched curiously and hoped he would escape, but drew in a breath as she saw a man in a top hat and frock coat put out his arms to bar his flight.

Poor lad's probably starving, she thought regretfully, but continued on her way, glancing in the shop windows in Lowgate with little interest. Even if there had been anything she would have liked to buy, she couldn't have done so for she still didn't have a penny to her name.

When she reached the square it was starting to rain. The police constables had gone but the old woman was still sitting on the steps with her head bent and her hands clutched round it. Lily stopped and stood in front of her. The woman unfastened her fingers and looked up. Her eyes had a cloudy film over them but Lily could see that once they had been blue.

'What 'you looking at?' she croaked. 'I ain't doing nowt. I'm minding me own business.'

Lily nodded. 'I just wondered if you'd like a cuppa tea. You've been sitting here a long time.'

The old woman's mouth dropped open and she stared. 'Tea! What do you mean?'

Lily smiled. 'How long since you last had a cup? Have you forgotten 'taste?'

The woman grunted and worked her lips together, pressing them hard as if trying to savour some long gone flavour, then ran her tongue over them. 'Can't remember when,' she muttered. 'All of a month; since I left 'workhouse, but then you can't call that coloured water tea. Barely a sprinkling o' leaves.' She squinted up at Lily. 'Where's 'catch?'

'No catch. Come on,' Lily said, bending down towards her. 'Let me help you up. I'm in need of a cup and I'm sure you are.'

The woman's joints creaked as Lily took her arm to pull her up, and she bent double for a moment. 'Ooh! Just a minute,' she groaned. 'Wait till everything's gone back into place. By, that step's hard.' She slowly straightened up, apart from her neck and shoulders which seemed to be permanently bent. 'You want summat from me,' she groused. 'Nobody does owt for nowt. Not any more.'

Lily led her towards the corner house and the woman gave a cackle. 'Can't see you wanting me to work here,' she

135

mocked. 'Not in this brothel. Worst bawdy house in town.'

'Not any more it isn't.' Lily led her up the steps to the door. 'There're going to be some changes.'

'Don't Miss Emerald run this place? She allus did.' The old woman ran her hand across her nose. 'She was a right madam, that one. I used to sit on her steps to catch a bit o' warmth from 'sun, but she allus moved me on.'

'No,' Lily said. 'She doesn't. I run it now, though it belongs to Jamie. At least, he pays 'rent.'

'Jamie!' Again the woman cackled. 'Full o' bright ideas is Jamie. You watch him.' She shook a finger at Lily. 'Don't trust him any further than you could throw him. He's a bad 'un, that one. What's your name?'

'Lily. What's yours?'

'Mrs Flitt,' she said. 'And that's me real name as well as being me nature. Righty-ho,' she said. 'So where's that tea you promised, Miss Lily?'

Mrs Flitt knew Lizzie and Alice already, but not Cherie or Betty. 'I heard you 'other night,' she told Alice. 'Heard you blubbering as you ran back here. There was nowt I could do to help you. I was stuck in a doorway across 'square and couldn't move. Somebody had to help me up when 'morning came. Me bones had set,' she said.

She drank appreciatively of the tea which Cherie had made and looked round at the parlour. 'Nice place you've got here,' she said approvingly. 'Is it going to be for haccommodation?'

'Not exactly,' Lily said, thinking that it could well be. There was a cheerful fire burning in the grate. The big table had been moved out and an old sofa was covered with colourful shawls. Several chairs and small tables which Jamie had acquired from somewhere were scattered about the room ready for receiving visitors once they started to come. 'They'll need somewhere to put down their gloves or drinks,' Lily had told him, 'while I assess their character. I'll not have them thinking they can dash away upstairs straight away.'

The room at the front of the house which had been Alice's was now Lily's. She had moved the sofa nearer the window so that she could see anyone coming up the steps to the house. There was also a small desk in which she would keep a list of regular customers, and a sofa bed, covered with shawls and covers and cushions during the day, where she would sleep at night.

Cherie cleared away the cups when they had finished and carried them to the kitchen on a tray. Mrs Flitt watched her go. 'Bonny girl, that,' she commented. 'Weak, though. Hope she's not going to be a jade like 'other lasses; she'll not last.'

'What do you mean?' Lily asked, knowing that Cherie did look frail with her pale face and languid air.

'She'd be tekken advantage of.' Mrs Flitt sniffed. 'And she don't look well to me.'

Lily hid a smile. Mrs Flitt was hardly the picture of health herself with her grey face and thin body, but she was right. Cherie had a fragile air.

'Can I have a look round?' Mrs Flitt asked. 'In 'kitchen, I mean. Not upstairs.'

Lily took her through to the kitchen which was now warm from the heat of the range, and smelt deliciously of the onion soup which Betty was cooking in a large iron pot. Mrs Flitt licked her lips. 'Would there be enough for an extra one?' she asked. 'I can't pay you but I'll scrub 'pan out afterwards. I used to work in a kitchen,' she added. 'When I was young.'

Betty glanced at Lily, who nodded. 'It's not ready yet,' Betty said. 'It won't thicken.'

Mrs Flitt peered into the pan. 'Have you put a chopped tatie in it? That'll thicken it up.'

'No, I haven't,' Betty said. 'I've never made it before. I asked Jamie to bring summat in for supper. He's not keen on spending money so there's no meat. He brought a basket of vegetables from 'greengrocer.'

'Let's have a look.' Mrs Flitt rummaged amongst the

137

mostly scabby potatoes, onions and carrots. 'I'll just scrub these.' She held up a couple of potatoes and a carrot. 'They'll be all right when they've had a glance at some water.'

As they ate their supper later, Mrs Flitt looked towards the range and pointed to a long cupboard at the side of it. 'What do you keep in yon cupboard?' she asked.

'Nothing,' Lily said. 'I think it was a warming cupboard. It goes well back. It'll do for storage.'

Mrs Flitt paused with her spoon up to her mouth. 'Can I 'ave it?'

Lily laughed. 'What'll you do with it?'

The old woman put down her spoon. 'Sleep in it,' she said in a pleading small voice. 'I'd not be a bother.'

'It's not big enough to sleep in,' Lily objected. 'It's onny a cupboard!'

Mrs Flitt gazed at her. 'You wouldn't believe some of 'places I've slept in. Pigsties, coal cellars, dog kennels. That cupboard would be a palace compared to some of 'places I've laid me 'ead.'

It could have been me, Lily pondered. She looked round at the young faces, Alice, Cherie, Lizzie and Betty, watching her and the old woman. Or it could be any one of these girls. 'Yes,' she said softly. 'Course you can.'

In no time, it seemed, Mrs Flitt had swept and washed the flight of front steps, cleaned the windows, dusted down the stairs and scrubbed the outside privy. 'You're very fortunate to have this,' she told Lily, 'and you onny have to share wi' folks on both sides, not 'whole street.'

'It's still six of us plus whoever's next door,' Lily said. 'It's enough.' When she had lived in Hollym and Seathorne, they had had an earth closet at the bottom of the garden for their own use.

Mrs Flitt shook her head. 'You're lucky,' she said. 'I know some courts where all 'houses had onny one. Sometimes as many as thirty folk sharing a privy and hardly ever seeing 'night-soil men.'

Lily had offered Mrs Flitt the attic room which was not yet in use when she realized how useful the old woman would be. She was always willing to do any job or run any errand, but she had refused the offer. It was warm in the kitchen cupboard, she had said, and she could keep the fire going all night. She had found an old blanket and Lily had given her a cushion for her head. The only possession she had was an empty tobacco pipe which she kept on a shelf.

Jamie was less than pleased to see her. 'Are you going to invite all 'waifs 'n' strays in town to live here?' he bellowed at Lily after meeting Mrs Flitt on the steps with a broom in her hand.

'She's helpful,' Lily retaliated. 'She'll keep 'house tidy and she'll stop out of 'way when she has to. I've told her that already.'

'Mek sure she does,' he grumbled. 'She does nowt for 'tone of place. Old ratbag,' he muttered.

'She doesn't care much for you, either,' Lily answered caustically. 'But she comes free; she onny gets her bed and board in return for all 'work she does. She's up early and in bed by eight.'

She agreed privately that Mrs Flitt looked a sight. She was skinny and her clothes were merely rags, but Lily intended to do something about that, and already the old woman looked brighter, bustling about all day, cleaning, dusting, stoking the fire and generally making herself useful.

Jamie just grunted and then unfastened a large parcel that he'd brought. 'Lizzie chose these at Rena's and I've got them on sale or return.' He unfastened the string and tipped out a pile of gowns. 'She said if they don't fit she'll change 'em.' He held one up: a red velvet gown with a low-cut neckline. He ran his hand over the cloth. 'I've seen this on somebody. It looks good. Might suit you, but 'girl who wore it wasn't as tall as you so it might not fit.'

'A lady friend was she, Jamie?' Lily enquired.

'No,' he answered shortly and with a note of bitterness. 'She wasn't. A whore who did well for herself.'

139

'It won't fit me,' she said. Whoever had worn it wasn't as well built as she was, though she knew she had lost weight after losing the child and with all the worry and anguish. 'Colour will suit Lizzie, though. Leave them wi' me and we'll try them on.'

He nodded. 'Is 'house ready?'

'Just about,' Lily said. 'We could do wi' some flowers to brighten 'place up, and perhaps you'd bring some wine and biscuits for 'customers. Or a cask of ale,' she added. 'I know how to draw it.'

He gave an exclamation. 'I hope you know how much this is costing me!'

'I don't know,' she said, 'but I'm sure you'll tell me. But you'll get it back if you bring 'right sort of customers. Don't bring riff-raff, cos I'll turn 'em away. I onny – only want gentlemen or good-class business men.'

'I know, I know,' he said irritably. 'I've been putting 'word out, and I'll bring a couple more women in. Be ready for Saturday,' he said. 'Day after tomorrow.'

CHAPTER EIGHTEEN

Lily was very nervous as Saturday approached, but Lizzie, Betty and Alice were full of excited anticipation. Cherie had been pale and trembling at the prospect until Lily had told her that she was to help her with greeting the gentlemen and serving them with wine if they wanted it.

'You're not going upstairs,' she had told her quietly. 'That's not for you, Cherie. I want you to blend into 'background and be ready with their coats and gloves when they leave.'

Cherie's face flushed with relief. 'Oh, I can do that, Lily,' she said. 'But I'd be so frightened to do the other. That's why Lizzie's allus looked after me.'

Lily smiled. 'We'll all look after you now, Cherie. But Jamie will expect you to do your bit, so we'll have to show him how important it is for 'gentlemen to be looked after too. You'll have to smile at them and mek 'em comfortable so that they'll want to come back again.'

'But I hate to think of what Lizzie and 'others have to do just to earn a living.' Cherie's eyes filled with tears and her lips trembled. 'It's not right.'

'It isn't right,' Lily agreed. 'But it's what happens when a woman has no other means of mekking a living.' She took hold of Cherie's hand. 'But they'll be safe here,' she assured her, 'and it's not as if they haven't done this sort of thing before. They know 'ways of men and what to expect.

141

That doesn't mek it right, I know, but 'men who'll come have a need, for whatever reason, and 'girls can satisfy that need and mek 'em pay well for it,' she added with some satisfaction.

Lizzie had tried on the red dress and it fitted and suited her, a perfect contrast against her dark hair. The bruises from her arms and face had faded; she had washed her hair and bathed in the tin bath which they had brought down into the kitchen where it was warm and to save carrying the hot water upstairs to the attic, and already she was looking healthier than when she had first arrived.

They had all bathed in the tin tub: Cherie first, before Lizzie; then it was topped up with more hot water and Alice and Betty took their turns. Apart from Cherie none of them were bashful and they washed each other's hair and scrubbed each other's back, giggling and chattering as they did so. Lily smilingly watched them; she felt very maternal towards them even though she was too young to be considered their mother substitute, but they all turned to her to ask questions as if she might have been an older sister.

Alice's bruises hadn't faded but were turning yellow; her face was still swollen and her eyelids were puffy, so it was decided that she wouldn't be seeing any gentlemen just yet, but with a touch of powder on her face would help Cherie serve the drinks on Saturday. 'I shan't earn any money,' she wailed. 'And I still owe Jamie for last week's rent.'

They had spent an afternoon trying on the clothes which Lizzie had chosen and Jamie had bought. Alice had selected a pale blue gown with an overskirt of white lace and short puff sleeves; she and Betty had almost come to blows as Betty had wanted it too. Lily stepped in to resolve the argument. 'Alice should have it,' she decided. 'The pale blue suits her fair skin and hair. Your hair's more golden, Betty, so will suit this other blue; look,' she said, holding up the dress. 'See how vibrant it is.'

And she was right, as Betty admitted when she tried it

on. It was a rich deep blue with a flounced skirt piped with a satin edging and a bow at the back, with long sleeves coming to a point at the wrist.

Cherie had stood back waiting for her turn. She didn't expect much as she wasn't to be working, but Lizzie held up a dress that she had previously put over the back of a chair. 'Try this, Cherie. I picked this out specially for you.'

Cherie pressed her lips together as she slipped off the grey dress. She wore just her cotton chemise and put up her thin arms for the new gown to be put over her head. 'It's lovely, Lizzie,' she said shyly. 'Can I really wear it on Saturday?'

'Whew!' the other girls screeched. 'Cherie, you look *lovely!*'

The sprigged muslin gown seemed to bring out Cherie's innocence. The skirt was full, the high-waisted, boned bodice, which laced at the back, not too low, having a lace fichu at the neckline, and satin ribbons floated from a bow at the front.

All the gowns were second- or even third- or fourth-hand, and some were worn in places or had a hem hanging down, but Lily was adept with a needle and was able to repair them; she'd always had to make her children's clothes out of whatever material she could find, and in various cupboards or drawers in the house she managed to unearth what she needed, needles and thread or skeins of silk.

'What about you, Lily? What'll you wear?' Alice asked her. 'We've all found something, so now you must.'

'There are two that I like,' Lily confided, 'and I don't know which to choose.' Lizzie had done well in gathering such a splendid selection. There was a fine wool gown in lilac, full with a stiffened underskirt and cut off the shoulder. The other one she liked was in a soft purple-black shot with a silver vein, with a deep neckline and a nipped-in waist and a full trailing skirt.

'You must have 'em both,' Lizzie said. 'You can't wear

'same frock every time you go to 'door. Try 'em on,' she urged. 'Let's see.'

Lily had bathed the night before after everyone else had gone up to bed. She had lain in the tub in front of the range with her wet hair pinned up and reflected that this wasn't her, not Lily Fowler formerly Leigh-Maddeson, a countrywoman with two children. This was someone entirely different.

She took the two gowns now and went away to her room and dressed in the black gown. She gazed at her reflection in the spotty cracked mirror. 'No,' she murmured. 'It's definitely not me.'

The person looking back at her was tall and stately, without the ruddy rosy cheeks that came from living by the sea, but paler, making her amber-coloured eyes seem larger and more intense. Lily lifted her hair away from her face and pinned it up on top of her head, pulling down just a few strands around her ears to hang in tendrils at her cheeks.

'Shoes,' she muttered. 'I haven't any shoes!' She only had the boots she had come in. 'I can't wear this wi' my old boots.'

She picked up her skirt and went through into the parlour where the others were waiting and stood poised in the doorway.

The four young women turned to look at her. For a moment they said nothing, just gazing in silence. Then Lizzie said, in a hushed almost reverential whisper, 'Lily! You look magnificent. Like a duchess!'

Betty took in a breath. 'I can't believe it's you!' she said. 'When I first saw you at Hope House, you were so – so dowly. I know you'd just lost a bairn, but even so you were . . .' she struggled for words, not wanting to be offensive.

'A peasant?' Lily suggested, smiling at the astonishment on their faces.

'Well, yes,' Betty admitted. 'But now you're so – so grand!'

'Glorious,' Alice said.

'Lovely,' added Cherie.

'What's going on?' Jamie's voice came through from the hall. 'What 'you all up to?'

He stopped as he saw Lily and his eyes opened wide. 'Whew!' he said. 'Who's this?' He circled round her. 'You look tremendous.' He grinned slyly. 'The gents will be mad for you, Lily. Are you sure you won't—'

'Quite sure,' she said firmly. 'Don't ask.'

'Well, when they see you at 'front door they'll know they're in for a treat.'

'I haven't any shoes,' she said, lifting her skirt to show her bare feet. 'I've onny – only got my boots.'

He sighed. 'Is there no end to spending money? Can't any of you lend her a pair?'

They all shook their heads. A second pair of boots or shoes was unheard of.

'Black slippers,' Lizzie suggested. 'They won't cost as much as shoes.'

Jamie reluctantly agreed and put his hand in his pocket to bring out some money. 'Go to Rena's, then. I'm just off to fetch 'wine and a cask of ale. There's a couple more girls due to come.'

'Who are they?' Lizzie asked. 'I hope they're decent.' She had become proprietorial, not really willing to admit any-one else to their group.

'Who do you think you are?' Jamie admonished her. 'They're all right. Been around a bit. Hope you've saved 'em summat to wear. Anyway,' he said, 'I've got some book-ings. You lot can have gents and they can have whoever else comes.'

'Which rooms shall these women have?' Betty asked. 'We've all chosen ours.'

He gave an exasperated exclamation as he went out. 'Whichever's free,' he said. 'I don't really care.'

Lily took off the dress and carefully draped it over the back of a chair. So this is it, she thought. Tomorrow night my life changes. I still don't know if I'm doing right. I'm

145

not. It's abhorrent to me. But the girls don't seem to mind too much. Perhaps they just accept what is to be.

She asked them, Lizzie, Betty and Alice, what they thought of when they were with strange men.

'If they're married, I wonder why they're with me,' Alice said softly. 'I wonder what it is that drives them from home to search out a girl like me. If I had a husband I'd make sure he stayed at home.'

'I don't think about them at all,' Lizzie said sourly. 'I onny know what idiots they are to part wi' their money.' She gave a smirk. 'But while they're at it, I add up what I'm earning and what I'll do with it.' Her expression changed to a wistful one. 'But there's never enough, not after I've eaten or paid for a room to sleep; there's never been enough left to put by for owt else.'

Lily glanced at Betty who was sitting quietly listening. She was the odd one out, not quite one of the girls, not always joining in their chatter, and, although not aloof, tended to be rather reserved. Lily hesitated, not wanting to pry into what her thoughts were as she sold her body to strangers.

'Aren't you going to ask me?' Betty said. 'Don't you want to know what I think about?' She looked at each of them in turn, her final glance lingering on Cherie.

'Onny if you want to tell us,' Lily said softly. 'You don't have to.'

'You're 'onny family I've got now so why shouldn't I tell you?' Betty swallowed, and then said huskily, 'My father disowned me and my ma went along with his decision. That's why I'm what I am; but when I'm wi' a stranger' – she pressed her lips together – 'I think about my babby.' Her eyes filled with tears. 'I loved his da, and I thought he loved me. I was onny about 'same age Cherie is, and I trusted him – was persuaded by him – and when I knew I was expecting I was so excited; I thought, fool that I was,' she added bitterly, 'that we'd be married. But he didn't want to know.'

Her voice caught on a sob. 'I managed at first, even though my da had turned me out. I found a room and got a job but it didn't last and that was when I went on 'streets.' Her eyes glistened; a tear slid down the side of her nose and she brushed it away with her fingertips. 'I loved my babby but as he got bigger I couldn't leave him by himself all night, so I took him to this woman; she looked after lots of bairns and I thought he'd be all right. But one night he was very fretful. He had teeth coming through and I told her to give him some Godfrey's Cordial or Daffy's if he couldn't sleep.'

Her breath caught in her throat and for a moment she couldn't speak. When she did her voice was thick with emotion. 'But when I went back to collect him 'following morning – he was dead.' Her mouth opened and she began a distressing sobbing wail. 'She'd given him laudanum! She said she couldn't stand 'racket he was mekking and swore she'd onny given him a drop to mek him sleep.'

Betty put her head down to her knees and sobbed and sobbed, her shoulders shaking. Alice went towards her but Lily put out her hand to stay her and shook her head. Betty had to cry out all her sorrow. Sad enough to have lost a child before full term as she had, but to have known one and loved him, to have dandled him on your knee and sung a lullaby, and then to have lost him must have been heartbreaking.

They all stayed silent; Cherie wept. Alice had her fingers clutched to her mouth and Lizzie stood with her arms crossed tightly in front of her staring into the fire, whilst Mrs Flitt, who had been busying herself in the kitchen but had come into the parlour to see Lily in her finery, slipped back into the kitchen, crept into her cupboard and closed the door.

Betty lifted her head. Her eyes were red and swollen. 'Sorry,' she whispered. 'So you see, I think about my Tommy and how he was made with love and passion, mine at any rate, and these *men*,' she spat out the word, 'they think of

147

nowt but themselves and their pleasure and nowt of what they're doing to us, and yet we're the ones who get 'blame. It's us who have to go to court and are called vile names and get sent to prison, and it's us who get diseased.'

She took a deep breath. 'Sometimes,' she said in a low voice, 'sometimes I wish I was dead.'

CHAPTER NINETEEN

Lizzie was the first to respond. Though she wasn't usually demonstrative, she gave Betty an awkward kiss on her cheek. 'Don't talk like that, Betty,' she said in a low voice. 'We wouldn't want owt to happen to you and it'd mean that they'd won.'

Alice hugged her. 'You deserve something good, Betty,' she whispered. 'And we all have to stick together and look after each other.'

Cherie was weeping so much that Betty had to comfort her and wipe her tears away. 'Don't worry, Cherie,' she whispered. 'We'll mek sure that nowt bad happens to you.' Then she looked at Lily. 'I'm sorry, Lily,' she said, her eyes filling again. 'I didn't mean to upset everybody, but I've not spoken about it afore, not properly, I mean.'

The others went out of the room and into the kitchen as Lily went to sit next to her, taking hold of her hand. 'It's been building up for a long time, I reckon, and now it's out you can begin your life again. You'll not ever forget your bairn,' she said softly, 'but you'll think of him wi' happiness one day.' She patted her cheek and smiled. 'This sort of life won't last for ever, and I said I'd another plan for you.'

Betty nodded and wiped her eyes. 'You did, but you didn't say what it was.'

'I've not quite got it fixed in my head,' Lily said. 'But you remember when you brought me my breakfast in bed when we were in Hope House?'

'Yes. What about it? Mrs Grant sent me up with it.'

'I know that. But it was 'way you gave me the tray all nicely set out, and you opened 'curtains at 'window to let in 'daylight; why, I felt just like a lady with her maid coming in!'

Betty gave a tearful laugh. 'I was pretending that's what I was,' she said. 'Mrs Grant said to set it and tek it up to a woman who'd just lost a bairn. I guessed that you'd be a street woman like me and I was going to reckon on that I was summat else, like an upstairs maid. But I saw straight away that you weren't 'usual type – if there is one,' she added.

'I thought you were a maid until you started to talk to me,' Lily smiled, 'and told me that you'd been brought there as well. But,' she said quietly, 'you've got 'knack. I've watched you. It's as if you know what to do. You can set 'table and you can make soup, and though I know we've not got much to cook at 'minute, as soon as we're earning some money we can buy some food and you can learn how to cook it.'

Betty's face brightened. 'I'd like that,' she said, her mind running on towards better things. 'But I don't know who'd employ me if they knew 'sort of job I'd done before.'

'We won't think of that just now,' Lily said. 'Let's just think of one day at a time and how to get through it.'

Mrs Flitt had put the kettle on and made a pot of tea when they joined the rest in the kitchen. 'Nowt like a cuppa to tek your mind off things,' she said. 'And you've all told your stories.' She put the pot on the table, first putting a tin plate beneath it. 'It's an owd table, I know,' she muttered, 'but owd habits die hard.' She looked up at Lily. 'And now I'll tell you my story. I used to work in a kitchen; I told you that already. I was a bright young thing. You'd nivver think it to look at me, would you?' She raised her sparse grey eyebrows at Cherie, who giggled.

'Well I was, and I worked me way up to be cook in a big house here in Hull.' She sighed. 'Aye, I had me own little kingdom. Two maids under me and onny 'butler over me. Plain food I cooked, nowt fancy. Master nivver wanted owt else. Mistress was a tartar though and I had to watch me ps and qs with her. Anyway, 'butler died, sudden like, and they took on another. Very smart he was, very handsome, and we took a shine to each other. Now I can see you don't believe that' – Cherie was chortling into her hand – 'but I used to be a right bonny lass. Anyway . . .' Mrs Flitt rubbed at her nose. 'He asked me to marry him and I said yes. But 'onny thing was that 'mistress didn't want us both working there, said it wouldn't do, so as soon as we was wed I had to leave and find another position, which I did, as I'd got a good reference.'

She took a deep breath and poured the tea. 'But that's when 'trouble started. While 'cat's away, you know, and while I was working across 'other side of town he started eyeing up one of 'parlour maids, who being young and inexperienced thought that he was serious about her and started planning that they'd move away together and find work somewhere else. When she discovered that wasn't what he had in mind, she went to 'mistress crying and bawling and told her about his philandering. He was given 'sack straight away and then they discovered that he wasn't who he said he was and that he'd been pinching silver and jewellery, not onny off them but other work places as well; but 'worst thing was he told 'police that I'd put him up to it. I had to go to court and swear that I knew nowt about it, and then 'next thing was that his wife turned up! His real wife who he'd married five years afore he'd bigamously married me.'

The only sound in the kitchen was a piece of coal shifting in the range as they sat silently listening to her story. Mrs Flitt drew her narrow shoulders up to her ears in a big shrug. 'So after that, nobody wanted to employ me. Stigma, you see. Folks were whispering that I probably knew all

151

about it. I got jobs in kitchens as a maid of all work, but not as a cook. Couldn't be trusted they said, not for bargaining with butchers and bakers and suchlike. They reckoned that I'd tek a few sweeteners for giving 'em 'trade. So for 'rest of my life,' she continued, 'until I got too old to work, I did a bit o' this and a bit o' that and then went into 'workhouse every winter and lived on 'streets every summer, scrounging whatever I could to keep breath in me body.'

'Did you never meet anybody else you wanted to marry, Mrs Flitt?' Alice asked wistfully.

The old woman sipped her tea. 'Nah! Once bitten, you know.'

'Lucky you didn't have a bairn,' Betty said. 'At least you onny had yourself to fend for.'

'Aye, well he wasn't all that good in that department.' Mrs Flitt frowned. 'At least I don't think he was, not that I knew much about that sort o' thing. Still don't,' she added. 'Very uncomfortable,' she commented to general laughter. 'Can't think what all 'fuss is about. I'd rather go to bed wi' a cup o' hot cocoa.'

'What a mixed bunch we are,' Lily said. 'And what happened to him? Did he go to prison?'

'Oh, aye.' Mrs Flitt slurped the rest of her tea. 'But not here. He was sent to Australia. He'll have done well out there if he survived 'voyage.' She sniffed. 'Good riddance to bad rubbish, I say.'

On Saturday morning Lily went into the town; Jamie had given her money to buy slippers and she also needed to buy food for all of them, and sweet biscuits to offer with the wine and ale. Jamie had brought in some bottles of wine and a cask of ale as Lily had suggested. She had left the girls preparing and tidying their rooms and Mrs Flitt was sweeping the steps.

Lily was very tempted to call at Mr Walker's and ask to see Daisy again but she knew it wouldn't be acceptable. Daisy had to stand on her own two feet; she couldn't expect to have her mother calling in on a whim when she was supposed to be working. But I'm the one who needs to see *her*, Lily mused. I worry about her, but more than anything I don't want her to know the type of work I'm doing. Mud sticks, and even though I'm not selling myself, who's going to believe that?

She went first to Rena's shop to buy a pair of evening slippers. She also wanted to take a look at the person who sold such magnificent clothes. Gowns were draped in the shop window, hats and shoes too, and a notice which stated that only the very best material was used for the garments. *Theatrical Attire*, it stated, and *Ball Gowns of the Nobility*.

Hmm, Lily pondered. Didn't know there was any nobility in Hull, but perhaps I'm mistaken. I suppose there must be, she conceded. There are plenty of landed gentry in Holderness, but I can't think that their wives would hock their clothes.

She went inside, feeling very shabby in her old skirt and shawl, for of course she hadn't come out in the grand clothes she was going to wear that evening. Rena was showing a dress to a young woman who was saying, 'You're sure that it hasn't been seen in Hull?'

'No, ma'am.' Rena's expression was one of disdain. 'It has been worn only twice before and then on 'London stage.'

The young woman said that she would think about it and left the shop and Rena, sighing, hung the dress on a rail. She shook her head. 'Why do they come here if they want new?' she muttered. 'What can I do for you?' she said to Lily, who noticed that she didn't address *her* as ma'am.

'I've come for a pair of evening slippers – black,' she said. 'Jamie said to come to you. You supplied him – us – with some clothes 'other day. Lizzie came to choose them.'

'Ye-es!' Rena looked Lily up and down; she was an exotic-looking woman in spite of being quite elderly and wore a black gown trimmed with red and a fringed lace shawl about her shoulders. 'So I did. Please sit down.'

Lily sat down and put out her foot for Rena to measure. She probably won't have any to fit me, she thought despondently. Her feet were long with slender straight toes and a high instep. They were also callused because she often went barefoot to save the cost of shoe leather; the boots she was wearing had once belonged to her mother.

'So what are you going to be doing?' Rena gazed at Lily's feet and then lifted down some shoe boxes from a shelf. 'Jamie's got some grand scheme planned, hasn't he?'

'I'm a sort of housekeeper,' Lily said, and was piqued when Rena raised her fine plucked eyebrows and made a slight moue with her painted mouth. She thought I was only fit to be a cleaning woman, she surmised.

'Oh, really.' Rena glanced again at Lily's shabby clothes. 'And which gown will you be wearing?'

'The lilac,' she said. 'And the black.'

'And for daytime?' Rena queried. 'What will you wear when 'constables come knocking on your door, as they inevitably will?'

Lily hesitated. It was a question that had crossed her mind several times. But she hadn't any other clothes than those she was wearing.

'You see, Jamie doesn't think things through,' Rena went on without waiting for an answer. 'He only thinks of the moment. He doesn't realize that there's 'day to get through as well as 'night.'

'You know about Jamie then?' Lily asked. 'You know what his business is?'

'Good gracious, yes.' Rena sat beside her on a stool and opened up a shoe box. 'Known him since he was a barefoot lad with torn breeches. He first came to me to buy a gown for his mother. Told me he was setting her up in business.' She gave a dry laugh. 'He asked if I'd give him credit. I was so taken aback that I said yes! He thought he was going to make his fortune out of her. But she had other ideas. Married a grocer.'

'So I heard,' Lily murmured.

'Then he tried again with another young woman who was down on her luck. Huh,' she snorted. 'He knows how to pick them. Just bends down into 'gutter and there they all are. But,' she picked up Lily's foot and slipped on one of the black evening slippers with a silver bow, 'he was let down again. There!' she said, sitting back. 'He doesn't stay down for long doesn't Jamie, I'll say that for him. How do they feel? Finest leather and hardly worn.'

'I don't know if I shall have enough money.' Lily loved them but they looked very expensive. She counted out the money in her pocket. 'I was wondering about getting another skirt.'

Rena got up and riffled through a rail of garments. 'I'll never make *my* fortune at this rate,' she sighed, taking out a grey wool dress. 'Try this. Come on,' she urged as Lily hesitated. 'I can see you're not going to be one of Jamie's girls so you'll need to be presentable during 'day. You can still wear those boots, if you must,' she said, 'and save the shoes for the evening.'

Lily tried the dress on in a curtained alcove. It was very plain, with a buttoned, high-necked bodice. Very elegant, she thought, and very respectable. No one would ever guess. She drew back the curtain.

'Perfect,' Rena exclaimed, nodding her head in satisfaction. 'Quite the lady of the house.'

Lily kept the grey dress on and gave Rena all the money she had been allocated for the shoes. 'You can pay 'balance when you're earning,' Rena said. 'That's if Jamie ever pays you.'

'Oh, he will,' Lily said firmly. 'Otherwise we'll all leave. I'll tek 'girls with me.'

'And set up in opposition?' Rena gave a cynical smile. 'Be careful,' she said. 'Jamie would report you to 'authorities. He'd spread rumours about you.' She handed Lily the shoe box and began bundling up the old skirt and shawl.

'I'll tek those,' Lily said. 'I know somebody who's wearing worse rags than mine.'

155

Rena nodded, and taking a shawl from a shelf wrapped it round Lily's shoulders. 'What happened to you?' she asked softly. 'Why are you doing this? You're not from Hull?'

'No.' Lily's mouth trembled. 'I'm from another life. I've been propelled into this one through no wish of mine. Everything has happened so fast,' she confided. 'I was a married woman, then I was sold like a prize pig at 'market. I lost a babby I was carrying. My young daughter has gone to work for someone as a lady's maid, my son has run away to sea and now I'm to run a brothel.'

Rena patted her arm. 'I'm sure there are worse things.'

Lily's eyes filled with tears. 'If there are I've never known them. Never in my wildest dreams did I think that I'd come to summat like this.' She took a deep breath. 'But I have and I just have to mek 'best of it.'

CHAPTER TWENTY

Ted stood pondering at the side of the narrow waterway. He had been directed there by a man in the street whom he'd asked the nearest way to the docks.

'What kind o' ship do you want, lad? Cargo ship, whaling ship, fishing smack, barge, ferryboat?'

'Erm.' He'd hesitated. 'One that sails to foreign countries.'

'What sort o' country?' The man started to grin, which had irritated Ted. 'A cold country like 'Arctic? Sweden? Plenty o' ships going to 'Baltic.'

'Yeh,' Ted nodded, anxious to be rid of him. 'Them countries. Where will 'ships going there be docked?'

The man directed him to the Old Harbour. 'You'll find plenty o' ships in 'Old Harbour, but whether you'll get work is a different matter. If there's nowt doing there then go to 'New Dock.'

There were dozens of ships; keels, cutters and barges, packed so tightly that Ted wondered how they would ever get out and make their way to the Humber. But they're not ocean-going, he thought. Most of these are river and canal boats, and although he didn't want to go to the frozen wastes of the Arctic and, he considered, was unlikely to be taken on for a whaling voyage without seagoing experience, neither did he want to sail only in inland waters.

Nor did he want to go fishing; the cold dark waters of

the German Ocean he knew to be dangerous to those who didn't know its moods.

A merchant ship, he thought. One that takes merchandise to other countries and brings goods back from theirs. That would be all right.

Ted was in blissful ignorance of the world at large as he stood there dithering. He was a country lad whose world had been bounded by his surroundings and the seasons of the year. Spring was when the cowslips came up, and sticklebacks, minnows and frogspawn appeared in the pools and ponds, and it was time for planting out the new season's vegetables or digging up the first new potatoes. Summer was when white blossom speckled the rich green of the hedgerows, and he woke every morning to trilling birdsong and the sight of young corn swaying in the fields, growing faster and more golden as the weather grew warmer. Then there was autumn and harvest time, with the smoky aroma of fires and the wheeling swallows practising for their departure, and a few weeks later the rushing sound of birds' wings as the early geese, fieldfares, snipe and the rest flew in across the sea towards the feeding grounds of the Humber. Then came winter when the cold nipped cheeks and noses and the ground was too hard to dig, and wood had to be fetched in for the fires.

Ted could read for his mother had taught him, though he had spent little time at school, preferring to skive off and spend his days out of doors; but he had no interest in books or newspapers and so he had missed the talk of foreign revolution and the social struggle between liberal bourgeois and radical republicans. Had he been older he might, in a local hostelry over a glass of ale, have discussed with other men the tales of great unrest in central Europe.

He might have heard tell of the conflicts in France, Germany, Hungary, Austria and Italy, countries which were all confronted by political problems. Hungary's relations with the Serbians and Croatians were at their lowest point. Austria was at odds with Northern Italy. The previous year Franz Joseph of Austria had appealed for help to the Russian Tsar Nicholas I but the tsar was fearful that the revolution would spread to Russia. Fighting raged between France and Italy and Garibaldi's troops were driven away. And as Ted stood debating his choices, France was introducing freedom of religious education, and there were ominous rumblings of nervousness, disquiet and discontent.

I'll walk round to the New Dock, he thought. There'll mebbe be bigger ships there. A harsh voice called to him. 'Oy! Catch, will ya?' A rope came whistling towards him from the deck of a barge and instinctively he put up his hand and caught it.

'Fasten it round that bollard,' a seaman on board called to him. 'Make it fast till I get there.'

He did as he was asked; how to make a clove hitch was one of the first things he had been taught when he started work on a farm. He secured it firmly. The seaman jumped from the deck to the dock. 'Thanks, lad,' he said. 'Well done. Are you an apprentice?'

'I'm – I'm not!' Ted stammered. 'I've come looking for work.'

'Oh, yeh? Been sailing afore?'

Ted shook his head. 'Onny pottering about. But I'm willing to learn.'

The man surveyed him. 'You can come wi' me to Driffield, if you like. My crewman's broke his arm and I need some help wi' hauling. What do you say?'

'Driffield!' It wasn't what he had in mind. He'd been thinking more of a trip abroad. 'I don't know,' he muttered. 'I was thinking of summat bigger.' This was a Humber keel, a flat-bottomed goods carrier, built for shallow river beds and canals, though he had seen them hugging the coastline close to Seathorne.

'She's big enough,' the skipper told him. 'And fast when 'wind is right. She's sailed up 'Aire canal, Sheffield, up 'Trent and 'Ouse. And 'Humber. She can do all of them

159

even if she is an owd lass. So make up your mind. I'm sailing as soon as I get a lad.'

'I'll come,' Ted said swiftly. 'I've nowt to stop me. What 'you carrying?'

'Coal. We've to collect it, get it weighed and then we're off. Are you a country lad?' The skipper's eyes narrowed. 'You don't sound like Hull.'

'Yeh,' Ted admitted, 'I am. I wanted a change of occupation. There's nowt much doing on 'land at 'minute.'

'What? This time o' year? I'd have thought there was plenty of work about.' He eyed him up. 'Not in trouble, are you? I'll not have you if you are. I've enough to do wi'out 'constables climbing all over me.'

'No. No,' Ted said hastily. 'It's just that I've got nobody, so I can please myself what I do.' It feels like I've got nobody, he thought, so it's not really a lie.

The skipper nodded. 'All right,' he said. 'Go stow your gear and we'll be off. You'll find Bob, me mate, below. He'll show you what to do.'

Ted had no gear, only his blanket, which he slung over his shoulder as he climbed down through the hatch. The mate Bob had his arm in a sling and was drinking a mug of tea. 'Who are you, then?' he said brusquely.

'Erm, Ted Maddeson. I'm coming to Driffield wi' you.'

'Are you? Have you sailed afore?'

Ted shook his head. 'No. But I was looking for a job.'

'You'll not last 'week out,' Bob grumbled. 'Why's he tekken on somebody who knows nowt.'

'Because.' The skipper slid down the steps making the space below very crowded. 'I want to be off and I won't be able to tek on a regular lad. Can't afford it for one thing, unless you're thinking of retiring,' he added sarcastically.

'Does that mean I'm onny doing this one trip?' Ted asked boldly. 'You won't just drop me off in Driffield, will you?'

'No. You can do 'return trip with us, but I onny want somebody to tide me over till Bob's arm's in use again.'

160

'Will I get wages?'

'Aye, some, but you'll get food and lodgings on board so you won't earn much. Are you coming or not?'

Ted shrugged. 'Might as well, I suppose. I've nivver been to Driffield.'

Bob laughed. 'You'll not have time to see 'sights,' he said. 'We'll unload, load up and be back again.'

'What, in 'same day?' Ted was astonished.

'No, you daft lump! As long as it teks. Might be three days, might be three weeks. Depends on wind and how good you are at hauling. But we'll mek time for a glass or two whilst we're there. How old are you?'

'Thirteen,' he said, and then wished he'd said older.

But the skipper, who said to call him Ken, nodded and said, 'Old enough.'

The next morning Ted stood on deck, his hands in his pockets, whistling softly. He had been first up and had brewed a pot of tea for the men. They had set sail last evening after loading up with coal and were now on their journey towards River Head at Driffield where they would unload, swill down and pick up a return cargo. It was a beautiful morning and he mused that this was just about as good as living in the country. On each side of the bank contented cows had their heads down in the meadow grass and he gave a fleeting thought to their cow at Seathorne and hoped that John Ward had milked her.

He had been dead tired last night after the journey into Hull and the work on board as he'd helped to load the coal, and he was asleep in minutes as the motion of the keel – *Daisy*, it was named, the same as his sister – rocked and soothed him. He was awakened by the honking of geese and for a second he didn't know where he was. The guilt of Billy Fowler's accident was fading, and as he gazed out along the waterway he thought that this was possibly a good kind of life, although not as adventurous as he might have wished for. Bob had said he would show him how to operate the locks when they reached the Driffield canal and the skipper had told him he'd teach him how to handle the sails.

He looked up as a flock of wigeon flew over. The sky was a brilliant blue with only a scattering of soft white clouds; a family of moorhens were busying themselves in a nest by the bank, half hidden by a drooping willow whose branches touched the water, and as he watched a bevy of ducks up-ended and dipped their heads. He gave a deep sigh. Yes, all in all, he thought, I reckon I made a good decision. For 'time being anyway.

John Ward did as he said he would and rode into Withern-sea to report a missing woman and her daughter. 'I don't trust yon fellow,' he'd whispered to his wife outside the door. 'There's summat not quite right.'

Billy Fowler was sitting by the fire wrapped in the blanket whilst his clothes steamed on a wooden horse. His head was sunk on his chest and he seemed to have fallen asleep.

'Will you be all right on your own wi' him?' John Ward asked his wife. 'It shouldn't tek me all that long to find 'constable and he can mek 'decision over what to do.'

'I'll get me rolling pin out,' she'd said in a low voice. 'But he'll not try owt; he asked to stop here for 'night, didn't he? He's nowhere else to go.'

Ward notified the constable and told him of his suspicions. 'House has gone ower 'cliff,' he said. 'But I don't know for sure if his missis and bairn were in it. I've not seen 'em about for a day or two.'

'Well, what 'you telling me?' The constable was peeved at having his evening disturbed. 'Have they or not?'

'Well, Fowler says they have. He said they were in 'house wi' him.' He shook his head. 'But his story's all wrong. He said as lad were there as well, but I saw him ride off on 'hoss.'

'Well, mebbe he came back,' the constable said irritably. 'You weren't watching all 'time, were you?'

'No,' he admitted. 'I wasn't.'

'So why isn't Fowler reporting this incident? Why's he sent you?'

'He didn't send me,' Ward answered sharply. 'That's just it. He didn't want me to do owt. He just said they were drowned.'

'All right,' the officer said reluctantly. 'I'll have to ride down to Spurn to notify 'Humber lifeboat men and tell 'em to look for two bodies. Can't think they'll put off tonight, though, and in any case if they are in 'sea it'll be too late to do owt for 'em.'

John Ward gave an exasperated grunt. The constable wasn't getting the point. Mrs Fowler and her daughter were not drowned. They were missing, it was true, but he was convinced that harm had come to them at Fowler's own hands.

The next morning Billy Fowler dressed in his dry clothes and prepared to walk into Withernsea. He'd breakfasted on porridge and a slice of bread. He'd hoped for a rasher of bacon but Mrs Ward wasn't offering any. 'Mr Ward has summat a bit later,' she said, answering Billy's hints, 'after he's finished wi' 'animals. But you'll not want to stop that long, will you? You'll be off to mek enquiries about Mrs Fowler and her bairn. It's a mystery about 'lad, though, isn't it? You'd wonder where he was off to at that time o' day, 'specially when it was so wet.'

'They're a law to themselves,' Billy muttered as he put on his jacket. 'But where's my hoss? That's what I'd like to know.'

Mrs Ward related this to her husband when he came in later, after Fowler had gone. 'He wanted to know where his owd hoss was,' she said. 'He didn't seem that bothered about his poor wife and 'bairns.'

'There you are then,' he answered. 'Isn't that what I said? I reckon that lad was leaving home, or,' he nodded significantly, 'he was going off looking for his ma.'

Fowler searched out the parish clerk. 'I'm homeless,' he said pitifully. 'My lovely little house has gone ower cliff, aye and my wife and daughter wi' it.' He decided not to mention Ted, as John Ward had spoilt that part of his story, and in any case he reckoned that the boy had scarpered when he saw him go over the side. 'I'm a poor widower. Everything I owned has gone.'

'That's terrible,' the clerk said. 'Is somebody looking for 'bodies?'

'Oh, aye.' He nodded. 'Humber lifeboat's been notified.' Then he shook his head sorrowfully and wiped his eye. 'But they'll nivver find 'em.'

CHAPTER TWENTY-ONE

When Lily returned from Rena's the fire was blazing merrily in the tidy parlour, a small table had wine bottles and glasses on it and the cushions on the sofa had been plumped up.

'Can we have a glass of that?' Lizzie asked. 'We need summat to boost us up.'

'Why?' Lily asked. 'What would you normally have?'

'Gin,' Lizzie said. 'Or sometimes a glass of beer, but you're better wi' gin cos some of 'landlords water their beer.'

'Yes, they do,' Lily agreed. 'I've seen 'em do it.'

'I'm so hungry!' Cherie complained, and the others agreed that they were too; they'd had little to eat but soup and bread.

'I've no money left,' Lily told them. 'I gave 'last to Rena. Is there nothing to make soup of, Betty?'

Betty shook her head. 'Nothing,' she said. 'We shan't be able to eat till we've been paid and Jamie will want his share first.'

Mrs Flitt had been listening. 'I'm just going out,' she said. 'What if I 'appened to find some money? What would you like to eat?'

'Meat pie!' Lizzie said.

'A nice piece o' cod,' Alice said.

'Chicken.' Lily smiled. 'But you'd need a miracle. Where will you find any money?'

Mrs Flitt tapped her nose and picked up her old shawl. Lily had given her her old clothes but she wasn't wearing them yet. The skirt was much too long and wide and she would need to take it in and shorten it; the sleeves on the blouse were so long that they hid her hands completely, but she was well pleased with them.

'I'll be back in a bit,' she told them. 'Don't mess 'place up.'

'Where's she going, do you think?' Lily asked.

'Stealing,' Lizzie said.

'Beggin', shouldn't wonder,' Alice said. 'I've seen her many a time down Whitefriargate.'

The afternoon stretched long and they'd nothing to do. Lily took the skirt she'd given to Mrs Flitt and unpicked the seams. Cherie and Betty brushed each other's hair, Alice dozed in a chair and Lizzie went upstairs. Then they heard the front door open. 'Jamie!' Lily said. 'Or Mrs Flitt.'

It was Jamie and his arms were full of flowers. He beamed at them all and let his gaze fall on Lily in her grey gown. 'You look nice,' he said. 'Did I buy that?'

'On credit,' she said. 'From Rena.'

'Good old Rena,' he said, 'you can allus rely on her.' He thrust the flowers towards her. 'Lilies,' he said. 'We're going to call you Miss Lily, so I reckoned we should allus have lilies in 'house. Just smell 'em,' he said. 'They're lovely.'

Lily breathed in the heady perfume. 'They are,' she agreed. 'I've never been bought flowers afore.' She suddenly felt emotional. The only flowers I've ever been given were from Johnny. I was sixteen and he plucked a wild rose from the hedgerow and put it in my hair.

'Ah well,' he said, spoiling the moment, 'this is business. They're to mek 'house smell nice.' He wrinkled his nose and sniffed. 'It don't smell of damp any more, anyway.'

'It's been scrubbed out, that's why,' Lily said. 'And we've had 'doors and windows open.'

'Right, I'm off,' he told her. 'I'll be back tonight at eight o'clock with 'first customers. Be ready.'

Lily sat clutching the flowers after he had gone and looked at the other girls. Alice was examining her bitten nails; Betty was pinning up Cherie's hair. Cherie seemed nervous.

'It'll be all right, Lily,' Betty said calmly, glancing at her. 'Don't worry about it. It's not as if we haven't done this before. And we're not out on 'streets.'

'I think I'll be all right for tonight,' Alice remarked. 'My face isn't so swollen, and besides they wouldn't notice.'

Lily nodded and swallowed nervously. 'We'll draw 'curtains,' she said. 'And light 'lamps.'

'Yes,' Cherie said. 'They won't want anybody looking in at 'em. Customers, I mean.'

Lily got up to put the flowers in water. There were several vases and a jardinière in a cupboard and she busied herself filling these and arranging the lilies as best she could, just to take her mind off what was happening tonight. Then she heard the door open again and Mrs Flitt rushed towards the kitchen, calling them all to come and eat.

'Chicken pie.' She grinned. 'And meat pie; but I didn't buy any fish,' she told Alice. 'It didn't smell fresh; it was yesterday's catch. And I was given these hot potatoes by a fellow in 'market who knows me.'

'Where did you get 'money from?' Lily asked.

'Beggin',' Mrs Flitt said, and Alice gave a told you so look. 'And then I found a tanner in 'gutter, and then,' she gave a triumphant grin, 'I accidentally on purpose fell to my knees, right in front of a nice lady and gentleman, who helped me up. Leave me, I cried. Leave me to die! I haven't got long for this world.' She raised her eyes to the ceiling, clutching her bony fingers together. 'I told 'em I hadn't eaten for a week, which is nearly true,' she added. 'And they give me a shilling to go and buy summat hot to eat and drink.'

They all dived into the food, and Lizzie, with her mouth full of pastry, said, 'Can we open a bottle o' wine, then? It'll put us in 'right sort o' mood for tonight.'

'Yes, let's!' they all said, and Lily, gazing at the excited expectancy on their faces, agreed. What does it matter? she thought. Why should we save it all for the men who are coming, who probably have a glass of wine every night of their lives?

'I'll get a bottle,' she said. 'But we'll drink it out of cups and save 'glasses for when 'customers come.'

She went to fetch a bottle from the parlour and by the time she came back with it opened there were six cups ready and waiting on the table. 'There'll onny be enough for one cup each,' she said as she poured. 'But it's enough, we can drink a toast.' She sat down again and raised her cup. 'Here's to all of us. May we have good fortune.'

'And money,' Lizzie added. 'Lots of it.'

'Good health,' Alice said, adding, 'and meet somebody nice.'

Lizzie snorted derisively. 'Not a chance,' she said. 'Don't fool yourself, Alice. Nowt's really going to change.'

'It has already,' Betty butted in. 'We're here, aren't we? We're not outside hanging about in 'street. We've just eaten; we've got nice clothes to wear, and we've met Lily.' She blinked and raised her cup again. 'You're 'best thing that's ever happened to me, Lily. I think we should drink to Lily.'

'Hear hear,' Mrs Flitt said. 'I'll go along wi' that.'

The others agreed and smilingly raised their glasses. 'To Lily.'

They were all changing into their finery when there was a knock on the door. 'Oh, no!' Lily was in her room by the door and just putting on her black slippers. 'Not yet! It's onny seven o'clock. We're not ready!'

Another knock came, louder and more persistent, and she smoothed down her hair, which was still hanging down her back, and went into the hall. Cautiously she opened the door. It wasn't a man standing there, but two young women who by the look of them were women of the streets.

168

'Yes?' she said.

'Jamie sent us,' one of them said. 'He said there'd be a place for us here. Let's come in,' she added, staring at Lily. 'Can't stand 'ere all night.'

'Well, we could.' The other one laughed coarsely. 'But we'd tek all your trade!'

Lily opened the door wider. Whatever was Jamie thinking of, asking women like this to come here? He said he wanted a better class of woman. These were as low as could be; they showed it by their dress and demeanour. One of them, who had brassy fair hair, was chewing tobacco, her inside lip stained dark brown; the other had a glazed look to her eyes as if she had been drinking heavily, and her blouse was open, showing her thin ribs and loose breasts.

'This place has changed a bit,' the fair woman said, chewing open-mouthed. 'Not like when Miss Emerald had it.'

'Oh, you knew her, did you?' Lily said. 'Did you work here?'

'Yeh,' she answered, looking round. 'We did. On and off. When some of her regular girls were off sick.'

'This is not 'same,' Lily asserted. 'This is a better class establishment.'

The other woman laughed. 'That's what they all say. But they're all selling 'same thing.'

'I know that,' Lily said. 'But we're aiming for something better. A better class of customer. Do you have any other clothes?' she asked briskly. 'You can't wear those you've got on.'

The tobacco woman glanced down at her shabby skirt and then up at Lily. 'Don't mek any difference,' she said. 'They don't notice your clothes.'

'You can't work here if you don't change,' Lily said firmly. 'And you need to wash your hands and faces and brush your hair. We'll find you something else to wear.'

The two women stared at her as if she was mad; then they looked at each other and grinned.

'What's up?' A voice came from the top of the stairs and they all looked up to see Lizzie dressed in her red velvet gown; her hair was brushed and hanging loose about her face and she'd put a touch of rouge on her cheeks. She looks lovely, Lily thought. You'd never think it was the same Lizzie.

The other two women seemed to think the same, for they stared and stared as if Lizzie was an apparition. Then the drunken one pointed a finger. 'I know you,' she mumbled. 'Where've I seen you afore?'

'It's Lizzie!' the other one said, and moved towards the stairs. 'Crikey! Look at you! Who do you think you are, dressed up like a shilling dinner?'

Lizzie moved slowly down the stairs. 'What 'you doing here, Flo? And you, Poll? Who dragged you in here?'

Flo continued to chew. 'Jamie,' she said. 'He said he needed some more women.'

'And are you two all he could find?' Lizzie sneered. 'What was he doing down in 'gutter?'

Flo launched herself towards Lizzie, grabbing hold of her by the hair. 'Who do you think you're talking to, you drab,' she yelled. 'Just because you're wearing fancy clothes doesn't mean you're better than 'rest of us.'

'I'm better than you any day, you she-cat,' Lizzie yelled back, aiming a punch at Flo's nose. 'I allus was and allus will be.'

'Stop it. Stop it!' Lily screeched at them, and pushed away Poll, who was hurling herself towards them to join in the rumpus.

Doors opened upstairs and Betty, Alice and Cherie appeared. They too were dressed in their gowns for the evening.

'God almighty!' Flo exclaimed, stopping her onslaught on Lizzie. 'What's going on? Where do you think you're all at – 'queen's palace?'

'No, we don't think that,' Lily said steadily, though she felt anything but calm. 'But now do you see why I want you to have a wash and change your clothes?'

'Will we earn more?' Flo's eyes narrowed. 'And who pays for 'fancy frocks? I en't paying for 'em, I'll tell you now.'

'You don't have to,' Lily said. 'Jamie got them for us, but you can't keep them,' she added hastily. 'They're onny borrowed.'

'Where're you from?' Flo asked. 'Not round here. Why don't I know you? I know all 'tarts, whores and harlots in this town.'

'You don't know me!' Betty piped up from the stairs. 'And I'm a tart. But Lily isn't a whore!'

'Huh! And I'm a vestal virgin,' Flo scoffed. 'So what's she doing here then, in this bawdy house?'

'Don't you talk of Lily in that way,' Cherie said angrily. 'She's fallen on hard times, that's all.'

'And who are you?' Flo turned on Cherie. 'Little Bo-Peep in your clean frock! You'll soon get that soiled in a place like this.'

'Do you want to stay or not?' Lily interrupted. 'If you don't, you'd better go now. We're expecting customers and I don't want you here looking like you do. If you stay, you get changed as I've said, and,' she added, 'you watch your language and your manners. You'll stop in 'kitchen till I tell you to go upstairs and *I'll* choose 'customers for you. I want no trouble,' she said firmly. 'If there is, you leave.'

Flo and Poll looked at each other. 'I'll not have her lording it over me,' Flo said, pointing at Lizzie. 'She's no better'n any of us even if she thinks she is.'

'Is it yes or no?' Lily asked. 'Mek up your mind.'

'All right,' Flo said. She seemed to be the one who made the decisions. 'We'll see how it works out. Who pays us?'

'Not the customer,' Lily told her plainly. 'I collect 'money and Jamie will pay you.'

'What if she' – Flo shifted her head towards Lizzie – 'what if she gets more customers than me? What do I do for money? And I suppose you get all 'extra tips when they leave?'

'I might,' Lily said tight-lipped, trying not to lose her temper. 'But I'm at 'door and it's me who decides who's suitable for 'customer.'

Flo and Poll both burst out laughing. 'We'll tek anybody,' Poll said. 'We don't care who it is as long as he pays.'

Lizzie turned away with an exclamation. 'Jamie's crazy to tek these two on. We'll have a bad reputation even before we start.'

Flo raised her fist to Lizzie and Lily quickly intervened. 'Go and get changed. Betty, tek a couple of frocks into 'kitchen. They can try them on in there, but mek sure they get washed first; we might want to take 'dresses back.'

She took a deep breath as Betty led the two women from the hall. The last thing she wanted was for them to be in the parlour to greet the customers. They would immediately let the tone down, and, she thought, I can't imagine that putting them into clean clothes will make much difference. They look like what they are, coarse and dissolute harlots. Whereas my girls . . . my girls, she thought affectionately, are simply fallen angels.

CHAPTER TWENTY-TWO

At a quarter to eight they were all ready. Cherie and Betty were making last minute arrangements at the drinks table; bottles of wine were opened; Lizzie and Alice were prowling about, and Mrs Flitt was keeping an eye on the two women in the kitchen, who surprisingly did look better after a wash and in their clean clothes. She'd made them a pot of coffee in an attempt to sober Poll up and they were sitting at the table grinning and whispering together.

Lily had positioned herself in her room so that she could see down the street. There were only a few people about: some girls strolling arm in arm, but no men. It's early yet, she thought, and still light. Perhaps the men don't come looking for girls until it gets dark. They'll be afraid of being seen. Then she saw Jamie hurrying down the street; he was carrying a top hat and trying, it seemed, to keep up with a hansom cab which was trundling before him.

She went into the hall and to the parlour door. 'Get ready, girls,' she said in a hoarse voice. 'I think 'first customer is arriving.'

'It's odd,' Lizzie whispered to Alice. 'But it feels like it's my first time.'

'I'm scared,' Alice confided. 'I've never entertained gentlemen afore. It's allus been – well, like, in a hurry.'

Lily watched Jamie run up the steps, ring the bell and then dash down again to the cab. He spoke to the driver and then opened the cab door. Lily took a breath. This is it then, she thought. Here is where my life changes. I'm no longer the woman I was. I must pretend that I'm someone else.

She opened the front door as Jamie and an elderly man arrived on the top step. 'Good evening, gentlemen,' she said softly. 'Won't you come in?'

'Miss Lily,' Jamie said suavely, 'may I introduce Mr Smith? Lily will be looking after you this evening, Mr Smith. Anything you want, anything at all, just ask her.'

Mr Smith silently appraised her as he handed her his top hat and unbuttoned his coat. 'Mmm,' he murmured. 'Fine figure of a woman. Very striking.'

'You're most welcome, sir.' Lily gave Jamie a warning glance as she took Mr Smith's coat. He was well dressed in a silver grey frock coat and striped trousers, and had white hair and sideburns.

'Yes.' Jamie caught her look. 'Lily will know just how to please you, but perhaps I should mek clear . . .' He leaned towards him and whispered into his ear.

'Is that so?' Mr Smith gazed in astonishment at Lily, who smiled sweetly at him. 'Well, we shall have to try to find some inducement to make her change her mind, won't we?' He laughed heartily and took her arm, patting it endearingly. 'There'll be something she's set her heart on, I'm quite sure!'

Jamie winked at Lily behind Mr Smith's back. 'I have to be off,' he said. 'I'm meeting another friend. I'll be back in fifteen minutes.'

Lily led Mr Smith into the parlour. It looked very cosy, she thought; a bright fire was burning in the grate, the curtains were partly drawn, for this room looked out on to the yard at the back of the house, and the lamps were lit, giving a warm glow. Lizzie and Alice rose from the chairs where they had been sitting, and Betty and Cherie dipped their knees as Mr Smith entered.

'By Jove,' he uttered. 'This is jolly nice. Not at all what

I expected. Now then, introduce me, won't you, to these pretty gels?'

Alice came forward first and dropped a slight curtsy. 'Good evening, sir. I'm Alice. How nice to meet you. Won't you sit down?'

'I will if you'll sit by me,' he said, taking the chair he was offered, and Alice pulled up a stool beside him. 'What's happened to your face?' he asked. 'You've taken a bump by the look of it.'

'That's exactly what happened,' Alice said. 'I tripped over the cat and fell. I hit my face on 'kitchen table. That's why it's bruised. I bruise very easily,' she said, looking up at him.

He patted her shoulder. 'We must be careful with you then,' he whispered.

'I'm Elizabeth.' Lizzie came forward, extending her hand, which he grasped tightly. 'But my friends call me Lizzie.'

He kissed her hand. 'Forgive me if I don't get up, Lizzie,' he said. 'But now that I'm down it'll take the two of you to get me up again.' He leaned forward with a lascivious twinkle in his eyes. 'But you shan't mind that, shall you?'

Lizzie grinned merrily. 'Certainly won't, will we, Alice?'

Alice put her hand to her face as if embarrassed. 'No we won't, Mr Smith, not a bit.'

'Call me Leo,' he confided. 'Never mind this Mr Smith business. I can see you're the type of young women to keep your counsel.'

Betty came forward holding a tray with glasses of red wine. 'I'm Elizabeth too,' she said. 'But everyone calls me Betty. Won't you take some refreshment?'

'Well, well,' he said. 'This is a treat!' He took a glass of wine. 'Won't you join me, ladies? I can't possibly drink alone. And I shall call you Elizabeth,' he said to Betty. 'The name suits you very well, whereas Lizzie,' he said, turning to Lizzie, 'is perfect for you. It's a merry kind of name.'

He took a sip of wine and Betty handed glasses round to the others. 'Now who's this little maid?' he said of Cherie. 'Come here and let me look at you.'

Cherie, who had been standing back, came forward reluctantly. 'I'm Cherie,' she said in a low voice, dipping her knee again.

'Cherie,' he said softly. 'Pretty little thing. You remind me – well, never mind. You remind me of someone.' He took a drink and lapsed into silence for a moment, and then the front door bell rang again.

Lily excused herself and went to answer the door. A man stood there, holding his hat in his hand and looking cautiously about him.

'Henry,' he said. 'Jamie invited me.'

'Do come in.' Lily smiled. 'I'm Miss Lily. Jamie will be here shortly; he had to slip out. Shall I take your hat?'

He nodded, eyeing her. 'Have you been here long? In this house, I mean?'

She hung his bowler on the hat stand and turned towards him. He was in his mid-thirties, she supposed; dark hair, slightly streaked with silver, not very tall but exceedingly handsome.

'No,' she said. 'Hardly any time at all. Would you like to come through?'

He cleared his throat. 'Erm, yes. Erm, I'm new to this kind of thing,' he said. 'Don't know the procedure.'

She smiled at him. 'I'm new to it too,' she said in a confidential whisper. 'But don't tell anyone!'

'Really?' His face brightened. 'That's a relief.'

'Think of it as a sort of club,' she advised. 'A meeting with friends.'

'Lady friends?'

'Yes, of course,' she said. 'That is why you're here?'

'Oh, it is,' he said fervently. 'It most certainly is.'

She took him through to the parlour where she introduced him to the girls and Leo. Leo looked up at him from his seat and said, 'How de do, young feller.' Betty gave him a glass of wine and as they stood together chattering the bell rang again.

It was Jamie with another customer, middle-aged and dressed soberly in a dark frock coat, and Lily wondered how Jamie had managed to ensnare these obviously well-to-do gentlemen.

As she took the newcomer towards the parlour, Lily said to Jamie, 'Don't go just yet, Jamie. There's a matter I need to discuss.' She indicated that he should go to the kitchen. 'A matter of staff,' she added.

'Kendall, you old dog,' Leo greeted the visitor. 'Fancy meeting you here.' He put up his hand and the other man shook it.

'How are you, Leo?' Kendall said. 'All the ruffians keeping you busy?'

'Yes, yes,' Leo said. 'Lots of villains about.'

Lily felt her heart sink. Who were these men? Not the police, surely? Whilst Cherie introduced herself and offered a glass of wine, which Kendall refused, saying he'd have a glass of ale instead, Lily hurriedly went to the kitchen where she could hear Jamie's voice.

'I never asked you to come here,' he was saying angrily. 'So you can get those glad rags off and get back where you belong in 'gutter!'

Lily opened the door in time to hear Flo yelling at Jamie using very choice ripe language. 'Didn't you invite them?' Lily asked. 'They said you'd sent them.'

'I did no such thing,' he said. 'Pox-ridden harlots. I wouldn't touch 'em wi' a barge pole.'

'And I 'eard you wouldn't touch any woman unless it was wi' 'flat of your 'and,' Poll butted in. 'That's what I 'eard out on 'street.'

'Get out!' Jamie spat out at them. 'Now!' He glanced at Mrs Flitt. 'Mek sure they tek those frocks off afore they go. Lily, you go back to 'customers. I'll see these two off 'premises.'

Lily heaved a sigh as she went back to the parlour, putting

177

on a smile as she entered the room. All seemed to be well. Kendall, who had seemed such a sobersides, was telling a rather risqué joke to the other men, had taken off his frock coat and was unfastening his cravat. Henry seemed relaxed and had his free arm round Betty's waist and a glass in his other hand, and Alice had given up the stool to Lizzie and was sitting on Leo's knee.

Lily poured more wine, whilst Cherie handed round a plate of biscuits. Kendall took several. 'I am rather peckish,' he said, taking a bite. 'Not had my supper yet.'

'Working late at the office, are you?' Leo guffawed. 'Well, I don't need to make those excuses any more, thank God. Not now I'm a widower. I can do as I damn well please.' He jiggled Alice on his knee. 'I can stay all night if I want.'

Alice smiled adoringly at him and kissed his cheek. 'Of course you can,' she breathed, but raised enquiring eyebrows in Lily's direction.

'Now, Leo,' Lily said playfully. 'Surely Jamie has told you you have to leave by four?'

'Four, is it? I must have forgotten! Well, somebody will have to send for my cab. I have a regular fellow, he knows where I live. He'll get me home.'

'Oh, but not yet,' Lily said. 'We've lots of time. The night is still young.'

'Anybody else coming?' Kendall asked. 'Anybody we know?'

'Possibly,' Lily said, not knowing the answer to either question. 'Jamie teks – takes care of that side of things.'

'Quite right,' Leo said. 'You need a man for that. Don't want any ne'er-do-wells crashing in, spoiling things. It's very nice to come to a place like this and know there won't be any trouble. Not a good area, of course,' he said, taking a rather large gulp from his glass. 'Surprised really when Jamie said the house was in Leadenhall Square. More gels come up in front of me from round here than anywhere else.' He took another drink. 'They're a bad lot, some of them.'

They heard the sound of voices and the front door crashing.

'Trouble?' Leo said, and the men were instantly alert.

'I don't think so,' Lily said placidly. 'We've been having problems with 'kitchen staff and Jamie's seeing them off 'premises.'

'Ah!' Leo said. 'My wife had the same problem. Very difficult to get reliable help.'

Jamie came into the room. He straightened his cravat. 'Sorry, gentlemen. Just a little domestic problem. Is everything all right? Got all you need?'

'We will have!' Kendall drank the last of his ale and handed the glass to Lizzie, who had come towards him. She put the glass on the table and raised her eyebrows enquiringly, putting her hand on his arm.

He nodded and she led him towards the door, closing it behind them.

'You know what you need, Jamie,' Leo bellowed. 'You need a piano! That's it. That's what you should have, and then we could have a sing-song.'

'But who would play?' Alice asked. 'None of us can play.'

'I can play,' Henry said. 'I can bash out a tune or two. My guardian insisted I learn to play.'

'There you are then,' Leo said. 'What about it, eh?'

'Mmm,' Jamie murmured. 'We'll see.'

'Oh, come on!' Leo urged. 'They don't cost all that much. Tell you what. I'll buy you one.' He jiggled Alice on his knee again. 'And then you can sing to me. Dum-de-dum-dum-dum!'

'You are so nice, Leo,' Alice said sweetly. 'How generous you are. I've never known anyone so generous.'

'Well, I've nothing to spend my money on, no wife, and no family. Might as well give some pleasure, eh?' He patted her cheek and whispered into her ear.

Alice smiled and got up from his knee. 'Come and help Leo up, Jamie,' she said. 'I've said I'll show him round 'rest of 'house.'

'So is that how it's done?' Henry whispered to Betty, as Alice, with Leo hobbling after her, went out of the door and into the hall. 'Just slip away like that?'

She gazed enquiringly at him, her lips parted. 'What do you mean, Henry?'

'Well, you know.' He looked embarrassed. 'If you want to go upstairs!'

Betty lowered her lashes. 'Would you like to go upstairs?'

'Erm . . . I suppose so.'

'Is that why you've come?' she asked. 'You don't have to. We can just stay here and talk if you like.'

'I'd like to talk to you,' he murmured, looking about him at Cherie, Lily and Jamie who were standing together. 'But not here where the others might hear. I'd like to ask you things, sort of – privately.'

'We can do that,' she said softly. 'Would you like to come to my room?'

'I think I would. I've not done this sort of thing before.'

'What sort of thing?' she asked innocently.

'Well, come to a . . .' He took a handkerchief from his pocket and wiped his brow. 'A house like this, you know . . . to meet women.'

'I understand,' she said softly. 'Would you like to tell me about it?'

He nodded. Taking his arm, she led him out of the room.

CHAPTER TWENTY-THREE

Alice came quietly down the stairs. 'Lily,' she said softly, 'Leo's asleep. Should I leave him for a bit, do you think? He's flat out!'

'When Jamie comes back I'll ask him to order a cab; but on the other hand,' Lily mused, 'Leo did say he didn't have to go home early. Perhaps when he wakes up he'll stay and have another glass of wine and a spot of supper.'

'The longer he stays the more he'll have to pay, is that it?' Alice asked. 'I must say that's 'easiest night's work I've ever done.' She was quite unruffled, with not a hair out of place. She sighed. 'If they were onny all like Leo.'

They heard the sound of voices coming from Lizzie's room and moved into the parlour as Lizzie and Kendall appeared at the top of the stairs. Lizzie's face and neck were flushed and Kendall was whistling softly, fastening up his cravat as he hurried down.

Lizzie handed him into his coat. 'It's a pity you have to leave so early,' she murmured.

He nodded. 'I'll try to get away from the office a little earlier another time.' He stared down at her, his face as tight-drawn and arrogant as it was when he'd first arrived. 'Great romp, though, Lizzie. You're a good sport!'

She put her chin up and surveyed him, her bottom lip pouting. She nodded. 'Yeh, great fun. Come again.'

'I will,' he said carelessly. 'As soon as I can get away.' He

181

looked round for Lily. 'Have to be off,' he said, and Lily came towards him.

'I'll see you out,' she said. 'Do you need a cab?'

'No, I'll walk to my club and get one from there.' He took his pocket book from an inside pocket as Lily opened the door and looked out.

'It's quiet,' she told him. 'Hardly anybody about.'

'Good,' he said, handing over some money. 'This is what I agreed with Jamie. I've given the girl some extra; don't let him take it from her.'

'I won't,' she said fervently. 'Jamie needn't know about that.'

He nodded. 'Good night, then.' He ran swiftly down the steps and Lily watched him as he marched down the street.

What a cold fish he is to be sure, she thought. I bet he's a pillar of society, rules his wife and family with a rod of iron and is seen in church or chapel every Sunday.

Lizzie was lounging in a chair with her head back and her eyes closed when Lily went back into the parlour. 'Is everything all right, Lizzie?' she asked.

'Yes.' Lizzie sat up. 'I've just asked Cherie to mek me a cup o' coffee. Give me my strength back,' she said half-heartedly.

'Was it bad?' Alice said anxiously.

'I could tell what he was like 'minute I saw him,' Lizzie muttered. 'That's why I went with him, though I rather think he wanted you.' She looked at Alice. 'He's a foul-mouthed rampant goat and if he'd caught sight of your bruises he'd have added to them. That's 'sort of whelp he is. Don't tell Cherie,' she added softly as Cherie brought in a tray of coffee. 'It's not for her ears. Where's Betty?' she asked aloud. 'Not still upstairs with Henry?'

Lily put her hand to her mouth. 'Should I go up, do you think?'

'No.' Alice and Lizzie answered together. 'She'll be fine.'

They were finishing their coffee when the door bell rang

and Lily rushed to answer it. It was Jamie with two young women and three men. The men were in naval uniform and already in a state of alcoholic merriness.

'Here we are,' Jamie said. 'These are 'girls I was expecting. Them other two had got wind that summat was happening and thought they'd turn up. And these gents are sailors. Look after 'em, Lily.'

Jamie wasn't putting on any style in front of these men. He obviously reckoned he didn't need to, Lily thought. The three customers who had arrived first were residents of Hull and needed to be impressed, whereas these were visitors and would probably be sailing away the next day.

The young women were Mary and Sally, fairly presentable and not too obviously street women. 'Go in 'kitchen,' Lily told them. 'There's some clean clothes in there. Get changed, wash your hands and faces and brush your hair.'

The two women stared at her and glanced at each other. 'Those are the rules,' Lily said. 'This is a decent house.'

Mary gave a cynical laugh, but took Sally's arm and headed down the hall. 'Been some changes,' Lily heard her say. 'But I couldn't stand that Miss Emerald or her pander. Mebbe this one'll be better.'

Lily turned to the naval men, who were swaying and rocking on their heels. 'Gentlemen,' she said, 'would you like to come through and meet the ladies?'

'Where are we?' asked one thickly. 'Are we afloat?'

'No sir. We're ashore,' said another.

'Sun over the for'ard, then,' said the third, grabbing Lily's arm. 'Show us the grog and the girls.'

'Three sheets in the wind all right,' Lily muttered. 'Jamie, go and fetch Mr Smith's cab and ask him to wait in case he decides to go home.'

Lily took the three men to the parlour and introduced them to Lizzie and Alice; the other two young women appeared in their clean finery and they chatted for a time while the men gazed bleary-eyed at them all. Then she suggested that Mary, Sally and Alice take the men upstairs.

'I hate this,' she said to Lizzie as she heard the ribald drunken sound of them crashing on their way. 'Hate it! Hate it!'

Lizzie shrugged. 'What else is there? We're stuck, en't we? What other sort o' living is there for such as us? Such as me, anyway,' she added. 'At least you've had a better life.'

'Kendall gave you extra, didn't he?' Lily asked her. 'He said not to tell Jamie.'

'I won't,' Lizzie said determinedly. 'It's hidden where he won't find it. That's 'start of my pot o' gold. Where's Leo? Is he still asleep in Alice's room?'

'I hope so,' Lily said. 'Unless 'sailors have woken him.'

'I'll go up.' Lizzie rose quickly from her chair. 'Don't want to upset him, do we? We want him as a regular.'

'I suppose so,' Lily said.

'Course we do,' Lizzie said over her shoulder as she went into the hall. 'He's a magistrate. We need him on our side!'

A magistrate! Lily breathed. Here?

From outside there came a sudden crash and crack of breaking glass and strident shrieking voices. Lily rushed to look out of her window. There was a raucous commotion going on and a crowd of people were watching a fight, and not just watching but lustily urging on the participants and throwing the occasional blow. Drunken brawling women were fighting each other as well as men, shouting and screeching as they pulled hair and tore clothes.

As Lily watched she saw a black horse cab arriving at the top of the street. Several police constables got out and started running towards the miscreants. 'Black Maria,' she murmured and hoped that Jamie wouldn't come back yet with Leo's cab. She went to check that the front door was locked.

Lizzie was coming down the stairs holding tight to Leo's arm. She gave a quick grin at Lily before saying softly to Leo, 'Let's take one step at a time, Leo; otherwise we'll both fall arse ower tip!'

He started to laugh. 'I said you were a merry sort of girl, didn't I? Keep hold of me – I'll get you down all right.' When they reached the safety of the hall floor he asked her, 'Did I go up with you or somebody else?'

'You went up with Alice,' Lizzie told him. 'But you fair wore her out so she's gone for a lie down.'

The old man sighed. 'Ah, well! That's the way it used to be in the old days. Where's my coat and hat?'

'Won't you wait awhile?' Lily asked. 'Why not have some coffee until your cab comes? I'm sure Alice will be disappointed if you go without seeing her. Besides,' she bent down and lowered her voice to a confidential whisper, 'there's a commotion going on outside and 'constables have arrived.'

'Oh!' His lips pursed and he looked anxious, but she reassured him.

'It's all right,' she said softly. 'Door's locked and there's no reason for them to come here.'

'I should hope not,' he said. 'Has Kendall gone? It wouldn't do for him to be caught. Not in his position. Don't matter so much for me.' He gave a satisfied smirk. 'Some of the fellows would be envious, I should think. At my age and all that, you know!'

Lily and Lizzie glanced at each other and smiled. From what Alice had said, Leo had fallen asleep as soon as his head had touched the pillow. She had taken off his shoes and trousers and carefully laid them on a chair and he hadn't even stirred.

Mrs Flitt knocked on the parlour door and asked Lily to come to the kitchen. 'Jamie's come to 'back door,' she said in an urgent whisper. 'He says if Mr Smith wants to go home he's got a cab at 'back. He says police are all over 'place.'

Alice had come downstairs and placed herself once more on the stool next to Leo. Lily repeated Jamie's message to him.

'Oh, what a shame, Leo.' Alice seemed disconsolate. 'Just

when we were going to have a nice chat. Still,' she added, 'we don't want any trouble, do we?'

'Indeed we don't.' Leo patted her cheek. 'There now, still warm from sleep, aren't you? Now I'd better get off. I'm on the bench in the morning so I need my wits about me. How shall I get out? Round the back?' He gave a chuckle. 'A real cloak and dagger affair, eh? Running the gauntlet and all that! Well, ladies.' He puckered up his lips to give them each a kiss, Alice, Lizzie and Cherie. To Lily he crooked his forefinger. 'I'll see you in a moment, Miss Lily. Perhaps you'd be so good as to get my coat?'

Lily helped him on with his coat and handed him his top hat and cane. 'Do take care,' she said. 'Jamie's waiting at 'back door. I hope you've enjoyed your evening.'

'I've had a splendid time,' he said, patting his coat pocket for his pocket book.

'Here it is sir.' Lily handed him his leather wallet. 'I took 'liberty of locking it in my desk drawer. I can't be sure of all our clients as yet. There are some dishonest people about and I wouldn't want my regular girls to be accused of stealing.'

'What a remarkable woman you are,' he said quietly, opening up the wallet and counting out some money. 'Whatever are you doing in a place like this?'

She smiled. 'It's a long story, Mr Smith,' she said. 'Perhaps I'll tell you some time.'

He nodded. 'Perhaps you will. I'll see you again, at any rate. And I won't forget the piano!'

Lizzie and Alice were laughing together when she returned to the parlour. 'I was just saying, Lily,' Alice giggled, 'there's another one upstairs that I rocked off to sleep. Or mebbe there's summat in the wine! Anyway that jolly jack tar was asleep on his feet. I just gave him a little push on to 'bed and he was snoring in a minute!'

Jamie returned, having safely deposited Leo in his cab and seen him being driven off. 'It's a riot out in 'street,' he said. 'If there's anybody else here mek 'em stop for a bit.

If you open 'door you'll have 'police in like a shot. They're rounding everybody up. There'll be no more customers tonight. Not till 'police have gone, anyway.'

'The seamen are still here,' Lily told him. 'And Henry.'

'Is he still here?' Jamie said in astonishment. 'Charge him more, then. He can't stop all this time without paying for it. Anyway, I'm off. I might be back if things quieten down, otherwise I'll see you in 'morning to collect.'

'Yes,' Lily said sarcastically. 'I expect you will. You won't want to risk us spending your hard-earned money!'

He cast her a disdainful glance and left, going through the kitchen and out into the back yard. Mrs Flitt carefully bolted the door behind him. 'Whoremonger!' she hissed as she turned away. 'Pander!'

The constables had left and the crowd dispersed by the time two of the navy men and the two other women came down. 'Don't forget your friend,' Lily said as she took money from them. 'He's asleep. Will you pay for him?'

One of the men put his hand to his head. 'He can pay for himself,' he muttered. 'Can somebody fetch him down? I daren't climb those stairs again.'

'We'll go,' Alice and Lizzie said and darted upstairs again. They came down a couple of minutes later, Lizzie steering the seaman down whilst Alice kept hold of his shoulders. Whilst the two girls held him up Lily put her hand in his pocket.

'Look,' she said, speaking to the other men. 'This is what I'm taking. Just 'standard rate.' She glanced at the man's face. He was still asleep. 'I'll tek a bit extra,' she said, taking two more coins. 'That's for Alice.'

The other two men shrugged. 'Whatever you like,' one hiccuped. 'Plenty more where that came from.'

They were propelled towards the door. 'Can you find your way back to your ship?' Lily asked. 'Go down to 'bottom of 'street and turn left. What?' she said, turning round as she heard all the women burst out laughing.

'Just listen to you, Lily!' Alice spluttered, whilst the

others doubled up with laughter. '"Can you find your way back to 'ship!"' she parodied.

'Who cares?' Mary grinned. 'Don't matter to us if they fall overboard.'

'I don't suppose it does,' Lily said despondently. 'I'm 'odd one out here.'

Mary and Sally told her they were going home. They didn't want to stay the night and Lily guessed that they had business elsewhere.

'We'll be back tomorrow for our money,' Mary told her. 'Mek sure that Jamie leaves it for us, won't you? I have to have it; I've a bairn to feed. We don't want any excuses or we don't come again and we'll spread 'word he's a bad payer.'

Lily nodded and let them out of the door. She wrote down in a notebook how long the women and the men had stayed so that she could tell Jamie, then she entered the names of the other gentlemen and who had entertained them.

'Henry!' she muttered. He was still upstairs with Betty. She went into the hall and looked up. Should she go up? Alice and Lizzie had said before that she shouldn't. Perhaps they've both gone to sleep, she thought. But the customers were not supposed to stay the night.

Alice and Lizzie both came yawning into the hall. 'What's up?' Lizzie asked. 'I'm off to bed in a minute. Don't suppose anybody else'll come, do you?'

Lily was just about to voice her fears about Betty and Henry when there came a sudden shout from one of the bedrooms. It was a triumphant victorious vociferous blast of sound and they all looked up. Alice and Lizzie eyed each other and Cherie came out of the kitchen holding a cup in her hand.

'Whatever's happened?' Lily put her hand to her mouth, then they all looked at each other and grinned.

A door upstairs opened a few minutes later and Betty appeared at the top of the stairs. She looked exhausted.

Her hair was tousled and hanging free, her face and neck were red and her gown was unbuttoned. They heard a sort of crowing and Henry emerged from the room behind her. He gave a whoop, kissed her on the cheek and raced downstairs. His shirt was hanging outside his trousers, his cravat was in his hand and his bootlaces were undone.

He planted a kiss each on Alice, Lizzie and Lily, and headed for the door. 'Goodbye,' he said. 'I'll be back! Thank you. Thank you. Thank you!' He opened the door and let himself out, slamming the door behind him.

'He hasn't paid!' Lily gasped, but as she spoke the door bell rang. She opened it. It was Henry with a huge smile on his face.

'I forgot,' he said, thrusting his pocket book at Lily. 'Take it,' he said. 'Take it all!'

She closed the door after him as he ran down the front steps, his shirt tails flying. 'Betty!' she said, turning. 'He's forgotten his coat.'

Betty was hanging on to the bottom newel post as if her life depended on it. She blew out a breath. 'He's lived with a maiden aunt since he was a child. She's just died leaving him her fortune. It was his first time with a woman!' she gasped. 'He's thirty-five years old and it was his first time! Heaven help us when he's had some practice!'

CHAPTER TWENTY-FOUR

A week later Lily walked into town to visit Rena. She was wearing the grey gown and thought how uplifting it was to be well dressed. I feel as if I can hold my head up with the best of them. I don't look poverty-stricken or down at heel and of no account. One or two gentlemen had lifted their hats to her to bid her good morning, and she wasn't sure if it was because she looked elegant, or because they recognized her from a night-time activity. The house had been busy most evenings. Jamie seemed to have a constant supply of customers; either that or the word was getting round that it was a very discreet establishment with some very respectable gentlemen using the services there.

'I need a pair of everyday shoes, Rena,' she told the older woman. 'These old boots are worn out. And I'd like a new bonnet for when I come into town.'

'Quite right,' Rena agreed. 'I wondered when you'd get round to buying one.'

'I've not had any spare money,' Lily said. 'The money Jamie pays me is for essentials, like food.'

Jamie was not very generous with his wages. 'It's me who brings 'customers in,' he'd said when she complained. 'And I pay 'rent; five bob a week it costs me.'

'And I'm the one who teks 'risk,' she retaliated. 'If 'house was raided it'd be me who'd tek 'blame.'

She knew that for a fact because Leo had told her. 'You

must be very careful,' he had said. 'Jamie can claim that he has no knowledge of what you and the girls are doing in his house. He's only the landlord – the sub-landlord, at any rate. I know he doesn't own it. You would be the one to be prosecuted.'

'But . . .' She had been confused. 'He brings 'customers here. He even brought—' She'd stopped. Benevolent and big-hearted as Leo was to them all – and true to his word he had had a piano delivered – the expression on his face had warned her that he would deny all knowledge of her or the house.

'I was given a big tip 'other night,' she told Rena. 'So I decided that after I'd paid you what I owe, I'd buy myself a new hat or bonnet. I've never had one. I allus – always made my own bonnets out of old frocks.' She was trying to improve her manners and speech, having become very conscious of how countrified she was. 'But I've never owned a hat. Never had 'call for one.'

'Every woman should have at least one hat in her lifetime.' Rena smiled. 'I have twelve of my own, and even then sometimes I'll use another from my stock. Let's have a look and see what suits you.'

They spent a pleasant half-hour trying on shoes and hats and bonnets and eventually Lily chose a pair of plain black leather shoes, barely worn, and a straw bonnet lined with grey silk. Rena also insisted that she have a pair of silk gloves and a beaded purse.

'There,' she said, putting her head on one side. 'You could be taken for a prosperous tradesman's wife quite easily.'

'A tradesman's wife!' Lily said. 'Gracious! Really? How about an apothecary's wife?' She laughed. 'Mrs Walker is nowhere near as elegant as me!'

'Mrs Walker?' Rena looked startled. 'You know her, do you?'

'My daughter Daisy works for her and Mr Walker was very kind to me when I first came to Hull. He took me into his care when I was in labour. Mrs Walker wasn't so keen to have me there, nor to have Daisy at first, but now, oddly enough, she's taken to her and wants her as a lady's maid.'

'Does she indeed,' Rena muttered. 'Ideas above her station!'

Rather a strange thing to say, Lily pondered as she walked back to Leadenhall Square in her new attire. I would have thought that Mrs Walker as an apothecary's wife had a good status in life and would need a personal maid; though now I think about it, she doesn't have the manners or the voice of a lady, whereas Mr Walker is obviously a gentleman, and their son will be the same.

It was a very warm day and she was conscious of the many strong smells of the town. A stench of fish offal and glue, of open drains and sewers, an odour beyond imagining from the charnel house, and a reek of rotting meat, decaying vegetables and overflowing privies. She put her hand over her nose as she hurried back and saw that many other women had their handkerchiefs to their faces.

'Oh, what a stink out there!' she gasped as she went indoors. 'Summat should be done about it. It can't be healthy. There's no wonder there's disease everywhere.'

Lizzie looked up. She was sitting on the parlour sofa with her feet up. 'Hadn't noticed,' she said.

'We're used to it,' Alice said. 'But sometimes it makes me cough.'

Lily had noticed that Alice coughed, especially at night.

'You must've had bad smells where you lived, Lily,' Cherie said. 'Didn't you?'

Lily shook her head. 'Not like these,' she said. 'Nowt at all like these. But you forget, I lived near 'sea. That was a smell worth sniffing.'

'Tell us, then.' Cherie moved Lizzie's feet and sat beside her. 'Tell us what it was like where you used to live.'

'I'll just tek my hat off. Has anybody noticed?' she

asked, turning her head this way and that to show off her bonnet.

'I did,' Alice said. 'It's lovely. Have you been to Rena's?'

'Yes.' Lily unfastened the ribbons at her throat. 'And look – gloves, bag' – she lifted her foot and twirled it – 'and shoes.'

'Have you come into a fortune?' Lizzie grinned. 'Or have you been stealing our customers when we weren't looking?'

'No, I haven't,' she said. 'Though I've been asked, so you'd all better watch out.' When Lily was asked a 'favour' by the customers, she simply sweetly and politely refused. How very charming they seem, she would think as she smilingly declined, yet she knew they were concerned only with their own gratification.

'I'd give a fortune for a cuppa tea. Ask Mrs Flitt, will you, Cherie, and then I'll tell you about 'sweet scents of home.'

Lily slipped off her new shoes; they were pinching her toes just a little and she thought that whoever they had belonged to previously hadn't worn them much for there was barely a scratch on them. Her old boots she had handed over to Mrs Flitt who had opened the door to her and who had almost grovelled with delight; her own footwear had cardboard soles which she replaced every few days.

'Tell us then, Lily,' Cherie pleaded, when she came back from the kitchen with a tray of tea. 'What was it like where you lived? Did you have shops? And were you very poor?' Cherie was almost childlike in her eagerness to know.

'Everybody I knew was poor.' Lily sipped her tea appreciatively. This was a luxury; there had been times when she couldn't afford to buy tea, and when she did she used it sparingly. 'But in 'country, folks shared what they had when they could, especially if they thought you were on your uppers. Most folks grew their own food, potatoes, beans, cabbages and suchlike, and there was a butcher's van came once a week for them as could afford to buy meat. But sometimes I'd be given a rabbit or a boiling chicken and they'd last for a couple o' days. But you asked about 'smells of 'countryside, and,' she drew in a breath, 'I miss them a lot. I've not smelt a sprig of hawthorn or apple blossom – and they'll be in full flower now – since I came to Hull. There are no gardens round here, or at least none that I've seen.

'The village I lived in when I was a bairn and where my ma and da lived all their lives was about a mile from 'sea. We used to walk there regular, and when I was courting Johnny we walked there every Sunday until we wed. After he joined the army I still used to go with my bairns. Our village wasn't very big, not compared with this town, and we knew most folks. They'd lived there all their lives, you see. Farming folk, they were mainly; labouring men.'

'But the smells,' Cherie interrupted. 'What about them?'

Lily smiled. 'In 'spring, the smell of blossom was so heady that you felt you could get drunk on it. I've telled you about 'hawthorn; 'trees and hedges would be covered in white blossom, and sometimes it was pink – Flowers of May, it was called. Then 'hedge rose and elder would be in flower about 'same time and 'smell from 'em used to nearly knock me over! Did you know that you can mek champagne with elderflower?' Without waiting for an answer, she went on, 'My ma used to mek it and then elderberry wine in 'autumn when 'berries came out. By, that was potent!'

'Would you like to go back?' Alice asked. She was sitting curled up in a chair, looking rather fragile, Lily thought.

'I've nobody to go back to,' she answered. 'When Johnny didn't come home I married again and went to live in Seathorne. I thought I was going to summat better than I had, but it was just a hovel right on 'edge of 'cliff. The village is disappearing into 'sea.' She wondered uneasily about Billy. Was he really dead? She sighed. There was no point in enquiring. He hadn't wanted her – that much was obvious. She was better off without him.

She looked round at all the faces watching and listening to her. 'But 'smell of sea was lovely,' she added brightly.

194

'Sharp and salty, and sort of pungent. You felt refreshed when you took a breath. That was one of 'best smells ever.'

The door bell rang and they all looked up. 'Who's this?' Lizzie frowned. 'At this time o' day!'

'Mrs Flitt can go,' Lily said. 'It can't be a customer.'

Mrs Flitt was allowed to answer the door during the day. She looked much more respectable than before in her newly fashioned skirt, made from Lily's old one, and she always wore a clean apron.

'Somebody for you, Miss Lily.' She put her head round the parlour door and sniffed disapprovingly. 'A woman.'

Lily raised her eyebrows. 'Wanting work?'

'Shouldn't think so,' Mrs Flitt grunted. 'She's waiting in 'hall.'

Lily slipped her shoes back on. 'It's all right. I'll see her in my room,' she said, as the girls stood up to leave the parlour and go into the kitchen.

A pretty middle-aged woman in a hooped cream day dress worn with a short cape and a flowered bonnet stood in the hall looking round her and up the stairs. 'Good afternoon,' she greeted Lily. 'I'm sorry to disturb you. I wondered if Jamie was here.'

Mrs Flitt could have told you that, Lily thought. Why didn't you ask her? 'He isn't,' she said. 'He doesn't live here.'

'No, I know he doesn't. He lives in our old house in Middle Court.'

Lily waited. She didn't know where Middle Court was, but who was this?

'I'm Jamie's mother,' the woman said. 'Nell.' She left it at that, not giving out her married name. 'I wanted a word with him.'

'Why didn't you go to his house?' Lily asked. 'That's where you'd find him.' She must know he runs a brothel. Why else would she be here in this notorious square?

'I can't go back there,' Nell said. 'My husband forbids it; it's such a run-down area. Neither does he know I've come here. He doesn't approve of Jamie, and he doesn't like me to see him. He thinks he's a bad lot. Which he is,' she added. She gazed at Lily and said softly, 'But he's still my son.'

'Come through.' Lily led her into her room. The afternoon sun was shining through the windows, brightening up the room. It looked nice, she thought with satisfaction. Very neat and cheerful, with a vase of flowers on a small table.

'This is lovely,' Nell said. 'I often used to wonder what this house was like inside.'

'You never came in, then?' Lily asked astutely.

'Oh no!' She gave a little shrug and smiled and Lily thought how much Jamie was like her; both had fair hair and blue eyes, but his mother had softer features, and, Lily guessed, was more vulnerable than he was. 'You'll have heard I was in this line of business, I expect?'

Lily nodded, but said nothing. Who was she to judge?

'Jamie used to look after me,' Nell said softly. 'That's 'hardest thing to live down; a son being pander for his mother. Every woman who knows me despises us both for it.'

'I'm sorry,' Lily said. 'I understand how they feel. I wouldn't want my son to know I'm working here and I don't even—'

Nell looked at her curiously. 'Don't even . . . ?'

Lily cleared her throat. 'I don't – well, I just look after 'girls and tek money for Jamie. Nothing else.'

'How very odd.' Nell gave a girlish laugh. 'Nobody'd believe that, of course.'

'I don't suppose they would,' Lily replied sharply. 'But it happens to be true.'

'I made some good men friends over the years,' Nell said. 'They don't acknowledge me now, of course. But I don't mind – I've got a husband who cares for me.'

'Then you're fortunate,' Lily said. 'Does he know about your past?'

'Oh, yes! He was a customer.' Nell folded her hands together. 'I didn't come just to see Jamie,' she said softly. 'Though I would've liked to. I came to see you. I've heard about you – and I wanted to warn you.'

'Warn me? About what? Who?'

'Jamie,' she said. 'You're probably making money for him now, but if he thinks you're getting 'upper hand, he'll get rid of you and bring in somebody else in your place. I know he would,' she added, 'because he tried it with me, with somebody younger. He's allus been full o' big ideas has Jamie.'

'Well, thank you for telling me,' Lily said. 'I appreciate that. But there's nothing I can do about it, and in any case I don't intend to stay here for ever. I hate this kind of work; it's degrading and disgusting and I'm onny here because I'd nowhere else to go. Jamie found me when I was at my lowest ebb and threw me a lifeline.'

'Be careful, then,' Nell advised, 'that 'lifeline doesn't drag you under.'

CHAPTER TWENTY-FIVE

Alice was unwell all summer. She was pale and listless, though the cough which had bothered her in the early months had subsided, except at night when she was kept awake by it.

'It's nowt. I've allus had it,' she told Lily, who was worried about her. 'My ma did too and two of my sisters. Where we lived, near to 'factories, there was allus thick smoke and soot and Ma said that was what caused it. She used to buy milk from a yard down 'street to build us up.' She grimaced. 'I never fancied it, but I was made to drink it. Cows were that thin and scrawny and 'cowman looked as if he'd never had a wash in his life. He used to milk 'cows into a mucky old pail and we were sent with a jug for him to fill.'

'My bones ache,' she complained on another occasion. 'That beating I got from that seaman has damaged me.'

'You've got a sore on your face,' Lizzie told her one morning. 'You'll have to cover that up.'

Alice looked in the mirror and saw the festering sore at the side of her mouth. 'What can I put on it?'

'Lavender water,' Lily told her. 'I used to mek it. But where can we get lavender round here?'

Alice shook her head. 'Don't know. Chemist's shop?'

Mr Walker, Lily thought. I'll ask him and maybe I'll see Daisy too. She had seen her daughter only twice during the summer and those had been chance encounters. Daisy

198

had grown and was filling out, and she had told her mother that she had started her flux. 'Molly showed me what to do,' she said, and Lily thought sadly that Daisy was growing up without her influence.

When the shop door bell rang, Mr Walker looked up from what he was doing at the counter. He didn't recognize her at first, but then his face showed surprise and pleasure. 'Mrs Maddeson!' He smiled. 'How very nice to see you. Are you keeping well? You look well. Your new position is suiting you, I gather?'

'For 'time being, yes it is,' she replied. 'It puts bread in my mouth, at least.'

'An honest job of work is what we all strive for,' he acknowledged. 'And if it feeds us and clothes us as well, then we are fortunate.'

She doubted if he had ever been in the position of worrying whether his work was honest or not. Would he consider running a brothel honest work? I think not, she decided. I'm sure he would consider it corrupt. Which it is.

'I've come on a mission for one of, erm, 'kitchen staff,' she said, 'but I was also wondering about Daisy.' She guessed that dealing with servants wasn't his domain, but it was he who had suggested that Daisy should stay with them. 'Is she proving satisfactory?'

'My wife seems pleased with her, and sometimes she helps behind the counter. Not on her own, of course,' he hastened to add. 'But she helps Oliver with counting the tablets and so on, and she dusts the jars,' he pointed behind him at the shelves of bottles and jars, 'and keeps things tidy.'

'So,' he said. 'What's the trouble with your servant? What are her symptoms?'

'Well, she allus has a cough. She says she's had it since she was young, and her sisters and mother were afflicted as well. But,' she frowned, 'she's got a nasty sore on her face that I don't like 'look of and I wondered if you sold lavender water?'

He gazed at her. 'A running sore? That's not something you want in a kitchen. You must tell her on no account to scratch it or it will become infected and spread further. Her cough? Hard to say. It could be caused by any number of ailments, but there are many people in the town with tuberculosis and it does seem to run in families.'

He turned to bring down a bottle from the shelf. 'I can make up a cough syrup to ease her throat, but if she has tuberculosis or scrofula then I can do nothing except advise her to go to live by the sea or take walks by the pier on her days off. But that is probably not an option open to her. I must also caution *you*, Mrs Maddeson,' he looked at her with grave intent, 'that she should seek advice, for if she does have the disease it is highly contagious and it would be prudent to give her notice immediately.'

Lily took a breath; this was a blow and not something she had thought of. 'And . . . lavender water? Do you sell it?'

He nodded. 'Yes, but I think you should send her in to see me. There may be another underlying cause; perhaps she's run down because of the cough and needs a tonic. Use lavender water by all means, and if it doesn't clear ask her to come in.'

Agreeing that she would pass the message on to the mythical servant, she hurried away clutching the cough syrup and the bottle of lavender water, bought at a price she thought exorbitant – she had previously made her own and used honey for coughs; she was disappointed too that she hadn't caught even so much as a glimpse of Daisy.

'Alice,' she said, handing her the bottles on her return, 'has anybody in your family had tuberculosis?'

'Yes,' Alice said. 'Two of my brothers and one of my sisters. There were eight of us, bairns I mean. One brother died when he was nine and 'other one when he was eleven. My sister lived to be sixteen.' Her mouth trembled. 'That's why my ma made us drink milk; she said it would mek us strong. She'd seen her own ma die of consumption, you see.'

'Yes, she would be worried, of course,' Lily said slowly. There had been nothing like that in the village when she was growing up – not that she knew of, anyway. But then, she thought, Mr Walker said you should live by the sea and breathe in the salty air to be healthy. So he must be right. 'Have you any money put by, Alice? Enough to see a doctor?'

'No!' Alice exclaimed. 'Course I haven't. A doctor? Why? It's onny a cough, Lily. Nowt more than that.'

Alice wasn't earning much money. Leo was a regular customer and he used to slip her something extra, but she was inclined to be lazy and would always suggest that Lizzie or Betty, or Mary or Sally if they were there, took any new customers. 'I'm too tired,' she would say, 'and besides I'm scared of men I don't know.'

Jamie had noticed, and complained to Lily. 'She's not earning her keep. This isn't a charity and if she doesn't do more she'll have to go and I'll find somebody else.'

'She's not costing you anything,' she retorted. 'She buys her own food and she keeps Leo happy and he's important to us.'

Lily felt that Leo added tone to the house. There had never been any trouble, even though occasionally unsavoury characters had rung the door bell demanding to be let in. Lily always closed the door on them, telling them they had mistaken the address, and directing them elsewhere in the square.

There was a storm early that evening, torrential rain and a thundering overhead as the heavens opened. 'I hate thunder,' Cherie said, holding her hands over her ears. 'And look.' She pointed out of the window at the lightning. 'It's like daylight.'

'I used to like to watch storms over 'sea,' Lily said. 'When I was at Seathorne we were right on 'edge of 'cliff and it was as if we were sitting in 'middle of 'storm. The sea'd churn as if a giant hand was stirring it and 'colour would change to muddy brown and grey-green, and 'tops of waves would be thick with white frothy foam. Sky would light up,' her eyes sparkled, 'flaring and flashing and showing everything up in silver.'

'How lovely.' Alice was listening intently. 'I'd love to see that. How lucky you are, Lily. I've never been anywhere else but Hull.'

'Nor me,' Lizzie said, and neither had Cherie or Betty. They'd spent all of their young lives in the town.

'If we'd enough money we could go on a train,' Betty said, and then laughed. 'Perhaps I'll ask Henry to tek me to Bridlington!'

'Where's that?' Cherie asked. 'Is it far?'

Lily glanced at Betty. Henry came regularly, at least twice a week, and always asked for Betty. 'It's up 'coast,' she said. 'There's a train service running there now. Would he tek you, do you think, Betty? If he will you should go.' She sighed. 'It would be nice if we could all go.' She longed to see the sea and realized how much she was missing it.

'I'll ask him when he comes next time.' Betty grinned. 'Mebbe he'd tek me on Sunday.' Then the smile left her face. 'But mebbe he wouldn't want to be seen wi' me. He hasn't any family but I expect he's got friends who'd turn their noses up if they saw him out walking wi' somebody like me.'

They all fell silent. It was true, Lily thought, they would be considered low and unworthy, but then, she mused, Jamie's mother had risen above the stigma. If she could, why not Betty and the others?

The girls went upstairs to get ready for the evening, though Lily considered that not many customers would come in such weather. She lit her lamp and, going to draw the curtains, looked out on to the square and saw that the road was flooded and the rain still pelting down. The door of one of the other houses opened and several young women came running down the steps. They were scantily dressed and shrieking at the tops of their voices as they splashed in the water. Other windows and doors opened and heads popped out, and within minutes other girls had dashed out of the houses to join them in splashing and sloshing in the puddles.

As Lily watched, some of them took off their skirts and threw them on to the steps, and then as if at a signal they all took off their clothes and ran naked up and down the street, laughing and screeching, pushing and pulling at each other until they fell over.

Shouts came from the end of the street and a group of men called to the women. 'Come on then,' one of the women yelled. 'Come for a swim.' The men without hesitation rushed towards them, dragging off their coats and shirts as they ran.

'Heavens!' Lily breathed. 'I hope 'constables don't come or we'll all be in trouble.' Then she drew in her breath and closed the curtains. The men had reached the women and what they were up to now was not for public display.

'What's going on?' Lizzie came down and into Lily's room. 'What's that row?'

'Don't look,' Lily said sharply. 'It's disgraceful.'

'Sounds like a riot.' Lizzie peeked out anyway. 'God! Police are here! They're rounding them up! Oh!' She swivelled, showing a scared face to Lily. 'I hope none of our regulars turn up or they'll catch 'em.' She peered out again, holding the curtains close to her head so that no light showed outside. 'They've brought 'Black Maria! Quick,' she said, turning away. 'Get your sewing basket out. I'll tell 'others.'

'What? What?' Lily asked. 'Police won't come here!'

'Course they will.' Lizzie dashed towards the stairs. 'They'll come banging on everybody's door.'

Lily was seized by a sudden panic. If the police came she would be the one to be accused of running a brothel. Would they lock her up? Jamie wouldn't appear, not if he saw what was happening out in the square. He would be in the clear just as Leo had said.

When Mrs Flitt announced the sergeant and his constable,

Lily was sitting with her sewing basket at her feet, a needle and thread in her hand and a piece of linen on the lap of her grey gown. Lizzie was curled up with a book in her hand; Betty and Alice were in quiet conversation, whilst Cherie was coming through from the kitchen with an apron over her dress, carrying a tray of tea cups and saucers.

'Telled yer, didn't I?' Mrs Flitt said to the sergeant. 'This is a respectable 'ouse. Not like them thieves' cribs and brothels up 'street!'

'Thank you, Mrs Flitt,' Lily said calmly, though her heart was racing. 'That will do.'

'I'm sorry to bother you, ma'am,' the sergeant said. 'But you must realize this is a notorious area.'

Lily sighed. 'Of course I do, but what can a poor woman do? There's very little accommodation for someone with limited means. I didn't know what it was like until I moved in and then it was too late.'

'Who's your landlord?' he asked bluntly and Lily hesitated, convinced that the police would know Jamie's name.

'Mr Broadley,' Lizzie said. 'He owns most of 'houses round here.'

'I know you.' The constable stared at Lizzie. 'Where've I seen you afore?'

Lizzie shrugged. 'Around, I expect. I've lived in Hull all my life.'

He patted his mouth with his finger and then pointed at her. 'I remember. You were brought up to court. Assault and stealing a shilling from a seaman.'

'Self-defence!' Lizzie snapped. 'He gave me a slap and wasn't going to pay what he owed.' She stopped, her face flushing, aware that she had given herself away. 'I've turned over a new leaf now,' she muttered. 'I'm not a street woman any more. I've seen 'error of my ways,' she added piously.

'I don't think so.' The sergeant took out a notebook. 'Do you all live here? How many of you? Five women plus 'rough.'

''Ere! Who're you calling rough!' Mrs Flitt had been listening out in the hall. 'I'll have you know I'm a cook and a good one.'

'Five women plus 'cook.' The sergeant without a flicker of expression licked his pencil and amended his notes. 'And your name?' he asked Lily.

Lily swallowed. She wouldn't, couldn't defile Johnny's name. She didn't care about Billy's and anyway, he might be dead so it wouldn't matter. 'Fowler,' she said. 'Lily Fowler.'

'Well, Mrs Fowler. I have reason to think you are running a disorderly house.'

'How can you say such a thing?' she demanded. 'There are no men in here.'

The sergeant gave a thin smile. 'Not at 'minute there aren't. But there's one waiting at 'door and I dare say there'd be others if they hadn't seen us in 'street.'

'Who?' Lily asked. 'Who is it at 'door? We were expecting a friend to call.'

'Claims his name is Henry,' the constable said. 'Refuses to give another name.'

'Henry!' they all chorused.

'He's my intended,' Betty said.

'They're engaged,' Lizzie added.

The sergeant frowned. 'That's what he said. Let him in,' he told the constable.

The officer came back a moment later with Henry, hand-cuffed to another constable.

'Dearest,' Betty said piteously. 'What have they done to you?'

'I'm all right, old girl,' Henry said in a brave tone. 'I say, what's going on? These fellows jumped on me as I came up the steps. I told them I was visiting my fiancée but they didn't believe me. There's some kind of riot going on outside. But not anything you ladies would want to see. Quite degrading.' He turned to the sergeant. 'Take these things off me, would you? Otherwise I might have to make a complaint.'

The sergeant signalled to the constable and Henry was

released. 'Sorry, sir,' the officer said, 'but please understand we have to do our duty. There've been some immoral acts in this square tonight.'

'Indeed that is true.' Henry rubbed his wrists. 'I saw them with my own eyes, but that does not give you any reason to question these ladies.'

'No sir.' The sergeant turned to Lily and eyed her keenly. 'I'm sorry to have taken up your time, Mrs Fowler. I'll bid you good night.'

Lily inclined her head but didn't speak. She was shocked to the core. The sergeant didn't believe them, that was obvious. It was only Henry's plausible and timely intervention that had saved them.

CHAPTER TWENTY-SIX

There were no other customers that night and Jamie came in by the back door. He was soaked to the skin. 'I've been stuck in a shop doorway,' he groused. 'Daren't come out till 'police left. Did they come here?' He sniffed, wiping his nose on his sleeve. 'Get me a cup o' coffee,' he said to Mrs Flitt, who had let him in on hearing his tap on the door.

'They did come,' Lily told him, 'and if it hadn't been for Henry I don't know what might have happened. I was scared witless.'

'They can't get you for keeping a brothel. Not that this is one,' he added hastily. 'It's a bordello.'

Lily gave an impatient sigh. 'It's 'same thing,' she said irritably.

'Well, anyway, they can't. There's no law,' Jamie went on. 'But they can get you on keeping a disorderly house, which is what they'll charge that lot out there with; silly beggars all dashed inside when they saw 'police and they caught 'em red-handed. Half dressed, most of 'em.' He laughed.

'Yes, we don't need 'details, thank you!' Lily interrupted.

'Ooh, Miss Prim!' Jamie said caustically. 'Anyway, watch out and mek sure 'girls don't get drunk cos they can get 'em on that as well, and,' he wagged a finger, 'no pinching money off customers.'

'They don't,' she said indignantly.

'Don't you believe it,' he said. 'Course they do!'

'Police asked me who was 'landlord,' Lily told him. 'Should I have said you?'

'Broadley.' His answer was swift. 'Not me. He owns 'house. He's 'one who gets 'rent. And he's got a lot o' clout and friends in 'right places so he'll never get prosecuted. Anyway, I'm off; don't forget to tek money off Henry.'

'I won't. Don't you want your coffee?'

'Nah, I'm going home to get dry. Be good.' He winked cheekily and sped off down the hall and she heard Mrs Flitt chastising him.

''Ere you are, Miss Lily.' Mrs Flitt came through with the coffee pot. 'You might as well drink it. Can't afford to waste it, can we? You all right, dearie?' She bent anxiously towards her.

'I suppose so, Mrs Flitt,' Lily said despondently. 'I just keep on wondering what I'm doing in this kind of life.'

'You've just got to keep your head above water and below 'parapet,' Mrs Flitt said sagely. 'That's what I allus say.'

Lily vaguely wondered how she could possibly manage to do both these absurdities, but she smiled and took the offered drink and sat quietly thinking.

'Henry,' Betty wheedled, stroking his hair. 'I want to ask you something!'

Henry grunted. He was lying face down with his head in the pillow. 'As long as you're not going to ask me to do anything exhausting,' he muttered. 'I'm shattered. Oh my! What a girl you are!' He half turned towards her and opened one eye. 'Just let me get my breath back.'

She laughed. She had never known anyone with as much stamina as Henry; neither had she ever looked forward so eagerly to seeing a man. 'Silly,' she said. 'I didn't mean *that*!'

He rolled over and grabbed her. 'And why not?' He straddled her with his strong thighs and she thought that although he was the sort of man you wouldn't notice if you passed him in the street, once he was disrobed he was magnificent. 'Tired of me already, are you?' He bent to nibble her neck, and as his hands clutched her hips she knew he was ready to ride her again.

'Never,' she breathed, arching her body beneath him. 'I'll never get tired of you, Henry. I've never met anyone like you before.'

Later, as he was dressing, he asked, 'So what did you want to ask me?'

'Erm.' She hesitated. When she and the others had been talking about going to see the sea, and she had blithely said she would ask Henry to take her, she now realized she was asking the impossible. 'Oh, it's nothing,' she said. 'It doesn't matter. You wouldn't anyway.'

He looked keenly at her. 'I wouldn't what? Come on, tell me. Don't be shy. You can ask me anything.' He kissed her on the cheek as he buttoned up his shirt: 'After all we've done together, surely there's nothing you can't ask?'

'Ah, well, that's just it.' She felt tears welling. 'It's not as if I'm an ordinary sort o' girl, after all.'

'Phew! You're certainly not.' He ran his fingers down her throat to her breasts. 'Don't get me started again, Betty, or I'll never get home tonight.'

She smiled. She hadn't done anything, yet here he was becoming amorous again; she recognized that gleam in his eyes. 'It's just that 'other girls and me were talking with Lily and she was telling us about living by 'sea; and we'd never seen it—'

'Never seen the sea!' he broke in in astonishment. 'What? Never?'

She shook her head. 'No. How could we? We've barely had money to scrape together to buy a bit o' bread, let alone a train ticket.'

Henry sat down on the bed and stared at her. 'Is that what you wanted to ask? If I would buy train tickets for you all?'

'No. No! Not for all of us!' She looked pleadingly at him. 'Onny me. I wondered if you'd tek me.' She pressed her lips together and shrugged. 'It was a stupid idea. I know that you can't.'

He reached out and drew her towards him. 'Why can't I? It's a splendid idea! I could hire a carriage if you like and we could jog along in fine style along the coast; or I suppose you'd rather travel by train if you've never done it before. Where to? Bridlington?'

'Oh, yes! Please!' She jumped into his lap. 'Yes, please!'

'Oh, heavens! There, you've done it again.' He began to unbutton his shirt, using one hand whilst with the other he stroked her thigh, seeking pleasure with his fingers. 'I can't get enough of you, Betty. You're going to have to come back into bed again.'

'Lily!' Betty crept into Lily's room after she had let Henry out of the house. 'Henry said to give you this.'

Lily sat up in bed. She'd given up waiting for Henry to leave. 'Has he onny just gone?' There was astonishment in her voice. 'Wherever does he get 'energy from? Put it on my desk. I'll see to it in 'morning.'

Betty put the money down and said, 'Oh, we've been talking! That's why he was so late leaving.'

Lily gave a snort. 'Well, I don't believe that for a minute, but as Jamie would say, as long as he pays it doesn't matter what he does.'

'He can't come for a few days,' Betty said in a low voice. 'He's got some business to attend to; but Lily, I asked him if he'd tek me to Bridlington and he said he would.'

'Really? Oh, you lucky girl! The others will be wild wi' jealousy.'

'I hope he meant it,' Betty murmured, 'cos after he said he would, he remembered he couldn't come again till next week. Now I'm worrying that p'raps I shouldn't have asked. That mebbe he thinks I've got a bit above myself and he's mekking an excuse not to come back.'

Lily got out of bed and, wrapping a shawl round herself, came to Betty's side. 'He won't be doing that,' she said. 'Men do have businesses to run or other commitments, but he's been coming here regular as clockwork. Why, there's nobody else been so often and he's never asked for any-body but you.'

Betty began to weep. 'I know,' she said. 'But it's just . . .'

'You're not getting over fond of him, are you?' Lily asked anxiously. 'That won't do, Betty. You'll get hurt.'

'Yes,' Betty sobbed. 'And I never wanted to care for anybody ever again, not like I did for my babby's father. I vowed I wouldn't after he said he didn't want me.'

'He was young, I expect,' Lily soothed her, 'as you were; and he didn't want 'responsibility of a wife and child.'

Betty lifted the hem of her skirt and wiped her eyes. 'That's what he said at 'time, but it didn't help me when I was carrying his bairn.' Another tear slid down her cheek. 'My poor little Tommy. I think about him all 'time. I'll never get over losing him.' She sniffed and drew a sobbing breath. 'Sorry! Funny thing is, though, Henry teks my mind off what's gone before. He meks me laugh, and – and I do care for him, Lily, and I just hope that I haven't asked for more than I deserve and frightened him off. After all, there are plenty of other women like me who'll ask a man for nowt more than the price of a cup o' tea or a loaf o' bread.'

'Yes,' Lily said gloomily. 'That's a woman's misfortune; unfortunate women, that is, who have no other means of mekking a living and are corrupted by unscrupulous men.'

'Henry isn't unscrupulous!' Betty sprang to Henry's defence. 'He's 'nicest man I've ever met.'

'Betty,' Lily said thoughtfully, 'would you go back to Hope House?'

'What? Why would I do that? I like it here, and besides, I'd want to see Henry.'

'You just said that he won't be coming till next week, and it's just – will you trust me, Betty? I've wanted to do some-thing to help you and I think that now I know how I can.'

The next morning Lily dressed in her grey gown, put on her bonnet and walked out of the house. In Lowgate she hired a hansom using money she had taken out of Henry's generous payment. He had stayed for several hours, but, she reckoned, Jamie didn't know that and what he didn't know about he wouldn't miss. Am I becoming underhand? Dishonest even? I think I probably am, she thought, but that's what life has made me.

The hansom drew up outside the address she had given and she paid the driver. She would have to walk back; the money wouldn't stretch to two journeys. Mrs Grant opened the door to her knock and asked politely, 'Can I help you, ma'am?'

Lily suppressed a smile; the housekeeper hadn't recognized her. What a poor thing she must have looked when she was first brought here. 'Good morning, Mrs Grant,' she said. 'Might I speak to Mrs Thompson?'

She was invited in and she could see that Mrs Grant was puzzled that Lily should know her by name. 'What name shall I say, ma'am?'

'Mrs Maddeson,' Lily said, and was taken through to Mrs Thompson's room.

Mrs Thompson was sitting behind a desk writing in a ledger. She looked up and smiled at her visitor as she was announced. 'Good morning.' A little frown appeared above her nose. 'We've met. You're not on the committee? No? Then where – I know,' she said intently. 'My word. Mrs Maddeson! What a surprise. Please take a seat.'

'You remember me? Mrs Grant didn't.'

'Mrs Grant has so many young women passing through her door that it's not surprising that sometimes she forgets. But I didn't think I would see you again. You were not the usual kind of woman to come here.'

'Is there a usual kind of woman?' Lily asked. 'It seems to me that any woman can fall on misfortune and end up in 'gutter.'

'Yes.' Mrs Thompson sighed. 'Forgive me. That is very true. Sadly, women are not in charge of their own lives; but what I really meant was that you seemed more capable than most of managing to fend for yourself.'

Lily nodded. 'Generally I am and I've survived, but not in 'manner I'd wish.' She went on to give brief details of what had happened to her and how she was presently employed.

'I'm very sorry to hear it,' Mrs Thompson said in her quiet manner. 'I had hoped for better things for you.'

'It's a temporary situation,' Lily assured her. 'I don't intend to stay in my present occupation. It's degrading and humiliating,' she said bitterly. 'But I'm not living on 'streets and neither are my girls.' She took a breath. 'There's one young woman in particular that I'd like to discuss with you. She's been here and you mebbe thought that you'd had success with her.'

She told Mrs Thompson about Betty and how she was becoming fond of one of her customers. 'I think,' she said, 'that Betty can be saved from 'kind of life she's presently in, and that this gentleman might well see her in a different light if she's not always available for – well, you know – for his pleasure. I'm asking you, Mrs Thompson, if you'll have her back for a week and attempt to . . . shall I say knock off some of her rough edges. She does know how to behave; I noticed that when I first met her, but she needs to be told that she isn't worthless, that she has something else to offer as well as her body.'

'We normally prepare young women for other types of work,' Mrs Thompson said doubtfully. 'What had you in mind for Betty?'

'Show her how to act in front of a man without trying to entice or allure him. Teach her to behave modestly. What I'm hoping is that this man, who's already smitten with her, might, just might, offer her summat more permanent.'

'Something more permanent?' Mrs Thompson raised her eyebrows. 'A week, you say?' At Lily's nod, she said, 'Well, there's a challenge! All right. We'll do it.'

Lily smiled. Good, she thought. That's Betty. Next is Lizzie!

CHAPTER TWENTY-SEVEN

Jamie often brought in other girls. Some of them came regularly, whilst others whom Lily considered unsuitable for their clients were asked to leave. 'We've got to be particular,' she told him when they had had an argument over two women whom she had found objectionable. 'And we don't want any more women like those two harlots Flo and Poll who crashed in the first night; they'd really let 'side down.'

He was torn, she knew, between running a first class establishment with fewer clients and bringing in customers whom he didn't know and making more money.

'But we need more girls! Where's Betty?' he asked suspiciously. 'I haven't seen her for a day or two. And that customer, Henry? Don't tell me he doesn't come now?'

'He's away at present,' Lily said. 'But he'll be back. And Betty's about somewhere,' she lied.

He grunted. 'Mek sure she teks on some others, then. Don't let her slack. We can't let 'em have favourites.'

'You have to mek your mind up, Jamie,' she said impatiently. 'If you want a first class house for 'gentry, you've got to have first class girls that 'gentlemen will ask for. They pay plenty for having 'same girl available to them every time.'

Kendall, for instance, always asked for Lizzie, and although Lily knew that Lizzie detested him she didn't ever let it show; Leo always went upstairs with Alice and never asked for anyone else.

Betty had agreed to go to Hope House and the others covered for her. Lizzie was scornful about the plan when Lily had explained it to them. 'You think that Henry's going to offer for her, don't you? What a laugh! Course he won't. He'll find some dull little woman to marry and come here to bed Betty when he's bored wi' married life.'

'What a cynic you are, Lizzie,' Lily said. 'Don't you believe that married life can be good?'

'No!' Her lips curled pettishly. 'I don't believe in owt but getting from one day to 'next.' She gave a discontented grunt. 'I wonder sometimes what I've been put on this earth for.'

'To give pleasure to men.' Alice yawned. 'Nowt else.' Her eyes looked huge in her pallid face. 'Leo says he's glad he met me.' She shrugged and smiled. 'Sometimes we onny talk, you know, but I'm happy wi' that.'

'What!' Lizzie's face was a picture of disbelief. 'He pays you just to talk? I wish I'd tekken him upstairs instead of that serpent Kendall!'

'Lizzie, I can tell Kendall you're not available,' Lily told her. 'He can go with Mary or—'

Lizzie shook her head. 'No. I know what to expect from him now.' She gave a little shudder. 'And he gives me extra,' she glanced at Lily, 'that I don't hand over.'

Poor Lizzie, Lily thought. Is it too late for her? Is she so embittered that her life will never be satisfactory? God knows I feel downhearted most of the time, yet there's still a spark of hope within me that makes me think that life will get better. That I won't be in this pit for ever.

Henry rang the door bell one afternoon a few days later. 'I'm back.' He beamed at Lily. 'My business affairs didn't take as long as I'd thought.' He came inside and vigorously rubbed his hands together. 'Betty?' he enquired.

'She's not here at present,' Lily told him, and watched his disappointment show and his ready smile disappear.

'Oh! Of course she won't be expecting me just yet, and I usually come in the evening.' He heaved a breath. 'Mmm. She'll be here tonight though?'

'No. She won't be back for a day or two.'

He looked puzzled. 'But – where has she gone?'

'I'm not at liberty to say. It's something private. If she wishes to tell you on her return, that's up to her.'

'I see!' His eyes clouded. 'Oh. Well. I suppose I'll just have to wait.'

Lily lowered her voice. 'Would you – would you like to talk to one of 'other young ladies? Or perhaps stay for tea,' she added brightly.

He looked bewildered. 'Why would I want to talk to any of the others? Betty's my friend, and I've something to discuss with her.'

Lily felt a flutter of excitement. 'Will it keep?' she asked. 'I could get a message to her.'

'You know where she is? So can't you tell me?'

'I'm sorry,' Lily apologized. 'I can't.'

'She's not in trouble?' Henry said anxiously. 'Or it's not that she doesn't want to see me?'

Lily smiled. 'No. She only ever says how much she enjoys your company.'

'Ah!' His eyes brightened a little. 'She's a grand girl, you know. I'm very fond of her. I'll come back tomorrow,' he said decisively. 'Tell her to wait for me, won't you?'

'I'll ask her, certainly,' she said.

'Yes. Yes, I meant ask, of course. I shouldn't presume.' He frowned. 'Does she – erm, well, I suppose she sees other gentlemen when I'm not here?'

Lily didn't answer, but quizzically raised her eyebrows.

'Sorry.' He patted his hands together, making a hollow clapping sound. 'Of course. Shouldn't ask! Right. I'll come back tomorrow. Thank you so much, Miss Lily. Goodbye.'

Lily shook her fists joyously after she had closed the door behind him. Was her plan going to work? What was he going to discuss with Betty? She'd half a mind to send a

216

message to Betty to ask her to come back, but she refrained. No, she thought. Henry can wait a little longer.

He came back early the following evening and sat despondently drinking a glass of wine and ignoring or not noticing Lizzie's blandishments or flirtatious behaviour. Lily sat down beside him. 'I did say she wouldn't be back for a few days,' she said gently.

'Yes. Yes, you did. But I just hoped that perhaps she'd come back early. Tomorrow, do you think?'

'Perhaps. More likely 'following day.'

'But you still won't say where she's gone?' Henry gazed at her appealingly.

What a nice man he is, Lily thought. So guileless. You'd really want to please him.

'You see, Miss Lily,' he dropped his voice, 'I'd never been with a woman until I met Betty. And it's – it's just wonderful. I had no idea!'

'How is it that you hadn't – hadn't been to an establishment like this before?' she asked. 'Young men do.'

He nodded gloomily. 'When I was very young, my aunt gave me books which cautioned of sinful practices before marriage. Of course, what she really wanted was for me to stay with her and never get married. I was working as a clerk in a bank and didn't get the opportunity to meet very many young ladies, and those I did take home she warned off. I was constantly at her beck and call and made to feel grateful that she had given me a home after my parents died. I wasn't allowed to go away to school where I might have found out about, erm' – he glanced sheepishly at her – 'sexual activities, but had to attend a local school. I could have left her when I was twenty-one, but by then she was hinting that I would receive all of her estate, providing I didn't do anything to forfeit it.

'I suppose that might be considered acquisitive, but I wasn't earning much money, not enough to set up a home, and I decided that I could hang on a bit longer and then do as I wished when she had gone.' He put his chin in his hand. 'Didn't think she would live so long, though,' he said dejectedly. 'She was nearly eighty when she died.'

Lily hid a smile. 'Well, you can kick over 'traces now,' she said. 'If she left you all her possessions.'

'I suppose I can.' His spirits didn't seem to lift. 'But I'm an ordinary kind of man, Miss Lily; never been very ambitious, and I don't really know what to do next.'

The door bell pealed. Henry drained his glass and got to his feet. 'I'll be off,' he said. 'You don't want to hear about me. That's the thing about Betty, you see. She always listens to me.'

He didn't say if he'd come back tomorrow, Lily worried as she let him out and another gentleman in. Perhaps I'd better fetch Betty back.

There were a lot of customers that night. Some were regulars, others were strangers. One man in particular seemed familiar, but Lily couldn't place him. She sent him upstairs with Mary but he didn't stay long; nor did he leave Mary anything extra, which most of them did.

'He was an odd sort of cove,' Mary told Lily. 'Real jumpy he was, as if he thought his wife might come in and catch him. Didn't tek his coat off neither, and kept asking me questions about how long I'd been working here and was I on 'streets; and he asked about you, did you have any favourite customers 'n' that.'

'I hope you told him I didn't.' She was alarmed and wondered why he wanted to know.

'I told him he'd have to ask you.' Mary sniffed. 'Said it was nowt to do wi' me what you did.'

Lily felt unsettled. There wasn't the usual jolly mood tonight: no Henry to play the piano, and neither Leo nor Kendall had come. They generally lightened the atmosphere, giving the feeling of a social occasion with their witty banter and repartee.

I'm fooling myself, she censured herself as she let a customer in. Pretending it's a party of friends getting together when it isn't at all. The men are here for one thing only and I'm degrading myself and the girls by tolerating it.

The next morning Jamie arrived with two young girls. 'Look after these two, will you, Lily? They've just got off a ship and don't speak English.'

'What am I supposed to do with them?' Lily gazed at them. One was dark-skinned; the other had high cheek-bones and an oriental look about her. They were about sixteen, she thought, and both seemed very frightened.

'Get 'em cleaned up and put 'em to work, what else?' he said sharply. 'That's why they're here.'

'But where have they come from? Have they worked before? They're very young.' She was suspicious that something was not quite right.

'Yeh, course they have. They came looking for work. A fellow I know brought them over from Holland. He picked 'em up in Rotterdam. He says there's loads o' women over there wanting to come over.'

'All right, leave them wi' me,' she said, anxious to be rid of him. 'They can have a bath and I'll find them some clean clothes for a start.'

The two girls were filthy and their clothing was torn. They huddled together and clutched their arms across their chests. Their hair was matted and unkempt. As soon as Jamie had gone they both started talking; their incomprehensible speech was racked with sobs and shouts, and the dark girl pushed at Lily with her fists.

'It's all right, it's all right,' she soothed them, and beckoned with her hand to lead them into the kitchen. They both turned and headed for the door which Lily had locked after Jamie, putting the key in her pocket. They screamed and shouted and rattled at the lock, banging with their fists against the wood.

'What's happening?' Cherie came out of the kitchen with a cup of coffee in her hand. She looked very sweet and innocent and had a sleepy glaze in her eyes, for she had only just got up. 'Who's this?'

The two girls dashed towards her, gabbling furiously and pointing towards the door. The oriental girl licked her lips as she smelt the coffee. Cherie held it out to her. 'Want some?' she said. 'It's onny just been made.'

The girl took it and at first sipped it slowly, as if she thought it might poison her, and then as she tasted the sweetness, for Cherie always added sugar, she drank it eagerly.

Mrs Flitt came out of the kitchen. 'Who's mekking all that row?' Lily smiled. Mrs Flitt was wearing a voluminous apron and a cotton cap on her head and looked a picture of domesticity. 'Who's this then?'

'Jamie brought them. But they obviously don't want to be here. Have you got more coffee, Mrs Flitt? I think they're in need of it.'

'A jug full,' she said, turning back into the kitchen. 'And some bread just out of 'oven.'

The two young women tore into the bread that was offered and drank the coffee jug dry. The dark girl kept clutching Cherie's arm and telling her something.

'I don't know what she's on about!' Cherie said. 'It's double Dutch!'

'Dutch anyway,' Mrs Flitt remarked. 'That's what it sounds like to me.'

'Jamie said they'd come over on a ship from Holland,' Lily told them. 'He said they'd come looking for work.'

'Not our kind o' work, I bet.' Lizzie spoke from the doorway where she was lazily leaning, still in her nightshift. 'Reckon they thought they were coming for some other kind o' work, domestic or summat like that.'

The two girls looked at Lizzie and then at Cherie, and back to Lizzie again. 'No! No!' the dark girl said, shaking both hands in front of her.

'You see!' Lizzie was quite unperturbed, though her mouth turned down. 'They can tell what I am just by looking at me.'

'What nonsense, Lizzie,' Lily said, though she was

inclined to agree. Lizzie looked as if she had been up all night, which was almost true. It was four o'clock before the last customer had gone. 'They're frightened. They don't understand 'language.'

Lizzie came into the kitchen, looked into the empty jug and sighed. 'Mek us a cup o' coffee, Mrs F, will you? No, 'fact of 'matter is, Lily, that our dear Jamie is up to summat. Word is out on 'street that foreign girls are being brought in from Germany and Holland, and women from Hull are being tekken over there. There's a ton o' money to be made. For 'men that trade 'em, that is,' she added cynically. 'Don't suppose lasses'll mek much and they'll probably finish up in one of 'canals if they don't do as they're told.'

'Lizzie!' Lily breathed. 'Is that true?'

'As true as I'm waiting here gasping for a cup o' coffee.' Lizzie sat down and put her feet up on a vacant chair. She looked at the strangers. 'They're scared all right. They probably thought it'd be a lark to work abroad and didn't know what they were getting into. They've got innocence written all over 'em; and they look different, don't they? Men'll pay a load o' money to bed girls like them.'

CHAPTER TWENTY-EIGHT

By midday the two girls had been bathed and fed and put into clean clothes which had belonged to Alice and Lizzie but which had been washed and mended and were fairly presentable. By means of sign language and gestures Lily told them that they should go with her. She pointed to both of them, at herself and then at the door, and Cherie nodded and grimaced to show it was all right.

'Where do you intend to take them?' Lizzie asked. 'Jamie's going to be right mad if they're not working for him.'

'Jamie can go jump in 'river,' Lily said vehemently. 'These girls are far from home and I've no means of getting them back, but I know somebody who might. I just hope they don't run off when we get outside. We'll never find them if they do.'

'I'll come with you, Lily,' Cherie said. 'They seem to trust me. I'll get my shawl and I'm ready.'

'If Jamie comes you don't know where I've gone or where the girls are either,' Lily told Alice and Lizzie. 'Are you listening, Mrs Flitt?'

'What, m'dear? Didn't hear a word you said. What girls? I ain't seen no girls.'

Lily nodded. She could trust them, she knew, but she was furious with Jamie.

The girls didn't attempt to escape as they went out but

walked at Cherie's side, holding her hands and looking nervously at the adjoining houses where the prostitutes sat on the doorsteps in the sunshine and shouted abuse at them as they walked by.

'Don't look at them, Cherie,' Lily said firmly. 'Keep your eyes in front. We don't want any trouble.'

But one of the women got up from her place and strolled towards them. 'Hey,' she said. 'What 'you up to then?' she asked Lily. 'You're running that brothel over yonder. Got some foreign lasses now, have you, tekking our jobs?' Her mouth and teeth were stained and flecked with brown strands as she chewed on a wad of tobacco. 'You should send 'em back where they've come from!'

'You're mistaken,' Lily said politely. 'They're not in your line o' work and neither am I.'

'What about her then?' The woman pointed with her thumb at Cherie, who shrank behind Lily.

'No. Her neither. Sorry.' She gave a thin apologetic smile. 'Can't stop to talk. Got an appointment.'

'Oh, aye! Wi' 'magistrate, I bet.'

Lily shook her head and they moved away. The dark girl grabbed her arm and urged her on, muttering anxiously. Lily patted her hand. 'It's all right,' she murmured. 'At least I hope it will be.'

They climbed into a hansom and Lily mused that she would soon have no money at all if she had to keep paying out fares. Jamie paid her a small percentage of the takings, and the customers usually gave her something as they took their leave; but after buying food she had little left. Still, she thought, I've never had money, so there's nothing different.

As the vehicle drew to a halt outside Hope House the foreign girls jabbered vigorously to each other, their eyes fearful. 'They're frightened,' Cherie said. 'They won't know where they're coming to.'

A maid opened the door and took them through to Mrs Thompson. 'Mrs Maddeson! I didn't expect to see you again quite so soon, though I think Betty is anxious to talk to you. She's come to a decision.'

'I didn't come to see Betty,' Lily said. 'I came about these two young women.' She turned to the two girls who were cowering behind Cherie.

'Cherie!' Mrs Thompson beamed. 'You've come back!'

'No, not me,' Cherie said hastily. 'It's these two.'

Lily explained the situation and Mrs Thompson frowned. 'It's not the first time this has happened,' she said. 'Just a moment.' She rang a hand bell and the maid returned. 'Ask Lottie to come through, will you?

'I have two other young women here at present,' she told Lily. 'They were induced to come to England from Holland. They were promised housekeeping situations, but on arrival were told that they were to work in brothels. One of the other prostitutes told them about us, and as soon as they could they made their escape. Unfortunately they spent some time within those establishments and one of them is extremely distressed after her experiences.'

A blonde woman of about twenty knocked and came into the room. 'You want to see me, yah?'

'We have two of your fellow countrywomen here, Lottie. Could you explain to them that they are safe and will be able to go home?'

Lottie turned to the girls and spoke quickly to them, whereupon they both burst out weeping and clung to her. She nodded and said something else and finally put her arms about them both. 'Come,' she said, and to Mrs Thompson said, 'I'll take them to see Ellie. They will know then that they have lucky escape. They are not hurt.'

They all went out of the room, but then the oriental girl came back. '*Sank* you,' she said to Lily. '*Sank* you.'

'I'm trying to arrange a passage back,' Mrs Thompson told Lily. 'The police have been informed and it's to be hoped they can catch the people who take such advantage of vulnerable young women.' She sighed. 'It's a very big problem. There are moves afoot to organize a society for the protection of foreigners who are stranded here, and to send them back home. Perhaps it's something that you might care to become involved in, Mrs Maddeson?'

Lily shook her head. 'I'm more concerned over local young women,' she said. 'Those that I know, anyway.'

'Like Betty, you mean?'

'Yes, like Betty. Girls who come into this kind of life through no fault of their own and are caught up in it with no means of getting out.'

'Like yourself, in fact?' Mrs Thompson said quietly.

'Yes,' she answered, her voice faltering. 'Just like me.'

When Betty appeared, she said that she would like to return to Leadenhall Square with Lily, and asked if Henry had been to the house. 'I'm going to change my life,' she told her. 'Mrs Thompson has shown me how to go about things and how to conduct myself and she says I can work here until I find something else.'

'You can,' Mrs Thompson confirmed. 'But I don't think you'll be long finding other employment. It might not be much to begin with, shop work or housekeeping, but you can stay here until you earn enough money for a room.'

Lily smiled. 'Thank you so much. We're very grateful. I allus thought that Betty had 'ability to pull herself up.'

'I have.' Betty nodded. 'But when I came here last time I was lonely and I couldn't be bothered to look for owt – anything else. Now, after being with 'other girls, even though we've had a laugh together, I've realized that what we do is degrading. We should all try to get out, cos it's humiliating and shameful and – and besides,' she bit on her lip and ran her fingers around the neck of her dress, 'I don't want to be with any other man but Henry.'

She looked at Lily, and said, 'I know what you're going to say – that he's a customer and I shouldn't get fond of him, but I couldn't help it and I have; so I'm coming back to explain to him that I won't be seeing him any more cos I'm leaving. I've seen 'error of my ways, just like that old parson in 'Market Place was allus telling us we should.'

I remember him, Lily thought as she waited for Betty. That first day I came to Hull. Billy Fowler gave him sixpence for the loan of his box. He said all he wanted was a square meal and a place in heaven. I wonder if he got either of them.

Betty was quiet on their walk back, but when they reached the square she said, 'Well, I shan't miss this pit at all, but I'll miss seeing 'girls, and especially you, Lily. I'll really miss you.'

'You can still come and see us,' she told her. 'And mebbe you'll persuade Cherie to go back with you to Mrs Thompson's.'

'Not without Lizzie,' Cherie broke in.

'You've got to stand on your own feet, Cherie,' Lily urged her. 'Lizzie has to look out for herself.'

'What do you mean?' Cherie's eyes became moist.

'I mean,' Lily said, as they reached the steps of the house, 'that Lizzie has to go forward before it's too late for her to do owt else with her life.'

'Are you saying that I'm holding her back?' Cherie muttered petulantly.

Lily patted her cheek before putting the key in the door. 'She won't think of doing anything that doesn't involve you. She worries about you and thinks that you can't manage without her.'

'I can't.' Cherie began to sniffle.

'You can,' Lily said firmly. 'Of course you can.'

As Lily changed for the evening, she thought about Cherie and how she clung to Lizzie, and then she thought of Daisy. Though her children were always in her thoughts, she was more anxious about Ted than she was about Daisy. At least I know where she is, she thought as she brushed her hair and pinned it up. And anyway, 'young minx has squirmed her way into Mrs Walker's employ without any help from me. She could always fend for herself.

She smiled as she remembered how Daisy, when still a baby, had learned to feed herself, pushing away from her breast and snatching a spoon from her hand to share in whatever Lily herself was eating. Whilst Ted, even at four, would wait expectantly for Lily to cut up his food or open his mouth like a little bird for her to feed him. I spoilt him, I suppose, she mused. I took comfort in doing more for him while Johnny was away instead of letting him grow up. She sighed. I wonder where he is. Poor lad, he'll be growing up now without me there to do for him.

The door bell rang and she frowned. Who's this? It's too early – there'll be nobody ready. She put the last pin in her hair and went to open the door. It was Henry.

'I know it's early, Miss Lily.' He clutched his bowler hat in his hands. 'But has Betty come back? I really do need to speak to her.'

'She has, as a matter of fact,' Lily said. 'But . . .' How do I tell him that she's not available any more, and how will Betty feel if he says he'll take one of the other girls instead? But then Betty came tripping daintily down the stairs which saved her from having to make any further response. Betty had her hair tied modestly in the nape of her neck and wore the grey dress that she had worn at Hope House.

'Hello, Henry. How nice to see you,' she said, and glanced at Lily, who indicated with a nod of her head that they should go into the parlour where a fire was already lit in anticipation of the evening's company. 'Won't you come through and have a cup of coffee?'

'Yes. Yes, thank you.' He handed Lily his hat in a distracted manner and followed Betty. 'It's very nice to see you too,' Lily heard him say. 'I've missed—'

Betty closed the door behind them. 'I'm pleased you came early, Henry,' she said. 'I was hoping to see you before I go.'

'Go?' Henry looked bewildered. 'Go where? I've come specially to tell you something and you're going out again!'

'It's not that I'm going out, Henry,' she said gently. 'It's just that I'm leaving. Leaving here. This house. I'm going to live somewhere else.' She looked down and locked her fingers together. 'I'm giving up this line o' work,' she whispered. 'I don't want to do it any more. I've rediscovered a pride in myself. I'm worth more than this degrading life I've been living.'

She raised her eyes to his and saw how Henry stared at her, his mouth slightly open. 'So I'm sorry,' she said. 'Really sorry that I won't be able to see you again, because I've enjoyed your company. You made me feel special, even though I know I'm not, and I'll always be grateful for that.' She put out her right hand. 'Goodbye, Henry. I hope you have a happy life.'

'W-wait. Wait!' Henry took her proffered hand and held on to it. 'But where are you going? And I wanted to tell – ask you something. And – you are special,' he stammered hoarsely. 'I wanted to tell you that you were – are. I came to ask if you would leave here. I can't bear to think of you being with other men.'

They gazed at each other and she waited for him to continue, but he didn't, seeming to be lost for words. 'I won't be with any others, Henry,' she said softly. 'I just said I'm giving up. I'll not sleep with another man until I marry.'

He gave a small moan. 'Betty! You're not getting married? But *I* want to marry you. That's why I came. That's why I was away. I've been to talk to the bank about my inheritance and I've been to see about renting a house.' His eyes filled with tears. 'Give him up,' he choked. 'And marry me!'

Betty took a deep shuddering breath. 'I didn't say I was *getting* married.' She gave a little hiccuping laugh. 'What I should have said was that I won't sleep with another man until I *get* married.'

'So you're not? So will you?' He knelt down on one knee. 'Will you marry me, Betty? I love you and I'll try to make you happy.'

'But don't you mind about me being – you know, a . . .'
She shrugged; there was no point in evading it. 'A tart? A prostitute? I've sold my body for money!'

He clambered to his feet. 'I wouldn't have met you, would I, if you hadn't been? I might never have known such delight, such happiness.'

'You mean it, don't you?' she said slowly. 'It's more than I ever hoped for. More than I ever thought I deserved.'

He kissed her cheek. 'You deserve everything you wish for and I'll try to give you it. A home. Children.'

'Children!' Tears cascaded down her face. 'To make up for my little Tommy.'

'Yes.' He kissed away her tears. 'To make up for. Not to replace. So is it yes?'

CHAPTER TWENTY-NINE

Lily and the girls were thrilled for Betty. 'I can't believe it,' Alice croaked the next morning when Lily broke the news. 'Oh, Lily. Do you think there's hope for 'rest of us?'

Lily grinned. 'I have to say quite honestly, Alice, that I don't think Leo is 'marrying kind.'

'No, you're right,' Alice agreed. 'He's too old.' She pouted. 'Mebbe he'll remember me in his will.'

'No chance of that either,' Lizzie remarked. She was sitting with her legs draped over the arm of a chair. She looked tired and pale and though she had said she was pleased at Betty's prospects, she hadn't been as enthusiastic as Alice or Cherie. 'I think Leo would drop you, or anybody else for that matter, if it suited him.'

'You're such a killjoy,' Alice complained. 'It doesn't do any harm to dream.'

Lizzie shook her head and then got up. 'I'm a realist,' she muttered. 'No point in dreaming.' Lily thought that she seemed keyed up about something. She's never jealous of Betty's good fortune? Not Lizzie.

'And anyway,' Lizzie went on, 'it's a million to one chance that summat like that'll happen again. It's just a fairy tale and Betty's found her prince. But it won't happen to you or me, Alice, so don't get your hopes up. Betty's different from us and she's not been in this game for long.' She looked searchingly at Alice, who was very pale and languid.

'We're just whores, you and me. We're fit for nowt else but men's pleasure.'

'Lizzie!' Lily admonished her. 'Don't talk like that. Of course you are.'

'No, we're not. Sorry, Lily.' Lizzie swallowed and when she spoke again her voice was husky. 'We've got to accept facts. We're stuck in this hellhole for good.' She went towards the door. 'I'm going out. I'll be back later.'

Lily frowned. It was raining and Lizzie hated going out in bad weather. 'Are you going far?' she asked.

'No. I just need some air.'

'I'll come with you.' Cherie got up from her chair. 'It won't tek me long to get dressed.'

'No.' Lizzie was sharp in her response. 'I need to be on me own.'

'Oh!' Cherie slid back down into her seat. 'All right,' she said in a small voice.

'There are times when we don't want company,' Lily said after Lizzie had gone. 'Is Lizzie worried about something?'

Cherie shrugged. 'Don't know. But she wouldn't tell me anyway. She allus hides 'worst things from me.'

'She's been out of sorts for a day or two,' Alice said grumpily. 'Sometimes there's no pleasing her. Do you think it's true what she said, Lily? About her and me not being fit for owt else but this life?' She coughed and winced. 'I get ever such a pain when I cough,' she murmured.

'Did you go to see Mr Walker?' Lily asked her, ignoring her question, for how could she answer it. 'I said you should go.'

'No.' Alice leaned her head on the back of the chair. 'I didn't have 'energy. I'm allus too tired. I've to save up my strength for when customers come. I hope Leo comes tonight. He doesn't tek a lot o' pleasing.'

Lily felt restless and anxious. Something was not quite right. It was unlike Lizzie to go out during the morning and Alice looked so pale and drawn Lily was sure she was

231

ill. She also had to break the news to Jamie that Betty had left and he would be angry about that.

He was and reacted strongly, blaming her and saying that she encouraged the girls to get out of the business. 'Bring them foreign lasses downstairs for me to see,' he told her. 'I'm bringing some new customers tonight and they can go with 'em.'

'They're not here,' she said. 'They've gone. Slipped out of 'door when my back was turned,' she lied.

'Damn and blast your eyes,' he swore. 'I paid good money for them! You should've looked after 'em better. I'll tek it out of your wages,' he bellowed. 'It'll tek me weeks to get any more girls like them.'

'Well don't bring any back here,' she shouted back. 'They're too young. Those girls hadn't been in this vile trade! They were innocent.'

He put his face close to hers. 'That's why I brought 'em,' he said in a vicious whisper. 'But they were old enough. I'll not bring anybody under sixteen.'

'You say you won't.' Lily gritted her teeth in temper. 'But sooner or later somebody will ask you to and you will. You'll be tempted and I'm telling you now, *don't* bring them here!'

He stabbed a finger at her. 'And I'm telling *you*! Don't go too far or you'll be out.' He indicated the door. 'I gave you a roof over your head, don't forget, and I can put you out into 'street as soon as I like.'

He would too, she thought, as he slammed out of the house. He wouldn't care. She thought of what Jamie's mother had said about him, that he would turn her out if he thought she was getting the upper hand.

Mary and Sally arrived in the early evening. 'Can we work here tonight, Lily?' Mary asked. 'It's raining cats and dogs out there.'

'And there are a couple of foreign ships just in,' Sally added. 'All 'whores in town are waiting for 'em.'

'Yes.' Lily nodded. She didn't mind these two so much,

and they were short of girls with Betty gone and Lizzie not yet back from wherever she had gone this morning. 'Jamie said he was bringing some new customers so go and get changed.' The girls were not allowed to go out in any of the better clothes but had to keep them only for use at the house. She hoped that Rena might exchange them for others some time.

'Where do you think Lizzie's got to?' she asked Cherie. 'She's been gone all day.'

'I don't know,' Cherie said. 'I'm getting bothered about her.'

Lizzie had seemed very dejected, Lily remembered. But surely not because of Betty? She wouldn't – she wouldn't do anything drastic, would she? she asked herself.

Lizzie still hadn't come back by the time the customers started arriving. Alice went straight upstairs with one of the new gentlemen, but the others seemed content to have a glass of wine and chat with Cherie, Mary, Sally and Lily. Then the door bell rang and Kendall arrived.

'Lizzie's not here,' Lily told him pleasantly. 'I'm not expecting her back until late.'

He grunted. 'I can't wait,' he said. 'I'm expected at home. Who've you got, then? What about that girl – Alice, is it? Pale face – fair hair.'

'She's busy at 'minute,' Lily said, hating this man, but hating herself more. 'Sally is free.'

'All right.' He took off his coat and top hat and handed them to her. 'Fetch her.'

She wanted to spit at him. He didn't give a thought to these girls. They were here just to be used. All he cared for were his own carnal desires.

'Is Leo here?' he asked her.

'No,' she said stiffly. 'We haven't seen him all week.'

'Huh.' He gave a thin smirk. 'Getting too old, I suspect.'

Lily didn't answer; it didn't do to discuss the clients. She excused herself to fetch Sally, who was in the kitchen eating a hunk of bread.

'Kendall usually sees Lizzie,' she whispered to her. 'If you're not comfortable with him mek an excuse to come down.'

Sally wiped crumbs from her mouth. 'What do you think I am?' she said caustically. 'I'm not likely to turn down his money, am I? I'm better off in here than out on 'street.'

Lily shrugged and turned away. She could help some people, she thought, but there were others who didn't want her help. She watched as Sally joined Kendall in the hall and saw how she gave him a saucy wink and tucked her arm into his as she took him upstairs; saw too how his face brightened and how he licked his lips as she murmured something in his ear.

Someone was playing the piano and she peeked into the parlour. One of the new men was sitting on the stool playing with one hand. Cherie was on his knee, her fingers on the keys and the man's free hand over hers guiding it to pick out the notes.

Lily quietly closed the door on them and leaned her head against it. She swallowed, close to tears. Was this the beginning for Cherie? Was she about to be seduced by some man's endearments? She had done her best to protect her, but how could she continue? She was working in a brothel and men expected the services of such.

She heard a tapping on the front door. She took a breath and went to open it, wondering why whoever it was hadn't rung the bell. Somebody new, she thought. But it wasn't anyone new and it wasn't a man. It was Lizzie. Lizzie leaning on the door jamb, her face pale as death and soaked to the skin.

'Whatever's happened, Lizzie? Where've you been? Have you had an accident?'

Lizzie shook her head and all but fell into Lily's arms. Lily practically carried her into her own room, the nearest to the front door, and helped her into a chair, unfastening her wet shawl and taking off her boots. Lizzie started to sob. 'Don't tell 'others I'm here, will you? I don't want 'em to know. Don't tell Cherie!'

'I won't. I won't,' Lily comforted her. 'But you have to tell me or else how can I help you?'

'Nobody can help me.' Her body was racked with sobs. 'I'm done for this time, Lily. I'll end up in 'workhouse.'

The front door bell rang and Lizzie clung to Lily's skirt. 'Don't tell anybody I'm here,' she beseeched her. 'Please! I can't work tonight.'

'I won't,' Lily whispered. 'But I have to go to 'door. I'll be back in a minute. Get into my bed.'

Lily went to the door to greet a regular customer and take him through to the parlour, where Mary invited him to take a glass of wine. Alice came downstairs and sweetly said goodbye to her customer, who took out his pocket book to pay. He gave Lily an additional half-guinea and whispered to her that he had given Alice a shilling. How generous, she thought cynically as she closed the door on him, and on impulse gave Alice the half-guinea.

'Put it away,' she murmured. 'That's between you and me, Alice. Now will you go and entertain them in 'parlour and don't let anybody tek Cherie upstairs.'

Alice beamed at her. 'Thanks, Lily. You're an angel. And don't worry about Cherie. I'll get her to mek us all some coffee.'

Lily went back to her room. Lizzie had stripped off all of her wet clothes and climbed into Lily's bed where she lay shivering. 'I'll get you a hot drink,' Lily told her. 'But do you want to tell me what happened? I thought you'd fallen in 'river.'

'I nearly did.' Lizzie's mouth trembled. 'Jump in, I mean, not fall. I've never felt so low, Lily. Never in my life. But then I thought about Cherie, and how she needed me, and about you, and how I'd be letting you down.' She started to weep again. 'And I hadn't 'courage either, that's top 'n' bottom of it. I'm just a coward.'

'No you're not.' Lily smoothed her wet hair, which was

starting to spiral into dark curls. 'You're 'bravest lass I know. You don't ever let owt get you down and God knows we've all got good reason. But why now?' she asked softly. 'What's happened to distress you? Not Betty? You're not upset that she's gone and you're still here?'

'No.' Lizzie gave a choking laugh. 'No, I'm glad for her and I hope she'll be happy wi' Henry.' She wiped her tears on the sheet. 'He's so nice he'd drive me barmy, but he's just right for Betty.'

She half sat up, leaning on her elbow. Her bare shoulders had plumped out since she had come here and were smooth and soft. She's so young and lovely, Lily thought as she gazed at her. Yet so hardened and bitter. Surely there's more for her in life than this?

'I'm pregnant, Lily,' she said quietly. 'That's where I've been today, trying to get rid of it. I've tried myself, but it's too late. Everywhere I've been they said they wouldn't tek 'chance of me bleeding to death.' She was quieter now and more composed, though she kept giving deep sighs as if she couldn't take a breath.

'It's not 'first time,' she admitted. 'It's one of 'hazards of this job. I had an abortion when I was fifteen, but I've never had a proper flux since then and so I was caught out this time. I haven't even been sick. So,' she said. 'I'll have to have it and then give it away or hope it's a still birth.'

'Don't!' Lily said. 'Don't hope that! It's a life when all's said and done.'

Lizzie shook her head. 'What sort of a life will it have? What can I offer it? Nowt, that's what!'

'Love,' Lily whispered. 'That's your gift to a child, no matter how the begetting of it.'

Lizzie lay down again. 'Can I stay here till everybody's gone?'

'Course you can.' Lily smiled down at her. 'In any case, Kendall's in your room wi' Sally.'

'She's welcome to him,' Lizzie muttered. 'It's probably his bairn anyway. Damned barbarian!'

'Try to get some sleep,' Lily said. 'I'll lock 'door so's you're not disturbed and I'll come in later with a hot drink.'

Outside her door was a curtain pole holding a dark velvet curtain. Usually she left it draped to one side, but now she pulled it across, hiding the door so no one would disturb Lizzie. What shall we do, she wondered as she went towards the parlour, where she could hear the sound of singing. Alice had a sweet clear voice and one of the customers was singing with her. Then the door bell rang again.

This'll be Jamie back again, I expect. He'll want to know if we're making him a fortune. She opened the door ready with a sarcastic retort, but stopped and took a breath. It was the police and they pushed her aside as they barged in.

'We've reason to believe you're running a disorderly house.' The sergeant, the same one who had been here previously, spoke brusquely. 'And we need to question you, and all who are in here.'

CHAPTER THIRTY

Lily was shocked into silence as the police charged in, making for the parlour and the stairs. Then she said hoarsely, 'We've just got a few friends in, that's all.'

'Pull the other leg,' the sergeant said, bringing out a notebook from beneath his rain cape. 'We've reason to believe there's been disorderly conduct in this establishment.'

Lily put her hands on her hips. 'And what's that supposed to mean?'

'Noise,' he said, not looking at her, 'riotous behaviour, conduct likely to disrupt 'neighbourhood.'

Lily laughed; she couldn't help it even though she felt nervous. 'This neighbourhood!'

'Yes, madam.' He took a pencil from his pocket and began to write. 'Residents of Lowgate have complained to 'magistrates of importuning females and their indecent conversation in 'area of Leadenhall Square.'

Well, I can understand that, she thought. If I were a respectable citizen of Hull I wouldn't want to live round here. 'But no one has complained of *us*,' she said. 'Who would do that? We live very quietly.'

He raised his bushy eyebrows. 'I don't mek rules.' He handed her a slip of paper. 'I just carry out orders and I'm here to tell you to be at 'magistrates' court on 'date so written here. Can I have your name, please?'

'You know my name,' she said. 'You took it last time you came on a fool's errand.'

He looked at her without speaking. 'Lily Fowler,' she said faintly. I'll damn Billy Fowler's name for ever, she silently vowed. He's brought me to this. What shame.

A constable came downstairs with a lopsided smirk on his face. 'Nobody up there, sarge.'

Kendall's up there with Sally, Lily thought. He's bought him off! Damn him! It would be almost worth going to court just to see him there as well. 'I know you,' she said abruptly, and then stopped. He was the man who had been here one night whom Mary had said was an odd cove. Now she realized that he was one of the constables who had come before. But how could she confront or accuse him? He knew they were running a brothel and he would also know that they couldn't be prosecuted for it. There wasn't a law against it, so they would find some other reason to charge her.

Another constable came out of the parlour. 'Drinking and playing music in here, sir. I've tekken names.'

'There's no law against that,' Lily said indignantly.

'Intoxicating liquor,' the sergeant muttered, writing in his book. 'Selling without a licence.'

'No, we're not!' She almost shrieked at him. 'There's no money changed hands. Who's put you up to this? Why don't you go down 'street to 'other houses and see what they get up to?'

The police officer put away his notebook. 'Have done!' He wore a satisfied smile as he spoke. 'We've done a round-up. That's why we're here. We're visiting every house in 'square.' He tipped his top hat with his forefinger. 'I'll wish you goodnight, *madam*,' he said with heavy emphasis.

She closed the door behind them. The police had no valid reason to come here, she thought. Unless one of the other women who lived in the square had suggested they should. Perhaps out of spite because we don't talk to them. Some of the women used to shout after her if they saw her; derogatory expressions like 'stuck up bitch' and 'Lady Whore'.

They called after Lizzie too, who always retaliated and gave them back a mouthful of abuse which made Lily cringe. Or, she thought, maybe a client had spoken of them and word had got back to the police.

She gave a deep sigh and looked at the warrant. She had to appear at the magistrates' court the following day. At least they didn't arrest me, she considered. I could have been spending the night in a cell.

Two of the customers appeared from the parlour. 'Erm, can't stay, I'm afraid,' one said. 'Have to be off.' The other one hesitated for a moment, then said, 'Well, I'm going to stay. They'll not prosecute me and you'll need the money to pay the fine. Come on,' he said to Alice and Cherie. 'No point in wasting time.'

'Not Cherie,' Lily said. 'I need her for something.'

The man shrugged and went upstairs with a reluctant Alice.

'Mek a pot o' chocolate, will you, Cherie?' Lily said. 'Lizzie's back and in my room. She's not well.'

She pulled aside the curtain and opened the door to her room. It was in darkness; Lizzie must have turned out the lamp.

'It's all right, Lizzie,' she whispered, fumbling on the desk for a candle and match. 'It's onny me.'

Lizzie put her head above the covers. 'It was 'police, wasn't it? I'd recognize 'sound of them clodhopping boots anywhere.'

'Yes.' Lily held up the lighted candle. 'But they've gone now. I'm accused of keeping a disorderly house. I've to appear in court tomorrow.' Her voice trembled no matter how she tried to keep calm. What if Daisy heard of it, or Mrs Walker? Would her daughter be dismissed because of her?

Lizzie sat up, frowning. 'Why here?' she muttered. 'This is a well kept house. Somebody's got a grudge.'

'That's what I thought.' Lily sat on the edge of the bed. 'But I can't think who. One of 'customers has left; he decided not to stay, but 'others are still here, including Kendall. Constable who went upstairs came down and said there was nobody there.'

'Bribe!' Lizzie said caustically. 'Not that Kendall'd have been prosecuted; men get away with it every time. But 'word would have been put about that he was here, and he wouldn't want his wife finding out what he gets up to.'

'So Sally's all right, and Alice, Cherie and Mary were only singing.'

'They could mek summat o' that,' Lizzie said. 'They'd say they were singing vulgar ditties.'

'It must have been 'other women who told of us,' Lily said. 'Sergeant said they'd been doing a round-up.'

'Meks us sound like a pack o' horses, doesn't it?' Lizzie gave a wry grin. 'Fillies!' Her grin faded. 'And that's what we are.'

Cherie knocked on the door. She'd put a pot of chocolate on a tray with two cups and saucers. 'Where've you been, Lizzie?' she said. 'I've been that bothered about you.'

Lily glanced at Lizzie and raised her eyebrows. 'Lizzie will tell you later,' she said. 'Right now she needs to rest.'

Lizzie took the cup from Cherie and sipped the chocolate. 'That's good,' she sighed, and took another sip. 'No, I'll tell her now,' she said, 'and get it over with. I'm pregnant. I've been out all today trying to find somebody to help me get rid of it. But there was nobody, so I'm stuck wi' it.'

Cherie's mouth opened and then closed. Then she whispered, 'I'll help you look after it, Lizzie. I like little bairns. And – and I'll go wi' men instead of you, or we can tek it in turns once you've had 'babby. We'll need 'money to feed and clothe it.'

Lizzie nodded, but tears trickled down her cheeks. 'Yes,' she said huskily. 'I suppose we could do that.'

The next morning Lily presented herself at the door of the magistrates' court. She had dressed neatly in her grey gown and a plain bonnet and the usher asked politely, 'What can I do for you, miss?'

When she showed him the papers he seemed taken aback. 'Would you come with me, Mrs Fowler?' he said. 'There's someone here you might like to speak to. Your case won't be heard just yet. There are twenty women before you.' He must have noticed her surprise for he added, 'Some are charged with robbery and violence and will be heard first.'

He took her along a corridor and she heard the raucous sound of singing and swearing coming from a room off it. She shrank back. Dear God, she thought. Please don't put me in there with those women. They'll eat me alive. But he continued along another passageway and opened a door. 'Wait here and I'll send somebody to you.'

He locked the door behind him and Lily sank down on to a wooden chair, one of two which were placed at a table. There was nothing else in the room: no furnishings and no curtains against the narrow barred window. She clasped her hands together. What if I'm sent to prison? I'll be in a worse position than when I first came to Hull.

She'd waited about fifteen minutes before she heard a key turn in the lock. The usher opened the door to admit a man, then closed it behind him and locked it again.

'Good morning, Mrs Fowler.' The man greeted her pleasantly. 'My name is Thomas Fulton. I'm sorry you find yourself in such an unfortunate situation. The usher asked if I would speak to you as you didn't appear to him to be the usual type of offender. I'm generally here at the courts when charges of indecency or disorderly conduct are heard.'

'Are you a lawyer, Mr Fulton?' Her voice trembled. 'Can you help me?'

'I'm not a lawyer, Mrs Fowler. I'm a member of the Society

for Enforcing and Improving Laws for the Protection of Women.' He gazed at her solemnly. 'But I might be able to help you. Would you like to tell me your story?'

She told him, as succinctly as she could, for she was aware that she might be called before the magistrate at any time, all that had happened to her since she came to Hull with Billy Fowler; of Jamie paying her husband and of her being obliged to him for giving her shelter after she had lost the child. He made a moue with his lips when she mentioned Jamie's name as if he knew him, although he made no comment, either then or even when she said that she had in fact been running a brothel.

'One of my girls has done well,' she choked, for she felt very emotional. 'She's going to marry one of her clients. I've rescued two young foreign girls. If I could onny do something about 'others – well, three of them anyway – I'd feel that all of this hadn't been in vain.'

'Tell me, Mrs Fowler,' he asked quietly. 'Amongst your clients, do you ever have any eminent gentlemen, or are they mostly from the lower classes?'

'Oh, they're gentlemen mostly,' she said, wiping her eyes. 'So called,' she added bitterly. 'Men of law and business, though we've had Navy men. Officers, not crew.' As she spoke she thought of Leo. He was a magistrate. Suppose he was to try her case? He would never admit to knowing her, of course.

'If by chance,' Fulton was speaking, 'just supposing that a clerk to the court or a magistrate or lawyer might have been a client and you saw him here today. What would you do? Would you greet him as if you knew him or would you pretend that you'd never met him?'

She gazed miserably at him. Whatever she did, the odds were against her. There was the police constable who had visited the house. Was he gathering evidence or indulging himself? There was Kendall; he certainly wouldn't stand up for her. She was convinced that Mr Fulton was going to advise her not to display any recognition of such men. 'I'd have to treat him like a stranger,' she muttered. 'What else could I do?'

'Stand up to them,' he said severely. 'Women need greater protection. There should be no need for women to prostitute themselves just to survive. Laws should be implemented to crush this vile trade.'

'I know,' she said irritably. 'But as long as there are men willing to pay for their services, then there'll allus be women willing to take their money. It's a vicious circle, Mr Fulton, and not one that we can change, no matter our good intentions.'

He gazed at her. 'You're an articulate woman, Mrs Fowler. We could do with you on our side. These men should be denounced.'

She heaved a sigh. 'I'm doing my best,' she said. 'But I can't do it from inside a prison cell.'

The key turned in the lock and the usher opened the door. 'Mrs Fowler is to be called next,' he announced. 'Would you come with me, please?'

Lily could hardly stand. Her legs felt like jelly and she swayed from side to side as she followed the usher back down the corridor. The women in the cells were still shouting and some were singing in a raucous drunken manner. Have they been here all night? she wondered. Were they drunk when they were brought in?

'They're regulars,' the usher commented. 'They'll spend a night or two in jail and then go back on 'streets again.' He glanced back at her. 'This your first time?'

'Yes,' she said hoarsely. 'And I hope it's my last.'

She was led into a crowded courtroom as two street women were being brought out. 'Don't bring them before me again,' the magistrate called out. 'I don't want them in my court with their filthy obscene language!'

Lily raised her head and looked towards the bench. It was Leo, and she didn't know whether to be glad or sorry.

CHAPTER THIRTY-ONE

Lily licked her dry lips as she stood in the dock and Leo Leighton sifted through the notes in front of him. At his nod the clerk to the court asked Lily to give her full name.

'Lily Fowler,' she whispered.

'Would you speak up, please,' Leo said, with no sign of recognition or any other emotion on his face.

I wonder if he's nervous of what I might reveal, Lily thought. Though I suppose he's used to accusations or abuse, especially from women like those who have just left. 'Lily Fowler,' she said more loudly.

'And you live in Leadenhall Square?' He glanced again at the notes in front of him. 'Have you lived there for very long?'

'Only a few months, sir.'

'Have you fallen on hard times which have necessitated your living in such an undesirable place?'

'Yes, sir,' she said. 'I was left stranded in Hull without any support.'

'Have you a husband?'

'I did have. But after he abandoned me I heard that he'd died.'

Leo leaned forward. 'Your husband left you here? Why was that?'

'He brought me from Holderness and sold me in Hull market. He wanted rid of me.' She tried to swallow but her throat was parched. 'Might I have some water, please?'

Leo indicated that water be brought. He frowned. 'He sold you? To whom?'

'A resident of Hull, sir, who gave me shelter. I – I'd just lost a child; it didn't go full term,' she explained. 'I was desperate. I didn't know anyone here. Didn't know where to turn.'

Leo ran his hand over his chin. He had said on first meeting her that she was a remarkable woman and asked what she was doing in Leadenhall Square; now she was telling him.

She took a drink of water from the glass that was brought and gazed directly at him as he said, 'You stand accused of running a disorderly house and selling intoxicating liquor without a licence. Is this true?' He too raised his head and gazed at her.

'No, sir. It's a quiet house. There's no riotous behaviour from any of our visitors. We do have music; piano playing,' she added evenly, 'and some singing, and we offer our guests a glass of wine or beer. But there's no charge for that.'

She thought she saw Leo's lips twitch when she mentioned the piano and was rather cheered by that. Perhaps after all he would treat her leniently, even though she expected him to follow the rules.

'I would have thought, looking at you, that there would be other avenues of employment open to you, without your having to stoop to the level of running such an establishment; even though,' he consulted his notes again, 'the police state that it falls into a category between a first and second class house and does not contain any criminal element or employ street walkers.'

Lily's mind raced. Lizzie, Alice and Betty had all walked the streets, as Mary and Sally still did. 'The girls don't go out on 'streets, sir,' she said. 'They feel safer inside. One of them had been beaten up; she's very nervous, but she has no other means of surviving. It's very hard for young women,' she said passionately. 'If they can't get work in a factory or a mill then they can't pay rent for a room or buy food.' She spread out her hands. 'How are they supposed to live? Workhouse won't allus tek 'em. They wouldn't tek me because I was from out of 'district.' There was a catch in her voice which she couldn't control. 'They turned me away and I was in labour.'

There was a silence in which no one spoke or shuffled or rustled a paper as Lily wiped her eyes; then the magistrate said quietly, 'It seems that you have been badly done by, Mrs Fowler, and I don't wish to add to your misfortune. I have here a recommendation from Thomas Fulton, who represents a society which aims to improve the laws regarding the legal protection of women and considers that this case should not have been brought to court, and I am inclined to agree with him. However . . .'

Lily had begun to feel an uplifting of her spirits as he spoke, but now it was checked as Leo went on, 'It is our duty to stamp out this trade in the town. Women so employed attract criminal elements; in fact many of the establishments are run by unscrupulous men. You have not denied that young women in the house are employed in prostitution and you are to be recommended for your honesty; but as a deterrent to others who might seek to make their living in such a manner, I shall order you to pay a fine of five pounds for a first offence, the charge being that of supplying alcohol without a licence. You may stand down.'

Lily stared across at the bench. *Hypocrite*, was her first thought, but as she was led out of court she wondered whether, had it been any other magistrate, the fine would have been greater. I suppose he had to make an example of me, but how could he say such things? How could he let those words fall from his lips? *It is our duty to stamp out this trade*! When he has been enjoying the pleasures of it!

Thomas Fulton was waiting for her at the outer door. He gave a thin smile. 'You got off quite lightly,' he said.

'You think so, do you?' she answered bitterly. 'Five pounds is a fortune and I don't know how I shall find it.' She gave a disgruntled snort. 'I suppose I could sell myself to earn it. It's a vicious circle, Mr Fulton. If women are fined for such offences how else can they afford to pay?'

He nodded. 'I know,' he said. 'I do understand. That's why the laws have to be changed. And they will be. In time.'

'But not in time for me,' she hissed. 'I have a week to pay.'

'My society does have a little money with which to help,' he said. 'I'll put it to committee and get in touch with you before then. But believe me when I say that you did get off lightly. Had it been another magistrate you might have gone to prison. This one had some sympathy with your circumstances.'

'Yes,' Lily said with some irony. 'He obviously did!'

They stepped outside the courthouse together and Mr Fulton greeted a man waiting on the footpath. 'Good day to you, Walker,' he said, and Lily took a sudden breath as Charles Walker turned round. He lifted his hat. 'Good day,' he answered. 'Good morning, Mrs Maddeson. Or should I call you Mrs Fowler for the time being?'

Thomas Fulton raised his eyebrows enquiringly and she looked from one man to the other. Did Mr Walker know why she was here outside the court? If he didn't then she would have to tell him before Mr Fulton did.

'I'm using Fowler for this,' she said, her voice trembling. 'I don't wish to foul my first husband's name. It's very dear to me, and I'm in a great deal of trouble due to Billy Fowler.'

'So I understand,' he said sympathetically. 'I belong to the same society as Fulton, and he told me of your difficulties whilst you were before the magistrate.'

'What about Daisy?' she whispered. 'You won't tell her? Please don't!'

'Certainly not,' he said. 'I have no intention of telling her, but I would like you to come home with me to talk to my wife.'

'I'll be off then,' Fulton interrupted. 'Please excuse me, but I've some urgent business to attend to.'

Lily was horror-struck. How can I talk to Mrs Walker? She's sure to dismiss Daisy the instant she hears about me. What'll I do then? Daisy will have to come to Leadenhall Square and live with me there.

'You don't need to worry,' Charles Walker was saying. 'You'll find her well disposed towards you.'

'I don't think so,' she said, as he firmly took her arm and led her towards King Street.

'Come in, Mrs Maddeson.' Mrs Walker greeted her at her sitting room door; there was no sign of Daisy or Molly. Mr Walker had taken her through from the shop to the house himself. Oliver was in the shop and he looked up and smiled a greeting.

'I'm using Fowler now,' Lily told Mrs Walker.

'You can use whatever name you want,' Mrs Walker said abruptly. 'It doesn't matter to me.'

She was neatly though dowdily dressed in dark colours, and Lily thought she would be very handsome if she made more of her appearance. I wonder why she doesn't? She has a very handsome husband and Daisy said she had lovely underwear, so why not outer wear?

'There's coffee,' Mrs Walker said. 'Would you like some? I've sent Daisy out on an errand and I've told Molly I'm not to be disturbed.'

Lily frowned. 'Were you expecting me, Mrs Walker?'

'Oh, yes.' Mrs Walker poured the coffee. 'Whenever there's a worthwhile case my husband brings them here for me to talk to.' She handed Lily a cup and then sipped at her own. 'I'm to show them 'error of their ways.'

'You don't need to talk to me about that, Mrs Walker,' Lily said sharply. 'I know 'difference between what's right and what's wrong. I'm a grown woman, not a vulnerable young girl. All I'm concerned about just now is my daughter and that she doesn't find out about how I'm living.'

'I'll not tell her, you can be sure of that,' Mrs Walker said calmly. 'You need have no fears there.'

She drank again from her cup and Lily waited for her to continue.

'Do you want to know why I kept Daisy on?' she asked after a pause. 'Are you curious about that or just relieved that she's safe?'

'Well, both,' Lily admitted. 'At first it seemed as if you were against her stopping here. It was Mr Walker who said she could.'

'That's right, it was,' Mrs Walker said. 'I didn't want her. I felt resentful of her and jealous of you.'

'Why?' Lily asked softly. 'A woman in your position? You have so much more than I have.'

Mrs Walker reached forward as though to ring the servant's bell, and then abruptly sat back as if remembering that she had asked not to be disturbed. 'Because,' she said, 'if my daughter had lived she would have been about Daisy's age and I didn't want her reminding me of what I'd lost.'

She gave a smile which in spite of its wistfulness lit up her wan face. 'But Daisy could charm 'birds off a tree,' she said gently, in a voice so unlike the one she usually used that Lily was totally bemused.

'I'm sorry about your daughter,' she said. 'But you have a son and you know where he is. I've no idea where my son might be.'

Mrs Walker looked at her. 'Yes I have, and I'm very proud of him. He'll do well.'

Lily nodded. 'Like his father.'

Mrs Walker's head shot up abruptly and she glared at Lily. 'What do you mean?'

'I – I meant that he'll – I expect he'll do well at his studies and become an apothecary like his father . . .' her voice trailed away as Mrs Walker continued to stare.

'He's like me,' she said fiercely. 'Through and through.'
She lowered her voice. 'Shall I tell you something, Mrs
Maddeson – Mrs Fowler or whatever you call yourself.'

'Lily,' she answered on a breath. 'Call me Lily, if it's
easier.'

'Very well, Lily. I'm sick of this farce!' She licked her
lips and her eyes narrowed and Lily became uneasy. The
woman had become malicious, unhinged almost.

'Don't tell me anything you might regret,' she told her,
'though I'm not one to tittle-tattle.'

'Well, I'll tell you anyway.' Mrs Walker heaved a great
sigh and leaning back against her chair she closed her eyes
for a moment. When she opened them again she looked
straight at Lily, who saw how deep a blue the irises were,
and how long her lashes. 'Oliver is not my husband's son,
though neither of them know it.'

'Why are you telling me?'

'Because for years I've wanted to tell somebody and
there's never been anyone I saw fit to confide in.' She
closed her eyes again, and although Lily felt flattered that
she had been the one chosen she also felt uneasy with the
knowledge.

'I was working in Leadenhall Square when I met Mr
Walker,' Mrs Walker said, opening her eyes. 'In a house such
as the one you are in, though I imagine it was in a worse
condition. It was fit only for 'dregs – 'scum of humanity.'

Lily said nothing. What was there to say to such a
statement? But as the silence drew on, she ventured, 'So
Mr Walker rescued you from there?'

Martha Walker gave a throaty laugh. 'Rescued me! Ha!
He was a client!'

CHAPTER THIRTY-TWO

'Surprised are you, Lily? Doesn't seem 'type, does he? Pillar of society 'n' all that.'

'Nothing surprises me any more, Mrs Walker,' Lily answered. 'Though I have to say I didn't expect it – of either of you.'

Martha Walker gave a shrug. 'He doesn't frequent those places now – at least I don't think he does. He doesn't need to, not since he married me.' She lifted her chin and observed Lily closely as if gauging her reaction. Then she gave a lopsided smile. 'He wouldn't want anyone to know about it, but some do remember him. Jamie's mother, for instance.'

'Does she know about Oliver?'

'No, she doesn't, and I wouldn't tell her in case it got back to Jamie. He's a snake in 'grass as I'm sure you've found out. But Mr Walker,' she went on, 'although he's a very professional man, likes to keep in touch with that side of things, hence his involvement with 'society for 'protection of women.' She gave a caustic grunt. 'He gets some kind of thrill out of it, I expect, even though he doesn't touch 'em.'

'I don't want to hear any more, Mrs Walker.' Lily felt sickened. Charles Walker had been so kind to her and she had been about to bring Alice to him for a consultation. Now she couldn't. Was there not a man anywhere whom she could trust?

'I haven't finished.' Mrs Walker's eyes were wide, the pupils dark and large. 'I want to tell you about Oliver and the baby I lost. Sit down,' she said, for Lily had risen to leave. 'Please.'

Lily sat again. 'I can't stay long,' she said.

'I was expecting Oliver when Mr Walker first came to Leadenhall Square.' It was as if she hadn't heard Lily. 'I was lovely then, beautiful even, and I used to wear such pretty clothes.' She glanced down at her drab gown. 'I went to Rena's whenever I could afford it, and I looked after my things, dressed them up, you know. I had some pride. Mr Walker was taken with me right from 'start. Besotted, he was. Told me he wanted to save me from 'life I was living. So I said that I wanted to get out of that pit and make something of myself. I didn't tell him I was pregnant and you couldn't tell. I hadn't put on any weight.'

'Surely he must have guessed?' Lily said disbelievingly. 'He's an apothecary, for goodness' sake!'

Martha Walker laughed and shook her head. 'I told him I'd keep myself pure once I'd left. I knew he was mad for me and it paid off: he applied for us to get married straight away. Oliver was late and he never guessed.'

'But your little girl, the one who died?' Lily interrupted. In spite of not wanting to discuss what she considered a private matter, she was anxious to know about the baby who died, and how it tied in with Daisy, for whom she was now very concerned.

'There were about fifteen months between her and Oliver.' To Lily's surprise, Martha Walker's eyes filled with tears. 'I wanted—' There was a catch in her voice. 'I wanted a child by my husband. I was grateful to him for giving me a new life. It would have made us a proper family and it would've proved to him that I was done with 'old ways for ever.' She licked her lips. 'We loved her, but she didn't live long and Charles changed. He blamed me and he treats me like a whore again whenever we're alone.' She heaved a breath. 'But I have to dress in these dreary clothes so that no other man will be attracted to me.'

'How does Daisy come into it?' Lily asked. 'I don't understand.'

Mrs Walker stared at her. 'Well, don't you see? Eventually it will be like having a daughter here. She'll become part of our family.'

'But she's a servant, Mrs Walker.' Lily was aghast. 'And besides, she's my daughter, not yours.'

Mrs Walker gave her a condescending look. 'But you'd give her up. She'd have a much better life with us, and 'chance of a good marriage. Surely you'd agree to that?'

'Does Mr Walker know about your plan?' Lily asked faintly. 'Has he agreed to this without consulting me?' She's crazy, she thought. Unhinged. Why would she think I'd give Daisy up?

'Why, no! Not yet I haven't.' Lily knew then for sure that the woman was unbalanced. 'I haven't discussed it. I won't, not until Daisy is ready.'

Lily walked back towards Leadenhall Square in a daze, then abruptly turned round and went back in the direction of Rena's. Mrs Walker needed to talk to someone, she had said, and now so do I, she thought. I must try to find something good about this day for otherwise it'll be the second worst day of my life.

Rena was sitting in an easy chair in her shop. She had her feet up on a footstool but put them down as Lily entered.

'Please don't get up,' Lily said. 'I haven't come to buy anything. I've come to talk if you can spare me a minute.'

Rena waved a lazy arm towards another chair. 'Sit down, do. Trade is quiet today. The round-up by 'police has quietened everybody down. All my regulars, I mean.' She arched her fine eyebrows. 'I still have my fine ladies' maids coming in to sell me their mistresses' old gowns.'

'How does that work out?' Lily said curiously. 'Do they tek a commission for selling them?'

Rena laughed. 'Bless you, no. A lady gives her maid any old gowns she doesn't want any more, or which have been made over so often that she's sick of them. Then, because they're totally unsuitable for 'kind of life a maid leads, 'maid brings them in to me. I buy them and she keeps 'money.' She sighed. 'But then I have to unpick them and turn them into something unrecognizable.'

'Do you do your own sewing?' Lily asked.

'Oh, yes.' Rena nodded. 'I'm a good seamstress, and I should be sewing now instead of sitting here being lazy. But sometimes I want to do nothing! What I would like to do is go out of the shop for a day and see what's happening elsewhere. I'm fifty years old and tied to these four walls. You might think I'm lucky to be in such a good position; but I used to be an actress and led a varied and exciting life, and now I get so *bored*!'

Lily felt a flurry of hope. 'Would you ever consider taking on an assistant?'

'Couldn't afford to pay you, m'dear,' Rena said patiently. 'I've been asked countless times to take on young girls, but 'shop doesn't make enough to warrant anybody else's wages.'

'Not me!' Lily said. 'I don't understand fashion. But Lizzie,' she said. 'She does, and she can sew.' She gazed pleadingly at Rena. 'She's expecting a babby. She can't stay wi' us once Jamie finds out and there's onny 'workhouse for her.' She swallowed hard. 'She'd work for nothing. Just her bed 'n' board. And she'd be an asset. She's got such style.'

'But what would we do with a young baby here?' Rena objected, sitting up straight in her chair. 'I know 'girl you mean, and yes, she does have a certain style from what I've seen of her. Some women do. I had it myself when I was young.'

'You still do,' Lily murmured. 'And Lizzie does too. She trimmed an old hat of Mrs Flitt's, our cleaning woman; she used a scarf and pigeon feathers and you wouldn't have known it for 'same hat. Her dream – not that she's likely to achieve it – is to have her own shop. Selling new clothes,' she added, though not telling her that Lizzie had dismissed Rena's own stock as second-hand tat.

'Ah, well,' Rena said. 'I had that dream once, but it didn't materialize. I didn't have the money or anyone to help me.' She pondered awhile and then murmured, 'I feel sometimes that I haven't achieved what I'd have liked to. But I know nothing about children,' she added fervently. 'I couldn't cope if it cried.'

Lily waited, her heart pounding, for Rena to say more. She was considering the proposal, Lily could tell. Rena was gazing round her shop as if rearranging it; then she glanced towards the door which led to her private rooms. She looked up towards the ceiling, stroking her long neck as she thought.

'I do have a spare room as it happens,' she said at last. 'It's full of boxes and lengths of material that I keep thinking I'll fashion into something when I've time to spare or be bothered. Is the girl sick? Has she long to go?' she asked. 'I can't be doing with sickness.'

'No. She's very healthy. I didn't even know she was expecting. Knowing Lizzie as I do,' she added, 'she'll just get on with it. She wouldn't be a trouble.'

Rena toyed with the rings on her fingers and made expressive gestures with her lips, pouting and pressing them together. 'All right,' she said abruptly. 'Send her to see me. I'm not promising anything, mind. If we don't take to each other then the answer is no. If I say yes then she can stay for free and I'll feed her in exchange for help in the shop and some sewing. After she's given birth we'll review the situation, cos I'm not one for babies, as I said.'

Lily heaved out a sigh. '*Thank* you! Thank you so much. I'm sure you won't regret it.'

'I hope not,' Rena said wryly. 'You'll be to blame if I do.'

Lily smiled and rose to go. 'I shan't mind that. Were you never married, Rena? Did you never love a man?'

Rena started to shake her head, but then said, 'I did once love somebody, but he let me down very badly and I vowed that it wouldn't happen again. I can do without a man in my life.'

'Just like Lizzie then,' Lily murmured as she took her leave.

What will Jamie say? she wondered as she walked back. He'll be mad at me when Lizzie leaves. Whether Rena takes her on or not she'll have to go. He won't let her stay, not if she's not earning her keep. So that will mean just Alice and Cherie left of the original girls, and Alice isn't well. I heard her prowling about during the night as if she couldn't sleep. Cherie, well, how much longer can I keep her safe?

A platoon of soldiers came marching towards her and she stood by the tower of St Mary's church to watch and let them pass. The road was very narrow here and Mrs Flitt had told her there had been talk of widening the road and building a new town hall for years, but the plan had never been developed. So many old buildings and narrow streets, she thought as she saw the build-up of hansom cabs and horses and carts also waiting for the platoon to pass. How I miss the open views of the countryside and the salty smells of the sea.

Though the soldiers marched eyes front as they came past, one of them, without moving his head, glanced her way and gave her a saucy wink. He was very young and an unbidden spurt of tears came to her eyes as she was suddenly reminded of Johnny. He had been seventeen when he joined the army. He could see no future in being a farm labourer, he'd said, and besides, he wanted some adventure. We were both so young, she thought, as tears ran down her cheeks. Perhaps we should have waited. But he was so eager to be married. He wanted to be sure that I'd wait for him, he said; didn't want me to love anyone else whilst he was away. I wouldn't have done, Johnny. I never did. But you were away so long. You had no idea how hard it was for me to bring up two children without you.'

She gave a small sob and turned abruptly as someone took hold of her elbow. 'Are you all right, Mrs Fowler?' a quiet voice asked. 'Can I help you?'

It was Thomas Fulton. He wore a dark frock coat and top hat and carried a small leather case. 'You seem distressed. Are you still anxious about finding the money for the fine? I told you we could probably help you.'

'No.' She sniffed, feeling in her pocket for a handkerchief. 'No, it's not that. It was seeing the soldiers that upset me. I was reminded of my husband. My first husband, I mean.' She took a deep sobbing breath. 'I still miss him, you see, and not knowing how or when he died is a hurt that never goes away.'

Thomas Fulton nodded. 'You made all the usual enquiries with the military authorities, I suppose?'

'Yes.' She blew her nose. 'But they didn't know anything much. They just said he was missing somewhere and presumed dead.' She gave a watery smile. 'Sorry. It just comes over me sometimes – 'memory of him, I mean. I'll be all right, but it's been a strange kind of morning.'

'If I can help you at all,' he said, bringing a printed card out of his pocket, 'don't hesitate to send for me. I live not far away and if I'm out on a call my wife or housekeeper will know where I am.'

He touched his hat as he moved away and she mouthed her thanks and glanced at the address. He lived in the High Street, which ran parallel with Lowgate and alongside the Old Harbour. *Dr Thomas Fulton*, she read. 'He's a doctor!' Not just a charitable man who fills his time helping unfortunates. Would he see Alice? Could we afford him?

'Doctor!' she called after him. 'Dr Fulton! Please, wait!'

CHAPTER THIRTY-THREE

Dr Fulton said he would call at the house later that afternoon. In the meantime Lily had passed on to Lizzie the
news that Rena would like to see her with a view to her
helping out in the shop. 'She has a spare room, Lizzie,' Lily
said eagerly. 'I think she'd be willing for you to have it until
your babby comes.'

Lizzie had stared open-mouthed. 'No!' she said disbelievingly. 'You're kidding me. Why would she? She doesn't
know me; and besides, what would I do after it's born? I'd
still be out on 'streets.'

Lily looked at her. 'It's a chance,' she said softly. 'It's a
helping hand. Don't reject it.'

Lizzie raised her fingers to her trembling mouth.
'Nobody – nobody's held out a hand to me afore,' she
whispered. 'Onny you, Lily.' A single tear trickled down
her cheek and she dashed it away. 'I'll do it all wrong,' she
muttered. 'I'll rub her up 'wrong way and she won't want
me.' The bold, defiant Lizzie was showing how vulnerable,
how frightened, she really was. 'Will you come wi' me?'

'You don't need me, Lizzie. You need to see Rena on your
own and talk it over together. Besides, I have to wait for Dr
Fulton. He's coming to see Alice.'

'I don't need a doctor.' Alice turned large eyes, deep in
their sockets, towards Lily. 'It's nowt. Onny a cough. It's
allus wi' me.'

Lily nodded. 'He'll give you summat to ease it.' Though I don't know how we'll pay for it, she thought. And it was only now as she looked at Alice that she berated herself for not finding the means to send for a doctor long ago, or take her to Mr Walker as she'd said she would. She saw how thin the girl had become, how her clothes hung upon her and how very pale her skin was. The sores on her face had spread much further. Alice, she thought, is very ill.

When Dr Fulton came, she took him into her room and went to fetch Alice. 'Stop wi' me, Lily,' Alice said imploringly. 'I'm scared to see him by meself.'

'He's already asked me to stay with you,' she consoled her. 'He won't want to see you on his own. It wouldn't do.'

Alice nodded and nervously followed her down the hall and into the room at the front of the house. 'I've onny got what my ma had,' she began as soon as she saw him. 'We all had bad coughs; every winter we had 'em.'

'But it's not winter now,' he said gently. 'This is just the beginning of autumn.' He took a stethoscope out of his case and asked her to sit down and unbutton her blouse. 'I just want to listen to your chest,' he explained. 'It's easier without too many layers. No,' he said as she began also to unfasten the small buttons on her cotton under-bodice. 'That's fine, thank you.'

Alice is so used to undressing, Lily thought, noticing that Alice had flushed at the doctor's remark. She must think that all men expect it of her. Poor girl, she's never known courtesy or respect.

After listening to Alice's chest, the doctor turned her round and tapped her back with the tips of his fingers. He glanced at Lily and, looking grave, gave a little shake of his head. Then he stood in front of Alice. 'Button up your blouse,' he said quietly.

She did so, keeping her eyes averted from him.

'Do you have a home or family where you could have a week or so of rest?'

She gave a small laugh. 'No. This is my home – onny

one I've got, anyway.' She glanced at Lily. 'And everybody here's my family. I've got nobody else who'd be bothered about me.' She looked candidly at Dr Fulton. 'I've got consumption, haven't I?'

At his nod, she said, 'I knew I had. Onny I've been pretending I hadn't. That it was just a cough.'

'But did you know that it can spread?' he asked. 'That you might have passed it on?'

Alice looked away from him. 'I've been keeping my own cup so that 'other girls and Lily didn't catch it. I'm not bothered about 'customers,' she said bitterly. 'They pass on all kinds of disease to us and don't care a jot!'

'It's not my place to preach to you, Alice,' he said softly. 'But I'm asking you not to continue with this kind of life. Take a month or two off if you can, until you recover.'

'An' what'll I do for money?' She gave a sudden cough as she spoke and put her hand to her mouth; when she drew it away it was spotted with blood. 'How will I live?' She stared at him from her sunken eyes. 'Will I live?' she whispered.

He didn't answer for a second, and Lily almost held her breath. Dear God, she thought. Alice is dying.

'Sleep with your window open,' he answered. 'Get as much fresh air as you can. As for earning a living,' he pressed his lips together. 'I'm sure your friends will help you until you've recovered.'

'How long?' Alice breathed. 'How long will it tek?'

He gave her such a kind, gentle smile that Lily wanted to weep. So there are some good men after all, she thought. 'A month,' he said. 'Perhaps two.'

'We can manage.' Lily's voice was choked with emotion. 'That's not so long.'

Dr Fulton left, asking Lily to call at Mr Walker's for some syrup which he would prescribe for Alice. He paused at the front door. 'The medicine is useless,' he said quietly. 'You could give her honey just as well. You realize, don't you, that she won't recover? She has advanced tuberculosis and the sores on her face are probably caused by a venereal disease.'

He saw the shocked look on Lily's face. 'Mrs Fowler,' he said, 'you're in the wrong business if you're not aware of the hazards of this vile trade. You should have preventative aids available for the men who are willing to use them. Pregnancy is not the only thing that can be caught. You are all vulnerable.'

'Not me,' she gasped. 'I don't – I'm not . . .'

He frowned. 'What?'

'I run this house,' she said in a whisper. 'I'm a sort of housekeeper and I tek care of 'money. I don't – I don't go with any of 'customers.'

His eyes opened wide. 'Never?'

She shook her head. 'Never.'

She saw the beginning of a smile as his lips turned up. 'Forgive me, Mrs Fowler. I know this isn't a laughing matter and I've just delivered some tragic news, but' – his face broke into a grin – 'that's the oddest thing I've heard in a long time!'

She closed the door behind him and leaned against it, letting out a sigh. But perhaps I might have to, she mused. With Betty gone and soon to be married, Lizzie going to Rena's and Alice – she pushed to one side the thought of what would happen to Alice – well, we shall be very short of girls. Would it be very bad? she wondered. We have to earn some money somehow and I could charge more for my favours than the others. Mentally she started to work out how much she would need to charge to be able to cover their expenses.

'You all right, Lily?' Cherie had come out of the kitchen and was regarding her seriously.

Lily sighed again. And then there's Cherie. She pulled away from the door, giving a forced bright smile as she answered that she was. A rattle on the letter box made her turn round and she picked up an envelope. 'A bit late for 'postie,' she muttered, and opened the door to look out. A young lad with a grey shirt hanging out of his ragged trousers was running back towards Lowgate.

'What's this?' She slit open the envelope with her finger nail. Inside were five shiny gold coins with the queen's head on them. There was no note or indication of who had sent them. She held them up to Cherie. 'Sovereigns! Our ship's come in,' she said haltingly. 'Whoever can afford to give us these?'

Cherie's face lit up. 'Can we have a feast?' she asked eagerly, not bothered about where the money had come from. 'Or go into 'town and buy summat nice?'

Reluctantly Lily shook her head. 'It's for my fine,' she thought of Dr Fulton, who had said his society might be able to help her, 'or to help Lizzie and her babby; or for Alice,' she added.

'For Alice?' Cherie whined. 'Why Alice? That's not fair!'

'Life isn't,' Lily told her. 'But Alice is sick. She'll need extras. Eggs and fruit and another blanket.'

Cherie's eyes opened wide. 'If Alice is sick and can't work and Lizzie's going to Rena's, then – then that means I'll definitely have to go upstairs.' Her voice trailed off into a whisper. 'I know I told Lizzie that I would, but . . . Unless I can get other work! What can I do, Lily? Nobody would take me afore. I've tried all over Hull.'

Lily pulled her to her and gave her a hug. 'We'll think o' something, Cherie. Course we will.'

Alice had asked Lily not to tell Lizzie or Cherie how bad her illness was, only that she had to rest for a short while, but Mrs Flitt guessed. 'I knew,' she told Lily. 'That lass has had that sickness on her for a long time. She'll not last 'year out, you know that, don't you?'

Lily sank down on a chair in the kitchen. 'Yes, I do know,' she said miserably. 'But Lizzie and Cherie don't and I'd rather keep it from them for 'time being, Mrs Flitt.'

'We'll be short on women,' Mrs Flitt said, rubbing her nose with the back of her hand. 'Jamie'll want to cover 'rent.' She wrinkled her nose as she considered. 'He'll not have any sympathy. In fact,' she added, 'don't say owt about Alice or he'll turn her out.'

'He wouldn't!' Lily couldn't believe that even Jamie could be so heartless.

'I'm telling you.' Mrs Flitt waved a finger at her. 'He will. So,' she shut one eye and screwed up her face as she concentrated, 'how will we get ower that? You can't just say you need more girls. There's Cherie, of course.' She gave a sigh. 'Seems a shame, though. We've kept her pure all this time.'

'I will say I need more girls. Lizzie will be leaving us too.' She explained that Lizzie was pregnant and that she was going to Rena's. 'I'll use Lizzie as an excuse and not mention Alice just yet.'

'She doesn't show.' Mrs Flitt was peeved that she hadn't noticed. 'Must be a little bairn!'

'And then I'll . . .' Lily heaved a breath. 'Then I'll bring in some money too.'

'You will! How?' Mrs Flitt stared at her. 'There's no work anywhere in Hull. All 'mills and factories are standing folk off.'

'Same way as 'others do. It's going to be 'onny way we can survive.'

Mrs Flitt shook her head. 'No,' she said. 'No, Miss Lily. Not you!'

CHAPTER THIRTY-FOUR

Johnny Leigh-Maddeson hoiked his pack further on to his shoulders and, grimacing, rubbed his right elbow, which was paining him considerably. He'd never again be able to lift his arm high, that was for sure, or take aim with a rifle. Shan't want to anyway, he told himself. I've had enough fighting to last me a lifetime.

As a young soldier, with Victoria newly on the throne, he had been sent on a tour of duty to Ireland. After spells away with only short trips home to see his wife and young children, he had been recalled and posted first to Kandahar and then to Kabul, which was occupied by British forces; after much bloody fighting from which he considered he was lucky to emerge alive the British were forced to retreat from Kabul.

He wrote a hasty letter to Lily telling her that he was being posted to India; order was to be maintained as the native culture and way of life were repressed and Western ideology and principles put in their place. The wives and children of merchants, administrators and army officers came out with their husbands to make a home in this British outpost, but the ordinary soldier was sent all over the colony to put down simmering uprisings and minor skirmishes.

Johnny wrote several more letters but he could never be sure whether they would reach their destination and one, unfinished, was still in his pocket as his regiment was transferred to the Punjab when the Sikh leader, Ranjit Singh, died and disorder began. In the fighting that ensued between the army of the East India Company and the Sikh Darbar, a group of soldiers became cut off from the main body. A detachment of rebel sepoys, riding fast and furiously towards them, fired a random shot which sheered off Johnny's elbow and hit the soldier behind him, killing him instantly. That fellow was the lucky one, he remembered thinking, as he and three other members of his troop were taken prisoner by the most dangerous-looking group of fanatics he had ever come across in all his years of warfare.

The Sikhs lost the battle and most of their army, the Treaty of Lahore was signed, and the group of sepoys which had captured Johnny and his compatriots withdrew to the mountains with their prisoners to maintain their own brand of guerrilla warfare. They were totally opposed to the handing over of Kashmir and the establishment of a British residency in Lahore, and vowed they would continue the fight.

Two of the British soldiers captured with Johnny were shot as they tried to escape from the hideout in the mountains. Johnny couldn't see the sense in holding him or his surviving companion prisoner as they were just foot soldiers in the British army and of no use to the Sikhs as a bargaining tool, but decided that he would make the best of the situation and hope that the Sikhs wouldn't behead them with their swords as they threatened to do if they tried to escape.

His captors bandaged his arm, and he knew that even if he didn't die of blood poisoning or gangrene he wouldn't be able to straighten his elbow again. He made a play of firing with his left hand which the sepoys seemed to find amusing, and they fired a succession of rifle shots in the air with both their right and their left hands just to show him how superior they were.

Some of the sepoys spoke English and Lal, who bandaged him, said, 'There will be another war. Then you can go home. You are of no use to the army any more.'

'Why not let me go now?' he asked. 'I'll put in a good word for you.'

He grinned as he said it, but the man only shook his head and said, 'We might need you.'

'For what? There won't be another war,' he said. 'The British have won.'

'The British have won this time because we have been betrayed by our commanders,' the sepoy said fiercely. 'Not because the Sikhs can't fight. We are the best fighters in the world!'

Johnny hastily agreed that they were. The ground he was on was far too shaky for him to disagree. Besides, he had a sneaking regard for their cause. Britain was seeking to rule the world and impose its influence on countries it considered inferior, and to his way of thinking that wasn't right.

They were moved from place to place as the rebel Sikhs continued their skirmishes. Johnny considered how laughable it was that his army could be picked out so easily in their reds or blues, whilst the Sikh dissenters blended into the mountains in their camouflaged rags. He made himself useful to them, never giving them any trouble, whilst his sullen companion Blake plotted their escape.

'We'll never get out alive,' Johnny told him. 'Even if we escaped this camp we'd never find our way back to the regiment. We've no idea where we are. If another war starts, as they seem to think it will, they'll move nearer to the river crossing, which is where the army will come to capture the ground there; then we'll try to make our escape.'

But the war was a long time coming and they spent twelve months hiding out in the mountains with the guerrillas as they made their spasmodic attacks; the first winter he was sure he would die of the freezing cold and the following summer he thought he would succumb to the fierce heat;

the next winter, when he was becoming acclimatized and the group trusted him enough to use him as a lookout with one of their men, he alerted them to a movement down the mountain. It was a rebel from another group coming to tell them that a second war was about to begin.

Blake stole out of the camp that night. They slept in the same cave as their captors and hadn't been tied up for some months as the Sikhs were now so used to their presence. Blake shook Johnny's shoulder to wake him, and indicated with a toss of his head that he was leaving.

'No,' Johnny whispered. 'Wait until we see some troop movement. Besides, they'll be able to follow your tracks in the snow.'

But Blake didn't want to wait. He crept out and Johnny lay awake listening for any sign that he had been recaptured. Twenty minutes or so passed and then he heard a shot. He heaved a sigh and, feigning sleep, waited to be hauled out of the cave at gun point. He held his left arm high in surrender as he was dragged out and his right up to his chest. He had some movement back in his arm but he wasn't going to show his captors that.

Blake knelt on the ground with his arms tied behind his back and blood oozing from his mangled leg. 'For God's sake get on with it,' he growled at the men standing over him. And they did. With a bright moon lighting the scene and one swift stroke of a sword before he could even blink, he was beheaded.

Johnny drew in a whistling breath as Blake's head rolled down the hillside and came to rest against a boulder. The man who had executed the deed put the bloody tip of his sword against Johnny's chest. Johnny gave a shrug of his shoulders in resignation and lifted his damaged arm to show them how handicapped and disadvantaged he was. To his amazement one of them, the one who had bandaged his arm, said something he didn't understand and the others all burst out laughing.

'What?' he said. 'What did he say?'

268

'You are sad about your friend?' the leader, Teg, asked.

'He wasn't my friend,' Johnny answered; in truth he hadn't much liked Blake. 'He was a soldier like me. But it seems a waste of a life.'

'Lal says just now that as the second war has started we should let you go before you get killed. That's why we laugh. He says that he told you this.'

'He did. But why've you kept me? Nobody would be bothered. My regiment won't even know that I'm missing. They probably think that I'm dead.'

'We kept you because we could!' Teg growled. 'But now you must do something for us in exchange for your life. You will take a message back to the British that will tell them that this time they will not win.'

Johnny nodded. 'All right. Fair enough. When shall I go?'

'Tonight, after dark.' He gave a sly grin, but without humour. 'Don't think that you can tell them where we are, for we will have moved on.'

Johnny frowned. 'I won't do that. You have my word.'

One of the other sepoys grunted. 'The word of the British means nothing. They are liars and usurpers.'

'Some of them are,' Johnny agreed. 'Up at 'top they are. But I'm just an ordinary foot soldier. I'll give you my word as a Yorkshireman that I won't tell 'em where you are.'

'What is this Yorkshireman?' Teg asked.

Johnny stood up straight. 'It's where I hail from. Best place in 'world. After 'Punjab, of course!'

They'd tied both his arms to his sides with a rope. They would have tied them behind his back but he couldn't move his right arm so far, and he considered that they were not completely without feeling, as they could have forced it back if they'd wanted to. They stuck a stave of wood into his trouser waistband and tied a piece of white rag on to it.

'We don't want you to get shot by the British,' they joked, and then tied a bloody sack round his waist containing something which bumped against his legs as he moved.

'Give that to the officer in charge when you meet up with a regiment.'

He'd staggered down the mountain, often knee deep in snow, falling and crashing down the rough terrain as he had no means of balancing himself; as he'd reached the river a silver dawn was breaking.

He walked all day without seeing any other sign of life; he was desperate for water and dipped his head into pockets of snow to take a mouthful. When he reached a stream which ran into the river, he fell to his knees and lying prostrate on the frozen ground managed to put his head into the water and take a drink. He rolled over and sat up, his bloodstained bundle rolling with him. He had a horrible suspicion that he knew what was inside it.

As night began to fall and he was considering climbing up to higher ground and finding shelter from the cold, he heard the rhythmic drum of horses' hooves and saw in the distance a platoon of British cavalry riding towards him.

It's been a long journey home, he thought, as he got off the train in Hull railway station. I was beginning to think I'd never get here. The nerves in his arm were shattered, the army doctor had said, and the commander of the regiment he had reported to had opened the sack in Johnny's presence, looked in at Blake's mouldering head and asked, 'Who's this?'

'His name was Blake, sir,' Johnny said, and the commander had tossed the sack aside and said that if it was meant as a warning it hadn't succeeded. He told Johnny he was of no use to him if he couldn't hold a rifle, but that if he could find his own unit perhaps they'd have him back.

He had given some thought to this as he'd wandered about the camp and talked to the other soldiers as they'd queued for food at the canteen. He had been captured south of Ferozepur and gathered that his regiment was in the Multan area where there was heavy fighting. He asked an officer if he might look at a map in order to make his way there; he had seen one on the commander's table when he had reported to him.

Having looked at it, he decided that the war could continue without him and he would take a risk and head south instead, following the Sutlej River to Hyderabad and the Arabian Sea, where he would hope to take a ship home to England.

Throughout that winter and the following spring he travelled on foot, by bullock cart and finally on horseback when he found a horse roaming free with the body of a cavalryman hanging from the saddle. He'd lifted the soldier down and placed him near a rocky outcrop with his hands folded over his bloody chest. 'Rest easy, lad,' he'd said, before mounting the horse and continuing his journey.

His period with the warriors had taught him how to hide in the mountains and survive on little food; he had stolen extra rations from the army canteen. Each time he saw a division of British soldiers in the distance, he took off up the hillside in case he was ordered to join them, for he knew in his head and heart that he had had quite enough of fighting in a foreign land and was ready to go home.

Following the river, he finally arrived at Hyderabad and reported to a British mission that he had been captured by the enemy, and that not only had he lost his papers in a skirmish, but he had become lost and disorientated and didn't know where he was. By this time his clothes were in rags and his hair, beneath a turban, was long; he was emaciated and footsore and he walked with a limp. His arm he allowed to hang uselessly by his side, though in fact it had strengthened on the journey.

He was directed to a civil servant who, astonished that he had travelled all the way from the Punjab, told him that the second Anglo-Sikh war was practically over and the British were once more the victors. Rather than send Johnny back to his regiment, he signed papers for his passage and directed him to a ship which was leaving for England within the next few days, with the directive that he should report to his regimental office as soon as he arrived.

He went on board, hid out of sight in case anyone should change their minds and order him onshore again, and emerged two days later when the ship was out at sea. He reported to his regiment as suggested when he landed in England and heard the news that the war was indeed finally over. The Sikh army had surrendered at Rawalpindi.

There was a further wait as the regimental clerk checked with his superiors, as the records showed that Johnny had been reported missing and possibly killed in action. During questioning he gave again the story of his capture and after some deliberation was discharged on medical grounds. A week later he was on a train and heading for home.

He looked round him as he stood on the Hull railway concourse, and wondered what was the quickest way to get to Holderness. Having walked across India he didn't find the small detail of walking a distance of twenty-five miles or so in the least daunting. He just wanted to get there as quickly as possible. All I want is to see my Lily again. I want to put my arms round her, feel her soft warm body next to mine and look into her eyes. He smiled to himself. Those beautiful amber-coloured eyes which turned green when she was passionate or angry; the colour of brandy when she was loving and tender.

He put his hand in his pocket to stroke a piece of amber, one of several which he'd found on his journey through the mountains; these were the colour of honey or the sap they had once been, with pollen and seeds trapped inside. He'd visited a jeweller in London before he caught the train and saw the man's eyes widen, though he'd tried to disguise his pleasure and greed. Johnny had refused his first offer and wrapped the stones up again, only opening the package once more when the jeweller doubled his price. 'For one,' Johnny had said firmly, and then offered a second stone for a slightly smaller sum.

This will see us all right for a bit, he thought. We can set up in a little business. The bairns can help us when they're old enough. And it was this thought which reminded him of how long he had been away. It took him aback. They'll be – how old will Ted be? And the little bairn – Daisy? He took a deep breath as he worked it out. And Lily? Will she still be at home in Hollym? How has she managed all these years without any money?

He began to be depressed and agitated. What if something had happened to her? Suppose she and the bairns had been turned out of the house? What if they were in the workhouse? He hoisted his pack more securely, rubbed his painful elbow, turned his back on the station and headed off in the direction of the Humber, to follow the road to Holderness and home.

CHAPTER THIRTY-FIVE

'Daisy! Daisy, come here,' Mrs Walker called down the stairs.

'Yes, Mrs Walker.' Daisy ran up to her employer's room. 'Sorry, I was about to go in 'shop to help Oliver.'

'Where is Mr Walker?'

'Gone on an errand, I think. Would you like me to brush your hair, ma'am?'

Mrs Walker was sitting in front of her dressing mirror. 'No. I want to tell you something, Daisy. We're going to have a different carry-on.' She smiled at her. 'It's a sort of secret between us, so I don't want you to tell Mr Walker or Oliver either. Not just yet, anyway.'

Daisy's mouth turned into a round O. Mrs Walker had been hinting at secrets for a few days but they hadn't amounted to much so far.

'You've enjoyed being here, haven't you, my dear? Feel comfortable, don't you?'

Daisy hesitated for a second. She did, though Mrs Walker could be very fussy and demanding, and sometimes so clinging and emotional, wanting to know where Daisy was every minute of the day, that she felt suffocated.

She had grown up as a child in Hollym with a certain amount of independence; she was expected to help in the house but her mother had trusted her to do what was right without constantly badgering her. Now, the thrill of being a lady's maid and of constantly having to dance attendance on her mistress was beginning to pall. Besides, she missed her mother.

'Yes, ma'am,' she said meekly, for she knew that was what Mrs Walker expected her to say. 'Of course. I hope I've pleased you.'

'Oh, you have indeed!' Mrs Walker was effusive. 'So much so that I'm going to elevate you.'

Daisy's eyes grew wide. What did that mean? She already slept on the top floor.

'Come here.' Mrs Walker reached out to bring her closer, and dropped her voice to a whisper. 'How would you like it if we adopted you, Daisy? If you came here to live as our daughter?' Mrs Walker nodded her head in a mysterious fashion. 'I've been thinking of it for some time.'

'Oh, but – what would my ma say? I don't think she'd like it.'

'I don't think she'd mind much. I've mentioned it to her already. She didn't make any objections.'

'You've seen my ma, Mrs Walker? When? Did she come here?' Daisy couldn't believe that her mother would have come without asking to see her.

'She's been having a bit of bother,' Mrs Walker said soothingly. 'She came to ask my advice.'

'What kind o' bother, Mrs Walker?' Daisy asked anxiously. 'She's not ill or lost her job or anything?'

'No. But her prospects are uncertain. That's when I mentioned about you becoming part of our family.' She smiled reassuringly. 'I do believe she thought it a good idea. It would take a weight off her mind, knowing you'd be well looked after.'

Daisy blinked. Surely her mother wouldn't give her up? 'Wouldn't Mr Walker have to agree to it?' she asked, trying to think of an excuse. 'He might not want to. He said I was very useful to him in 'shop, but . . .' her voice trailed away. Mr Walker had said that after Oliver had gone away to medical school she could do more to help in the shop if she would like to, and she had thought that she would prefer that to being at Mrs Walker's beck and call. But if they adopted her, what would happen then? Mrs Walker would probably want her with her all the time.

'He'll agree eventually,' Mrs Walker said softly. 'I know how to persuade him. But, for now, just be thinking about it and how your life would change for 'better. Now,' she said, 'I thought that you and I'd go out and have a little walk round town. See who's about, you know.'

Daisy sighed. This meant trailing after Mrs Walker as she looked in the shops but never bought anything. It meant going into coffee shops and sitting watching other people while Mrs Walker whispered that they were not as prim and proper as they made out. That she could tell a tale or two about them.

'Shall I tell Oliver that I can't help him after all?'

'Yes,' Mrs Walker said firmly. 'Tell him that I need you.'

Daisy suddenly felt very wise. She could see that if her mother agreed to hand her over to the Walkers, she wouldn't have any kind of life of her own. Not even when she was grown up. 'I won't be a moment,' she said, 'and then I'll get your coat, Mrs Walker.'

Mrs Walker smiled. 'And soon you can start thinking of me as Mama,' she said. 'Won't that be nice?'

Daisy dashed downstairs into the shop. 'Oliver, I'm sorry, I can't help you after all. I have to go out with Mrs Walker.'

'You're always in demand, aren't you, Daisy?' He seemed concerned. 'Daisy come here, Daisy go there! Never mind, you can help later if Mother doesn't need you.'

'Oliver,' she said appealingly. 'Do you know where my mother is? I really need to ask her something.'

'Mmm, no, I don't.' His brows knitted together in a frown. 'But I'm sure my father does. He brought her here to see my mother.'

'Did he? Where was I, Oliver? I didn't see her.'

'You'd gone off on an errand, I believe. Do you want to

see her urgently? I can ask my father when he comes in. Or you can ask him yourself.'

'Would you ask him for me, please?' she asked. 'Seeing as I have to go out. And – and perhaps you'd tell me later.' She gazed up at him. 'I'm very worried about her,' she said pleadingly. 'I really do need to see her soon.'

Oliver asked his father about Daisy's mother as soon as he came back. 'She's so young,' he said, referring to Daisy. 'I think she's really missing her.'

'That's what happens when very young girls go into service or get jobs away from home,' his father said. 'It's not a fair system. They should be at home with their mothers; but there we are, some parents have to put their children to work or the family wouldn't survive. It's a very hard life for some.' He pondered for a moment. 'But Daisy's mother wouldn't want her with her just now, or to see her place of work.'

Oliver glanced curiously at his father. 'Is she in trouble?' he asked.

'Yes. Well, no, but she's having a difficult time.' He glanced back at Oliver. 'She's living in Leadenhall Square,' he said quietly.

Oliver drew in a breath. 'I see.'

'I'll speak to the child,' his father said, 'and try to arrange a meeting for them. Away from here, if I can.'

Ted had landed back in Hull again. He had made several trips between Hull and Driffield but on this last journey Ken, the skipper, had been approached by a bargeman whose former skipper had died suddenly who was now looking for other work. He was an older man and experienced and was taken on as crew for the journey back to Hull. Ken had apologized to Ted, but explained that the other man was more suitable for taking his mate's place. 'I'm not saying that I'll even keep him on once Bob's back to full strength,' he said. 'I'll take you back to Hull because I promised I would, but you'd be better looking for summat more permanent, lad. It's harvest time; there's sure to be some work if you go back home to 'country.'

But where will I stop? Ted had thought. Where will I get my grub? If I could get work on a farm they'd feed and house me, but I can only get casual work at this time of year. I'll have to wait till Martinmas Hirings for a regular job. He pondered on the garden he had cultivated at Fowler's cottage. Maybe I could grow enough to feed myself, but where would I live? Bet that old house has fallen over into the sea, so I can't live in that. He wanted to cry, he felt so miserable and alone. I wish I knew where Ma was. She and Daisy'll be all right. Both of them working. Bet they're not bothered about me.

He was sitting brooding on a bollard at the side of the Old Harbour where he had left the keel, and glanced down the river to where it ran into the Humber. The sun was glinting on the water and he screwed up his eyes, for his long sight wasn't very good, and watched a platoon of soldiers marching across the bridge towards the citadel.

'If I'd had a father,' he muttered, 'I wouldn't be here on my own.' But then he considered that his father had left him and his mother and sister to manage on their own. 'Why did he?' His lips were barely moving. 'Was there no work on 'land? Is that why he joined up as a sodger?' I don't suppose he thought that he would be away for ever, he mused. I don't suppose he ever thought he would get killed and not come back.

Perhaps I'll go to the barracks and ask if I could be a soldier. If I tell them about my da they might take me on. He got to his feet and started to walk along the harbour-side. But then, what if I don't like it? And what if I get sent abroad and get killed? Ma won't know what's happened to me. He dragged his feet; he was beset with indecision. His mother had always made decisions for him. She seemed to know what he liked to do. I wish I could see her now. Just suppose I bumped into her, wouldn't she be surprised to see me?

He kept on walking and cut back on to the High Street and then on to the bridge. This would take me home to Holderness. He stood there looking down at the glinting River Hull and then turned to see the muddy waters of the Humber. Shall I go and try to find work? I could help with harvest and— His mind clicked, like a trigger. What if I go and see John Ward? He'll need some help and – and mebbe his missus will let me stop there. They've got room in their loft. He felt a sudden tingle of excitement. They've got our cow. That's what I'll do. He took a breath and put his shoulders back before he started walking forward. I will. There's nowt for me here. I'll go back!

Mrs Flitt scurried towards the Market Place. She was wearing her oldest clothes, not the ones Miss Lily had given her. Her ragged shawl was tied tightly over her grey head and her boots had flapping cardboard soles. She found a position on the pavement beneath a lamppost and sat down. Leaning against the lamppost, she took a tin plate from under her skirt waistband and placed it on the ground beside her. She took off her boots and hid them beneath her skirt and wiggled her bony misshapen toes.

'Spare a copper,' she whined, holding out her hand. 'Spare a copper for a bit o' bread.'

Someone dropped a coin on to the plate. It spun and then gave a satisfying clang. 'Thank you, sir,' she croaked. 'God bless you and may fortune allus smile on you.'

The man nodded and then as if in afterthought dropped another penny.

The people of Hull were generous when they had money to give and within half an hour she had several coins on the plate. She left one there and put the rest in her skirt pocket. 'Spare a copper,' she whined again, and then gasped as someone kicked her in the ribs.

'What 'you doing here?' Jamie stood above her. 'Beggar woman!'

'Well, you don't pay me,' she retaliated.

'I give you shelter, don't I?' he snapped. 'You don't pay owt for that.'

'I cook for them lasses. And I wash for 'em and keep 'house clean! Anyway.' She glared defiantly. 'This isn't for me. This is for Miss Lily to help pay her fine.' She shook a fist at him. 'Which by rights you should be paying. It's your brothel she's running!'

He bent down and put his face close to hers. 'It ain't a brothel! It's a first class establishment. And it's Lily's own fault. She was asking for trouble. If she'd offered 'police special terms they wouldn't even have come to 'door.'

Mrs Flitt snorted. 'You'll get your comeuppance,' she said. 'You'll see. You're tekkin' advantage of them as is low as can be. You're scum, Jamie. You allus have been.'

He leered at her. 'Am I?' he sneered. 'Then you'd better not show your face in my house again in case you get contaminated. Keep away,' he warned her. 'Do you hear? Or else I'll throw you out meself.'

As he turned away, she spat at him. 'Cur,' she growled. 'Mongrel! If your ma weren't no better than she should be, she'd be ashamed o' you.'

He turned round and put his fist in front of her face. 'Don't speak of my ma or you'll get this,' he snarled. 'Or mebbe even finish up in 'river.'

She laughed at him, even though she was seething inside. 'I wouldn't be 'first old woman you've beaten up, would I? But I'm not scared o' you, so don't think I am.'

There was a twitch on his top lip as she scored points over him. She was aware of what went on in this town and knew that Jamie worked alone. He didn't have anyone to do his dirty work. He was quite capable of doing it himself.

It was early when she got back to the house, for she had every intention of staying there, no matter what Jamie threatened. But she went in by the back door and crept in quietly in case he was there.

'Where've you been, Mrs Flitt?' Lily asked. 'I was getting

bothered about you. Fire wants lighting in parlour and 'lamps need trimming.'

Mrs Flitt grinned and handed over a handful of coins. 'Here!' she said. 'That'll go towards 'fine. Nearly five bob!' she said jubilantly.

'Wherever did you get it?' Lily asked. 'You didn't—'

'Steal? No. I don't do that any more. I'm not that desperate.'

'Begging,' Cherie said. 'I bet!'

Mrs Flitt nodded. 'I found a real good pitch in 'Market Place.' Then she wrinkled her nose. 'But Jamie came along and we had a few 'ostile words.'

'What you do has nothing to do wi' Jamie,' Lily told her.

'No; but he said I couldn't stop here any more. Said I hadn't to show my face here.'

'Or else what?' Lily asked slowly.

Mrs Flitt shrugged. 'I'm not scared of him.'

'Nor me,' Lily said. 'I'll tell him if you go, then so will I.'

'And me,' Cherie said. 'Though he won't be bothered if I leave as I don't earn him any money.'

'No.' Lily looked anxious. 'I hope Mary and Sally come tonight or I don't know what we'll do. I've sent Lizzie to see Rena. Alice is ill, so that leaves just you and me to see to 'customers, Cherie.'

Cherie's face drained of colour. 'I'm scared, Lily,' she whispered.

Lily gazed at her. 'So am I.'

CHAPTER THIRTY-SIX

The door bell rang as Lily and Cherie were finishing an early supper. Alice was having hers in bed and Lizzie had not yet returned from Rena's. Mrs Flitt went to see who it was. 'Shall I say it's too early?' she asked. 'It's not yet six.'

'It won't be a customer,' Lily said. 'It'll be Lizzie back from Rena's.'

But it wasn't, it was Betty and Henry, standing hand in hand on the doorstep. Mrs Flitt brought them through to the kitchen; Betty was looking radiant and Henry flushed and cock-a-hoop with excitement.

'We've had 'banns read,' Betty announced. 'Third time'll be tomorrow. Now we can get married!'

'But first,' Henry beamed, 'we've got a treat in store for you.'

'Oh, what?' Lily asked. 'We could do with summat good to happen.'

'Why, is something wrong?' Betty said anxiously.

Lily shook her head dismissively. Now wasn't the time to tell them of her fine, Alice's illness, or even Lizzie's pregnancy. 'Oh, nowt that won't keep,' she said airily. 'Tell us about you two!'

'Well, I'd like you to be my witness, Lily. Please,' she said imploringly. 'You will, won't you, and I'd like one of 'girls to be my maid of honour.'

Mrs Flitt gave a strangling croak which became a dry coughing fit as Lily glared reprovingly.

'But I wouldn't know who to choose,' Betty went on, unaware of her slip. 'So I'd like you to choose for me, Lily. I don't want to upset anybody.'

Lily nodded. 'Cherie, then,' she said, knowing that the others couldn't in any case. 'You'd like that, Cherie, wouldn't you?'

'Oh, yes!' Cherie clasped her hands together in her joy. 'Would I be able to wear 'muslin gown? I know we're onny supposed to wear our frocks here and not outside, but it's all I've got!'

'No,' Betty said. 'You'll have new.' She turned to Henry adoringly. 'Henry said he'll pay for new clothes for us; you too, Lily.'

'That's very generous of you, Henry,' Lily said breathlessly. 'How very thoughtful.'

'But that's not all.' Henry beamed even more widely than before. 'So that nobody feels left out we've arranged a treat for all of you. You too if you like, Mrs Flitt.'

They waited expectantly. 'What we thought,' Henry continued, 'well, Betty told me that none of you had ever been to see the sea, except for you, Lily,' he added. 'And so we thought that we'd hire a carriage and tomorrow go off for the day after we've heard the banns read. We'll go to Bridlington.' He looked at Lily and Cherie eagerly. 'What do you think?'

'All of us?' Lily asked, her eyes wide in amazement.

'Yes,' Betty said. 'There'll be plenty of room in 'carriage. Where are Lizzie and Alice anyway?'

'Lizzie will be back in a minute, she's onny gone to Rena's, and Alice has gone for a lie down.' Lily put on a show of unconcern. 'She's feeling a bit off colour.'

'That cough still bothering her?' Betty asked. 'A breath of fresh air is what she needs.'

'I think you're right.' Lily smiled, though she felt very tearful at Henry's open-heartedness. He couldn't have known how despairing she felt, or how much she needed this demonstration of human kindness.

The bell rang again, but this time they heard the door open and Lizzie's voice calling out, 'I'm back.'

She burst into the kitchen, and she too had an ecstatic grin on her face. 'Oh, hello!' she said, seeing Betty and Henry, and then she glanced at Lily, her eyes sparkling and obviously bursting to tell her news.

'Go on, then,' Lily urged. 'Tell us, and then you can hear about Betty and Henry.'

'Rena's tekking me on,' she crowed. 'We've been nattering away for ages and going over ideas 'n' that.' She turned to Betty. 'I'm pregnant.' She lowered her voice slightly as she remembered Betty's lost baby. 'I was that desperate,' she said. 'And Lily asked Rena if I could go there and work for my keep. And she said *yes*!' she shrieked, and they all laughed. This wasn't the acerbic sceptical Lizzie they were familiar with.

They exchanged the details of the trip to Bridlington, and as they were discussing it the kitchen door opened and a white-faced Alice stood there in her night shift with a shawl around her shoulders. 'I heard a noise,' she said in a breathy voice. 'What's going on?'

Lily got up and went towards her, putting her arm round her and drawing her into the room. 'We're planning a surprise, Alice,' she said softly. 'Henry and Betty are tekking us all to 'seaside, and because Cherie is going to be an attendant at their wedding, and Lizzie is going to work for Rena . . . well, you've been chosen to tek 'first look at 'sea when we get there.'

She glanced at them all in turn, an entreaty in her eyes, begging them to see what she could see and to give Alice this last chance of happiness. It was Lizzie who broke the short poignant moment.

'We've decided,' she invented, in a croaky voice, 'that when we get to Bridlington we'll all shut our eyes and you must keep lookout for 'first glimpse of 'sea, and then you shout out and tell us.'

Alice's pale face took on a wondrous glow which lit up her dark sunken eyes and they all saw how her thin chest heaved as she took a breath. 'Oh! Can I? Really? Can I really be 'first to see it?'

They all nodded and murmured and tried to put on brave smiling faces as they acknowledged and came to terms with the inevitable which they hadn't recognized before.

Mary and Sally arrived a little later, after Betty and Henry had left, and brought another young woman with them. 'This is Olga,' they told Lily. 'She's foreign but classy. Doesn't like working out on 'streets.'

Olga was older than the others, late twenties, Lily thought, and had a strong accent. She was quite exotic-looking with dark hair and eyes and a long sharp nose. She was dressed reasonably well, not shabby or unkempt, but wearing a colourful skirt and blouse and a long red scarf tied round her head and floating over her shoulder.

'I earn plenty money here, yes?' she asked Lily, and Lily told her that she probably could, and gave a sigh of relief that neither she nor Cherie would be called upon tonight. Here is a woman who has chosen this life, she told herself, and hasn't been forced into it through poverty.

At ten o'clock the next morning, Henry and Betty arrived in the square, Henry driving a four-wheeled two-horse brougham and Betty waving to them from the plush leather interior. He wore a dark green top hat which he lifted in greeting as they all crowded in the doorway.

He jumped down to help them all in and apologized that the vehicle was only an old Clarence. 'A Growler,' he said. 'But I knew there'd be plenty of room for everybody, and though it's a bit noisy it'll be comfortable.'

Mrs Flitt had come to see them off but declined to accompany them. 'I'd be sick,' she said. 'All that shekking about. No, I'll stop at home and have a clean through while you're all out.'

Lily smiled at her, knowing that the real reason was

because she wanted Alice to have more room. They'd brought pillows and a blanket in case she wanted to sleep on the way home.

'Won't you come, Mrs Flitt?' Betty asked. 'I'm going to sit up on top with Henry.' But still Mrs Flitt said no and urged them off whilst the weather was still fine.

'It's bound to be foggy out near 'coast,' she intoned.

'No, it's not – not always,' Lily said, 'but it might be cooler. Have you all got your shawls?'

They had, and Lizzie was also wearing a black and red skirt, with a separate top and matching jacket, which Rena had given her. 'Look,' she said to Lily. 'I can move 'buttons on 'skirt as I get bigger.' She seemed to have accepted the fact of her pregnancy, now that her future was more secure.

'Come along then, ladies.' Henry urged them to get inside. 'Let's be off.'

They all waved to Mrs Flitt as the carriage jerked forward and they fell about laughing. 'Oh, I just can't wait,' Alice said. She had a bright pink spot on each pale cheek. 'I can't wait to see the sea. Could we have a paddle in it, do you think, Lily? Have we brought a towel?'

'Yes.' Lily laughed. 'Of course you can. Today you can do whatever you want.'

Alice gazed eagerly out of the carriage window as they approached the town and the others, even Betty riding next to Henry, squeezed their eyes up tight until they heard Alice's shout of delight that she could see the sea. 'It's so big,' she exclaimed. 'Look how big! And look at those enormous waves! And there are people in the water! Swimming!'

They'd all opened their eyes and Lily was choked with emotion as she thought of her childhood home further down the coast, and then thought with bitterness of Billy Fowler who had ruined her life.

It was a warm September afternoon, with a slight onshore breeze which ruffled their hair. The sands were soft and golden with quite a few visitors walking beside the briny ocean, which was a rippling triple shade of blue, green and brown.

Lily, Lizzie and Alice took off their boots and held up their skirts as they paddled in the water, whilst Cherie and Betty chased about on the sands; then they all sat on blankets to enjoy the picnic which Henry and Betty had packed for them. Henry had beamed at them all and said that after he and Betty were married they must do this again. After they had eaten, Betty, Henry and Cherie went off arm in arm to walk by the quayside and harbour, whilst Alice, Lizzie and Lily lazed about on the blanket, running sand through their fingers and lifting their skirts to their knees to feel the sun on their bare legs.

On their way home in the evening, Alice, cuddled in a blanket, leaned against Lily's shoulder. 'I'm so happy, Lily,' she whispered. 'This has been 'best day of my life. I feel tired, but really, really well. I think I shall get better now.'

Lily stroked her cheek and hair, and glanced across at Lizzie who was biting her lip and Cherie whose eyes were filling with tears. 'You will,' she said softly. 'All that fresh air has done you good. There's nowt like sea air to give you energy.'

'Yes.' Alice smiled contentedly. 'And to be in 'company of friends. I feel – I feel as if I'm wi' folks who care for me. I'm not bothered now about having a man to look after me or my own little house, like I used to long for. It's enough now that I've got good friends like you, and Lizzie and Cherie. And Betty too; wasn't that kind of her to ask Henry to bring us?' Her eyelids started to flicker and Lily shushed her gently and bade her sleep, telling her that they'd wake her when they arrived back in Hull.

Dusk was falling as they arrived in Leadenhall Square and the street women were sitting on their doorsteps. Some of them wandered up to the carriage to see who was in it and one or two jeered and made remarks to Henry, who simply smiled and bade them good evening and wasn't in the least affronted. He opened the house door for them, and then he and Betty departed with fervent thanks following in their wake.

'Mrs Flitt,' Lily called. 'We're back.'

The kitchen door opened and a figure was backlit by the lamp inside. 'Not Mrs Flitt.' Jamie's voice came bellowing out. 'I thought I'd given her 'sack! Where do you think you've been all day?'

CHAPTER THIRTY-SEVEN

'We've been out,' Lily replied. 'What's wrong wi' that?'

'What if there'd been customers? Think of 'money I've lost!'

'It's Sunday!' Lily objected. 'We never have customers on a Sunday. Not during 'day. Occasionally somebody might come of an evening, but never during 'day,' she repeated. 'And anyway, it's onny seven o'clock, so what 'you on about?' She stared at Jamie through the gloom of the hallway. 'We've every right to go out if we want. It's got nothing to do wi' you.'

He shook his fist at her. 'This is my house and you run it how I say. You don't go gallivanting out.'

'Then if it's your house you can pay my fine,' she shouted at him in sudden anger. 'And don't you shake your fist at me! Don't think you can bully me cos you can't.'

'You watch out,' he snarled. 'Next time 'police come you'll go to jail and not just be fined. Just because Leo was 'magistrate you got away wi' it this time.'

'What 'you talking about, Jamie?' She was flummoxed. 'You sound as if you want me to be arrested and sent to jail.'

'It would serve you right, Mrs High and Mighty!' He put his face up to hers and she took a step back. 'It was a warning, so tek care.'

She narrowed her eyes as she gazed back at him.

Something was not quite right. 'Who told 'police to come here?' she said. 'They had no reason to. I run a quiet house. Look at me, Jamie.' He had turned his head away. 'Was it you?'

He snorted. 'Why'd I want to do that?'

'To teach me a lesson? Because I don't toe the line? Because I'm not frightened of you? I've made this hovel into a first class house and you're getting 'benefit o' that. Why would you bite 'hand that feeds you?'

'Because you're trying to tek over, that's why. You let those foreign lasses go! Somebody told me that they'd seen you tek 'em to Hope House. *She* was with you.' He pointed a finger at Cherie, who was standing behind Lily and shrank back next to Lizzie. Alice had slipped into Lily's room. 'And she doesn't pay for her keep either, so she can clear off. I'm not running a house o' charity. And another thing. I told that old hag of a cleaner to clear off and when I arrived she was still here.'

'Mrs Flitt?' Lily said in alarm. 'We can't manage without her. She cleans for us, washes 'steps, cooks for us, and she doesn't get a penny in return!'

'Well that's as mebbe, but I've sacked her again and seen her off 'premises.'

'But why? What's she done?'

'Gave me a load o' lip, that's why, and I'll not have it. She can get back to her beggin'.'

'She was beggin' to help pay my fine,' Lily shrieked at him. 'What's wrong wi' you, Jamie? I don't understand you.'

'There's nowt wrong wi' me,' he snarled. 'It's you lot o' whores – dissipated harlots that bring men down—'

Lily interrupted him. 'I think you'd better get off home. You've been drinking or tekking summat, haven't you? We're here providing you with a living, in case you've forgotten,' she added, lowering her voice. She'd seen the wildness in his eyes and the way his wet mouth trembled. 'Go home and we'll talk tomorrow. If you're still in 'same state o' mind then we'll all leave.'

An expression of panic crossed his face and his eyes switched from Lily to Lizzie and Cherie. 'Where's Alice,' he barked. 'Is she working?'

'She's gone to bed,' Lily said. 'She's got a cold and I've told you we don't work on Sundays.'

She walked to the door and held it open for him. 'Good night,' she said calmly. 'See you tomorrow.'

He walked out of the door and half stumbled down the steps. Lily closed the door and locked it.

'He's been on 'poppy,' Lizzie said. 'I bet he got a supply when those foreign girls came over.'

'What? Raw opium, do you mean?' Lily was alarmed. A dose of laudanum was safe enough if you were not well – so she'd heard, anyway. It wasn't the kind of medication that had ever been available to her. But the raw stuff was different.

Lizzie nodded. 'I've seen him chewing on it. He offered me some once. To buy,' she added cynically. 'He'd never give it away.'

They went into the kitchen and Cherie swung the kettle over the low fire. 'This'll tek ages to boil,' she said. 'Why didn't he put some coal on to keep it in?'

'I'm bothered about Mrs Flitt,' Lily said. 'I wonder where she's gone.'

There came a soft tapping on the back door and they all smiled. 'Who's there?' Lizzie called out. 'Friend or foe?'

'It's me!' Mrs Flitt's croaky voice rasped. 'Has he gone?'

'What if he hadn't?' Lily laughed as Mrs Flitt came shuffling in. 'What if Jamie had still been here?'

'I'd have thought o' summat,' she said. 'I'd have told him I'd come back for my belongings.'

'You haven't got any belongings, Mrs Flitt,' Cherie said, standing back whilst Mrs Flitt picked up the poker to riddle the fire.

'Nor I have,' she said. 'But Jamie doesn't know that. Anyway, he doesn't get rid o' me just like that.' She lifted her head and looked at them in turn. 'If you lot weren't here I'd have stopped away. But I know you need me, just like I need you,' she added croakily. 'And besides, I've got attached to me cupboard. It's 'best place I've ever had in me life.'

She busied herself warming the teapot and getting out cups and putting them on the table, whilst they divested themselves of shawls and boots, and then she muttered, 'It were me that upset Jamie. He saw me beggin' in 'Market Place. I told him a few home truths and he didn't like that. Told me to clear off out o' his house an' o' course I took no notice. When he came in today I was sweeping 'stairs and he took me by surprise. I'd no time to hide but by a stroke o' luck I had 'broom in my hand otherwise he might've belted me one.'

'Surely he wouldn't,' Lily said, remembering how he'd waved his fist in front of her face.

'He doesn't know what he's doing when he's on 'poppy,' Mrs Flitt said, and Lizzie gave a knowing glance. 'I reckon he came by just to check if I was still here.'

'And found we'd all gone out,' Lily murmured. 'Perhaps he thought we'd all gone for good.'

'Which I shall have tomorrow,' Lizzie said, her face creasing into a grin. Then her jubilance faded when she saw Cherie's stricken expression. 'I'm sorry, Cherie. But what else can I do?'

'So soon?' Cherie groaned. 'I didn't think you'd be going yet.'

'But she can't stay here,' Lily intervened. 'How can she? Jamie would turn her out anyway if he found out, but in any case it wouldn't be right, would it? She's onny got a few weeks before her babby's due.'

'And if Kendall or somebody like him should notice . . .' Lizzie let the statement hang in the air; but she looked vulnerable, frightened even, at the thought of it.

'I'm sorry.' Cherie burst into tears. 'I wasn't thinking straight. It's just that we've been like a proper family and now everybody's leaving. Betty's gone, and now Lizzie, and,' she gave a sob, 'we don't know what's going to happen to Alice.'

'Even in proper families people move out,' Lily said soothingly. 'They get a job somewhere or they get married. Look at me,' she added. 'My son and daughter are not here with me. We've all to make our own way, Cherie. Sooner or later we're on our own having to fend for ourselves.'

Cherie snuffled and then fished for a rag to blow her nose. 'I know,' she gulped. 'But I don't want to go upstairs with them men, and I don't know what else to do. Jamie's not going to let me just pour wine and offer 'customers drinks for much longer. Sooner or later he's going to mek me go upstairs.'

Lily climbed into Alice's bed that night, for Alice was fast asleep in hers and she didn't want to wake her, but she tossed and turned most of the night wondering what they would do if they had to leave Leadenhall Square. I could go back to Holderness, but what would I do about Daisy? She likes it in Hull and I suppose it's much livelier than 'country for a young girl. If she was in service at one of the farms she wouldn't have as much freedom as she does at the Walkers'. And what should I do about Alice? Or Cherie? And I don't even know where my poor Ted is. She shed a few tears at the hopelessness of her situation.

'Will you call and see Mary?' she asked Lizzie the next morning. 'Tell her I've got a proposition for her but if Jamie's here I won't be able to talk about it.'

Lizzie was in her room, still in her night shift, putting her possessions, such as they were, into a bag. 'I won't go today after all,' she murmured. 'I'll leave tomorrow. But I want to get it over and done with, Lily, because Cherie is going to be upset.' She screwed up her eyes and swallowed hard. 'Am I doing 'right thing? I feel terrible about leaving her in 'lurch.'

'It's 'right thing for you, Lizzie,' Lily said softly. 'You've to think of yourself and your babby. You've tekken care of Cherie, but she's not your responsibility. Time has come for her to tek care of herself. She has to stand on her own feet. You'll see; she'll grow up when you're not there to mek decisions for her.'

Lizzie nodded. 'I suppose so. But I still feel bad about it.'

Lily smiled. 'When I first met you, I thought you were so bitter and hard-hearted. You seemed angry and hostile towards everybody. And now I know you for what you really are,' she said. 'You're generous and compassionate and caring.'

A tear ran down Lizzie's face. 'I was angry, and I hated everybody for what I had to do just to live. But when I first saw Cherie she seemed lost and frightened like I used to be, and I knew I had to help her. That's why I took her to Hope House, but I knew that it wasn't 'place for me. I didn't belong there; they were good people but I was scornful of 'em. They didn't know what it was like to live out on 'streets. And they couldn't begin to guess how worthless I felt, giving myself to lecherous rogues who were more corrupt than I could ever be.'

Lily put her arms round her and hugged her. 'It's done with, Lizzie,' she whispered. 'It's all over. You did what you did in order to survive. And you have, and 'future is rosy for you and your babby. Rena's a good woman. She's had a hard life too. She'll understand and she won't judge you.'

She held her at arm's length and smiled. 'You're a beautiful young woman. Put 'past behind you. Get your things together,' she said briskly, 'and go today. Now! Ask Cherie to call and see you when you're settled in.'

Lizzie wiped away her tears and nodded. 'All right. I wanted to leave today but it seemed as if I was rushing off. I'll slip in and see Alice first, and I'll call and talk to Mary on my way to Rena's.'

After Lizzie had left, Cherie ran upstairs to her room. Lily could hear her crying but left her to sob out all her fears. She took Alice some hot soup to tempt her to eat, for she had refused breakfast.

'I'm not hungry,' she said, but was persuaded to take a few spoonfuls. Lily brought her an extra pillow and propped her up.

'Would you like to sit in a chair by 'window?' she asked her. 'You could watch what's going on out in 'street. You can have a pillow and a blanket.'

Alice smiled wanly. 'This is such a comfortable bed, Lily. I don't want to get out of it. Oh, I'm sorry. It's your bed. Where did you sleep last night?'

'In yours.' Lily smiled. 'This was your room before it was mine, wasn't it? This was where you were when Jamie brought me here that first night.'

'And you came to my rescue when that customer attacked me.' Alice shook her head. 'I don't know what I'd have done if you hadn't been here to let me in. I was terrified.'

'Try to forget that now,' Lily said, reflecting that her role in life seemed to be to console others worse off than herself.

'Will you let me stay here, Lily?' Alice asked.

'In my bed?' She laughed. 'Yes, all right, if you like.'

'No. I mean . . .' Alice reached for Lily's warm hand with her cold one. 'I mean – stay here and not go to 'hospital.' Her large eyes gazed imploringly at Lily. 'I'd be sent to 'workhouse hospital. I wouldn't be allowed to go to 'Infirmary. Not with consumption. And besides, somebody has to recommend you before they'll accept you in there. Please,' she begged. 'I'll try not to be a bother, and – I don't think it would be for long.'

Lily gazed at her and blinked her eyes rapidly so that tears didn't fall. 'Of course you can stay,' she said huskily. 'Why shouldn't you?'

Mary called as Lily was changing into her grey going-out gown. Thanks to their unknown benefactor she had enough money now to pay the fine, and intended to walk down to the magistrates' court to do so. 'Lizzie said you wanted to see me,' Mary said. 'What's up? She said she was off somewhere.'

'Lizzie's got a change of occupation,' Lily told her. 'She's going to work for Rena and she'll be living there.'

Mary's mouth dropped open. 'Lucky hussy! Does that mean she's not going to be working here?'

'Yes. Are you interested? Would you like to tek her place?'

'Oh, would I? Wouldn't I just!' Her expression brightened and became animated, but then her face fell. 'But I've got a bairn. Can I bring him? He's ever so good, hardly ever cries, and it'd mean I needn't farm him out when I'm working.'

Lily hesitated. Whatever would Jamie say? How could they keep a child's presence from him? 'How old is he?'

'He's onny nine months and he sleeps a lot. At night, I mean.' Mary gazed pleadingly at Lily.

'We wouldn't have to let Jamie know, or 'customers for that matter. But perhaps . . .'

'What?' Mary said eagerly.

'We could ask Cherie to keep an eye on him at night. Or Mrs Flitt. They'd like that.' It would give Cherie someone else to think about, Lily reflected. She wouldn't feel so abandoned if she had a child to look after.

'All right,' she said. 'But I also wanted to ask you to bring some other girls. You'd have to share a room, for sleeping I mean,' she added. 'Would Sally come? But maybe not Olga.' She wasn't sure about the foreign girl, didn't know if she could be trusted not to tell tales to Jamie.

'Sally will come like a shot,' she said. 'And I know somebody else. Out of top drawer she is, fallen on hard times. A bit toffee-nosed, but she'd do fine for gents.' She gave a frown. 'So Lizzie's gone, and what about Betty? Has she left as well? And Alice? Where's she?'

'Betty's getting married.' Lily smiled. 'So there's hope for you all. But Alice isn't well, and she has to rest for a bit.'

'What? Betty's marrying one of 'customers? Crikey. She must be mad or he is!' Mary was so astonished that she didn't even mention Alice.

Lily shook her head. 'He's very nice, as a matter of fact. No, really, he is,' she added as she saw the disbelief on Mary's face.

'Oh well, she's allus got a trade to come back to if it doesn't work out,' Mary said cynically. 'I got married and he cleared off within six months when he found out I was expecting. So I'm not looking for any other man except to mek my living. They're all poison as far as I'm concerned.'

Lily felt depressed after Mary had gone. How terrible that these young women had been let down and were no longer able to trust. Would I ever trust again, she wondered, after the way Billy treated me? And what about Johnny? Was he faithful to me when he was away? Or did he fall for the exotic charms of some foreign woman when I was out of sight? She gave a deep sigh and put her shawl about her shoulders, for there was a cool breeze blowing and a few drops of rain falling; she called to Alice and Cherie that she wouldn't be long and set off for the court with the money for the fine jangling in her skirt pocket.

CHAPTER THIRTY-EIGHT

The road on which Johnny had first travelled into Hull to report to the citadel all those long years ago was much improved. Then, he had walked from his home in Hollym towards the town of Hedon, down to the Haven waterway and along the muddy bank to Hull, following the course of the Humber. He could have taken the newly opened turnpike road from Hedon to Hull, but he was a sentimental youth and had felt in his heart that perhaps he wouldn't see the estuary for many years. As it was, he had come home several times and on each occasion, knowing his visits would be short, he had hitched a lift from whoever happened to be passing, be it carrier or farmer's cart.

Now he was in a sentimental mood again, and although he was anxious to be back in Hollym as soon as possible he walked first of all towards the pier, where he leaned on the railings to gaze at the barges and sloops tossing on the turbulent waters of the Humber and knew he was nearly home. He retraced his steps and crossed the bridge over the River Hull, looking down at the river traffic in the Old Harbour which led into the New Dock, where ships from every nation brought their goods.

'Right,' he murmured. 'Home I go. No more nostalgia. I'll keep to 'turnpike and should be there afore nightfall.' A grin creased his face. Won't Lily be surprised to see me! And 'bairns; why, they won't know me. I'll be a stranger to 'em. I hope they tek to me and don't blame me for being away so long. I shall have to explain to my lad that if you join the queen's army then you're committed to serve queen and country.

He thought back to the Sikhs who had captured and then released him. They showed me mercy, he ruminated, which is more than some of our men did to them during an attack. If I'd known when I joined 'military that I'd have to fight to take over somebody else's country and not just defend my own, I might have had second thoughts. Infidels, some of our fellows called them, but they had their faith, as I discovered when I was captured, and to my way of thinking they were defending their land against invaders. But if I'd dared to say as much I'd have been shot by my own side.

Further up the road he saw a horse and cart pulling to a stop. He narrowed his eyes. 'Mebbe I can get a lift,' he muttered and started to run. But then he saw a youth also running towards the cart, and jumping on board. The vehicle started up again and he slowed to a walk. Ah, well, he thought resignedly, looking back over his shoulder. There'll be somebody else trotting by before long.

The cart was always in sight ahead of him but too far in front for him to catch up. Dark clouds scurried across the sky and he turned up his collar as a few drops of rain fell, but, he thought, there were many times in India when he would have been thankful for gentle rain to ease the fierce unremitting sun.

Three or four miles along the road, he saw the cart stopping again. The youth jumped down and gave a wave of thanks. The cart turned off the road and the boy set off at a fast pace as if in a great hurry. 'He'll not keep that gait up for long,' Johnny muttered. 'Steady walking is what's needed for a long journey. I wonder where he's going.' But the boy's progress was constant and purposeful and Johnny couldn't gain on him.

He'd make a good foot soldier, he mused. He's intent on getting somewhere and nobody will stop him. Those were the traits he had discovered in himself on his journey through the mountains towards Hyderabad, when he had decided to leave the army and return home.

Johnny followed the lad as far as Hedon and there he stopped at an inn and had his first tankard of ale in years. He chatted for a while with the landlord, who wanted to know where he was heading and where he had been, but he cut the conversation short as he was anxious to be off. He kept the youth in his sights as far as Winestead on the Patrington road and then he lost him.

'He must have turned off for one of 'villages,' he murmured as he continued on towards the town of Patrington and the last few miles of the journey to Hollym. 'Pity I didn't catch him up. We'd have been company for each other. We could have had a chat and I'd have found out what's been happening since I've been away.' But then, he mused, he was onny a lad. He probably doesn't know much, any more than I did before I left home.

He arrived in his home village by the early evening; several laden farm waggons had passed him, reminding him that it was harvest time. There was an aroma of burning stubble and he sneezed several times as dust from the fields clogged his nostrils. He walked quickly to the cottage in the main street and rapped on the door, a grin of anticipation on his face. But the expression faded when a young woman with a child in her arms opened the door.

'Oh! Where's Lily? Is she in?' He tried to peer behind her into the room but it was dark inside, with no lamp or fire lit to show the interior.

'There's nobody here by that name,' she said, trying to close the door.

'But—' He put out his hand to detain her. 'We – she allus lived here, with our two bairns.'

She shook her head. 'We've been here for gone two years.' She turned her head as a man's voice called out, 'Who is it?'

'But she's lived in Hollym all her life,' Johnny said, a little desperately. 'You must know her. Lily Leigh-Maddeson.'

Again she shook her head and then moved aside as a man appeared behind her. 'Who're you lookin' fer?' His manner was rough. 'Somebody owe you summat?'

'No. I'm looking for my wife and bairns. I've been away in 'army. Just got home.'

The man glared at him. 'Mebbe she's gone off wi' somebody else then, but she don't live here.' He shook his thumb towards the neighbouring cottage. 'Ask next door, but they've onny been here a twelvemonth.'

'So where are you from?' Johnny was curious to know why these strangers were here. 'Not from these parts?'

'Holmpton,' the man groused, speaking of a village close by and nearer the sea. 'We were rehoused when 'cliff fell.'

Johnny turned away, murmuring his thanks. They were obviously people who kept to themselves and didn't get involved with anyone else. He didn't know them, although he had known several people from Holmpton in his youth as the villages were closely linked.

I'll go to 'Plough, he thought, feeling very deflated. There'll be somebody there who'll know where Lily is. She's sure to be somewhere in 'village. As he walked to the hostelry he felt an ominous shadow over him. I should have written when I got back to England, he thought. I should have warned her and then she would have been here waiting for me; she might even have told that dowly couple back there that I'd be knocking on their door expecting to see her.

He stood for a moment in the doorway of the Plough and thought that it hadn't changed. The old men of the village were sitting clutching tankards and still wearing the battered wide-brimmed hats which Johnny recalled they used to wear whilst working in the fields to keep away the insects. They looked up as he entered and paused in the act of supping their ale.

'How do!' Johnny greeted the landlord, who wore a

301

leather apron and was wiping a glass with a cloth. 'I don't suppose you remember me? Johnny Leigh-Maddeson?'

The landlord gazed at him for a moment, still wiping the glass, then his mouth dropped and his face took on an expression of incredulity. 'Young Johnny! But – we heard you was dead! Lily said—' He stopped and put his hand to his mouth.

'Who's this?' One of the old men got up from his stool and came to stand near Johnny. 'What did you say your name was?'

'How do,' Johnny said weakly, not knowing the old man and guessing that he wouldn't remember him either. It had been a long time since he was last home. 'Johnny Leigh-Maddeson. Who's been putting it about that I was dead?'

'She wrote,' the landlord interrupted. 'Your missus; she wrote to 'army. I know it for a fact cos she was working here at 'time and she told me.'

Johnny was bewildered. 'She worked here? When did she write? Didn't she get my letters?'

Another man got up and came to listen. 'You young sodgers! We all knew you were going to your death out there in that foreign land.' Soon there was a small interested crowd round Johnny.

Jack, the landlord, drew him a glass of ale. 'Have that, lad; you're going to need it when we tell you 'news of your Lily.'

Johnny took it but didn't drink. He licked his dry lips. 'She's not at 'cottage. Couple there didn't even know her.'

'Oh, them!' one of the listeners jeered. 'He's a bad lot from ower Holmpton way. They'd reckon on they didn't know even if they did.'

'So where is she? Have Lily and 'bairns gone to live somewhere else?' He stared at them in turn; why were they not telling him?

'You'd best sit down,' Jack said. 'Fetch him a chair,' he said to the room at large and someone obliged. 'It'll be a shock, but like I said, she heard you was dead.'

'What 'you saying?' Johnny stared at the landlord. 'Are you telling me that my Lily's got married again? That she didn't wait for me?'

'Wait for you!' one of the men burst out. 'How long was 'poor lass supposed to wait? Ne'er a word in years. She took 'best offer she could get, onny it turned out that it was 'worst—' He suddenly dried up as if realizing he had said too much.

Johnny took a long gulp from the glass. 'So she married somebody else? That meks her a bigamist, doesn't it?' He had never in his life felt so low, not even when facing death during his capture. 'Doesn't it?' He looked up to face the men, but oddly they were all looking away from him.

'What? For God's sake, what?'

'She's dead.' A woman's voice came from the doorway. 'That's what we were told.'

He felt as if he was going to keel over, as if all the blood in his body was being drained away. He vaguely registered that it was the landlord's wife who came across to stand beside him. 'What happened?' His voice was hoarse and cracked as he whispered the question. Not Lily, he thought. Not my beautiful girl. I could forgive her for marrying again if she thought there was no hope of my return, but not for dying and leaving me completely. 'And my bairns?' he went on, not waiting for her answer.

The woman drew up a chair and sat next to him. 'I'll tell you what we know,' she said softly, 'and what we heard; whether it's gospel we couldn't say, because there's a mystery that we can't fathom.'

She explained that Lily had written to his regiment several years ago when she'd had no word from him and had been told that he was missing and presumed dead. 'She was bereft, poor lass, and wi' two young bairns to bring up. She'd managed well, working all hours to feed and clothe 'childre', but I reckon she was lonely being on her own. You'd been gone a lot o' years,' she added harshly. She then went on to tell him of Billy Fowler who had started coming to the hostelry.

'He'd never been a regular here, just dropping in now and again whenever he was ower this way; till he spotted Lily, and then he started coming in on nights when she was here. He let on that he had this smallholding ower at Seathorne, onny we discovered later that it was just a hovel on 'edge of 'cliff.'

'So she married him,' Johnny said hoarsely. 'Then what happened? Was there an accident? He didn't kill her?' His voice suddenly rose. 'If he did, I'll swing for him if he hasn't swung already!'

'No, no,' she said quickly. 'It wasn't like that.'

He listened, his mind whirling, as she detailed what she had heard. That Fowler's cottage had gone over the edge taking Fowler, Lily and Daisy with it. 'We're not sure about your lad,' she said. 'John Ward who farms nearby at Seathorne swore that he'd seen 'lad ride off on Fowler's owd hoss when 'cottage was still standing.'

'So – Ted might still be alive, but 'others all drowned?' His voice came out of his mouth but he felt that it wasn't himself speaking. It was as if this was happening to somebody else. He was disembodied. His own mind had closed down and another taken over.

'No,' she said patiently. 'Billy Fowler got out of 'sea and climbed up 'cliff. He told John Ward that they were all in 'cottage when it went ower. It was Fowler who said that Lily and Daisy must've drowned.'

Johnny gave himself a shake. 'Did they find their bodies?' he asked in a low voice.

'No,' she said. 'That's just it. There's been no sighting of 'em. None at all.'

Johnny got to his feet and put his nearly full tankard on the counter. 'Where does he live now, this Fowler chap? I'll go and see him.'

'He's been rehoused, so we heard,' one of the men said. 'In Withernsea. But nobody round here's seen him.'

'He doesn't come in here any more,' the landlord commented. 'He became a bit of a nine-day wonder in Withernsea, getting out of 'sea in 'way he did; though he didn't like to be questioned, so they say. But John Ward used to come in,' he added. 'He was allus spouting off that summat odd had gone on that day. He was right upset when 'authorities didn't believe him.'

Johnny hesitated. 'So – what do you think? Where will I find 'truth?'

They all glanced at each other but none would be drawn. Then the landlord's wife spoke up. 'It's like this,' she said. 'Lily was one of our own and none of us liked Fowler. If it was me . . .' She pressed her lips together as she considered. 'If it was me looking for 'truth – then I'd go ower to Seathorne and find John Ward.'

CHAPTER THIRTY-NINE

Ted sensed that somebody was walking behind him when he left the carrier's cart and once or twice he glanced over his shoulder, but whoever it was was way back in the distance and wouldn't be able to catch him up, not without running. Nevertheless he increased his stride; he didn't want anybody talking to him and holding him up. He reckoned that having had a lift he would be back in Seathorne before it got dark.

He turned off at the village of Winestead, crossing the old bridge over the drain and continuing through wooded parkland, most of which belonged to the Hildyard and Maister families. Though he was not familiar with this territory he thought he could cut across country, common and pastureland to reach the hamlet of Frodingham and thence go on to Seathorne. The paths were not easily defined and at times he had to turn back until he found the proper track, but twice he saw carters driving waggons who advised him on the best way to go. He wanted to arrive before dark as he knew that if he didn't he would surely get lost.

But he was a country lad, used to living by the sea, and within a few miles of the coast he sniffed the air and knew he was almost there. A grey mist started to come down and he quickened his steps. He felt the wetness on his face and neck and the dampness on his coat, and as he followed the rise of Little England Hill he saw at last the grey waters of the ocean and drew in a deep, satisfying breath of salty sea air.

Another half-hour and he was knocking on John Ward's door and praying that someone would be in. His feet and legs ached and he was soaked to the skin as the mist enveloped him.

Mrs Ward opened the door and stood for a moment looking at him; then she gave a shout to her husband. 'Look here,' she cried. 'Young lad's back from 'dead! He's as quick as you and me, just as you said he was! Come in. Come in!' She flourished her hands to Ted, beckoning him inside. 'Dear Lord,' she flustered. 'How glad I am to see you. See here, Mr Ward; flesh and blood he is, just like you said.'

John Ward was standing in his stockinged feet by the fire; his boots, which he must have just removed, lay sole uppermost in the hearth. He gazed open-mouthed at Ted. 'Didn't I say, Mrs Ward? Didn't I say that he hadn't gone ower 'edge like yon fellow said? Where've you been, lad?'

Mrs Ward bustled Ted towards the fire. 'Move ower,' she ordered her husband. 'Can't you see 'lad's wet through? Come on,' she told Ted as he stood shivering. 'Tek those wet clouts off and get warm, and then you'll have some hot soup and taties afore you tell us what happened to you.' She shook her head. 'We never really believed what yon fellow said.'

Ted took off his jacket and came nearer the fire, where his clothes started to steam. 'What fellow, Mrs Ward? Who do you mean?'

'Why, Fowler o' course,' John Ward answered for her. 'He made out that you'd gone ower 'cliff in 'cottage along wi' your ma and 'little lass.'

Ted gulped and stared at the old cow keeper. 'Billy Fowler!' he said in a low voice. 'I thought – I thought . . .' He glanced with scared eyes from one to the other. 'I thought he'd fallen ower cliff – he did,' he asserted. 'I saw him go ower.'

'Sit down, lad.' Mrs Ward poured him a large bowl of soup and cut a hunk of bread. 'Get that down afore you say owt else, though I must say I'm right glad to see you and that you at least are alive.' She sighed and crossed her arms over her ample bosom. 'Though what's happened to your poor ma and sister will allus be a mystery.'

Ted dipped his bread into the soup; his nose started to run as he ate. He sniffed and rubbed it with the cuff of his shirt sleeve. 'Well, I don't think they'll come back, Mrs Ward, not after what happened, and 'specially not if Fowler's alive after all. I was sure he was dead,' he muttered, taking another spoonful of soup. 'I'm not sure whether to be glad or sorry, but at least it wasn't my fault like I thought it was.'

John Ward sat down beside him and his wife served him a bowl of soup and cut another slice of bread. He broke up the bread and dropped it into the bowl. 'He climbed up 'cliff,' he said. 'He told us that 'house had gone ower and he'd lost everything. He said that your ma and sister were in it and he might have said you as well, except I said no, I'd seen you wi' 'goats. But when I told 'constable, nobody believed me and they said you must have been in 'house as well, cos you hadn't been seen, and Fowler never denied it.'

Ted shook his head. 'Ma's in Hull,' he said. 'And Daisy as well. Fowler took her and sold her in 'Market Place. When he came back, he didn't tell me at first, and when he did I fought wi' him. I gave him a right drubbing,' he said with some satisfaction.

Mrs Ward clasped her hands together. 'They're alive! Oh, praise 'Lord. But that wicked man – mekking out they were dead!'

'That'd be so he didn't get found out,' John Ward said slowly. 'Though I'm not sure if there's a law against selling your wife.' He looked up and then blanched at his wife's fierce glare. 'Well, yes, I expect there is,' he added humbly. 'Or at least if there isn't, there ought to be.'

'So where've you been all these weeks?' Mrs Ward asked him. 'Did you go looking for your ma? Was that it?'

'When Fowler went ower 'edge I thought I'd killed him,' Ted confessed. 'So I let out 'livestock, and hoped as you'd feed 'cow; I took 'owd hoss and rode into Hull.' He told them of his chance meeting with his sister, of selling the horse and trying to find a ship. 'I finished up on a keel going to Driffield. It was all right,' he said. 'But I was laid off and decided to come back here, and . . .' He hesitated. Would he still want to stay in Seathorne if Fowler was here? 'Well,' he continued lamely, 'I was going to ask if you'd give me a job.' He gazed earnestly at them. 'I'm not bothered about wages if I could just have a bed and a bit o' dinner of a night, and a bit o' breakfast,' he added hastily.

John Ward silently nodded as he considered. He scratched his chin and rubbed his nose and then looked at his wife, who nodded back at him. 'I think we could manage that,' he said. 'I can't afford to pay you. There's no money in dairy and we're losing more and more land – at least 'maister is. I wouldn't mind tekking it a bit easier, though,' he added. 'Owd bones are playing me up.'

'I like working on 'land,' Ted said eagerly. 'I could mek you a vegetable patch.'

'Aye, I know that. I had a gander at yourn when I went ower to Fowler's to see what had happened to 'owd cottage. He's gone to Withernsea,' Mr Ward said. 'Been rehoused by 'parish, so they say.'

'We'll all have to be rehoused afore long, at 'rate 'cliff is going ower,' Mrs Ward said gloomily. 'I remember 'owd church going ower 'edge when I was just a bairn. My da took me to see it – there was coffins and owd bones and skulls scattered all ower 'sands. A terrible sight to see; not one I'll forget.'

'There's nowt much in Withernsea,' Ted chipped in. 'Onny an owd pier.'

'Not yet, there isn't,' John Ward responded. 'But it'll be

bigger than Seathorne. They've got plans.' He nodded again in a significant manner.

Ted had finished eating his plate of mashed potatoes and turnip and Mrs Ward was about to make a pot of tea when a knock came at the door. 'Why, who's this at this time o' night, Mr Ward?' She paused with the kettle in her hand. 'Are you expecting somebody?'

From his chair by the fire where he was lighting his pipe, he said that he wasn't. 'Go see who it is, lad,' he said to Ted. 'You might as well mek yourself useful if you're going to stop.'

Ted unbolted the wooden door and opened it. It was dark now and drizzling with rain. A man stood there with rain running down his hair and face. He wore no hat but was wearing a dark coat with the collar turned up.

'Is this John Ward's house?'

'Yeh,' Ted said. 'Shall I get him?'

'Who is it?' Mrs Ward called.

'A man, lookin' fer Mr Ward.'

John Ward got to his feet. 'Tell him to come in then,' he said testily. 'There's a draught blowin' in.'

The stranger gave himself a shake to rid himself of the rain and carefully wiped his feet on the mat before stepping inside.

'I'm sorry to disturb you at this time o' night,' he said. 'But I was told you might be able to shed light on some distressing tidings that I've come by, regarding a family by 'name o' Fowler.'

Ted looked again at the stranger. He was lean, with a craggy weathered face. Nobody that he knew; somebody Fowler knew, perhaps.

'I might be,' John Ward said. 'We've just been discussing Fowler, as a matter o' fact, but why come to me? I've nowt to add about that beggar. Nobody believed what I had to say in any case.'

'I've come from Hollym,' Johnny said. 'They said at 'hostelry that if I wanted 'truth I should come to you.

310

And that's what I want, no matter how painful it might be.'

Ted looked at the stranger. 'Are you from 'police?' he asked. 'Cos if you are, I can tell you about Fowler and what he's been up to.'

Johnny shook his head and gave a slight smile. 'No. I've come home to Hollym after being abroad with 'army.' His eyes clouded. 'Onny I discovered that my family weren't there. My wife thought I was dead and married again. And now,' he rubbed his hand wearily across his forehead and took a breath, 'they're saying that she's dead. That they're all dead. And I don't know which way to turn.'

There was a silence in the room, all eyes on the stranger. Mr and Mrs Ward knew little of the Lily's background, though they had heard that Fowler had married a soldier's widow. Ted had turned quite pale. His stomach churned and his ears buzzed. He barely remembered his father; he had been less than five the last time he had seen him, though he vaguely recalled being taken by him to a low-lying meadow to look at frogspawn in a dew pond. But could this be him? And how could it be? His mother had been told that he was dead. Suppose he was an impostor?

'Wh-what's your name?' he croaked, and put his hand on the back of a chair to steady himself. There was no one else he knew who used a middle name; his mother always said it was a hyphenated surname, but he didn't know what that meant. If this man used it, why then, it could mean . . .

'Leigh-Maddeson,' Johnny said. 'John Leigh-Maddeson, though everybody's always called me Johnny.' He gave a slight embarrassed shrug. 'Leigh-Maddeson's a hyphenated surname,' he said. 'My da and grandda said we should allus use it.'

Ted felt tears welling up in his eyes and he took a breath. He mustn't cry. He was too big to cry, though he'd wanted to several times recently, but now he was suddenly overwhelmed by emotion.

Mrs Ward broke in. 'I think you'd better come and sit

down, young man. There might be summat you want to discuss wi' this lad. Mr Ward,' she said, 'I'd like you to give me a hand out at 'back.'

'Aye.' John Ward nodded. 'Tek my chair and warm yoursen. And when you've talked things ower, Mrs Ward will mek us all a pot o' tea and we'll think on what to do next.'

Johnny looked from the old couple, who were heading towards another door, to Ted, who was snivelling and rubbing his nose on the back of his hand. He hesitated about sitting down, though he moved nearer the fire. Then he turned to Ted. 'What's up, lad? What's upset you? It's not me, is it?'

Ted fished in his trouser pocket and brought out a grey rag that served as a handkerchief. He blew his nose hard. 'Might be!' He inhaled. 'What's it mean – hyphenated?'

Johnny looked puzzled, and then explained. 'It's – a sort of bridge between two names – a connection, or – joining together.'

'Oh!' Ted said slowly. 'I've allus wondered.'

'Have you?' Johnny wrinkled his brow. 'Why's that?'

Ted looked directly at him. 'Cos that's my name as well. I'm Ted. Edward Leigh-Maddeson.'

Johnny returned his gaze but he put his hand to his face which had paled in its turn, while Ted's had now flushed scarlet. 'Ted?' he whispered. 'My lad? They said over at Hollym – they said – that 'rumour was that you'd disappeared and were probably dead along with Lily – your ma, and Daisy.' He sat down abruptly, and then got up again and put out his arms. 'Is it really you?'

Ted came towards him but didn't get too near. 'It's me,' he said hoarsely. 'But where've you been?' His voice rose and he clenched his fists. 'Ma was told *you* was dead. Why didn't you write and tell her that you was alive?' Tears began to fall and he didn't do anything to stop them. 'She married that blackguard Fowler who when he wanted rid of her took her to Hull and sold her!'

Johnny took a step back, dropping his arms. 'I did write!' he said hoarsely. 'Whenever I could; but I could never be sure that 'letters would get to England. I wrote from Afghanistan and 'Punjab. Didn't she get *any* of them?'

Ted shook his head. He was too full up to speak. He swallowed and mumbled, 'Onny when you first went out there. That's what Ma allus said, anyway, cos I was too young to know. Then one day she said to Daisy and me that she didn't think you'd be coming home again. That you'd been killed out in a foreign land.'

He started to sob and Johnny was reminded that he was still only a boy.

'An' I wanted you to come home,' Ted grieved, hiccuping in his weeping. 'I wanted to have a da that'd be here, and I didn't want her to be married to Fowler who I *hate*!'

'What did you say?' It was as if the facts had just registered in Johnny's mind. 'He *sold* your ma? Sold Lily! What manner of man is it that can sell a woman?' He looked down at Ted and felt his own eyes prickle. 'But she's not dead. So we'll find her and fetch her back, from wherever she is,' he vowed. 'And what I want you to remember, Ted, is that even if your ma's married to somebody else, you and Daisy still belong to me. I'm your father and allus will be, and you are my son.'

He held out his arms again and this time Ted went to him and put his face into his chest, to be encircled in his father's embrace.

CHAPTER FORTY

'Miss Lily! Good day to you.' The voice was pleasant but low.

Lily glanced over her shoulder. She had paid her fine and was making her way from the clerk's office at the magistrates' court towards the door. Leo was inside a half-open door, beckoning to her to come inside.

Slowly she walked back. She inclined her head and dipped her knee. 'Good day, sir.'

He opened the door wider, inviting her into his room. 'Come to pay your fine?' he asked, and when she said she had he replied, 'Good. Best to let the authorities know you'll pay your dues on time.'

'I hope there won't be another time,' she stated. 'I don't even know why I was called this time.'

'Somebody reported you,' he said softly. 'It could have been one of the other women in the square, or someone closer to home.' He took hold of her hand and pressed it to his mouth. 'You're a fine-looking woman, Lily. There will be any number of people jealous of you.'

'Jealous of me?' She tried to withdraw her hand but he held it fast. 'I don't see why.'

'Don't you?' He released her hand and invited her to sit down, which she did. 'Some of the women in the square will have seen the kind of customers who are coming to the house. A better kind of client than those who come to them. They might even have recognized some of them.' He gave a slight sardonic smile. 'Kendall for one.'

And you for another, she silently added.

'I'm sorry about the fine,' he continued. 'But I have to be seen to administer justice. You paid promptly. Did Jamie give you the money?'

So it wasn't you, she thought. So who was it? 'It wasn't Jamie,' she said bitterly. 'He wouldn't give a copper to-wards it.'

'Of course not.' Leo smiled. 'He'd want you to keep on working in order to pay it. But you got the money together very quickly. Does that mean – does that mean that per-haps you are now taking clients yourself? Because if you are – well, I'd be very interested.'

Lily rose from her chair. 'No, it doesn't, Mr Leighton. I have no intention of selling myself in order to keep body and soul together.'

He shrugged. 'But there's a need! The oldest profession, you know!'

'It's a man's need,' she retorted. 'None of 'women who work for me have a choice. They're doing it under suffer-ance.'

He lowered his eyes and looked at her from under the eyelids. 'But someone like you, Lily. Someone with your bearing, your style, you could be set up somewhere and make a good living. Think of it: plenty of money, clothes, a place of your own, and you could choose who to enter-tain.' He reached out and stroked her cheek. 'If you should change your mind . . .'

'I won't,' she said, turning her head away. 'I shall be out of this business as soon as I can.'

'And what about your girls? What about the lovely Lizzie and sweet little Alice, let alone the innocent Cherie.' He gave a knowing smile. 'They'd be back on the streets without you.'

'Lizzie has found another occupation,' she said. 'I'll take care of Cherie, and as for Alice . . .' She spoke slowly

315

in order to let her words sink in. 'As for Alice . . .' She swallowed, her throat aching as she held back the abuse she wanted to hurl at him and all men like him. 'Alice is dying. She won't be in this world for long. She's been deprived of a home and food and fresh air for too many years and now she's lost 'chance of a fulfilled life as well.'

She watched him pale. 'Not Alice,' he whispered. 'What's wrong with her? Has she seen a doctor?'

'Not until it was too late,' she said abruptly. 'What hope has a girl like Alice of paying for a doctor? She's got consumption,' she said, and had the satisfaction of seeing him start and involuntarily rub his hand on his chest.

'I'm sorry,' he said. 'Really sorry! It's a sad state of affairs, I agree, but you can't help the whole world, Lily. There'll always be some who fall by the wayside.'

'Yes,' she choked, knowing that she wanted to blame someone for life's misfortunes and Leo just happened to be there.

She left him abruptly and walked slowly across town towards the Market Place. The traders were packing up, though some were still shouting their wares and selling off cheap. 'Last minute bargains,' one called and Lily stopped to buy a bunch of asters. She buried her head in them and breathed in. A smell of autumn, she thought. The year will soon be over.

'Ma! Ma!' Lily turned swiftly and a smile broke out on her face as Daisy came hurtling towards her. She opened her arms and Daisy fell into them. 'Oh, Ma! I'm so glad to see you.' Daisy's face was puckered up as if she was about to cry. 'I've missed you so much. Ma, Mrs Walker says she wants to adopt me so I can live with her and Mr Walker. And I don't want to. I like being her maid, but I don't want to be her daughter and live with her for ever.' She blinked to stave off her tears. 'I want to live with you!'

Lily hugged her. 'She can't adopt you unless I say so, and besides, it can't be so easy to adopt somebody. Not a nearly grown-up girl, anyway. I dare say it's different wi' a babby.

316

But listen, Daisy. Right at this minute you can't live wi' me. I'll explain why when you're older. But will you be patient for a bit longer? Then when I've sorted out a few things, I'll come and see Mr Walker and tell him that you're leaving his employ.'

Daisy nodded. 'I'll be sorry about that,' she sniffled. 'I like working for him – he's really nice to me.'

'Is he?' Lily said suspiciously. 'In what way is he nice?'

'Well, he lets me help him in 'shop. I keep bottles dusted and count out 'tablets for him. He says I'm a good organizer.'

'Ah! That's all right then.' Any misgivings Lily had concerning Mr Walker were mollified, though she was very uneasy about what Mrs Walker had told her of her husband's morals. 'Off you go then, Daisy. Are you out on an errand?' Daisy said she was, so Lily urged her to go, with the promise that she would see her again soon, and then walked reluctantly back to Leadenhall Square.

She put the flowers in a jug of water and took them into Alice's room. 'Here you are,' she said cheerfully, though she didn't feel cheerful when she saw how pale and listless Alice was. 'Look what I've brought you.'

Alice turned her head. 'How lovely. You're so kind, Lily. You shouldn't spend your money on me.'

'They were being given away,' she lied. 'I couldn't resist them.' She smiled at her. 'We'll have a spot of supper before I get changed for the evening.'

'What if Jamie asks for me?' Alice gave a cough as she spoke. 'He'll be getting suspicious.'

'Oh, I'll think of something to say,' Lily said airily. 'He doesn't scare me.'

Just before supper, Mary arrived with her baby, Aaron. He was a quiet curly-haired child and Cherie immediately fell in love with him. 'After you've fed him can I get him to sleep while you get ready?' she asked. 'And then if he wakes up when you're busy, he'll know me.'

'If he wakes up, give him some pobs,' Mary said. 'And if

317

he's restless, give him a drop o' Godfrey's. That'll send him back to sleep.'

Cherie glanced at Lily, who gave a gentle shake of her head, remembering Betty's story of her child who had died because of taking laudanum. 'I'd rather not,' she said. 'I'll sing to him.'

Mary shrugged. 'Suit yourself. He's generally good anyway.'

'Just keep him out of sight in case Jamie comes,' Lily told her. 'Which he no doubt will.'

They all changed into their evening gowns after supper; Mary wore Lizzie's red gown which was a rather tight fit as she was much more buxom than Lizzie. She undid the fastenings on the bodice to show a tantalizing glimpse of white bosom. Lily stopped herself from disapproving. After all, she thought, this is why the customers are coming. They're not really coming for the wine and conversation.

The evening became busy. Mary and Sally were very merry and Cherie served the men with drinks as they waited their turn and Lily chatted to them. Then the door bell rang and a young woman stood on the step. 'Angelina,' she said to Lily. 'I believe you're expecting me?'

She didn't need to change her gown. She was already wearing a most presentable low-cut dark blue satin, which rustled as she walked; a sparkling necklace was clasped round her throat. 'Don't introduce me to anyone rough,' she said haughtily, 'because I'll refuse.'

'We don't have rough,' Lily reproved her. 'They're mostly gentlemen or high class trade.'

'That's all right then,' Angelina said languidly. 'Could I have a glass of wine?'

Lily shepherded her to the parlour. Kendall was there and his eyes lit up as he rose to his feet to introduce himself. But then Sally came down and greeted him warmly so he took her arm and was led upstairs.

The bell rang again and Lily went to answer it. A youth

was almost hidden behind an enormous bouquet of flowers. 'For Alice,' he said, thrusting them at Lily. Then he bent down and picked up a box. 'Where do you want this? It's heavy.'

'What's in it?' Lily asked, frowning a little. 'And who are 'flowers from?'

'Dunno,' he said. 'I'm onny 'delivery lad.'

The box was filled with fruit, a jar of honey, two bottles of wine and a box of candy.

Lily smiled. I know who's sent this, she thought. Someone with a conscience and a lot of money. She took the box and the flowers in to Alice. 'Look, Alice. You've got an admirer.'

Alice's mouth parted. 'No,' she said huskily. 'Of course I haven't!' She looked into the box and saw the gifts, and was astounded. 'Who would send me all this?' A smile brightened her face. 'Who would do such a thing?'

Lily shook her head and said she had no idea. She'd let Alice dream for a while; let her think that she had stolen someone's heart and not tell her that an old man who dispensed justice had discovered a still small voice of conscience and recognized his own failings.

Jamie arrived to collect money from Lily. 'Have you made much tonight? You seem busy.'

'We are,' she said, handing over some of the takings. 'I've not added it all up yet. I'll give you 'rest in 'morning when I've paid 'girls.'

'Who's upstairs?' he asked.

'Mary, Sally and Angelina. She's very classy,' she added.

'Where's Lizzie – and Alice? What 'they up to?' His eyes narrowed and Lily quaked a little, hoping he wouldn't lose his temper.

'Alice is using my room.' She implied that it was for illicit purposes, 'and Lizzie has left.'

'Left! What do you mean, left?' His eyes flashed. 'Has she set up somewhere else?'

'No. She's found other work, and accommodation.'

'With a man?' he asked suspiciously. 'One of our customers?'

She knew what he was thinking. If Lizzie was living as a customer's mistress, Jamie would want a part of her earnings. 'Not with a man,' she said. 'She's working in a shop. She's finished with this trade.'

'Ha! Pull 'other leg. That'll not last long.'

'I think it will,' she said quietly. 'Lizzie's expecting a child.'

He stared at her. 'Lizzie!'

'Yes,' she said sarcastically. 'It does happen, Jamie! Did no one ever tell you?'

His face was full of venom. 'Damned women! Why don't they tek more care?'

'And why don't the men?' she spat out. 'Women can't!' She recalled her conversation with Dr Fulton. 'We should have 'means to supply 'men with prevention.'

'I don't want to talk about it,' he snarled.

'It wouldn't cost much,' she said, knowing that he wasn't listening. His face was working furiously, his eyes flashing, and she realized that she had touched on some raw and sensitive spot. He turned away, crashing out of the front door.

The following Saturday was Betty and Henry's wedding day. They had all had fittings for new outfits, except for Lizzie who had said she would borrow something from Rena's and then she could put it back into stock after she'd had the baby. Lizzie looked well. Her hair shone, the plumpness suited her and there was a sparkle in her eyes.

Cherie was dressed in her gown as maid of honour and the only difficulty was going to be getting Alice to the church, for she was very weak, her legs hardly able to support her.

'I can't go, Lily,' she whispered. 'I won't be able to walk to 'church.'

'I'll slip out and hire a sedan to tek you there and back,' Lily said. 'It won't cost much, cos 'church isn't far.' Betty and Henry were to be married in St Mary's church in Lowgate, a five-minute walk away.

'Oh,' Alice said. 'Would you really? I do so want to see them married.'

Lily stroked her hair. 'We wouldn't go without you.'

But fifteen minutes before they were due to depart, a carriage rolled up to the door and a coachman got down. Removing his top hat, he said to Mrs Flitt, who answered the door, 'Transportation for Miss Lily, Misses Cherie and Alice, and Mrs Flitt.'

Mrs Flitt stood open-mouthed, for although she intended to watch the bride arrive she had never expected to travel to the church in a carriage. She flew in to tell Lily and then shot into the kitchen to tidy herself up, whilst Lily dashed to find her a bonnet since she hadn't a decent one of her own.

'Borrow my shawl, Mrs Flitt,' she urged, handing it to her with the bonnet. 'Go on, do.' She laughed. 'What a treat.'

'Aye.' Mrs Flitt patted her hair and put on the bonnet, a wide grin on her wrinkled old face. 'And don't we all deserve it!'

'You're right, Mrs Flitt.' Lily felt choked and emotional over Alice's frail state, but very happy for Betty and Henry; they'll do well together, she thought, and I wonder if Henry knows of the joy he's given to Alice and Mrs Flitt by this generous act of kindness. 'We do!'

CHAPTER FORTY-ONE

'Alice should really be in hospital.' Dr Fulton spoke to Lily in a low voice. 'Though she's probably better off under your care.'

'I promised she could stay here with us,' Lily told him. Alice had gone to bed after the wedding nearly a week ago, and hadn't got up except to use the chamber pot, and, holding on to Lily's arm, to take a look out of the window to gaze down the square. 'There seems to be a glow over everything,' she'd said breathlessly. 'As if the buildings are lit up.'

The late autumn days had been lovely; though there was a mist every morning and they could hear the hooting of ships' sirens out on the estuary, by midday the fog had lifted and the sun had come out, shining with a warm intensity.

'Give her whatever she wants,' Dr Fulton continued. 'I'll send you some more medication to ease her cough.'

Lily nodded. Whatever he had given Alice previously had always soothed her and sent her off to sleep.

Lily spent most of her days by Alice's bedside. Mrs Flitt had taken complete charge of the kitchen, doing the food shopping, cooking every meal, and disappearing into her cupboard or out of the door if she thought Jamie was in the vicinity. Cherie looked after baby Aaron during the morning whilst Mary caught up on her sleep.

'Tell me about your life, Lily,' Alice said one day. 'When

you were a child living in 'country, and then meeting your husband.'

'I was onny a bairn when we met.' Lily smiled. 'We went to 'same school in Hollym. There were onny a dozen or so of us and Johnny was already there when I started. Teacher put me next to him so he could look after me, but he was such a harum-scarum I was 'one who looked after him and kept him out of trouble. When I was seven and he was eight, he told me that he'd marry me when we were old enough.'

She blinked. The memory was still so strong. 'We used to walk across 'fields to 'sea shore and then play on 'sand or paddle in 'sea. Then he left school and started work on a farm and we didn't see each other so often.' She gave a shaky laugh. 'He didn't like that, me being so near and us not being able to meet. We married as soon as I was sixteen. He told my ma that we didn't want to wait. Which was just as well,' she added, 'as I was expecting Ted.' She sighed. 'But he was keen for adventure and wanted to join 'military and because I loved him I let him go. But when he was sent abroad, it nearly broke my heart.'

'Do you still miss him?' Alice asked wistfully. 'Even though you married again?'

Lily nodded. 'Every day I think of him and wonder how he died. And every day,' she said bitterly, 'I think of that beggar Billy Fowler who brought me down.'

Alice slipped her hand into Lily's. 'But if he hadn't brought you to Hull,' she said softly, 'I wouldn't have known you; nor would Lizzie or any of 'others. You've made a difference to our lives, Lily.'

Lily put her head down and screwed up her eyes. 'Yes,' she whispered. 'And I'd still be living a miserable life out on 'cliff edge, so it was meant to be. But I've lost my bairns. Daisy isn't happy and God knows where Ted is!'

Alice squeezed her hand. 'It'll come right for you, Lily. I know it will. Perhaps you were meant to be here, to bring me comfort.'

When Lily lifted her head, her eyes were brimming. Here was Alice offering her support when she herself had no future to look towards. 'Mebbe so,' she croaked. 'Mebbe so.'

Alice searched her face. 'Will you stay with me, Lily?'

Lily looked puzzled. 'I'm here, aren't I?'

'I mean – when 'end comes,' Alice said in a low voice. 'I know that it's coming so there's no need for us to pretend.' She licked her dry lips. 'Do you believe in Heaven, Lily? Do you think there's a better life waiting?'

'There's got to be.' Lily choked back her tears. 'This can't be all there is. And as for Heaven, if there's such a place then you'll go there for sure.'

'Do you think so?' Alice stared anxiously. 'Even though I've been wicked? I wouldn't have chosen this kind of life if I'd been offered another.'

'You haven't been wicked. We don't have a great deal of choice, do we? Not when we're down in 'gutter.'

Alice lay down on her pillow. 'I'm tired now,' she said.

'Too much talking.' Lily smoothed Alice's forehead. 'I'll give you a dose of medicine and then you'll sleep.'

'Yes,' Alice murmured. 'But don't give me too much. I want my life, such as it is, to last as long as possible.'

Lily closed the door quietly and drew the curtain across it whilst she went to eat some supper, though her appetite was flagging. She felt totally drained and not at all in the mood to entertain any customers.

'Come on, have a drop o' soup,' Mrs Flitt urged. 'It'll give you strength. And if you like I'll sit by Alice tonight while you're entertaining. I'll fetch you,' she added, 'if you're needed.'

Lily sighed. 'Thank you, Mrs Flitt. But what'll we do if Jamie comes? I've kept him at bay all this time but he's getting suspicious. Each time he asks about Alice I tell him she's busy.'

'I think 'time has come to tell him,' Mrs Flitt said. 'Poor lass isn't going to last long. Even he won't turn a dying girl away.'

'He won't, will he?' Lily said. 'Why would I think that he would? He couldn't be so heartless.'

She told him about Alice later that evening and he stared at her aghast. 'She can't stop here! She'll have to go to 'workhouse. They've got a hospital there for folks who've nowhere to go.'

'She's too sick!' Lily couldn't believe what he was saying. 'We can't move her. It won't be for long, Jamie!'

'You think I'm a bleeding charity,' he said venomously. 'What will 'customers think? They'll put off coming in case they catch 'disease.'

'They won't know,' she pleaded. 'We're hardly likely to tell them.'

'You'll have to pay for her room.' He scowled. 'She can't stop wi'out paying.'

'She's not eating and she's sleeping in my bed. But I'll pay,' she said angrily. 'I'd hate to think you weren't mekking a profit!'

A sudden plaintive squall came from upstairs and Jamie looked up. 'What's that?'

'What?' Lily said. 'What's what?'

'You heard! Somebody's got a bairn up there. God almighty! What sort o' place is this?'

'It's onny Mary's babby. We let her keep him with her last night,' she invented. 'I was going to talk to you about it. I was going to ask Mary to tek Lizzie's place now that she's gone.'

He leaned towards her, pushing her up against the wall. 'You're trying to tek over,' he said. 'You're mekking up all 'rules to suit yourself.'

'No, I'm not!' she shouted, thrusting him away. 'I'm mekking money for you. I'm not mekking it for myself. Who else would do this job and not put money into their own pockets? I'm sick o' this, Jamie! If you don't trust me then as soon as – as soon as Alice . . .' She felt herself on the point of breaking down. 'Well – I'll leave and you can find somebody else.'

'Just don't forget you still owe me.' He leered at her. 'You'll not go anywhere till you've paid me back.'

'I've paid you,' she gasped. 'Ten times over!'

He grinned. 'No you haven't. You've given me what you've earned and that's paid for your bed and board. You haven't given me what I paid when I bought you off your husband.'

Will I ever be free of him? she thought as she changed for the evening. I shall have to keep some money back from the customers. But then I've also to pay for Alice's keep. She felt utterly depressed and yet had to maintain a cheerful façade as she greeted the gentlemen when they arrived. She peeked in at Alice and found her sleeping. Mrs Flitt had left her post at the side of the bed in order to put more coal on the parlour fire and Cherie was preparing the wine and glasses.

The door bell rang at about eight o'clock and, calling upstairs to Mary and Sally to hurry, she fixed a smile on her face and crossed the hall to open the door. A man was standing on the doorstep with his back to her, looking down the square. When he turned, he lifted his top hat. It was Mr Walker.

Lily put her hand to her chest. 'Mr Walker,' she breathed, and a flood of emotions ran through her. Alarm, that Daisy might be ill and he had come to fetch her; shame, that he had found her here in this despicable place; and horror that he might be here for nefarious purposes.

'This might not be a convenient time to call, Mrs Maddeson,' he murmured. 'But daytime is not appropriate for me.'

'Wh-what was it you wanted, Mr Walker?' she stammered.

'Only to speak to you,' he murmured. 'It concerns Daisy.'

'She's not ill or in trouble?'

'No. May I come in?'

She apologized and let him in. 'I, erm, I didn't realize that you knew where I lived.'

326

He gave a small smile. 'I've always known,' he said. 'I made it my business to find out.'

Mary and Sally clattered down the stairs, greeted him cheerfully and went into the kitchen.

'I'm sorry, I can't take you into my room at the moment,' she said, 'but please come in here. No one else has arrived yet.' As she spoke she ushered him into the parlour, where a cheerful fire was burning. 'Alice is very sick and is using my room.'

'Is that the girl you asked me about?'

'Yes,' she said. 'Dr Fulton is treating her.'

'I see. Good. I'm pleased to hear it.'

'No, you don't understand,' she said. 'She's very ill and won't get better.'

He looked very grave. 'And she's using your room? You must be sure to come to me for carbolic. You can't be too careful about infection. Many people disregard it, but I'm a great believer in fumigation to kill disease; and you must take care to wash the bed sheets and curtains.'

She nodded. 'I hate to hurry you, Mr Walker, but there'll be customers arriving very soon and you might not wish to be seen here.'

He put his hand over his mouth. He seemed uneasy. 'I have a little difficulty, Mrs Maddeson. Regarding Daisy. My wife, erm, my wife has . . . well, she's told me of some plans that she has discussed with you, which apparently you found agreeable.'

Lily eyed him anxiously. He was going to talk about adopting her daughter, perhaps tell her that Daisy would be better with them than with her brothel-keeping mother. She suddenly felt angry. Well, I'm not having it! They're no better than me in spite of having money and position.

'You can't keep Daisy,' she said vehemently. 'I won't allow it. She's *my* daughter and I won't give her up.'

'I had no intention of asking you.' A small frown wrinkled his forehead. 'My wife is in no fit condition to adopt a young person. She is getting agitated because Oliver will soon be leaving home for medical school. She'll miss him and will want someone else to take his place. I came to ask you to meet Daisy – not here,' he added quickly, 'nor at my home or shop. Somewhere neutral where you can discuss her future.' He eyed Lily cautiously. 'I'm afraid I'll have to ask you to take her away from us. I'll give her a reference, of course, so that she will be able to obtain another position, but I must advise you to find somewhere else as soon as possible.'

Things are going from bad to worse, she thought. I don't know anyone who would take her on. If I couldn't find any work, what hope has Daisy? 'Why so soon, Mr Walker? Has she not been satisfactory?'

'Very satisfactory,' he said. 'But Mrs Walker is becoming obsessed by her. She will soon want her with her all day and all night, and if Daisy doesn't agree then I can't answer for the consequences. I hate to say this, Mrs Maddeson, but I'm afraid my wife is becoming deranged. We had a child,' he murmured. 'A girl. It was my wife's fault that she died and she is trying to find another to replace her.'

CHAPTER FORTY-TWO

Johnny slept on the floor by the Wards' fire and Ted slept in a chair. Ted said that he was willing to sleep on the floor but his father explained that after being captured by the sepoys he had slept on the ground in a cave without the luxury of a rag rug like the one in front of the Wards' fire. 'This is real comfort,' he said. 'And I'm in no danger of being shot or beheaded.'

They'd talked well into the night, for there was much catching up to do. Ted was nervous and reticent at first, but he was also keen to know why it was that his father had spent so many years away from home and they had never received a word from him.

'What you have to realize, son,' Johnny said, 'is that when I joined 'military I didn't expect to go abroad so soon, or that I would travel so far away. I knew that I would probably go to Ireland as there's allus trouble there, but I was ignorant, I suppose, of what 'army did or where it went. At that time, your ma and me didn't have any money; there weren't many jobs out in 'country and folks were going into towns to look for work. The army seemed exciting; I'd get food and clothing and pay every month. But I was wrong,' he admitted. 'It's a life for a single man, not for one wi' a wife and childre'. But I've got a bit o' money now, some of my back pay, and . . .' On second thoughts he decided he wouldn't tell Ted of the

329

amber he'd sold. That was for Lily's ears, if ever he found her.

'What we'll do in 'morning, Ted,' he said, before settling down to sleep, 'is make a contingency plan. We'll talk about where your ma is likely to be. She'll probably still be in Hull. If she'd come back somebody over at Hollym would have heard about it, but as it was they thought you'd all been drowned.'

'She is still in Hull,' Ted said urgently. 'And I know where Daisy is,' he added eagerly. 'I know where she works. I've seen 'shop.'

'Daisy working,' Johnny murmured. 'That little bairn! I can't believe that I've been away so long!'

'You have, Da!'

They grinned at each other then, at the acknowledgement that they were father and son. Ted reached out his hand to Johnny, who took it and squeezed it. 'Goodnight, son.'

'Goodnight, Da!'

The next morning Mrs Ward gave them a good breakfast of eggs and bacon, and then packed up a parcel of bread and beef to sustain them on their journey into Hull. 'I wish you luck,' she said, 'and hope to see you back in Holderness with your wife.'

Johnny thanked her, but when John Ward came to see them off he asked him in a quiet voice, 'Where will I find Billy Fowler? I need to see him before I set off for Hull.'

John Ward looked dubious. 'You won't do owt you'll regret, will you? I've no regard for him, never have had, and what he did to his wife was despicable; but I'm onny thinking that if you should set about him it'd not be good. You'd find yoursen in trouble wi' 'law.'

'I won't,' Johnny assured him. 'But I need to find out why he did what he did.' And I want to take a look at him, he thought. To find out why Lily married him.

He called on the parish clerk to find out Fowler's address but drew a blank. The clerk told him that Fowler had been to see him asking to be rehoused. 'But we had nowhere for him,' he said. 'He was after a new property, but we have none. There are great plans afoot for when 'railway line comes to Withernsea, as it will afore long – then we shall have whole roads of new houses. Withernsea will be 'Brighton of the north.'

'Can't see it meself,' Ted muttered.

The clerk glowered at him. 'Oh, yes! Mr Bannister himself is planning it. It's been in 'newspapers so it must be right.'

'Who's Mr Bannister?' Johnny asked. 'Sorry, but I've been out of circulation for a bit. I've never heard of him.'

'He's 'chairman of 'railway company that's going to build 'line! Two or three years and it'll be here.'

'So what about Fowler?' Johnny persisted. 'Do you know where he went?'

The clerk shook his head. 'He was right mad. I told him, onny empty property we've got is on 'Waxholme road and that's standing right on 'edge of 'cliff. Somehow he'd got hold of 'notion that he'd get somewhere new and he went off muttering and grumbling. So, sorry, but I've no idea.'

'Don't let's bother,' Ted said when they got outside. 'He's not worth worrying about.'

Johnny heaved a breath. 'But what's bothering me, Ted, is that he's married to your ma, and I don't know if it's legal. Were you there? Was it in church?'

Ted nodded. 'It was in choch, but we didn't go, Daisy and me. He said he didn't want us there. Didn't want a fuss, he said, so it was going to be him and Ma and 'vicar.'

'And nobody else?'

Ted shrugged. 'Don't know. Ma went right quiet after. I thought mebbe she was wishing she hadn't done it, and then when we went to Seathorne and saw 'hovel where he lived!' Ted screwed up his face in disgust. 'She had to clean it out afore we could live in it.'

'All right.' Johnny had made up his mind. 'We'll go to

Hull and look for them and then decide what to do after that.'

'Do we have to walk?' Ted said wearily. 'Can we tek carrier? I had 'owd hoss last time but coming back I didn't have much money, so I walked.'

Johnny grinned. 'I think I could find a copper to pay 'carrier if he hasn't left already. And if he has,' he tweaked Ted's ear, 'then we'll walk. It's nowt,' he said. 'Just a stroll.' He looked questioningly at Ted. 'When did you come back? Did you get a lift?'

'Yesterday. I'd onny just got to 'Wards' house when you knocked on 'door. I walked from Hull and then I got a lift on a cart.' He gazed straight at his father. 'It wasn't you following me, was it? Somebody was.'

Johnny grinned. 'I rather think it might have been. I kept thinking that if I could catch up wi' that young fellow we could have a chat while we were walking.'

Ted groaned and then he grinned too. 'And we'd have saved ourselves a walk back from Holderness, wouldn't we, if we'd known?'

The carrier had already left from Withernsea so they walked into Patrington where Johnny hired a horse and small cart for the rest of the journey. 'We can bring your ma and Daisy back in this, if they want to come,' he said as they set off.

'Daisy likes it in Hull,' Ted remarked gloomily. 'She's working for this apothecary. He lets her count tablets and run errands.'

'How come she's there?' Johnny asked. 'She'd have no references. And why didn't she stay wi' your ma?'

'Daisy said he'd helped Ma when she was – when she was—' Ted stopped in confusion. Bad enough for his father to hear that his mother had married again, but what would he say if Ted told him that Ma had been expecting Fowler's child? What if he didn't stay? What if he went off and they never saw him again? He half turned and searched his father's face. He didn't know him well enough yet to guess how he would react to that kind of news. Right now he had a frown just above his nose which made him look stern, though not aggressive as Fowler used to look if Ted said something to upset him.

'Come on, lad,' Johnny said patiently. 'I'll not bite thee. Spit it out! Whatever your ma did or didn't do doesn't affect you and me. I'm your da. I'll not let you down again.'

Ted lowered his head. 'She was expecting,' he mumbled. 'Daisy said that this man, this chemist, helped her to his shop cos she'd—' He swallowed. 'Cos she'd started to whelp 'n' there was nobody else to help her.'

Johnny swore under his breath. 'So Fowler took her to Hull when she was expecting a bairn and sold her! I'll search him out,' he muttered bitterly. 'I'll teach him a thing or two. And it's *labour*!' he bellowed at Ted, more in frustration than anger. 'Not *whelp*. She's not an animal, even though Fowler treated her as if she was!'

Ted jumped, then said eagerly, 'Can I watch, Da, if you go and find him and give him a good hiding? I told you, didn't I, that I fought wi' him, 'n' he went ower 'cliff!'

Johnny nodded wearily, wondering when this nightmare would end and what the outcome would be. 'So was your ma delivered safely? Was it a healthy child?'

'No,' Ted said. 'It was aborted. That's what Daisy said anyway. And I'm glad,' he said vehemently. 'Cos I wouldn't have wanted any brat of Fowler's to be related to me!'

'That's enough,' Johnny said sharply. 'It wouldn't have been 'bairn's fault.'

'No, Da.' Ted hung his head again. 'Sorry.' Yet even as he apologized, he felt an extraordinary exultation in his chest: that his father knew what was right and what was wrong and would tell him; and somehow Ted knew that from now on, if he was anxious or bothered about anything, he could ask without fear of the consequences, and his father would willingly advise him.

CHAPTER FORTY-THREE

Lily's head was reeling as Mr Walker quietly explained about his wife's condition. 'She has, no doubt, given you an account of how we met.' When Lily nodded primly, he gave a wry grimace and said, 'My version might be somewhat different.' He explained that he had not been in practice long when he was called to a house in Leadenhall Square to give medication to a young woman. 'There wasn't a doctor available, and besides, they were not in a position to pay for one.'

He gave a wistful smile. 'Martha came in whilst I was there: she took my breath away, she was so very lovely. Graceful, with a beautiful smile, and I was absolutely smitten with her, so if she's told you that, that at least is true. I kept on calling at the house, with the excuse that I was coming to see the sick girl. Then one morning I met her in the town and invited her to come with me to a coffee shop. She put on all of her charm and I knew I had to keep on seeing her; and with a young man's arrogance I thought I could rescue her from the life she was leading.'

He gave a deep sigh and gazed at Lily. 'And so I did. I arranged our marriage against the advice of all my friends, and just a few weeks before we were due to be wed I realized that she was pregnant. I also knew that it wasn't my child.'

'Oh!' Lily exclaimed. 'So you did know! Mrs Walker said that you didn't.'

'I knew; and Oliver knows that he isn't my son, even though I treat him as if he is.' He smiled. 'He's as good as. I've brought him up as my own and he thinks of me as his father. But the child we lost was mine. During the pregnancy my wife began drinking and stealing medication from my medicine cupboard. She took an overdose of tablets by mistake, and it affected the child.'

He looked so sad that Lily's heart went out to him. 'Now she's full of grief and anger and has lost sight of what really happened. And although at first she didn't want Daisy anywhere near her, she has now thought up this scheme that Daisy could be a replacement for the child we lost.'

'I'm so sorry,' Lily began, but was interrupted by a peal on the door bell. 'A customer,' she whispered. 'Do you want to go out 'back way?'

He nodded. 'Please. I might see someone I know and it would be embarrassing for both of us. I'll speak to you again, Mrs Maddeson.'

'Lily,' she said softly. 'And please tell me when I might see Daisy. But you were right – it mustn't be here.'

'Tomorrow,' he said urgently. 'By St Mary's. Two o'clock? I'll send her.'

There was a non-stop queue of customers that evening; all very merry and all wanting a drink and a little supper before going upstairs with the girls. They were also very generous and gave Lily gratuities on leaving as well as payment for the services of the girls, some of them whispering seductively into her ear, 'If only you would, Miss Lily.' But she only smiled and gently shook her head.

That night she slept in a chair at Alice's bedside. Tomorrow I must ask Dr Fulton to call again, she thought wearily, though I don't know how I'll pay for all his visits. The doctor had not yet presented her with his bill and she had kept back a portion of her earnings to pay him. Leo had sent another basket of fruit and wine the day before and it sat on the side table waiting to be opened. He's got a conscience all right, she thought wryly, before falling into an uneasy sleep.

The next morning she brought a bowl of warm water to bathe Alice, but only washed her hands and her inflamed and sensitive face as Alice was barely able to raise herself. She brought another pillow and called to Mrs Flitt to help her. They arranged the sheets and blanket and then Mrs Flitt whispered that she had to slip out. She nodded significantly at Lily, who was so tired she didn't realize at first that she was trying to tell her she was going to fetch the doctor.

Lily busied herself about the room and then began to empty Leo's gift basket. She took out a bottle of sherry, some apples and oranges, a box of sweet biscuits and a box of chocolates. At the bottom of the box was a white envelope with her name on it. *Miss Lily*.

She glanced at Alice, who was sleeping, and opened it. *Dear Miss Lily*, she read. The note on plain paper was written in a bold hand. *Please accept this offering* – she peeked inside and saw crisp banknotes – *towards any comforts that Alice might need. She is a dear sweet girl and doesn't deserve such misfortune. With best regards, L.*

I suppose he couldn't give his name, she pondered, fingering the money, and it's almost too late, but at least we can pay the doctor, and . . . She didn't dare think any further than that. Enough, she thought, to live one day at a time.

Later, after she had fed Alice some soup and had some herself, she changed into her grey gown, pinned up her hair and put on a bonnet. 'I have to go out, Alice,' she said softly. 'I'm going to see Daisy. Mrs Flitt will sit with you until I come back.' Mrs Flitt had returned with the message that Dr Fulton would call that evening.

'I wish I could meet Daisy,' Alice whispered. 'I'd like to know her.' She gave a hacking cough. 'But you can't bring her here, can you? It wouldn't be right.'

I might have to, Lily thought, while telling Alice that she

would rather not. What am I to do? She gazed at Mrs Flitt, who had raised her eyebrows. I'd like to go home. With both my children. But what would we do there? Where would we live? Would the parish house us? And how will I ever find Ted again?

Daisy crept into the shop. Mr Walker had told her in front of Mrs Walker that he needed her to go on an urgent errand, but then when she had put on her coat and bonnet, both of which Mrs Walker had bought her, he had told her that she was to meet her mother at St Mary's. 'Try not to be longer than half an hour,' he said, 'or Mrs Walker will want to know where you have been.'

'Daisy.' Oliver had been gazing out of the window. 'I thought I saw your brother earlier, but I might have been mistaken. It was someone who looked like him, anyway.'

'Not Ted,' she said. 'He's gone to sea, hasn't he? He said he was going to travel to foreign countries.'

'He might have only got a short trip, say to Holland or somewhere. Would he come looking for you, do you think?'

'No.' Daisy sighed. 'He'd be too nervous. He wouldn't want to get me into trouble.'

Oliver smiled. 'You wouldn't be in trouble. Not with Father, at least.'

'I know,' she said. 'But Mrs Walker wouldn't like it.' She was on the point of telling him that his mother wanted to adopt her, but then thought better of it. 'I'd better go,' she said. 'I'm on an important errand.'

He grinned. 'Yes, I know. Give your mother my good wishes!'

'Oh!' Sometimes she was surprised at how much Oliver knew about what was going on. His father must confide in him, she had decided. 'Yes, I will.' She opened the door and looked out. 'It's very windy. I'll get blown away.'

Oliver nodded and gazed out of the window again. Then he frowned. 'Look. That's the fellow I was telling you about.

Is it your brother? It looks so like him. There, sitting on the church wall talking to that man.'

Daisy looked across the square. 'It is!' she gasped. 'It's Ted! Oh, he can come with me to see Ma. She'll be so pleased! Thank you, Oliver. Goodbye. I'll be back soon.'

She raced across towards the church. 'Ted! Ted! It's me!'

Ted saw her, grinned and waved. 'Hey up, Daisy! We've been waiting ages to see you.'

'I'm going to see Ma! Mr Walker arranged it. He's given me time off. Mrs Walker thinks I'm going on an errand. You can come with me.'

She gazed delightedly at Ted, completely ignoring the stranger by his side, who had risen off the wall and was gazing intently at her. 'I thought you'd gone to sea! You've soon come back.'

'Onny went as far as Driffield,' he said. 'Took a keel, but they wanted somebody wi' experience. Daisy—' Ted's face flushed and he turned to his companion.

'Come on,' she said impatiently. 'I don't want Mrs Walker to see me. She might look out of 'window. Besides, Ma will be waiting. I'm to meet her by 'church.'

'Yes, but . . .' Ted followed as Daisy moved off, his companion following also. 'Daisy, wait. I want to tell you summat.'

'What?' She turned when they were out of sight of the shop window and at last looked curiously at the man standing beside Ted.

'You don't know who this is, Daisy?' Ted's face was now bright red.

She shook her head. 'No. Are you a seaman?' she asked the man.

'No, I was a soldier.' Johnny blinked. He could scarcely believe that the child he had left behind had grown up almost to the brink of womanhood. 'I've been away a long time, Daisy. A lot of years.'

'Oh!' She wasn't very interested. She wanted to get to her

mother and she had so little time. 'My da was a soldier. He was killed.'

'No, he wasn't!' Ted was almost shouting. 'He's here! This is our da, Daisy.'

Daisy went so white that Johnny thought she was going to faint and took a step towards her. Her eyes filled with tears and she looked frightened. 'He's not!' she said. 'Don't you fib, Ted Maddeson. My ma said he was dead!' She clutched her arms about her. 'I've got to go.' She turned round and sped off.

'Keep up with her!' Johnny said urgently. 'We shan't know where she's going otherwise.'

'She said she was going to 'choch,' Ted puffed. 'But not this big one here. There's another at 'other end of 'road.' They could see Daisy's skirt flying and her head bobbing as she ran.

'I know where she's going.' Johnny slowed down. 'St Mary's. We used to march past it when I first joined 'military.' He didn't want to rush to his first meeting with Lily, and he hoped that Daisy wouldn't blurt out the news. 'You go ahead, Ted,' he said. 'Go meet your ma.'

Ted glanced at him and nodded, moving ahead of his father. 'Shall I tell her?' was his parting shot.

'No.' He didn't know how Lily would react. Would she be pleased to see him after all this time, or would she reject him for being tardy at corresponding? But what is a soldier supposed to do? he thought. How was I supposed to know whether my letters ever reached home?

He followed slowly and saw Daisy crossing the narrow road towards the church tower, and Ted close behind her. Then he saw a tall woman, dressed in a grey gown and bonnet, waving to them. 'Lily,' he breathed. 'Is it really you?'

Lily walked slowly towards the meeting place by the church. It wasn't far from Leadenhall Square and it seemed wrong that such a dissolute area should be so near to an ancient house of worship. The church tower jutted out into the north end of Lowgate and pedestrians risked their lives as they stepped out into the hubbub of hansom cabs, horses and carts and riders to get past the tower. A flock of sheep being driven towards a slaughter house was causing congestion and confusion as they skittered, bleating, about the road.

Lily spotted her daughter dashing along the footpath. Why is she running so fast? She's not late. And then behind her someone else was running and for a moment she caught her breath as she thought that Daisy was being chased. Then her face creased into a smile. Ted! It was Ted. She lifted the hem of her skirt and scurried towards them, glancing both ways before hurrying across the road between the traffic.

'Daisy!' she called. 'I'm here! Look behind you! It's Ted! Ted! Is it really him?' He had grown taller though he looked thinner. Wherever has he been?

She scooped Daisy up into her arms for a quick hug, and then let go of her as she reached out for her son.

'I've been that bothered about you!' she exclaimed. 'Daisy said you were going to find a ship and go to sea! Is that what you did?'

'Not exactly, Ma. Ma—' He seemed flustered.

'Ma!' Daisy said plaintively and Lily pulled them both back to the safety of St Mary's wall, putting an arm round each of them. 'Ma, Ted said—' Daisy began again.

'Wait,' Ted implored. 'Don't say owt yet.'

'About what?' Lily smiled. They must have had a disagreement over something, but she didn't care; she could forgive them anything now that she had them both safely back again. Whatever problems she had she could deal with, now that she knew her bairns were safe.

A man was standing behind the children, hindering the progress of passers-by, and she glanced at him, wondering why he didn't move on. Daisy was pulling on her arm and Ted was shuffling from one foot to the other in the way he always did when he had something to tell her.

Her lips parted and she took a sudden breath as she looked again at the man in front of her. 'Hello, Lily.' His voice was soft but oh so familiar. 'Don't be alarmed. It's me!'

Lily fell back against the church wall, feeling it solid beneath her fingers as she clutched at it for support. 'Johnny! But – they said you were dead,' she whispered. 'They said you'd been killed! I wrote . . .'

She saw the upturn of his mouth, though it wasn't a smile, rather a wry grimace. 'As you see, I'm alive,' he said in a low voice. 'A bit worse for wear but still upright and breathing.'

A range of emotions threatened to knock her out and she felt that she would fall but for the wall behind her. As it was, her legs were weak and she fought to keep standing. Tears rushed to her eyes. He was alive. He looked the same, though older and without the boyish demeanour he had once had.

'I'm dreaming,' she muttered. 'It's not true!'

'It's true, Lily. It's me; feel.' He put out his hand. 'Flesh and blood.'

A sudden gush of angry passion swept over her. 'Why didn't you write? Why did you put me through such hell? Such sorrow!' She hurled herself at him, hammering him with her fists. 'You don't know what I've had to do; what I've been through; how I've had to live!'

He caught her by the wrists, though gently. 'I did write. Lots of times. Regiment thought I was dead. I was captured. I've walked across India to get home. Lily! Whatever's happened we can put right together. Say that we can.'

Through her tears she saw the uncertainty on his face and tears glistening in his eyes too, which she had never seen before. 'You don't understand,' she croaked. 'I married someone else because I thought you were dead!'

'I know,' he said softly. 'But I still love you, Lily. You were my wife and as far as I'm concerned you still are.'

She started to weep, and as Daisy and Ted looked on with

341

a mixture of concern and bewilderment Johnny gathered Lily up into his arms and, oblivious of the people passing by, kissed her wet cheeks until at last, sobbing, she put her head on his chest and felt that he was real and had come home to her.

CHAPTER FORTY-FOUR

Johnny led them back to Scale Lane, away from the traffic and pedestrians, for they were causing an obstruction. Daisy and Ted gazed anxiously from one to the other.

'Ma.' Daisy's voice quavered. 'I've onny got half an hour and I've to get back. Mr Walker said you wanted to see me.' She didn't look at Johnny but kept her eyes averted.

Lily took out a handkerchief and blew her nose. 'Yes.' She swallowed. 'We have to decide what to do. You can't stay wi' 'Walkers. But now,' she glanced at Johnny, 'now things have changed. Am I a bigamist? But Billy Fowler's drowned, so am I a widow?'

Ted stared at her. 'No, Ma,' he croaked. 'He's not. He climbed up 'cliff. He's still alive.'

'So I'm a bigamist,' Lily whispered. 'Will I go to prison?'

Daisy started to cry, but Johnny broke in, 'It's all right, Daisy. We'll sort it out. It wasn't your ma's fault.'

'It's *your* fault,' Daisy shrieked at this man who was claiming to be her father when she didn't remember him at all. 'You shouldn't have gone away and left us!'

'I know,' he said gently. 'But you don't understand how it was. I thought I was doing it for 'best. But I was wrong.'

'Hush now and listen!' Lily wiped her eyes and took a breath. 'Daisy, go back to Mr Walker's. Ted, you walk her back. Yes,' she said firmly when Daisy scoffed that she didn't need anybody with her. 'Go with her and explain

343

to Mr Walker what's happened and ask if Daisy can come out tomorrow at 'same time; and mebbe then we'll have decided what to do.'

'Meet me here again in an hour, Ted,' Johnny urged; he didn't want his son to disappear. 'We'll find somewhere to stay. Unless . . . ?' He glanced at Lily, who vigorously shook her head.

As the youngsters walked away, Lily said bitterly, 'It's you who doesn't understand! You can't possibly know what I've been through these last six months.'

'I know some of it,' Johnny said. 'Ted told me that Fowler brought you to Hull and sold you. I've been to Holderness,' he explained. 'That's where I found Ted; he'd walked from Hull to an owd farmer's at Seathorne. And I was told you'd all drowned, so I do know what it's like to be told that somebody you love has died!'

'Drowned! Who said that?' she gasped.

'Fowler,' he said. 'Your husband! How did you come to marry a man like him?' Suddenly he too was angry. 'Surely you must have guessed that he was a villain?'

'How?' she shrieked. 'How could I tell? I was lonely and poor. You don't know how hard it is to bring up two young bairns! All those years on my own, waiting for you to come home! There was many a time when I thought we'd end up in 'workhouse.' She put her hand to her head. 'It seemed a way out. Fowler told me he lived in a smallholding near to 'sea. He said he could provide for us.' Though he was reluctant about the children, she remembered. 'But he didn't say that it was a hovel right on 'edge.' Her voice became quieter and she let Johnny take her hand. 'He just wanted a woman,' she muttered. 'He didn't want a wife. He liked things to be left as they were. He was bad-tempered and a bully. He was forever on at Ted and generally ignored Daisy, until he realized that she was coming up to the age when he thought she should find a job of work. Then,' she added, 'he'd heard somewhere that he was within his rights to sell me. I was pregnant, so there'd be another mouth to feed.'

344

Johnny was quiet and just stood by her side. They were jostled from time to time by people trying to get past them down the narrow cobbled street.

'You'd better come wi' me,' Lily said when he made no response, and pulled her hand away from his. 'And I'll show you how low I've sunk.'

She led him back down Lowgate, away from St Mary's, and crossed the road towards Leadenhall Square. He glanced round. As a young soldier he'd marched along here. When they came to the square, he faltered as Lily turned in and on towards the houses.

'Wait,' he said. 'Where're you going?' There were women sitting on the house steps. Some were talking to each other, some were lying asleep across the steps, others were smoking pipes. They looked on idly as Lily and Johnny walked by.

One of them shouted to Lily, 'Bit early in 'day isn't it, dearie?' Another called out, 'Send him ower here when you've finished wi' him – I could do wi' a bit extra.' Yet another turned over and pulled up her skirts, shouting to Johnny to see what was on offer.

Lily glared defiantly at Johnny. 'You'll have seen this sort of thing afore, I expect? Soldiers, sailors; this is what they expect of women.'

Johnny felt sick to the stomach and wanted to weep. 'Not me,' he muttered. 'Not where I've been.'

They were approaching a house at the bottom of the square. It looked tidier than the others, with clean curtains at the window and well brushed steps. The door opened and an old woman looked out and beckoned urgently. 'Miss Lily,' she called. 'Come quick!'

'Miss Lily?' he breathed. 'Is that what you're called?'

She turned to face him. 'Yes. It's where I live – and work. It's a brothel, onny 'fellow who runs it likes it to be called a bordello; he thinks it sounds more refined. You can come in if you like. Have a look round.' Tears were streaming down her face. 'This is what I've come to, Johnny. I'm a madam

345

in a brothel. Are you sure you want to reclaim me as your wife?' Her lips trembled. 'I've got to go. I'm wanted. Somebody needs me more urgently than you do.'

She turned and hurried towards the house where the old woman, halfway down the steps, was frantically beckoning.

He watched her go. His legs wouldn't move. He saw her run up the steps and through the door and the old woman, glancing his way, closed it behind them. Was there some man waiting for her? It was someone special who didn't like to be kept waiting, judging by the antics of the old biddy who was hurrying her up.

Ted! He remembered that he'd asked Ted to meet him by the church. He turned round and walked back past the women, who looked blatantly and curiously at him.

'It's true then, is it?' one of them called to him.

'What?' He should have walked on, but instead he paused in front of her. 'Is what true?'

'That that snooty bitch doesn't go wi' 'customers? She onny teks money for her girls?' The woman, or girl, for she didn't look very old, wiped her nose on her sleeve. She gave a laugh which showed her black misshapen teeth. 'Some of 'em have left. I reckon she kept most of their money for hersen.'

'It's to be hoped Jamie don't find out then,' another one called out. 'She's likely to get beaten up if he does.'

Johnny hesitated, then said, 'Can I talk to you? I need some answers.'

The woman grinned. 'Aye, come on in.'

Lily stumbled through the door. 'Is she weakening?' She gazed with reddened eyes at Mrs Flitt. 'Will you run for Dr Fulton again? Tell him it's urgent.'

Mrs Flitt placed her wrinkled hand on Lily's arm. 'It don't matter if he comes or not,' she said. 'There's nowt he can do, and besides, it's you she wants. You've got troubles, I can tell,' she said softly, 'but put 'em to one side for 'minute. They'll keep for some other time.'

Lily nodded, wiped her wet cheeks, and vigorously blew her nose. Then she drew herself up, took a deep breath and opened the door into her room where Alice lay quietly sleeping.

She drew up a chair and sat beside the bed, taking Alice's pale hand in her own. Alice opened her eyes. 'There you are, Lily,' she whispered. 'I hoped you'd come.'

'Of course I've come.' Lily's voice had a catch in it. 'I was detained, and you'll never believe why.'

Alice gave a wan smile. 'Was it something nice? Has Lizzie had her bairn?'

'Not yet,' she said. 'I'll tell you 'minute I hear. Do you remember, Alice, when I told you about my husband Johnny?'

'Yes.' Alice's breathing was laboured. 'You loved him, didn't you?'

Lily nodded. 'Always. Since I was very young. Well, he's come back.' Her voice broke.

'In a dream?' Alice's voice was merely a whisper and Lily bent her head towards her. 'Sometimes I think my ma's here. I can see her, clear as owt, but then she disappears again.' She took a shuddering breath. 'Then I know I'm dreaming.'

'Not a dream.' Tears started to trickle from Lily's eyes again. 'Johnny was real. Not killed as I thought, but alive.'

Alice had closed her eyes but she murmured, 'I'm glad for you, Lily. You'll be able to go home now.' She half opened her eyelids. 'I'll go home soon, I think. But I'll miss you, Lily. You're 'best friend I ever had.' She closed her eyes again and Lily thought she had dropped asleep until she murmured, 'You'll tell me when Lizzie has her bairn? Promise? It's a new life starting over.'

'I'll tell you,' Lily choked. 'I promise I will. Rest now – save your strength.'

Alice gave a hint of a smile. 'Yes,' she breathed. 'I'll save it. Ma'll want me to help her, I expect. She was never able to do for herself. That's why I left. I was allus 'drudge.'

'But not now, Alice.' Lily stroked her hand. 'Here you are in a comfy bed with all your friends here to do for you.'

Alice gave a gentle nod of her head. 'Lucky. Very lucky.'

Lily stayed by her side as she slept. Mrs Flitt came in to bring her a cup of coffee. 'How is she, do you think?' she whispered.

'I wish 'doctor'd come,' Lily murmured. 'I know he can't do anything, but it'd be a comfort just to see him.'

'He'll come.' Mrs Flitt patted her shoulder. 'Try not to fret.'

'Stay with me, Mrs Flitt,' Lily said. 'Keep vigil wi' me. I can't do it on my own.'

Mrs Flitt pulled up a footstool and perched like a gnome at the foot of the bed. 'What'll we do later?' she asked in a low voice. 'You know, when . . . when 'customers come.'

Lily stared at her with wide eyes and bit on her lip. 'We'll have to lock 'door. They can't come in when . . . when—'

'I'll see to it,' Mrs Flitt interrupted. 'Don't you worry. Mary and Sally are in already. Shall I explain to 'em – and then, well, if they want to go out . . . ?'

'Yes,' Lily agreed. 'They won't want to miss any earnings. Tell Mary that Cherie will look after Aaron. Will you send Cherie in to me? Tell her I need to speak to her.'

Mrs Flitt rose painfully from the stool. 'By, my owd bones ache, and yet I'm still here, of no use to anybody – and here's this young lass!' She gazed pityingly at Alice. 'Don't seem right somehow.'

'You are of use,' Lily admonished her. 'To all of us; but no, it doesn't seem fair that Alice – so young!' She sighed. 'There's no point in asking why.'

Cherie came into the room. She was pale and trembling as she gazed down at Alice, so thin and wasted. 'I'm frightened,' she whispered.

Lily comforted her. 'She's resting, Cherie. There's no need to be afraid, and she's in 'company of her friends. It's not as if she's out somewhere on her own and lonely.'

'No,' Cherie was unconvinced. 'I wish I could go and see Lizzie,' she said plaintively.

'You can,' Lily said patiently, 'but not now. I want you to look after Aaron tonight, and then we'll see what tomorrow brings.'

There were few customers that night, and Mrs Flitt in a neat bonnet and clean apron opened the door to them and explained that they were closed for business for a couple of nights and gave them directions for finding Mary and Sally who had gone out of the square and into the High Street.

'They'll treat you right,' she said, giving a wink, and closed the door on them, muttering contentious suggestions on the different ways they might hang themselves. The doctor came and went but gave no advice except to say to Lily that they could only wait.

Mrs Flitt came quietly into the room and saw that Lily had dropped to sleep; she put a few pieces of coal on the fire and sat on the floor beside it. What'll I do next? she pondered. Lily will move on, I'm sure of it. She'll not stop here when her precious girls have gone. She too nodded in and out of sleep and woke with a start when the coals shifted in the fire. A wafting sigh came from the bed and she lifted her head. It was close on the midnight hour; a time, she believed, when souls departing peacefully from this earth gathered together for their last journey.

Groaning inwardly from the pain in her knees, she got to her feet and stood by Lily's side. Lily was awake and holding Alice's hand. 'She slipped away so silently, I barely knew she'd gone,' she said softly. 'But she smiled. It was as if she'd seen someone she knew. I hope she had.'

CHAPTER FORTY-FIVE

At seven o'clock the next morning someone banged on the front door. Lily and Mrs Flitt were already up and dressed. Cherie was asleep with Aaron tucked up beside her. Mary and Sally had arrived back in the early hours of the morning and slipped quietly upstairs on hearing about Alice.

'I'm coming, I'm coming.' Mrs Flitt hurried to the door. 'Shut that racket.'

A small boy stood on the step, unable to reach the door bell. He touched his cap. 'Message for Miss Lily,' he piped. 'I've been give a penny for coming!'

Mrs Flitt grabbed the note from him and shooed him away. She took it through to Lily who was sitting in the kitchen cradling a cup and gazing into space. She opened the envelope, scanned the contents and in a tearful voice said, 'It's from Rena.' She began to read it aloud.

'"Dear Lily, we have a most beautiful boy! He arrived at a quarter past two this morning giving us a vociferous greeting. Lizzie is feeling well and already in love with her son, Ethan, as I am too. She says to be sure to tell Cherie and Alice and Mrs Flitt, and that you must all come to visit as soon as possible. Your humbled and overjoyed friend, Rena."'

She got up from her chair and, taking the letter with her, went into her room and gazed down at the peaceful

Alice. How lovely she is. Her skin seemed smoother, the pox marks already fading. 'Lizzie has a son, Alice,' she murmured, and couldn't contain the sob in her voice. 'I promised I'd come and tell you as soon as I heard.'

They scraped together enough money for a coffin and burial at the new General Cemetery on Spring Bank just outside the town. All other burial sites within the town were closed due to overcrowding and unsanitary conditions.

'It's a disgrace,' Mrs Flitt grumbled as they walked behind the cart which held the coffin. 'Every churchyard full and nowhere for a decent body to lay his head.'

It was a long walk for Mrs Flitt, hobbling along beside Lily, Cherie, a pregnant Betty, and Henry. A huge bouquet of flowers had arrived that morning, sent without a name attached, but Lily knew that it was from Leo. They were the only flowers and Lily placed them in the cart with the coffin. The cemetery was laid out like a park with trees and pathways between beds of flowers. Mr Walker was there, and Dr Fulton. Jamie was absent, but he had called at the house the morning after Alice's death, and muttered that he wouldn't be attending the funeral.

Lily wasn't surprised to hear that, but later that day on answering the door bell was astounded to see Jamie's mother Nell on the step, calling to offer her condolences.

'Jamie won't attend 'burial, that I know,' she'd said. 'My son seems to be a hard-hearted unfeeling man.' She had turned her head away as she'd spoken. 'And that's my fault. You see, he's hurt inside; has been since he was a bairn and I left him alone to work out on 'streets. There was allus a man coming between us and at first he didn't understand that that was how I made my living. Eventually he did understand, and it was then that he decided that he'd choose my customers.' She sighed. 'He was looking for a better type, and I believe he was trying to rid us of the sort of man who might have been his father.'

'But he hates women,' Lily said. 'I'm sure of it, or he wouldn't do what he does. He would have seen me go to jail and not turned a hair.'

'Yes,' Nell had agreed, and turned soulful eyes to her. 'He would. That's why – that's why I paid your fine. I knew that Jamie wouldn't and that you couldn't afford to.'

'*You* paid it!' Lily was amazed. 'But why? You're out of this business.'

Nell nodded. 'I had a lucky escape; but I still blame myself for 'way that Jamie behaves. He's my son and it's my fault,' she repeated, 'and I can't let anybody else suffer for it.'

Lily and Mrs Flitt walked back together after the burial. Cherie had been given a ride in the carriage hired for the return with Betty and Henry and intended to visit Lizzie and her baby; Dr Fulton and Mr Walker had gone off together with their heads bent in serious conversation.

'You should have gone in 'carriage with Betty like she wanted us to,' Lily told the old woman. 'It's a long walk back for you.'

'It's no further for me than for you,' Mrs Flitt said wryly. 'It's exactly 'same distance.'

But I wanted to be alone to think, Lily pondered. I want to think about my future; if I've got one. I shan't stop at Leadenhall Square. Not now. Not with Alice gone and Lizzie gone, and Cherie – well, I have a feeling that Rena will take her. She'll be able to look after baby Ethan whilst Lizzie and Rena build up their new business. But what about Mrs Flitt? I can't just abandon her.

'I've been thinking,' Mrs Flitt puffed at the side of her. 'Thinking I might move on. I'll try for a job in a kitchen somewhere, or mebbe in an inn or hostelry, washing glasses 'n' that or sweeping 'yard.'

'Will you?' Lily turned to her. 'You'd have to live in.'

'Aye, I know. But mebbe there's another warm cupboard somewhere.'

If that is possible, if someone would set her on, that

would mean I'd just have to fend for me and Daisy, Lily thought. Daisy wasn't very taken with Johnny, though I think that Ted is. He'll probably stay with his father. He needs a man to mould him. I haven't done a very good job, though I did try to keep Johnny's memory alive for them. But he'll not want me now. I'll be soiled goods in his eyes. He wouldn't believe that I'm not. Nobody would; not living and working in that place. I'll have a debauched reputation just like those other women in the square.

But we shouldn't judge, she mused, reflecting on how touched she had been as Alice's coffin had been trundled through the square. The women from the other houses, the whores and pox-scarred hags, had stood silently on their steps, by their doors and windows, watching Alice's last journey. Some had clasped their hands together as if in prayer, and many of the others had wiped their eyes. One or two had gazed searchingly at Lily and nodded to her in sympathy.

But now she looked about her with fresh eyes as she returned to the square. Mrs Flitt had gone to the market to try to beg for some bread, for they were completely out of money. Mary and Sally would be sleeping and tonight they would be out on the streets, earning money only for themselves.

Lily saw the house as it was, grimy and run down, with broken window frames and flimsy torn curtains which no matter how many times she and Mrs Flitt had washed them were still a dingy grey. What must Johnny have thought when I brought him here? I was foolish to do that. I should have just explained to him about my circumstances, instead of showing him. Perhaps then we would have stood a chance together. But I was so angry. Angry with him for leaving me for all those years, and not a word from him. But perhaps it wasn't his fault. He's been in another world and not one I know anything about. Do they have post boxes in those remote places? Afghanistan:

I think of it as a desert land with rocks and mountains. And India; I think of dark-skinned people and spices and heat. Why should our soldiers be there, trying to take what isn't ours?

A tear rolled down her cheek. It had been a harrowing day and she felt very sorry for herself. Why did Johnny have to go there when I needed him by my side? Why did he leave me to succumb to the likes of Billy Fowler just to put bread into our mouths? I was weak, she thought; it was a moment of exhaustion and despair. *Never*, never again will I be ruled by a man.

Someone whistled, a piercing, ear-blasting shriek. She turned her head. Jamie! He was the last person she wanted to see today. She turned her back on him and continued on towards the house, but he came running up to her and grabbed her arm.

'Is it done?'

'Is what done?' she answered wearily. 'If you mean Alice's funeral, yes.'

'Good. Then you can open up tonight.' He rubbed his hands together. 'I'm bringing in Olga and Angelina, Flo and Poll. We're going to have a fresh carry-on.'

'Not Flo and Poll,' she objected. 'I thought you wanted a first class house?'

'Not bothered.' He smirked. 'I'll still bring in 'gents, but Flo and Poll can tek whoever comes to 'door. Put 'em at 'back of 'house, out o' sight, and you and Cherie, Olga and Angelina can deal wi' 'better off customers. Don't start,' he warned, when he saw her expression of protest. 'You still owe me what I paid for you, and your bed and board.'

'I'm leaving,' she snapped. 'And so is Cherie. And I owe you *nothing*!'

He grabbed hold of her again. 'You'll get a cut across that handsome face,' he whispered, holding her close to him. 'And I've somebody in mind for Cherie. Somebody who's willing to pay a lot of money for a virgin.'

She spat at him. 'Vile pimp!' she hissed. 'You'll not have her.'

He gave a thin smile and wiped his face. 'You'll pay for that,' he muttered, 'and so will she. I'll tell him he can do whatever he wants as long as her pretty face isn't touched. He's been waiting a long time.'

She stared at him and whispered, 'Who?'

He grinned. 'A customer. One of 'regulars.'

Kendall, she thought. It has to be him. He's not been satisfied since Lizzie left. I must get a message to Cherie to tell her not to come back. I'll tell Mary that she'll have to make other arrangements for Aaron.

'Get inside,' he snarled, giving her a shove. 'Get into your finery and be prepared to tek it off. Your time o' playing hard to get is over.'

'Don't you touch me!' She hurled a blow at him but he dodged and smacked her across the face, making her stagger. She gasped and put her hand to her smarting cheek.

'Just to let you know who's in charge here.' He gave her another shove, propelling her towards the steps.

''Ere! Leave 'er alone!' A shout came from the house next door where a woman stood in the doorway. She was dishevelled and slovenly and had a small dirty child standing by her side. 'Find one o' your own kind to beat up.'

'She is my own kind,' he shouted back. 'Mind your own damned business. She belongs to me. I paid for her and she owes me.'

The woman was silenced and Lily knew that she would fully understand the situation. She too would be in thrall to some man who controlled her earnings and her life.

Wearily she sat on the bed only recently vacated by Alice. Well, she's well out of it, she sighed. Nobody can get her now. She's at peace. She was tempted to lay her head down on the pillow, but she thought of Alice's consumption and disease. Can I catch it? She'd been careful about handling Alice, her clothes and her drinking cup. She hastily got up and stripped the bed.

I'll ask Mrs Flitt to take these to the washhouse, she thought, before remembering that Mrs Flitt was banned from the house when Jamie was around, and in any case they had no money to pay to wash the bedclothes.

Lily intended to leave, no matter what Jamie said; she had nothing to pack but couldn't leave in case Cherie or Mrs Flitt came back. But the day wore on and then the evening and she began to pace the floor. She had lit the fire in the parlour, though she doubted the room would be used for entertaining if Jamie was going to fill the house with undesirable customers. It was getting late and neither Mrs Flitt nor Cherie had returned. Lily was still wearing her grey gown and she smoothed the skirt and combed her hair, and waited.

The door bell rang, making her jump, and she hurried through the hall, hoping it was Cherie or Mrs Flitt so that she could warn them to stay away.

It was Jamie with Olga and Angelina. He glared at Lily. 'Why haven't you changed? I told you to get ready.'

'I *am* ready,' she snapped. 'Ready to leave.' I should have gone, she thought, feeling panicky, and let Mrs Flitt and Cherie manage for themselves.

Jamie shook his head. 'I don't think so! Where'd you go wi'out a penny to your name?' He turned to the two young women by his side. 'Angelina's going to be in charge,' he said. 'She's tekking over from you. Olga will look after 'gentlemen who've a fancy for foreign whores.'

Both women stared at Lily; then Angelina, glancing at Jamie, said loftily, 'I'm not a whore. I was a lady of means. It's unfortunate that I took a wrong turn.'

Olga gave a guttural laugh. 'You were a lady's maid, nothing more. It is unfortunate that your mistress's husband took you to his bed. And she found out,' she added.

356

'You can't mek me stay,' Lily told Jamie. 'I'm free to go if I want to.'

'You owe me money!' he snarled. 'I'll mek a charge against you. You've robbed me right, left and centre. I'll bring 'police in and tell 'em you've robbed 'customers.'

'You're running a brothel,' she shot back. 'Why should they believe you?'

'I didn't know what you were up to, did I? I was onny letting rooms.'

Lily shook her head. 'I protected you last time, Jamie. I won't do it again.' He looks sick, she thought. His skin was pasty and slightly yellow and his eyelids were swollen as if he was tired. He's taken something, laudanum or something. 'Your ma paid my court fine, did you know, Jamie? She told me she had. She knew that you wouldn't.'

She gave a small smile of satisfaction when she saw his startled expression. Then he sneered. 'Liar,' he said. 'She doesn't know you.'

'She does. She's been here. We've had a couple of natters together – about you.'

He lunged towards her and grabbed her by the throat. Angelina and Olga hastily stepped back. 'Don't you dare talk about my mother! Why would she talk to scum like you or any other whore, let alone pay your fine?'

'Perhaps because she remembers what it was like to be wi'out money or hope.' She felt the constriction of his fingers, but still went on. 'Perhaps in her heart she still remembers 'pain of belonging to the band of women who are at 'mercy of men like you. Like her son.'

The door bell pealed and Jamie took his hands from her neck. He raised a finger and shook it, keeping his eyes on Lily. 'Tell whoever's there,' he ordered Angelina, 'that he's very welcome and that there's a woman waiting for him. 'I'll show you, you slut,' he hissed in Lily's ear. 'You'll not get out of this one.'

Lily heard Angelina's voice murmuring a welcome and

saw her opening the door to admit someone. Jamie put his hand on her arm, his fingers pinching into her. Then he thrust her forward to meet her client. Her head swam and she felt dizzy. Her eyes flooded with tears as she gazed at the visitor. It was Johnny.

CHAPTER FORTY-SIX

'Here you are, sir.' Jamie pushed Lily forward. 'A nice clean woman. Barely been touched in years.' He pointed to the door of Lily's room and Angelina opened it.

'Can I take your coat, sir?' she asked, stroking Johnny's arm.

'No,' he snapped. 'And I don't want to be disturbed!'

'Pay by the hour, sir,' Jamie fawned. 'Can I tek 'liberty of asking you to pay up front?'

Johnny withered him with a steely glance, his hand on the door. 'No, you can't. I'll pay later. Isn't this a first class establishment?'

'Oh, it is. It is. It can be owt – anything you want. You onny have to ask.'

'Then I'm asking you to clear off and leave us.' Johnny scowled. 'I've been abroad. Haven't been with a woman in a long time.'

Jamie backed away, pulling Olga and Angelina with him. 'I understand, sir. Tek your time. Tek your time.'

Johnny grabbed Lily by the arm and pulled her into the room, closing the door after them. Then he put his finger to his lips and motioned her to the other side of the room.

'What 'you playing at, Johnny?' Lily began.

'I'm playing at being a customer,' he said in a whisper. 'I've been talking to your old friend.'

'What old friend?' she demanded. 'I haven't got any old friends.'

'Yes you have.' Johnny gazed tenderly at her. 'Mrs Flitt.'

'Mrs Flitt! Where is she? I've been waiting for her. That's why I'm still here. I'd have gone otherwise.'

Johnny sat down on the edge of the unmade bed. 'It's a long story,' he said softly. 'I've been to see Daisy. Ted had told me where she was working, so I thought I'd ask her employer if I could speak to her. I didn't think she liked me much when we first met.'

'She doesn't know you, that's why! You went off and left us!' she said resentfully.

He nodded. 'I realize that. But I spoke to Mr Walker, told him who I was and said I'd like to get to know Daisy again; mebbe even provide a home for her which you weren't able to, due to 'nature of your work.' He gave an embarrassed shrug as Lily glared at him. 'And he said he knew where you were.'

He reached for Lily's hand, but she pulled away from him. 'And he confirmed what those harlots next door said about you; or at least what they'd heard.'

She scowled at him. 'What? What have they said about me?' Her eyes widened and her lips parted. 'You've never been there!'

'Yes.' He gave a shudder. 'I've seen some sights in my time abroad, poverty and disease, but nothing to match 'conditions in that house. Those women have nowt; hardly any rags to their backs. There were bairns there crying out in hunger and they'd no food to give them. Young girls, no older than our Daisy, willing to sell themselves just for a crust o' bread.'

Our Daisy, she thought. He's laying claim to his children. 'It could've been us,' she said softly. 'It very nearly was.' Then she frowned again. 'So what did they say? That I was running a brothel?'

'Yes. That you kept a clean house and were mekking money for your pimp.'

360

He kept a straight face even though she raised her fist and shouted at him. 'He's not my pimp! I've earned money for him through my girls.' She lowered her voice, conscious that Jamie might be out in the hall. 'They were already working as street women. I stayed because of them. To give them a safe refuge. One of them,' she gave a sudden sob as she thought of Alice, 'got beaten up by a man. Awful thing was that they almost expected it; it was summat that happened all 'time. I thought – I thought that if I stopped here, then they'd have a better chance.' She sat down beside him, but not too close. 'But I was desperate too and didn't know where to go, and Jamie said that I owed him. He'd paid money to Billy Fowler for me and said that I couldn't leave till I'd paid him back.' She put her head in her hands. 'He still says I can't, but I was going to sneak out; I was onny waiting for Mrs Flitt and Cherie to come back so's I could tell them.'

'Mrs Flitt told me that Cherie had gone to stay wi' somebody,' Johnny said. 'Rena? To look after somebody's bairn, anyway.'

Lily nodded and heaved a sigh. 'That's all right then. But where's Mrs Flitt gone? She's nowhere to go. And how did she know who you were?'

'She was skulking about at 'end of 'square and came up to me. She'd seen you bring me to 'house, and asked who I was and could I help you. When I told her I was your husband she began shouting at me, thinking I was that Fowler chap. When I told her I was your *proper* husband come back from 'military, she started to weep and said that God was good after all. She said that 'last few months wi' you and 'girls had been 'best in her life and she'd never be able to better them.' He rubbed his chin, contemplatively. 'She seemed very determined about summat and said she knew what she had to do now that she knew you'd be safe.'

'Safe? How am I safe?' Lily gazed at Johnny. She still loved him but he needn't think he could just walk back into her life as if nothing had happened. 'I owe Jamie, but I

361

don't care about that. I'll still leave here and he can come after me if he will. But I'll get my life back; nobody will ever pull me down again. There are things you don't know about me. I'm a different person from 'one you left behind and you might not want to start over again, and I might not either. I was pregnant by Billy Fowler and he humiliated me by selling me in 'Market Place wi' folks standing by watching; I lost 'child and was tekken to a home for fallen women. And then I had to see my bairns go off to mek their own way before they were ready.'

Tears came to Johnny's eyes and he dashed them away. 'Mr Walker told me about 'child,' he said, 'and how his wife sent you to a refuge, thinking that you were a – a street woman.' His voice broke. 'I'm sorry, Lily. So sorry that this had to happen to you. All 'time I've been away I've thought about you; every day I thought about you and my bairns. And I did write. Whenever I could I wrote to you, telling you that I loved you and would to my dying day.'

He fished in his trouser pocket for a handkerchief and blew his nose vigorously. 'When you're in 'army, officers sometimes send for their wives, and whenever I saw one of 'em, I thought that none of 'em was a patch on you, and how I wished that you could've come out to me. But then I thought that I wouldn't want to put you in danger, never thinking that you were in more danger at home.'

He reached for her hand again and she let it lie limp in his. 'Will you let me make it up to you, Lily? I want you to be my wife again, a family again.'

'How can that be? I married somebody else. And I've just said, I'm not 'same person I was.' Her voice was tight and bitter. 'I was onny a young lass when you went away, even though I had two childre'. I'm a woman now; I've had to struggle on my own.' She stared him out, challenging him. 'I'm not sure that I want to put my life in anybody else's hands.'

'I'm not asking you to,' he said softly. 'Don't you remember when we were young that we used to agree to differ? We were allus equal companions even afore we were man and wife. I never made decisions for you.'

It was true, he never did, and he always listened even if he didn't agree with her.

'I need time to think,' she said. 'But first I have to get out of here. Jamie's going to bring customers to me and as soon as you're gone he'll be watching me all 'time.'

'Right!' Johnny stood up. 'I'll see to him. You get your things together and be ready to leave.'

'I've got nothing.' She gave a short laugh. 'Just 'clothes I'm wearing and even these are second hand.'

He gazed down at her. 'Lily! Will you let me kiss you? I've wanted to for so long. It was 'one thing that kept me going, just 'thought of holding you in my arms again.' His eyes were moist. 'I'm not 'same person as I once was either. I've seen things that I'd never want to tell you about; but one thing hasn't changed and that's my love for you.'

Lily's mouth trembled. She wanted so much to be loved and protected, but dare she let down her guard? For so long she had stood alone, guardian of her children, supporting herself until Billy Fowler had come along with his false promises. She gave Johnny her hands and he pulled her to her feet; then gently and caringly he kissed her on each cheek, and then, so tenderly, on her lips.

She caught her breath as she recalled how he used to tempt and tantalize her with his kisses before their passion brimmed over, engulfing them. She closed her eyes, ready to succumb, when she heard someone at the front door and remembered where she was.

'No,' she hissed. 'No! Not here. You might or might not be my rightful husband but I vowed no man would ever touch me in this house, and that means you too, Johnny.'

He drew away, his eyes searching hers, then he kissed her hand. 'You've just proved to me that you are still 'same woman you once were,' he said softly. 'If I'd had any doubts at all about your life here in this hellhole, they're gone for good.' He kissed her once more on the mouth, and then said, 'Come on. Let's get you out of here. I'll not let a little runt like Jamie stop us.'

It turned out to be easier than they expected. Johnny opened the door into the hall and found it empty. They could hear raucous laughter and voices coming from upstairs and from the parlour; but the front door was locked. 'I've got a key,' Lily whispered and went back into her room and opened the drawer to the desk where she had always kept a spare. They tiptoed back into the hall and slipped the key into the lock. As they opened the door Angelina came down the stairs.

'Wait!' she called. 'You haven't paid. *I've* to collect 'money now. Jamie said so.'

'There's nowt to be paid for,' Johnny said. 'She's not up to it.'

Lily saw fear on Angelina's face. 'He'll blame me,' the girl said. 'He'll say I kept 'money. Don't go out, Lily. You've got to be here for anybody, doesn't matter who; that's what Jamie said. Don't go. Please!'

'I'm leaving, Angelina.' Lily felt sorry for her, but knew she couldn't help her. 'And you'd be wise to do 'same.'

The girl gazed at Lily, her face creased with panic. 'But where will I go? There's nowhere!'

'Go to Hope House. They'll look after you.' Lily could feel Johnny's hand on her elbow, urging her to hurry.

'They're full. I've been there.' Tears started to spill from her eyes. 'Jamie was my last hope.'

Johnny pulled Lily out of the door, and as he locked it behind them and put the key in his pocket the image of Angelina's lovely distressed face was imprinted on Lily's mind.

'You can't help them all, Lily,' he said, leading her away. 'Come on, you've a son and daughter waiting for you. A new life to begin.'

CHAPTER FORTY-SEVEN

'Where're we going?' Lily ran alongside Johnny towards the bottom of the square. Most of the houses were brimming over with people. Women were standing in their doorways with lamp or candlelight behind them, calling out to men who were idling about in the dark road. 'Where are Ted and Daisy?'

'I've left Ted at 'hostelry where we've been stopping. Daisy went back to 'Walkers'. She said she'd leave and come wi' us.' He glanced at her. 'If you were coming too.'

'Mrs Walker won't let her leave. Not straight away. And she'll kick up a fuss. She's not quite right in her head, poor woman.' She pondered for a moment, not answering his implied question. 'We'd best go there first, and then I want to see Rena and Lizzie and her new bairn.'

'And then?' he queried. 'What then?'

'I don't know,' she said, shuddering. Would Jamie come looking for her? What would she do next and where would she go? With Johnny, or to live a solitary unloved life?

'Would you come back to Hollym? We were happy there – we could start again. Get a little house.' He hadn't told her that after selling some of the amber he now had some money to his name.

Lily slowed to walking pace. 'We can't go back. And anyway, you don't know what it was like. You were hardly ever there.' She stopped and put her hands to her head.

'I don't know what to do. I feel that there must be summat – something I can do to help women who've come to rock bottom in their lives, just as I did. I keep seeing Angelina's face.' When she saw his puzzled expression, she explained. 'That girl back at 'house. She was so frightened and she reminded me of Alice. My poor Alice.' She started to sob. 'She was lovely, just as Angelina is now, yet she got diseased and she got consumption, and then she died. And she was so young!'

'It happens,' he said quietly. 'All 'world over.'

'But don't you see,' she cried passionately. 'There should be more done to help them! Like Hope House, where I was sent. If onny there were more places like that. Where young women could find refuge and weren't at 'mercy of men!'

'Who pays for summat like that?' he asked. 'Where does 'money come from?'

'I don't know. Donations, I think,' she said vaguely. 'And people like Dr Fulton give their services free. And there are women who run the house, sort of matrons and housekeepers, and they help young women to find other work or go back home if they can.' She sighed. 'I heard they were trying to buy another house because there's such a need. So many young women in desperate situations!'

'Is that what you'd like to do if you had 'money? Wouldn't you rather have a little house of your own?'

'At one time, yes,' she said. 'That's what I wanted more than anything. But now . . .' She turned to him. 'I've seen decent young women having to sell themselves in order to live. And it's a downward path, Johnny. They think that it'll onny be for a short time till they get some money together. But it never is. They can never earn enough to get out, especially if they owe a man like Jamie.' She took a breath and exhaled. 'So if I ever came into money I'd use it to try to save some of these girls.'

Johnny said nothing. He didn't want his new-found wealth to be spent on women he didn't know, deserving or not. He wanted to set up a business, provide Lily and his children with security to make up for the years when he had let her down. He strode by her side as she hurried past St Mary's, which was in darkness, and Holy Trinity, whose windows were dimly lit, and on towards King Street. The street traders had gone, their empty stalls ghostly in the gaslight, but the local hostelries were brimming over with revellers, some of whom were spilling out on to the pavements.

The chemist's shop was closed, and a low-lit oil lamp glowed dimly in a back room. Lily tapped on the door and peered through the glass. Presently an inner door opened and Oliver Walker came through. He drew back the bolts and turned the key and opened the door. 'Can I help you?' he began, and then recognized Lily. 'Mrs Maddeson!' he said. 'I'm afraid my father isn't in.'

He looks agitated, Lily thought. He's upset about something. 'I wondered if I might have a word with Daisy.'

'She's with my mother,' he said. 'My mother is unwell and Father has gone to fetch a doctor. Would you like to come in?'

Lily hesitated. 'I'll come back,' she said. 'If your mother's ill she'll not want anybody else with her.' She bit on her lip. 'Is Daisy looking after her? It's not anything infectious?'

'No, it's not. Mother is rather overwrought,' he murmured. 'She – she doesn't want anyone else to be with her but Daisy.' He looked at her reassuringly. 'She's bearing up very well – Daisy, I mean – and Father won't be long.'

'All right.' Lily nodded. 'I'll come back. I, erm, Daisy will probably be leaving.' She made the decision. She'd move Daisy no matter what. There was something not quite right in this household.

'I'm sure that would be for the best,' Oliver agreed. 'In fact . . .' He hesitated as if unsure whether to explain. 'That is the reason my mother is unwell. Daisy told her that she would probably be handing in her notice. They're in my mother's bedroom with the door locked.'

'Then we'll wait.' Johnny spoke up. 'When your father gets back with 'doctor we'll force 'door.'

'This is Daisy's father,' Lily explained, seeing the startled expression on Oliver's face. 'He wants to take her back to Hollym, our old village.'

'You'd better come in and wait,' the young man said, and Lily felt some sympathy for him. He must have been anxious about his mother.

'Can I go up?' Lily asked. 'Just to see if everything's all right.'

Oliver agreed and led the way upstairs to his mother's room and knocked on the door. 'Mother,' he called. 'Mrs Maddeson is here. She'd like to speak to Daisy.'

'Well she can't,' Mrs Walker called back. 'Daisy doesn't want to speak to her.'

'I do. I do.' They heard Daisy's answering piping voice. 'Ma! I want to come home!'

Johnny moved both Oliver and Lily out of the way and put his shoulder to the door. It was quite firm; a good solid door. He stood back and with a great heave he put his foot to it and felt the lock break. Another heave with his shoulder and the door crashed open and they saw Daisy and Mrs Walker sitting on the edge of the bed.

'Oliver! What's happening? Oliver!' They heard Charles Walker in the shop below and he came running upstairs, followed by Dr Fulton. 'Mrs Maddeson! I'm so very sorry. Is Daisy all right?'

Lily nodded. Daisy was sobbing in Johnny's arms and Mrs Walker was gazing vacantly into space.

'Poor woman,' Lily murmured as she, Daisy and Johnny trudged across to Rena's. 'I hope she'll be all right. I've heard tell that those asylums are terrible places.'

'He'll send her to 'best there is,' Johnny said quietly. 'It'll onny be for a short time. They'll mebbe give her electric shock treatment to bring her back to normal.' He heaved a breath. On his travels he'd seen people with a craving for opium and Mrs Walker looked to him as if she had had quite a large dose. He'd helped the doctor to put her into his carriage whilst Mr Walker and his son had looked on helplessly.

Lily and Daisy went into Rena's to visit Lizzie and admire the new baby whilst Johnny waited outside. When they emerged half an hour later, Lily said, 'Daisy wants to stop wi' me. I expect that Ted will go back to Hollym with you.'

'But where will you go?' he stammered. 'Where will you live? Lily! Please!'

She sighed. 'I'm sorry, Johnny, but I can't go back. Billy Fowler's there for one thing and if I saw him I think I'd be tempted to kill him.' She looked at him and saw despair. 'And I'm not free, am I? Whose wife am I? Yours or his? You can sort that out, because—' Her voice broke. 'I can't.'

'Where will you go?' he said miserably. 'What will you do?'

'I'm going back to Hope House,' she said. 'I'll tek Daisy with me, and I'm going to ask if I can work there.'

Johnny trudged back towards the hostelry where he'd left Ted. He felt more dejected and dispirited than he had ever done, even during his captivity with the Sikhs. How could he win Lily back? How could they ever start again?

'Hey! Hey you!' somebody shouted and he automatically lifted his head and looked across the street. It was that pup Jamie shouting to an old woman. Johnny watched, his eyes narrowing, and then he walked towards them.

'You old hag,' Jamie was saying. 'Don't you come near my place again! Do you hear?'

'I hear you, you little toad,' she answered back, and Johnny recognized Mrs Flitt. 'Don't you tell me what to do! I do as I like. Not that I'll ever set foot through your door. Why would I want to?'

She flinched as Jamie came towards her with his fists raised and put her skinny arms up in defence. 'Don't you touch me,' she screeched, 'or I'll yell for 'constable and I'll tell what you're up to, you dirty little pander.'

She ducked as his fist came down, but he yelped as Johnny caught his arm and wrenched it back, hearing his shoulder click.

'You've broke my arm,' Jamie shrieked. 'You've damned well broke it. You! You owe me money. You never paid for that whore Lily.'

He shrieked again and staggered as Johnny's left fist struck his chin. 'That's my wife you're calling a whore,' Johnny growled, shoving his other fist in his stomach.

Jamie retched. 'Well, that's what she is!' He doubled over in pain. 'And she's not your wife. I met her husband and he was more than willing to be rid of her.'

Johnny grabbed him by the neck and putting his face close to Jamie's said menacingly, 'Don't ever breathe her name again, and don't ever threaten this old woman or I'll come after you. I mean it. Don't think I won't. Now get out of my sight. Hop it to whichever sewer you came from.'

Mrs Flitt dusted herself down. 'Thank you very much, sir,' she said. 'Much obliged.' She peered at him. 'It's Miss Lily's husband, isn't it?'

'Yes,' Johnny murmured, giving a wry smile. She was a tough old biddy and no mistake. 'Where're you off to?'

'To 'workhouse,' she said. 'I was on my way there. I'll get a bed and a bit o' food. I'll stop ower winter and then – well, I'll see what happens. If I survive, that is. When you see Lily, will you tell her? Tell her I'll be all right and that I hope as it works out for both of you.'

Johnny's eyes glistened. 'I'll tell her.' He swallowed. 'When I see her.' He turned about and walked in the direction of the hostelry. 'Well,' he muttered, 'I've got my son. And if I want my wife and daughter back I'll have to prove myself.' But first, he thought, I have to confront that blackguard Fowler.

CHAPTER FORTY-EIGHT

Johnny located Billy Fowler living in a run-down dilapidated cart shed which was teetering on the edge of the low cliff just outside Seathorne on the Waxholme road. He'd whistled as he approached to warn the man of his presence. Fowler came to the door. He had a sack draped round his shoulders and his breeches hung loosely on his legs.

'Who are you?' he bellowed. 'Don't come any nearer. You can't turn me out. Place was empty when I came.'

'I haven't come to turn you out,' Johnny said. 'Isn't it dangerous here? You're right on 'edge.'

Fowler gave a crafty grin. 'Aye, I know. But I'm not paying rent and besides, 'sea don't want me. I was saved afore when I went ower. I'll not drown,' he crowed.

'What 'you living on?' Johnny was puzzled. There was no garden, nothing growing, no pigs or hens. 'What do you do for food?'

Fowler's eyes narrowed. 'What's it to do wi' you? Who are you anyway?'

'Johnny Leigh-Maddeson. Lily's husband. I wasn't killed. I was captured.'

Fowler hugged his sack closer to him. 'Ha! Well, I don't want her. You can have her back.' He sniggered. 'If you can find her.'

Johnny came closer. Fowler was unshaven and his beard

371

was matted and dirty; his hair was long and greasy, hanging down into his neck. 'I've found her, no thanks to you. You left her to perish, her and my bairns. Shame on you! You're a blackguard, Fowler, and deserve to rot in jail.'

'It'll be her that'll go to jail,' Fowler retaliated. 'She shouldn't have married me if you was still alive. She's a bigamist, that's what!'

'And you're a cur.' Johnny felt his anger rising. 'You took her to town and sold her. You're not fit to breathe, you heathen.'

Fowler scoffed. 'She weren't worth much. I onny got ten bob for her.'

Johnny launched himself at him, pulling him out of the doorway. 'She was carrying *your* child and you left her and Daisy to fend for themselves. What kind o' man are you, for God's sake?'

'Gerroff me! Leave me alone.' Fowler struggled out of Johnny's grasp. 'I don't want anybody. Don't need anybody. You can have her and your whining daughter and recklin' son.'

Johnny punched him on the nose, making him stagger against the door. 'That's just for starters,' he warned him. 'I'll be back wi' 'constable and I'm mekking a charge against you for ill-treating a pregnant woman.'

He walked away back along the crumbling cliff top, dodging and striding over the cracks and fissures. He was seething but undecided about Lily's position, not wanting to make things worse for her. Was she a bigamist or would she be excused? She had, after all, written to the army and been told that to the best of their knowledge he had been killed.

I can't let Fowler get away with this, he fumed, and it seems to me that he's not right in his head. What's he living on out here? Is he stealing food? Begging? There were but few cottages in Waxholme and he thought it unlikely that any of the tenants would have food to spare for Fowler. He's going to fall off the edge anyway, he thought. The cliffs are low, but on a high tide he could be swept away. He looked down. The sea was battering the base of the cliff and a wind was getting up. 'Aye,' he muttered. 'Mebbe 'sea'll get him and that'll be 'answer to all our problems.'

But as the night drew on the wind blew stronger and the rain came down, and he pondered on Fowler's situation. He and Ted were staying at the hostelry in Hollym. Johnny had a few plans in his head after talking to his son, but he couldn't settle whilst he had Fowler on his mind.

'I'm going out,' he said, after they'd eaten supper. 'I'm going to tek a walk.'

'It's chucking it down, Da. You'll get soaked.' Ted was content. He'd had a good supper and had been listening to some of the old men in the inn telling their stories, and watching them play dominoes. 'Do you want me to come wi' you?' he asked reluctantly.

'No. I want to think. I want to think on what's best to do.'

Ted gazed at his father. 'Ma'll come round, you know,' he said. 'She was allus talking about you when me and Daisy were little. About what we'd do when you came home.' He sighed. 'That was afore Fowler, though.'

'Aye, well, things are different now,' Johnny said, putting on his top coat. 'I won't be long. I'm just going to get a breath o' sea air.'

'You're not going down to 'sea, are you?' Ted frowned. 'It's blowing a gale.'

'I might,' Johnny said. 'Don't worry.' He grinned at his anxious son. 'I know how to tek care of myself.'

'Aye.' Ted grinned back. 'I heard tell you could.' He was very proud of his soldier father, never tiring of hearing of his exploits.

Johnny strode across the fields of Hollym, treading the path that he and Lily used to take when they were young. There was a moon but the cloud was thick and black, hiding its brightness, and now and again he stumbled and slid on the muddy ground. Eventually he came to the cliff edge and walked along it, past the darkened windows of Withernsea village and towards Seathorne.

The sea raged below him, crashing against the cliff. He felt the sharp salt spray on his face as well as the drenching rain and kept well back from the edge, but still the ground was cracked and broken and he fell several times. What in heaven's name made Lily come out here to live? he wondered. She must have been desperate, or else Billy Fowler spun a cock and bull tale about his life. He kept on walking, through the village and on towards the Waxholme road to where Fowler was living.

Why am I here? If he goes over the edge, good riddance! But there was something about the man that aroused, not exactly pity, but an unease as to his state of mind. Ted had confessed to his feeling of guilt when he'd seen Fowler go over, and Johnny too felt a clawing of his conscience at having wished the man dead just to solve his own problems. But even if he was dead, Lily might not want me back, he thought regretfully. I've failed her. I did what I wanted and not what was best for us both.

As he approached the cart shed he saw that part of the roof had blown off and there was only a thin strip of land in front of the door, barely wide enough to stand on. He must have moved out. He can't surely still be living there.

'Fowler!' he shouted. 'Fowler! Are you there?'

A figure shrouded in sacks emerged from round the back. 'What do you want? Clear off! This is my property.'

'Are you all right? You ought to leave. It'll go ower any minute!'

'Who's that? Maddeson? Is that you again? I told you to clear off.'

'You should leave,' Johnny insisted. The gale was so strong he could hardly stand and he was concerned for his own safety as well as Fowler's.

'Not me!' Fowler drew back his shoulders and gave a harsh laugh. 'I told you last time, 'sea don't want me. It can come but I won't drown!'

To Johnny's alarm, Fowler put his head down against the wind and battled his way to the front of the shed. 'Look,' he shouted, and stretched out his arms, dancing about in a circle. 'Can't hurt me!'

Then, to Johnny's horror, Fowler pointed both arms in front of him as if preparing to dive. 'No! Stop!' Johnny darted towards him. 'Don't. You'll drown. Tide's running high.'

'Ha! Scared you, didn't I?' Fowler took a step backwards. 'Call yourself a sodger! I could eat you for breakfast and leave room for gruel!'

'Come away. Parish'll house you,' Johnny called. 'You can't stop there.'

'Mind your own bleeding business,' Fowler shouted. 'Get back to that wife o' yourn. She'll happen keep your bed warm. If she's a mind to, that is. She was nivver very willing in that department.'

Johnny turned and began to walk away. He wasn't going to listen to Fowler's abusive language. Let him go hang, or drown, whichever was his preference.

'Hey! Maddeson!'

Johnny kept on walking. He didn't want to hear.

'Maddeson! You'll have to buy her back if you want her. Yon fellow paid out good money, even if it didn't amount to much!'

Johnny turned, an oath on his lips and his fists clenched. The wind screeched and buffeted him, almost knocking him over, and as he began to walk back towards Fowler he felt the earth tremble beneath his feet. He jumped back, further away from the edge. 'Fowler,' he yelled. 'Don't be a fool. Cliff's going.'

'Ha!' Fowler gave a guffaw and stretched out his arms, shaking his fists at the elements. 'Can't get me—' His bragging outburst abruptly changed to a startled cry as the soft, wet and fissured clay beneath his feet gave way and he began to sway. 'I'll not drown,' he began to shout. 'Not me. You'll see.' But his cries were lost in the shrieking of the gale as he plummeted headlong over the edge into the sea.

Johnny fell to his knees and gingerly stretched out to look over the edge into the swirling foam which was battering the weakened cliff. Not only was the sea deep but the tide was high, a huge surge rushing towards the cliff. He'll not get out of that. He peered into the darkness. Though he did last time, so it was said. Then he saw a dark head bobbing in the water and he half rose to his knees. If I had something to throw, a spur, or – he looked towards the battered cart shed. If there was only something – but he felt again a tremble beneath him and instinctively drew back from the edge.

The cliff slithered slowly downwards and Johnny felt himself falling. He turned tipple tail and grabbed a clump of grass, and leaning backwards dug in his heels, remembering how, on his release from the sepoys, he had tumbled down the mountainside with his hands tied behind him. The clay suddenly stopped on its downward path to the sea and, clawing on the slippery slope, he hastily climbed back up.

'Beggar's gone,' he muttered. 'Can't see him.'

The moon slid momentarily from behind the clouds and Johnny keenly scoured the tossing, churning waters. 'Is that him?' He saw a dark shape in the water, an arm perhaps, well away from the shore; then it was gone. He saw it once more for barely a second before the moon disappeared again, leaving only blackness and a dark foaming sea.

CHAPTER FORTY-NINE

It was early May. In the countryside, the hawthorn was covered in white blossom, clumps of cowslips carpeted the drain banks, birds were singing and fledglings were stretching their wings in preparation for their first flight, and pale green corn swayed gently.

In the town of Hull, Lily knew what she was missing, and although she was busy every minute of the day there were times when she caught a scent of the countryside on a breeze, or the briny tang of the sea travelling down the estuary, and pondered on the life she was leading now. Events had moved fast since she had once more knocked on the door of Hope House, asking for shelter and a chance of work.

It was twelve months since she had been abandoned in this town which was no longer strange to her, but on the contrary, now that she was no longer without hope, felt almost like home. Mrs Thompson had agreed to take her and Daisy in for a short time only, for, as she explained, this was a place of refuge for fallen women. 'And you and Daisy,' she gently explained, 'are not in that category.'

Lily had told her that she wanted to help young women in unfortunate circumstances and Mrs Thompson had told her of their efforts to find money for a second house. 'But there is none at present. Should it ever materialize, then I would certainly recommend that you be offered the position of housekeeper.'

For a month, Lily and Daisy had worked for their keep, hoping that they wouldn't be turned away when young street women came begging for shelter. 'Winter is the time when they start arriving in large numbers,' Mrs Thompson had said. 'They think they can survive during autumn, but once the cold weather starts they have second thoughts.'

But Lily recalled that it was spring when she, Lizzie and Cherie had found their way to Hope House.

Johnny had written to her care of Rena, whose address he had remembered, telling her of Billy Fowler's death. His body had been washed up at Spurn Point. *We know for sure he's dead this time*, he wrote. *John Ward identified him. He told me that Fowler had been caught stealing his eggs. He must have eaten them raw for there was no sign of any fire's having been lit when they looked at what was left of the barn.*

He'd pleaded with her to forgive him and give him the chance to start their lives again. *I've got us a little house*, he wrote. *It's just outside Hollym. It's not much at the minute. Needs some work on it, but it's got land and Ted wants to work it and send stuff to market. He's a grand lad, Lily. You did a good job on bringing him up, but he still needs his ma, and I need you too.*

Lily had felt a flood of emotion, for she had often thought that she had spoilt Ted and what he needed was a father's stronger hand. She had written in return to Johnny, and told him that there were others, more unfortunate than him or Ted, whom she wanted to help if she possibly could. She explained that she wasn't ready to give him a commitment, even though she was probably now legally married to him and he could take her back by force if he wanted.

He'd immediately sent a terse note, saying that she obviously didn't know him well enough if she thought he would do that. *I love you, Lily*, he had added, *and I would never again do anything to hurt you.*

There was silence then, with no more letters, and she had begun to wonder if she had done the right thing in turning him down. Just when she was on the edge of indecision, on a cold and wintry morning a fortnight before Christmas, Charles Walker and Dr Fulton had called to see Mrs Thompson to tell her that they had at last found funding to buy the house next door.

Lily was called in to the discussion and offered the position of house manager. 'It will be run by committee,' Dr Fulton explained. 'It will be a house of charity, though,' he hastened to say, 'our benefactor, who has chosen to remain anonymous, requests that it be called Amber House.'

'An odd kind of name,' Mrs Thompson said. 'But he is entitled to call it whatever he wants. I assume it is a gentleman, and not a lady of means?'

Charles Walker had interceded. 'A male, certainly, but we are pledged to silence on the matter, Mrs Thompson. Mrs Maddeson.' He turned to Lily. 'We would be honoured if you would agree to serve on the committee. As manager you will be in the best position to know what is required.'

In some astonishment she had accepted, and wondered what kind of fate it was that had turned her from a madam in a brothel to a manager in a house of charity.

Amber House was now up and running and the official opening was to be performed by the Chief Magistrate of Hull the following week. One of the first young women to ask for admittance had been Angelina, who had appeared on the doorstep with a cut lip and a black eye. At Lily's suggestion, after she had recovered from her ordeal, Charles Walker had taken her to see his wife, who had now recovered from her breakdown and was ready to accept Angelina as her maid. They're well suited, Lily thought. They will understand each other, and now that Oliver is going away Mrs Walker won't consider her a threat.

Lily had sought out Mrs Flitt at the workhouse and found the old woman at low ebb. 'I miss all of you,' she'd said. 'You've been like family.'

'So would you come and join us at Amber House?' Lily asked her. 'I have a job for you and you can have a bed in one of the attic rooms.'

Mrs Flitt didn't need to be asked twice. 'I'm ready,' she said. 'Nowt to tek.' She was now in charge of cleaning the steps and windows at both houses, and running errands when needed.

As for Jamie, Lily had occasionally caught a glimpse of him, but whenever he saw her he scuttled out of sight, disappearing round a corner or into a doorway.

Charles Walker had requested a few words with Lily one day regarding Daisy. She was curious and wondered if he was going to suggest that Amber House was an unsuitable home for a girl of tender years. Lily had in fact given some thought to the matter already, but Daisy didn't mix with the residents and spent much time next door with Mrs Thompson organizing her paperwork or helping in the kitchen.

'I do hope you will forgive my intrusion on what is after all a personal matter, Mrs Maddeson,' he said. 'But I wonder if you have given any thought to furthering Daisy's education.'

'Why, no,' she said, surprised. 'Daisy did go to school in our village and did very well, but after we moved to Seathorne she didn't attend very often. It seemed as if she wanted to stay by me.'

'She's a very bright child,' Charles Walker said, 'and I think you should consider allowing her some private tuition.'

'Goodness!' Lily exclaimed. 'But wouldn't that cost a good deal of money? And what would she do with extra education? She's a girl. There aren't 'same opportunities for a girl as there are for a boy.'

Charles Walker smiled. 'For some there are. She could be a teacher. She could be a scientist.'

'A scientist! Surely not!'

'Opportunities are opening up for women; there are

female doctors, female inventors, women in industry. Sadly, many have to hide behind their husbands' names, but the time will come when they will be completely independent.'

Lily had stared at him. 'And you think that Daisy . . .'

He'd nodded. 'I don't see why not. I saw her potential when she came to live with us.'

'I'll have to write to her da,' she murmured. 'See if he's got any money.' Though she was getting a salary as house manager, it wasn't enormous.

Charles Walker had raised his eyebrows at that and Lily frowned. 'What?' she said. 'Oh. You think I should make 'decision?'

He hadn't answered, only smiled, and she took it as a challenge. Why shouldn't Daisy be educated 'same as a lad, she'd thought, and I'll pay for it.

But Johnny had sent her money when she wrote to tell him that Daisy was going to have tutoring. *She's my daughter*, he'd written, *and I want to provide for her, just as I'm providing for Ted.*

She had asked him to come to the opening ceremony, but he hadn't answered and she wondered if he would come. She wanted to see him, to assess her feelings, for she thought of him often and though her thoughts were confused, they were warm.

Now Lily stood in the doorway of Amber House welcoming the dignitaries and invited guests. Charles Walker and Dr Fulton stood in the hall shaking hands and greeting them. Lily had decided to invite Lizzie, Cherie and Rena to see the house. Lizzie and Rena had come but Cherie had stayed behind to look after Ethan.

Lily could hardly believe the difference in Lizzie. The girl had lost her aggressive defiant air, and had an aura of bright confidence, which couldn't have been due only to her fashionable appearance, but must have owed something to her future expectations regarding her business partnership with Rena.

Someone else had been invited, but not by Lily. Leo Leighton put in a brief appearance, but on recognizing Lily, had given his flustered apologies that he couldn't stay owing to pressure of engagements at the court.

Lily smiled sweetly into his reddened countenance and said she could quite understand. 'So many scoundrels deserving to be locked up,' she murmured. 'So many immoral sinners amongst us.'

Johnny hadn't arrived, and regretfully she was about to close the door and circulate with the guests when on a whim she stepped outside to look along the street. There were a few people about, but none looked as if they were coming towards Amber House. A horse and trap was trotting briskly towards her, but she turned away. If Johnny was coming he would be walking.

She closed the door and moved into the hall, mixing with the guests. None of them know, she reflected. Not one of these guests would guess that I was once an unfortunate woman needing help, just as the young women who will come here will need help and understanding. If it hadn't been for Charles Walker – and even Mrs Walker, for she had played her part – and Mrs Thompson, where would I be now?

The door bell rang and she jumped, forgetting for a moment where she was. She saw Lizzie smile at her as if she understood. How they had all hated the sound of a ring at the door in Leadenhall Square, although it was crucial to the lifestyle they were leading.

'I'll go,' Charles Walker said. 'Why don't you show people round, Mrs Maddeson?'

She nodded, but kept her eyes on the door. She had so wanted Johnny to come; to show him that her visionary notion of working to help other women in jeopardy was not just an impractical theory but a plan that could be developed. Of course, it wouldn't have happened without a benefactor, she mused, glancing at the assembled company and trying to determine who he was. She took a breath.

What if it was Leo! Just suppose he had had a crisis of conscience. She put her hand to her mouth. Who invited him? Was I rude to him? He left in such a hurry!

Then she blinked and took a breath. There was Johnny, and Charles Walker was shaking him vigorously by the hand and drawing Dr Fulton towards him to do the same. What's going on? Why the welcome? She watched the men talking, Johnny placing his fingers over his mouth as he spoke; and then he laughed. She saw the way his cheeks creased and his eyes crinkled at the corners and was suddenly touched by a feeling of almost overwhelming tenderness. Of course he would come, she thought. He might be late, but it's a long way from Hollym. He must have been up at daybreak to get here.

He came across to her and kissed her hand. 'Hello, Lily,' he said softly. 'You look nice.'

She felt herself blush. 'So do you,' she murmured. 'Very smart.'

Johnny was wearing a brown tweed jacket and trousers, and held a soft hat in his hand. Not at all the kind of thing the other gentlemen were wearing, but very suitable for a countryman. The kind that a farmer might wear on a trip to town.

He grinned and gave his cuffs a flourish. 'My other clothes were hanging off my back. I thought that for such a grand occasion I ought to treat myself. Didn't want you to be ashamed o' me, Lily.'

'I'd never be that,' she said, and swallowed. 'I always thought it would be 'other way round.'

He took her hand again and squeezed it. 'Never!' he whispered, mindful of other people milling about. 'Never, ever! Lily,' he said. 'Would you come? To look at 'house and land? Ted's got planted up and I've started on 'repairs.'

She hesitated. She was curious, she'd admit, as she couldn't quite place where it was from his description of it. But also she was ready for some time off. The last few months had been tiring in the run-up to getting Amber

House ready for occupancy. 'I don't know,' she said reluctantly. 'I'm needed here.'

'But surely they can manage for a couple o' days. You've got staff, haven't you?'

She had, and they were good. There was a housekeeper, several kitchen maids and a cook, as well as Mrs Flitt; the residents were expected to keep their own rooms tidy and do their own washing, to prepare them for life outside Amber House.

'I suppose . . . yes, I could.' She smiled. 'I'll have to make arrangements.'

'Why not come now? Today? We could drive back together.'

'Drive back? You mean wi' carrier? It'll be too late, he'll have gone.'

Johnny flushed. 'Erm, no. I've got a trap. Hoss is tied up outside.'

She stared at him, a question on her lips, but Charles Walker came up to them. 'Have you shown your husband the house, Mrs Maddeson? Your wife has done wonders,' he said to Johnny. 'Absolutely. She's worked like a Trojan.'

Johnny nodded. 'She allus was good at organizing, but I thought she looked a bit tired. I had it in mind to tek her home for a couple o' days. For some sea air, you know.'

'Excellent idea!' Charles Walker rubbed his hands together. 'Mrs Thompson can direct your housekeeper if required, though everything is working so well it will hardly be necessary. Why not take a week off and come back in time for the board meeting?'

'Oh!' Lily was astonished. Am I superfluous? Have I done so well that I'm no longer required? 'What about Daisy?'

'She can come home – back with us, I mean,' Johnny said.

'Or she can stay with us and help me in the dispensary after her lessons,' Walker said. 'It would be a shame to interrupt them. And,' he added softly, 'she would be perfectly all right with Mrs Walker. In fact I know my wife would be pleased to see her again. She was genuinely fond of her.'

'All right,' Lily said breathlessly, and, although ready to agree with the suggestions, wondered why she felt that she was being manoeuvred.

CHAPTER FIFTY

Dr Fulton gave a few words of welcome, thanked everyone for their contribution to the opening of Amber House and in particular Mrs Leigh-Maddeson, who had worked so tirelessly in her efforts to provide a home and support for young women who, for whatever reason, found themselves in an unenviable position without hope or succour. He then invited the Chief Magistrate to officially perform the opening ceremony.

After that, some of the assembly began to drift away, whilst others inspected the rest of the house. Lily went to collect her outdoor coat and left Johnny talking to Daisy, who had come in for the last quarter of an hour.

'I don't want to go back to 'country to live,' Daisy told her father. 'I don't mean that I don't want to see you' – she hung her head – 'or Ted; it's just that I prefer it here. There's more to do, and I like being back at my lessons.'

'But you'd come and stay sometimes, wouldn't you?' Johnny asked anxiously. 'And – what if your ma came back to live wi' me? How would you feel about that?'

'All right, I suppose. Would that mean I'd have to live with Mr and Mrs Walker? Cos I wouldn't mind that really.'

Johnny smiled. 'I don't know if they'd want you to live with them all 'time. We'd have to sort summat out.'

'I'd like to go away to school,' Daisy said eagerly. 'I'd be with other girls then.' She sighed. 'But I know we couldn't afford that.'

Johnny patted her head. 'Don't let's worry over that now. Your ma hasn't said she'll come back to Hollym to live. I let her down. I don't know if she'll forgive me.'

Daisy looked up at him. 'But you came back, didn't you? You returned from 'dead and that's what she always wanted. More than anything else.'

Daisy's given me hope, Johnny thought as he helped Lily into the trap, covered her knees with a blanket and set off for Holderness.

Lily glanced at him. He's soft-soaping me and I'm not used to it. I'm used to managing for myself. 'So whose is 'trap?' she asked. 'Did somebody lend it to you?'

'Erm, no. I bought it. I thought if we were going to be backwards and forwards to market I'd better invest in some transport.'

'Hardly big enough to load taties and vegetables in it,' she remarked. 'Besides, it'd be a shame to muck it up with soil.' The seat was wooden but covered in dark green leather.

Johnny gave a wry grimace. 'You were allus smart, Lily. Nowt much gets past you.' He laughed. 'How else could I come to Amber House? I can't keep on catching carrier, can I? Not if you're going to stop there. I bought it so that I could come and see you. We'll get a cart for Ted's stuff once he's ready for market.'

What's he doing for money? she wondered. Fine suit of clothes, horse and trap, talking of buying a cart! I'll not ask him; not until I've seen this house and land. He'll have leased it I expect from one of the landowners. Hope he knows what he's doing and hasn't landed himself in a load of debt.

The sun was lowering as they approached Hollym and Lily kept glancing over her shoulder to look at the sky. She sighed in satisfaction. 'There's nowt to beat a Holderness sunset,' she murmured. 'There are some good ones in Hull, but out here there are no buildings to get in 'way; nothing to detract from 'miles and miles of sky.'

Johnny agreed. 'I often thought of Holderness when I was up in 'mountains wi' 'sepoys,' he said. 'Sunsets were brilliant but they didn't linger the way they do here. There was a great splash of colour and then it was gone into darkness.' He shook the reins to urge on the horse. 'But out here you can watch them changing into a rainbow of colours, onny without 'rain. We're nearly there,' he said eagerly. 'You'll know 'house, Lily, when you see it. I remember it from when I was a lad and you'll remember it too. It's an old one and been derelict for a long time, by 'state of it.'

'There's the new mill!' Lily interrupted. 'Its sails are turning.'

'Aye, it's up and working,' Johnny said. 'I lost my bearings when I first saw it. I onny remember 'owd post-mill.'

'They hadn't finished it when I left to go to Seathorne. They still had to put on 'cap and sails.'

'You can see it from 'top window,' Johnny told her. 'And here we are!'

'Is this it?' She gave a gasp. 'Why, this was part of Barnard's estate at one time.'

'Aye, it was.' He drew up at the gate. 'But different lots have been sold on over 'past few years.'

Lily stared up at the old turreted house. She remembered it from childhood. It had always seemed unusual and fascinating, even though run-down and in need of repair. It had been empty for years. 'So, have you leased it? Are you a tenant or what?'

'Come in,' he said. 'I'll tell all in a minute, but I want you to see 'view from top window afore 'sun sets.'

'Where's Ted?' she asked. 'Is he here?'

'He'll be out tending beans or peas or whatever he's growing.' Johnny grinned as he led her inside. 'He's got a young lad from 'village to help him plant up. He keeps calling Ted "young maister"!'

A market gardener and a scientist, she mused. Whatever next? She followed Johnny up the staircase to a landing, and then up another flight of stairs to the top floor. He held out his hand. 'Come and see this.' He smiled. 'Prepare to be overjoyed.'

She stood beside him at one of the windows and took a breath as she saw the sea a mile away, the tops of the waves white and frisky. Johnny turned her round. 'Now look the other way,' he said softly. 'Isn't that a sight worth seeing?'

From the opposite window she saw the sunset in all its glory. Red, yellow, blue; a fusion of brilliance and splendour which coloured the fields below them and filled the room with a rosy glow.

'Like purple mountains and golden clouds. It's wonderful,' she whispered. 'However did you come to get it, Johnny?'

'I passed 'house one day and I remembered how curious I'd been when I was a lad. There was nobody about and it was empty. Back door had been broken open, by village lads I expect, and somebody, some tramp mebbe, had made a fire in 'kitchen. So I came in and came upstairs, and 'sun was setting just like now; it was as if 'sky was on fire, and I knew I had to have it.'

Lily looked at him. Then she licked her lips. 'You bought it? Wherever did you get 'money from, Johnny?'

He took a breath. His whole life depended on her reaction. Without her the house meant nothing.

'When 'sepoys released me I had my hands tied at my sides. So, as I came down 'mountain I dug my heels in to stop myself falling. As I skidded down, some of 'rocks and stones that I dislodged fell alongside me and some of 'debris got into my boots, which were in tatters. When I got to 'bottom, I banged my heels on to 'ground cos it was gritty and painful to walk on, and I noticed that some of 'stones had a colour to 'em. I couldn't pick 'em up cos my hands were tied, but when I was released by 'cavalry I decided that next time I was on my own I'd tek a closer look. Which I did,' he said, 'after I decided that I wasn't going back.'

'So, what was it, this gritty stuff?' Lily asked. 'Was it valuable, like diamonds?'

He shook his head. 'Not like diamonds. It's amber. It's a fossil which comes from tree sap.'

'A fossil! You mean like we used to find on 'sea shore?'

'Aye, except it comes in different colours, depending on where it's been and where it comes from, and sometimes has bits of leaf or flowers trapped inside it, insects even. Anyway, when I went on my journey across India I kept a lookout. I didn't really expect to find owt and at first I didn't; but at night I sheltered in caves halfway up 'mountain side and it was in one of them that I found some. It's millions of years old, Lily,' he said excitedly. 'Treasure of the earth.'

'So you used it to buy this place,' she said quietly, 'and to buy 'trap. So are you rich then, Johnny? Is that what you're telling me?'

He shook his head. 'No. Well, yes. Richer than I ever dreamed we'd be. Our own house, Lily! That's riches. Nobody can turn us out of it. And Ted will be set up now cos I bought fifty acres to go with 'house.' He gazed steadily at her. 'But it means nowt, Lily, if you won't come back to me.'

Her thoughts were in turmoil. To come here; to live with a view of the sea and the sky. To have her own home again. But what about Amber House? She'd be letting them all down. She was relied upon.

'I can't,' she said. 'I can't let those girls down. Amber House means so much to me. Just because you have money now doesn't mean – doesn't mean . . .'

She stopped, her glance flickering over his face and the eyes which were gazing with such intensity into hers. 'Amber House!' she whispered, and saw in her mind's eye Charles Walker shaking Johnny by the hand. 'Was that you? Are you our benefactor?'

He nodded, but said nothing, only holding her gaze as if his life depended on it.

'Why?' she croaked.

'Because it was what you wanted. It was your dream, and if it meant so much to you I was willing to give away a fortune if it meant that you'd give me another chance.'

'So you arranged that I should run it?'

'Yes – to be 'manager and on 'committee. You're a trustee. Those were 'terms I insisted on when we were setting it up.' He reached for her hand. 'It means that you'd allus have influence, even if you didn't live there. You'd still have contact and know what was going on. You'd be involved for as long as you wanted to be.'

The sun was almost down as they stood together in the room, the shadows growing longer. Lily took a breath and watched the sea getting darker; somewhere along the shore the cliff would be crumbling, but here the ground was solid and safe.

'Did you spend it all then?' she murmured. 'Money you got for 'amber?'

Johnny nodded. 'Yes, just about. Amber House took most of it. That's why I said I wasn't rich. I didn't think you'd want me if I tried to buy you wi' promises of riches, anyway. We'll have to work to mek this pay – this garden of Ted's, I mean. He hasn't got much of a head for figures or planning, though he can mek things grow.'

'No, he hasn't,' she said softly. 'He didn't care for learning, not like Daisy.' But I have, she thought. I'm good at planning and organizing. 'And you definitely haven't got any money left? You sold all of 'amber?' It'll be a challenge putting this place back together, she thought. 'Ceiling needs fixing,' she said, looking up.

He felt hope rising and thought he could tell a small white lie. 'Sold all that I had.' He mentally crossed his fingers. 'All of 'jewellers were mad for it! But I tell a lie, Lily.' He saw her frown and gave her a smile which made

391

her heart flip over. She had always known when he was teasing her.

'What, then?' She laughed, and felt her spirits lighten. 'You'd better own up!'

He put his hand in his pocket and brought out a piece of soft cloth. 'You've to tek care it doesn't scratch,' he murmured. 'That's what 'experts say, anyway.' He opened up the cloth and brought out a ring set with a pale gold stone.

'This was 'best piece, Lily. Finest colour there is. See – it's got flecks o' brown, probably tree bark. I had this made for you, so that even if you don't want me, this stone will allus be your safeguard. You'll never be poor if you have this.'

He slipped it on to her finger, above her wedding ring. 'Is this 'one I gave you, Lily?' he whispered. 'Say that it is.'

'Yes,' she breathed. 'I never had another. Never wanted another. But you don't think I'd ever sell this, do you? Even if I was as poor as a church mouse I wouldn't.'

'So will you keep it, and will you come back to me?'

'I've never been away from you, Johnny,' she said, and leaned towards him to kiss his lips. 'It was you who went away. I loved you so much and prayed for you to come back; but then I gave up wishing and hoping.' A tear trickled down her cheek. 'I should have had more faith. I should have known that you wouldn't let me down – but when they said you were dead I wanted to die too, and if it hadn't been for our two childre' I might have done.'

He held her close. 'But you didn't, and I didn't, and you've proved yourself to be strong, and didn't weaken.'

'Just that once,' she whispered. 'With Billy Fowler.'

'It's done with, Lily,' he said, kissing her wet cheek. 'It's all over. I love you just 'same as I allus did. What's passed was just an interlude in our lives. Will you have me back?'

A sudden bright shaft of light seared the room, highlighting them as they stood close, and they both blinked from its intensity. Lily saw Johnny just as he once was, with laughter lines round his generous mouth and a crease at the sides of his eyes as he gazed anxiously at her. They would need to get to know each other again, but she could look forward to that with pleasure.

She nodded, unable to speak; then she swallowed. 'Yes,' she whispered. 'I will.'

THE END

SOURCES

Books for general reading:

The Victoria History of the County of York East Riding, Volume V. Published for the University of London Institute of Historical Research by Oxford University Press, 1984.

Bernard Foster, *Living and Dying: a Picture of Hull in the Nineteenth Century*.

Anthony Wood, *Nineteenth Century Britain*, Longman, 1960.